SKY DARK

ASHES OF EDEN, BOOK 1

(Skyfall Trilogy, Book 1)

Written by Diane Kann

Brought to you by Volans Galaxy Press

Published by Kannceptual Creations LLC

An imprint of Volans Galaxy Press

ISBN: 978-1-969569-86-9

Printed in the United States of America

First Edition, December 2025

CONTENTS

DEDICATION

To those who find light in the encroaching twilight, whose hands mend what has been broken, and whose hearts beat with the persistent rhythm of hope.

This story is for the builders in the ruins, the gardeners in the ash, and the dreamers who look towards a horizon obscured by dust and despair, yet still dare to believe in the dawn.

It is for the resilience of the human spirit, for the quiet courage found in everyday acts of survival, and for the unwavering conviction that even in the darkest of times, the seeds of a brighter future can always be sown. May we never forget the lessons etched in the scars of our past, and may we always strive to build a world where community, ingenuity, and compassion are the foundations upon which we stand, strong and unyielding, against any storm.

This is a testament to the enduring power of connection, the boundless capacity for innovation, and the profound truth that even when the sky falls, humanity finds a way to rise.

For the children who will inherit this transformed earth, may they know the strength that lies within them, the wisdom passed down through generations, and the unwavering promise of a world reborn, nurtured by those who refused to surrender their dreams.

CHAPTER ONE

THE DAY THE SKY FELL

The world, as they knew it, had ceased to exist weeks ago, not with a bang, but with a suffocating whisper. Florida, once a vibrant tapestry of sun-drenched hues and humid air, was now a monochrome dreamscape, perpetually shrouded in a twilight born not of the sun, but of a sky choked with ash. This omnipresent veil muted every color, transforming emerald canopies into spectral silhouettes and azure waters into murky, uninviting pools. Sound itself seemed to be absorbed by the thick blanket of particulate matter that settled on every surface, muffling footsteps, dampening laughter, and reducing the cacophony of everyday life to a hushed murmur.

The air, once sweet with the scent of salt and citrus, now carried a perpetual metallic tang, a constant reminder of the cataclysm that had redefined their reality. Every breath was a conscious act, an inhale tinged with the gritty taste of pulverized rock and the lingering fear of unseen toxins. Buildings, once proud structures of glass and steel, now stood like forgotten monuments, their facades dusted with a uniform layer of grey, their windows staring out like vacant eyes onto a landscape stripped of its vitality. The vibrant greens of manicured lawns and wild mangroves were replaced by a somber palette of muted browns and endless shades of grey. What had once been a land of abundant life was now a desolate tableau, a testament to nature's immense, indifferent power.

In the immediate aftermath, the world had been teetering on the precipice. The ordinary, that comfortable cushion of routine and predictability, had become a distant, almost mythical memory. Gone were the traffic jams, the bustling malls, the predictable rhythms of work and leisure. In its place was a raw, gnawing struggle for existence. Survival wasn't just a goal; it was the only currency that mattered. Every sunrise, if one could even discern it through the perpetual haze, brought with it a renewed urgency. The question wasn't "What will we do today?" but "How will we make it through today?"

The oppressive atmosphere was more than just environmental; it was psychological. The perpetual dimness seeped into the collective consciousness, a constant reminder of the world's wounded state. Hope felt like a fragile ember, easily extinguished by the prevailing gloom. Yet, even in this suffocating twilight, a primal instinct for self-preservation flickered. It was in the cautious movements of those venturing out for dwindling supplies, in the hushed conversations about potential dangers, and in the determined glint in the eyes of those who refused to surrender to the encroaching despair.

The land itself, once so familiar, was now alien. Rivers that once meandered lazily through lush wetlands now flowed sluggishly, their banks lined with skeletal trees coated in ash. The vibrant coral reefs that had teemed with life were now obscured by a film of particulate matter, their vibrant colors fading into oblivion. The familiar chirping of birds was a rarity, replaced by the melancholic cry of unseen creatures or the rustle of wind through the brittle remains of vegetation. Even the familiar warmth of the Florida sun was a forgotten sensation, its rays diffused and weakened by the thick atmospheric veil, casting long, distorted shadows that played tricks on the eyes.

The silence was perhaps the most unnerving aspect. The usual symphony of nature – the buzz of insects, the rustle of leaves, the distant roar of the ocean – had been largely silenced. What remained was a hush, broken only by the wind sighing through the skeletal remains of forests, the crunch of ash underfoot, and the occasional, unnerving groan of stressed structures. This profound quietude amplified every small sound, making the survivors acutely aware of their isolation, of the vast emptiness that now surrounded them. It was a silence that pressed in, that seemed to hold its breath, waiting.

In this altered landscape, the remnants of civilization offered little comfort. Roads were cracked and buckled, some swallowed by encroaching ash drifts. Abandoned vehicles lay scattered like fallen soldiers, their windows opaque with dust, their interiors bearing witness to hasty departures or tragic final moments. Homes, once repositories of warmth and life, were now chillingly still, their contents coated in a fine layer of grey powder, each object a silent testament to the lives that had once inhabited them. The very air inside these abandoned dwellings felt heavy, stagnant, imbued with the lingering scent of absence.

The initial shock had given way to a weary resignation for some, a desperate tenacity for others. The rhythm of life had been brutally reset. Days were now measured not by hours of daylight, but by the cycles of rationing and the constant vigilance required to simply exist. The concept of 'normal' had been obliterated, replaced by a precarious balance of immediate needs and the ever-present threat of the unknown. The world was a canvas of muted tones, and survival was the only splash of color, a fierce, defiant hue against the overwhelming greyness. This was the new reality, the somber yet urgent prelude to whatever lay ahead in the ash-laden twilight of their broken paradise. The oppressive atmosphere was a constant companion, a heavy cloak that settled upon every soul, yet within this suffocating shroud, the seeds of resilience, however small, had begun to stir.

The silence in the small workshop was profound, a heavy blanket that pressed in on Mika from all sides. It wasn't the peaceful quiet of a world at rest, but the suffocating stillness of a world holding its breath. Dust motes, illuminated by the weak, diffused light that filtered through the grimy panes, danced in lazy currents, the only sign of movement in the room. This had been her father's space, a sanctuary of creation and quiet contemplation, now a mausoleum of his absence. The scent of motor oil and aged wood still clung to the air, a phantom perfume that both comforted and gutted her. Every tool laid out with meticulous care, every half-finished project resting on the workbench, was a monument to him, a stark reminder of the void he'd left behind.

She ran a calloused finger along the cool, smooth metal of a salvaged circuit board, her mind a million miles away, sifting through a maelstrom of memories and anxieties. Her father, a man of tireless ingenuity, a tinkerer with an almost magical ability to coax life from dead machines, had been her anchor. Now, adrift in this grey, muted world, his absence felt like a physical ache, a constant pressure behind her ribs. It was his workshop, his legacy, that kept her tethered, that gave her a semblance of purpose in the face of overwhelming desolation. She picked up a pair of pliers, the worn handles familiar and comforting in her grasp, and turned her attention to a tangle of wires. Her hands, accustomed to the delicate work of circuitry and the brute force of wrenching metal, moved with a practiced efficiency, a counterpoint to the turmoil within.

The world outside the workshop was a monochrome blur, a landscape drained of its vibrancy. But here, surrounded by the ghosts of her father's creations and the raw materials of her own nascent survival, Mika found a fragile solace. She was assembling something, a device she wasn't entirely sure would work, but the act of creation itself was a balm. Her father had always told her that innovation was the ultimate act of defiance, a way to push back against the darkness. She clung to that belief like a drowning woman to driftwood. Her hands moved with a focused intensity, stripping insulation, twisting copper strands, her brow furrowed in concentration. The only sounds were the gentle snip of wire cutters, the soft click of components being fitted, and the shallow rhythm of her own breathing.

Her mind, however, was a more chaotic place. Images flickered behind her eyes: the terrifying sky, a canvas of ash and shadow; the eerie silence that had descended after the great purge of sound; the gnawing hunger that had become a constant companion. These memories were like shards of glass, sharp and painful, threatening to shatter her fragile composure. She pushed them back, a skill honed through weeks of relentless anxiety. Her father's voice, calm and steady, echoed in her mind, "Focus on what you can control, Mika. The rest will have to wait." He had been so good at that, at dissecting problems, at breaking down insurmountable challenges into manageable steps. She tried to emulate him, to apply his logic to her own fear.

The device she was working on was a rudimentary atmospheric sensor, an attempt to quantify the invisible threat that permeated their existence. She'd scavenged the delicate sensors from an old weather station, the intricate workings of its internal clock from a discarded digital watch, and the power source from a surprisingly resilient solar panel she'd found tangled in the roots of a toppled oak. Each piece was a testament to her resourcefulness, a small victory snatched from the jaws of despair. Her father would have approved, she knew. He would have watched her with that quiet, knowing pride in his eyes, offering a word of encouragement or a subtly improved design. The thought brought a fresh pang of grief, sharp and unexpected, and she had to pause, her hands trembling, to take a slow, deliberate breath.

She forced herself back to the task at hand. The wires needed to be soldered, a delicate process that required a steady hand and a focused mind. She heated the tip of the soldering iron, the faint hiss a welcome sound, and watched as the molten metal flowed, binding the copper strands with a secure, silvery sheen. It was a small act, a tiny repair in a world that seemed irrevocably broken, but it felt significant. It was a demonstration of agency, a refusal to be a passive victim. Her father's lessons were etched not just in her mind, but in her very hands. He had taught her to see the potential in discarded things, to understand the language of machines, to find order in chaos.

The anxiety, however, was a persistent undertow, threatening to drag her down. It whispered insidious doubts:

What if it doesn't work? What if you're wasting your time? What if there's no point in trying anymore? These were the voices of despair, the echoes of the cataclysm that had reshaped their world. She fought them back, channeling her frustration into the precise movements of her work. She remembered another of her father's sayings: "A problem is just a puzzle waiting to be solved, Mika. Don't let fear stop you from picking up the pieces." She picked up a tiny screw, its threads impossibly fine, and began the meticulous process of fastening the sensor array.

The workshop was her refuge, but it was also a constant reminder of what she had lost. Every object, every tool, every shadow held a memory. She could almost feel his presence beside her, the comforting weight of his hand on her shoulder, the low rumble of his voice as he explained some intricate piece of engineering. But then the illusion would shatter, leaving her alone again with the humming silence and the gnawing ache in her chest. She would bite her lip, forcing the tears back, and focus on the task, on the next connection, the next component.

Her father's workshop was filled with a disorganized order. Shelves overflowed with salvaged parts: vacuum tubes, resistors, capacitors, lengths of wire in a rainbow of muted colors. Gears and sprockets lay in dusty piles. Old radios, their bakelite casings cracked and faded, sat alongside dismantled engines and mysterious metal contraptions whose original purpose was lost to time. It was a testament to his unquenchable curiosity, his belief that nothing was truly beyond repair or repurposing. Mika found herself drawn to a particularly intricate clockwork mechanism, its brass gears tarnished but still perfectly aligned. She remembered him spending weeks on it, a project born purely out of fascination with its complexity. Now, it was just another beautiful, silent artifact.

She traced the outline of a faded schematic pinned to the corkboard, a blueprint for a device she'd never seen him complete. It was a complex network of pipes and chambers, labeled with cryptic symbols and equations. Had it been for filtering water? For generating power? She would never know. The questions, like so many others, hung in the air, unanswered. Her father had been a man of many projects, many ideas, and he had taken so many of them with him when he left. She wondered if she would ever truly understand the full extent of his genius, or if she would spend her days piecing together fragments of his brilliance, forever chasing a ghost.

A sudden, sharp gust of wind rattled the workshop door, making her jump. Her heart leaped into her throat, a primal surge of adrenaline flooding her system. She froze, straining to listen. Was it just the wind, or something more? In this new world, every sound was a potential threat. The wind howled through the skeletal remains of the trees outside, a mournful lament that seemed to echo the desolation of their lives. She cautiously peered through a crack in the dusty window. Nothing but the grey, swirling ash, a perpetual twilight that obscured the world.

She returned to her workbench, her hands still unsteady. The anxiety, though momentarily suppressed, was a persistent hum beneath the surface of her concentration. She picked up a small, intricate circuit board, a piece salvaged from a drone her father had been trying to repair before... before. The tiny components were almost microscopic, requiring the precision of a surgeon. She had always admired her father's dexterity, his ability to work with such minute parts without a tremor. Her own hands, while capable, often felt clumsy by comparison, especially when her nerves were frayed.

She remembered the sheer joy on his face when he'd finally managed to get a stubborn old radio to crackle to life, its static-filled broadcast a ghostly whisper from a lost era. He'd danced a little jig around the workshop, his laughter echoing off the tool-lined walls. That joy felt like a distant, unattainable dream now. The world had become a place of hushed whispers and furtive movements, where laughter was a dangerous luxury. But she held onto those memories, cherishing them like precious relics. They were proof that joy had once existed, that it could exist again.

She carefully began to solder a connection, the heat of the iron a familiar warmth against the chill of her fear. The tiny bead of solder flowed smoothly, creating a perfect, glistening joint. A small victory. A tiny act of creation in a world that felt intent on destruction. Her father had believed in the power of small things, the cumulative effect of many tiny efforts. "One step at a time, Mika," he'd always say. "That's how you climb the highest mountain." She was trying to climb her own mountain, a daunting peak of grief, fear, and the overwhelming task of survival.

She thought about the people in the small, scattered settlements that were beginning to form. They were like her, clinging to life, trying to find a way forward. But she also knew that many were succumbing to despair, to the sheer weight of the loss. She saw it in their vacant eyes, in their listless movements. She didn't want to be like them. She wanted to honor her father's spirit, his unwavering belief in human ingenuity. She wanted to build something, to contribute, to find a purpose beyond mere existence.

The sensor unit was taking shape, a fragile assemblage of scavenged parts. It wasn't much, but it was hers. It was a tangible manifestation of her will to survive, a silent protest against the encroaching darkness. She held it up, examining the intricate wiring, the carefully placed components. It was imperfect, a little rough around the edges, but it was functional. Or, it would be, once she tested it.

A surge of hope, tentative and fragile, flickered within her. It was a dangerous emotion in this world, prone to swift and brutal extinguishment. But for now, she allowed herself to embrace it. Her father would have wanted her to hope. He would have wanted her to keep tinkering, to keep building, to keep looking for the light, however faint, in the pervasive gloom. She carefully placed the sensor on a shelf, next to a dusty, half-finished automaton her father had been working on. It was a silent promise to herself, a commitment to continue the work, to keep his spirit alive in the only way she knew how: through the relentless pursuit of creation, one salvaged part at a time. The anxiety hadn't vanished, but for a brief, precious moment, it had receded, pushed back by the quiet hum of purpose and the enduring echo of her father's voice.

The thin, acrid scent of ozone and something else, something earthy and faintly sweet, clung to the air even in the protected confines of the makeshift greenhouse. Luis traced the pattern of a cracked clay pot with his thumb, its surface rough and strangely porous. It had been his grandmother's, a relic from the Before Times, when pots held vibrant flowers and rich, dark soil teemed with unseen life. Now, it held... this. This mutated earth, this whispering soil that seemed to hold its breath, waiting.

His grandmother, Elena, her face a roadmap of wrinkles etched by worry and wisdom, knelt beside him. Her movements were slow, deliberate, each gesture imbued with a reverence Luis was only just beginning to understand. She held a small trowel, its metal darkened by countless encounters with the altered earth, and carefully scooped a shallow depression. "Patience, Luis," she murmured, her voice a low rumble, like pebbles shifting in a dry riverbed. "The earth remembers. It just needs coaxing."

Luis nodded, his gaze fixed on the scoop of soil Elena held. It was a curious thing, this new soil. Not the rich, black loam of old stories, nor the pale, sterile dust that had blanketed so much of their world after the Sky Fell. This was a peculiar shade of ochre, almost rusty, with a subtle shimmer that caught the weak, filtered light. Sometimes, when the wind was just right, or when the humidity climbed, Luis swore he could hear it. A faint, almost imperceptible hum, a chorus of whispers that seemed to emanate from the very ground beneath their feet. His grandmother called it the 'whispering soil.'

"What do you think it's saying, Nana?" he'd asked her once, his voice barely a breath.

She had looked at him, her eyes, the color of faded denim, holding a depth of understanding that both soothed and unnerved him. "It's singing a song of survival, Luis. A song of change. It's telling us it's still here. It's telling us it's trying."

He had wanted to believe her then, but the despair that clung to their settlement, a damp, chilling shroud, made such hope feel like a dangerous luxury. But Elena, with her quiet persistence and her uncanny connection to the remnants of the natural world, was slowly, painstakingly, planting seeds of possibility within him.

Today, they were planting seeds from a small pouch Elena kept carefully wrapped in oiled cloth. These weren't the robust, familiar vegetables of the old world. These were hardy, mutated strains she had managed to cultivate, coaxing them from stubborn pods that had miraculously survived the atmospheric upheaval. There were small, gnarled tubers that looked more like pebbles than food, and seeds the size of pinpricks, a deep, iridescent blue.

"These," Elena said, holding up a few of the blue seeds, "are from the Sky-Kissed Vine. They say it can grow in even the harshest conditions. Your grandfather... he remembered seeing them once, in the wild, before... before everything." She paused, a familiar shadow crossing her face, then squeezed Luis's hand. "He said they tasted like the first rain after a long drought."

Luis carefully took a seed between his thumb and forefinger. It felt impossibly fragile, a tiny promise held in his palm. He looked at the ochre soil in the pot, then back at his grandmother. "But how do we know it will grow, Nana? This soil... it's so different."

Elena smiled, a slow, gentle unfolding of her features. "We listen, Luis. We observe. And we give it what it needs. It's like learning a new language. You have to be patient, to pay attention to the subtle cues." She gestured to a collection of tools spread out on a worn, oilcloth-covered table: small rakes, delicate sifters, vials of strange-smelling liquids. "This is not like planting in the old days. This soil has its own needs, its own rhythms. We must learn them."

Over the next few weeks, Luis found himself drawn deeper into this strange, new alchemy. Elena's greenhouse, a ramshackle structure patched with salvaged plastic sheeting and bits of metal, became his sanctuary. The air inside, thick with the scent of mutated earth and growing things, was a stark contrast to the perpetual grey haze outside. He learned to sift the soil, to break down the larger clumps, to aerate it just so. Elena taught him how to test its moisture content, not with a finger, but with a small, makeshift moisture meter she'd fashioned from scavenged electronics.

"See this reading, Luis?" she'd say, pointing to a needle on a dial. "It means the soil is thirsty. But not *too* thirsty. Too much water, and it can become sluggish, unable to breathe."

He discovered that the whispering soil responded to different stimuli. Certain metallic objects, when placed near it, seemed to make the whispers louder, more insistent. Elena explained that trace minerals in the metal might be interacting with the unique composition of the soil, perhaps even triggering dormant life. She had a collection of old coins, some brass, some copper, some of a strange, dark alloy he didn't recognize, and she would arrange them around the planting beds in intricate patterns.

"It's like a little offering," she'd explained, her brow furrowed in concentration. "A way of showing the earth we understand it's not just dirt. It's alive, in its own way."

Luis found himself spending hours just sitting near the pots, listening. At first, the whispers were barely perceptible, a faint static in his ears. But as he focused, as he quieted his own mind, they began to take on a more discernible quality. It wasn't language, not as he understood it, but a symphony of subtle shifts in tone and pitch, a rhythmic pulse that seemed to mirror his own heartbeat. He started to notice patterns. The whispers would intensify when the temperature rose, or when a certain nutrient solution – a concoction of fermented plant matter and mineral-rich water Elena had devised – was added.

One afternoon, he was tending to a small patch of the ochre soil where he had planted the blue seeds. He had followed Elena's instructions precisely, creating a shallow furrow, placing the seeds, and gently covering them. He had then arranged a circle of tarnished copper coins around the patch. He sat back on his haunches, his eyes closed, trying to attune himself to the soil's song.

Suddenly, a different sound emerged, a tiny, almost imperceptible *crack*. It wasn't the whisper. It was something new, something distinct. He opened his eyes and leaned closer. There, pushing through the ochre earth, was a single, impossibly delicate shoot, a vibrant, almost startling shade of emerald green. It was so small, so fragile, that he almost missed it. But it was there. Life.

His heart leaped. He wanted to shout, to run and tell Elena, but a strange sense of reverence held him. This was a moment of profound intimacy between him and the earth. He reached out a finger, hesitant to touch, then pulled back. The shoot seemed to glow with an inner light. He looked at the copper coins, at the whispering soil. Had they helped? Had the offering been accepted?

Elena found him a few minutes later, still kneeling by the pot, a look of stunned wonder on his face. She followed his gaze, her own eyes widening. A slow smile spread across her face, brighter than any sunlight. She knelt beside him, her weathered hand resting gently on his shoulder.

"You heard it, didn't you, Luis?" she whispered, her voice thick with emotion. "The song of new beginnings."

Luis could only nod, tears welling in his eyes. It was more than just a sprout. It was proof. Proof that life, in some form, could endure. Proof that the earth, even in its altered state, held the potential for renewal. It was a fragile hope, a single emerald thread woven into the vast tapestry of desolation, but it was there, vibrant and undeniable.

From that day on, Luis's dedication intensified. He learned to read the subtle changes in the soil's texture, its color, even its scent. He discovered that certain mutated fungi, which Elena had cautiously cultivated, seemed to thrive in specific areas, their delicate, bioluminescent caps casting an eerie glow in the dim greenhouse. She believed these fungi were crucial to breaking down the soil's complex compounds, making them accessible to the plants.

"They are the cleaners, Luis," she'd explained, pointing to a cluster of pale blue mushrooms. "They are working tirelessly, breaking down the old, making way for the new. They are part of the whispers, too."

Luis began to collect samples of the fungi, examining them under a salvaged microscope. He marveled at their intricate structures, their alien beauty. He realized that this was not just about survival; it was about understanding a completely new ecosystem, one that had evolved in the ashes of the old.

He started to document everything, filling notebooks with his observations. He drew detailed sketches of the emerging plants, noting their growth patterns, their resilience to atmospheric fluctuations. He recorded the subtle shifts in the soil's whispers, trying to correlate them with specific environmental factors. He was no longer just following his grandmother's guidance; he was actively participating in the discovery.

His determination didn't go unnoticed. Other young people in their settlement, most of them hardened by loss and resigned to a life of scavenging and fear, viewed Luis's efforts with a mixture of bewilderment and suspicion. They saw his time in the greenhouse as a waste, a futile attempt to cling to a world that no longer existed.

"He's wasting his time with dirt," muttered a young man named Kael, his voice laced with a cynicism that had become the default setting for many. "There's nothing in that soil but dust and poison."

But Luis found solace in the quiet work, in the steady rhythm of the greenhouse. The whispers of the soil had become a comforting presence, a constant reminder that he was not alone. He began to see the world differently. He noticed the tenacious weeds that still managed to push through cracks in the pavement outside the settlement walls, their leaves a deeper, richer green than he remembered. He saw the mutated insects, their exoskeletons shimmering with an otherworldly iridescence, and understood that they, too, were adapting, finding a way to exist.

One evening, as a dust storm raged outside, the wind howling a mournful dirge, Luis sat with Elena in the greenhouse. The plastic sheeting rattled, and the faint hum of the soil seemed to deepen, as if in response to the storm's fury.

"They don't understand, do they?" Luis said, gesturing towards the settlement, where the lights were dim, and the mood was somber.

Elena nodded, her gaze fixed on a cluster of small, pale tubers that were just beginning to emerge from a pot. "Fear makes people blind, Luis. They see only what they have lost, not what they can still find. They are waiting for the old world to return, but the old world is gone. We must learn to live in this one."

"And this soil," Luis said, a sense of awe in his voice, "it's not poison, is it? It's... it's just different. It's trying to heal itself. And we can help it."

Elena reached out and squeezed his hand, her grip firm and reassuring. "Exactly, my boy. You're learning to listen. You're learning to speak its language. That's where the real hope lies. Not in rebuilding what was, but in understanding what is, and building something new from it."

Luis looked around the greenhouse, at the rows of carefully nurtured seedlings, at the shimmering fungi, at the ochre soil pulsing with a silent energy. He felt a profound sense of connection, not just to his grandmother, but to the very earth beneath his feet. The despair that had once threatened to swallow him whole seemed to recede, replaced by a quiet determination. He was a part of this new world, and he was determined to help it thrive. The whispers of the soil were no longer a mystery; they were a promise. A promise of resilience, of adaptation, of life, reborn. He knew the path ahead would be difficult, filled with uncertainty and the ever-present threat of failure. But as he looked at the tiny emerald shoot, bathed in the soft glow of the bioluminescent fungi, he felt a flicker of something he hadn't felt in a long time: a quiet, enduring hope. The earth, he realized, was singing. And he was learning to sing along.

He spent countless hours observing the Sky-Kissed Vine seedlings. Their leaves, small and heart-shaped, unfurled with a surprising speed, a vivid green against the ochre soil. He meticulously recorded their growth, noting how they seemed to thrive when positioned under a specific angle of the salvaged UV lamp, and how their growth slowed significantly if exposed to drafts. Elena had identified a peculiar nutrient deficiency in the soil, one that affected the development of chlorophyll, making the plants appear pale and stunted. Her solution was a painstakingly brewed tea, made from the fermented caps of the bioluminescent fungi, which, when diluted and applied, seemed to invigorate the plants, deepening their green hue and, miraculously, intensifying the blue of the nascent seed pods that began to form.

"It's a symbiotic relationship, Luis," Elena explained one evening, her hands stained with the purplish residue of the fungi. "The fungi break down the toxins in the soil, and in return, the plant roots provide them with sugars and other compounds. It's a dance they do together, one we're only just beginning to understand."

Luis, armed with his detailed observations and his grandmother's ancient knowledge, began to experiment further. He learned to measure the soil's pH with remarkable accuracy, using a salvaged colorimetric test kit. He discovered that the soil's acidity levels fluctuated wildly, often in response to atmospheric changes. He hypothesized that the 'whispers' were a form of bio-electrical communication, a way for the soil's microbial network to signal distress or well-being. He began to fashion crude antennae from salvaged wire, strategically placing them around the planting beds, hoping to capture and amplify these signals.

One particularly damp morning, as a thick fog pressed against the greenhouse panes, Luis noticed something extraordinary. The ochre soil seemed to shimmer with an unusual intensity, and the whispers, usually a low hum, were now a distinct, rapid chattering. He rushed to his homemade antennae, a jury-rigged contraption connected to a flickering oscilloscope. The screen, usually displaying a chaotic jumble of lines, was now showing a series of sharp, rhythmic pulses.

"Nana! Look!" he shouted, his voice hoarse with excitement.

Elena hurried over, her eyes widening as she saw the oscilloscope's display. She had never seen such organized patterns. For weeks, the whispers had been growing more complex, more insistent, and now, this. It was as if the earth itself was trying to communicate something vital.

Luis, remembering a passage from one of his grandmother's salvaged botany texts, about seismic activity and its effect on plant life, began to cross-reference his soil readings with atmospheric pressure data he'd been collecting. He noticed a correlation: a rapid drop in atmospheric pressure, often preceding a major dust storm, coincided with a surge in the soil's electrical activity.

"It's warning us, Nana," he said, his mind racing. "The soil... it knows when a storm is coming. The whispers... they're a warning system."

Elena looked at him, a profound sense of wonder in her gaze. "You've done it, Luis. You've learned to truly listen."

This discovery had immediate implications for their small settlement. Luis, emboldened by his success, approached the settlement elders, his notebooks and oscilloscope readings in hand. Initially, they were skeptical, accustomed to relying on instinct and the limited weather forecasts they could sometimes glean from salvaged equipment. But Luis's data was compelling, and Elena's quiet endorsement lent him credibility.

They agreed to test his theory. When the atmospheric pressure began to drop significantly, and the soil's whispers intensified, Luis, with the help of his grandmother, broadcasted a warning to the settlement – a coded series of bell strikes, a language they had developed for such emergencies. For the first time, the community heeded the warning. They secured their homes, gathered their dwindling supplies, and took shelter just as a ferocious dust storm descended, far more violent than anyone had anticipated.

When the storm finally abated, the settlement emerged to find minimal damage. Homes remained intact, and precious supplies were safe. The elders, humbled and amazed, looked at Luis with newfound respect. He had not just cultivated soil; he had cultivated hope, and he had, quite literally, saved them.

This validated Luis's continued work. He began to establish a network of these 'whisper sensors' throughout the settlement, carefully monitoring the soil's subtle communications. He discovered that different areas of the mutated earth seemed to have distinct 'voices,' suggesting variations in their composition and microbial life. He even began to identify specific patterns that seemed to correlate with areas where edible, mutated plants were more likely to be found, allowing their scavenging parties to be more efficient and safer.

His connection to the earth deepened with each passing day. He spent less time in the dimly lit workshops, and more time outdoors, feeling the hum of the soil beneath his worn boots, listening to its ever-evolving song. He understood that this was not just about survival; it was about rediscovering a lost harmony, about learning to coexist with a world that had been irrevocably altered, but not entirely destroyed. The whispering soil, once a symbol of their desolation, had become a beacon of their resilience, and Luis, the boy who listened, was its unlikely, but steadfast, guardian. His grandmother's quiet wisdom, combined with his own innate curiosity and unwavering determination, had unlocked a secret language, a language that promised not just to sustain them, but to help them truly *live* in this new, strange world. The seeds of hope he had sown, in that ochre soil, were beginning to bloom.

The clang of metal against metal echoed through the skeletal remains of what had once been a bustling marketplace. Kiley, her knuckles white as she gripped the worn, rubberized handles of her wheelchair, navigated the uneven terrain with a practiced ease that belied the inherent difficulty. Each jolt and bump was a familiar sensation, a testament to countless excursions through the fractured pathways of their settlement. Her gaze, sharp and appraising, swept across the debris-strewn stalls, cataloging the damage with an engineer's eye and a pragmatist's resolve. Twisted metal, splintered wood, and the ever-present dust, thick as a shroud, were the dominant features. But Kiley didn't see just ruin; she saw potential, she saw problems that needed solving, and she saw people who needed her direction.

Her wheelchair, a marvel of salvaged engineering—its frame a sturdy blend of reinforced metal alloys, its wheels a hybrid of solid, puncture-proof rubber and a few strategically placed, salvaged pneumatic tires for shock absorption—was an extension of her will. It wasn't a symbol of her limitations, but a testament to her adaptability. She had meticulously modified it herself, incorporating a small, multi-tool rack bolted securely to the back, its contents gleaming dully in the filtered sunlight: a compact wrench set, a spool of industrial-grade wire, a pry bar, and a variety of fasteners. These were not luxuries; they were essential components for her mission.

"More of the south quadrant bracing has collapsed," she called out, her voice carrying clearly above the muted sounds of scavenging and the distant whisper of the wind. She was addressing Jian, a wiry young man whose usual demeanor was one of quiet contemplation, but who now moved with a brisk efficiency under Kiley's direction. He was perched precariously on a heap of rubble, using a salvaged crowbar to dislodge a large, jagged piece of reinforced concrete that had fallen from a support beam.

Jian grunted, his muscles straining. "Saw it this morning. Looks like that last dust storm did more than just blow dust around. The main supports on the eastern edge are groaning, too."

Kiley nodded, making a mental note. "Groaning means they're close to failure. We need to reinforce those before the next significant tremor or another storm. Get a team over there. Focus on temporary supports, something that can hold until we can source the better materials from the old fabrication plant. Have them prioritize the structural integrity, not aesthetics. We can patch the cosmetic damage later."

Her words were crisp, efficient, devoid of unnecessary preamble. She had learned early on that in a world where survival was a daily negotiation, time was as precious as clean water. Hesitation or indecision could be as fatal as a structural collapse. She had seen it happen. Those who clung to the old ways, who waited for orders or hoped for miracles, often found themselves left behind, buried under the weight of their own inertia. Kiley, however, had always been a doer.

Her pragmatism was legendary. While others might lament the loss of ornate architecture or lament the scarcity of refined materials, Kiley saw only the functional. A collapsed wall was not just a loss of shelter; it was an opportunity to salvage bricks, mortar, and any intact structural components. A broken piece of machinery wasn't a relic of a bygone era; it was a potential source of usable parts, a puzzle to be dismantled and understood. She had a knack for seeing the hidden value in what others deemed worthless.

"How are the water conduit repairs progressing near the residential block?" she asked, her wheelchair gliding silently towards a section of the marketplace where several elderly women were meticulously sorting through piles of salvaged cloth, their nimble fingers transforming tattered remnants into usable patching material. She knew that even seemingly small tasks contributed to the overall resilience of their community, and she made it a point to check in on all aspects of their ongoing efforts.

A woman named Elara, her face a tapestry of fine lines, looked up from her work, her eyes crinkling at the corners. "Slow, Kiley. Very slow. The main junction beneath what used to be the baker's has sprung a leak. It's a tricky spot to get to, especially with... you know." She gestured subtly towards Kiley's wheelchair.

Kiley didn't miss a beat. She understood the unspoken acknowledgement of her physical challenges, but she also knew Elara's concern was genuine. "I know. But we can't let that water go to waste. Have you assigned enough people to that section? We need to bypass the damaged pipe and reroute the flow. I'll send some of the younger lads with their lifting gear. And Jian, once he's finished with the bracing, can bring his cutting torches. We'll need to sever the old pipe and weld in a new section."

Her focus was always on the solution, on the practical steps needed to overcome the obstacle. She never dwelled on the difficulty, never allowed herself the luxury of despair. Her willpower was a tangible force, a constant hum of determination that propelled her forward. It was this unwavering spirit that had earned her the respect of everyone in the settlement, from the grizzled elders who remembered the Sky Falling to the youngest children who had known no other world.

She steered her chair towards a collection of discarded metal sheeting, picking up a large, relatively intact piece. "This might work as a temporary patch for the baker's storefront," she mused aloud, running a gloved hand over its surface. "It's weathered, but it's solid. If we can get it secured properly, it'll keep the worst of the elements out."

Her mind was a constant whirlwind of logistics, resource management, and problem-solving. She had a mental inventory of every usable tool, every salvaged material, and every skilled individual within their settlement. When a need arose, she could, with remarkable speed, identify the necessary resources and delegate tasks effectively. This organizational prowess was invaluable. It transformed chaotic scavenging efforts into coordinated repair and rebuilding initiatives.

"I need a report on the structural integrity of the western watchtower by sundown," she instructed a young man named Finn, who was meticulously sharpening a salvaged blade. Finn, like many of his generation, had grown up amidst scarcity and danger. His hands, though calloused, moved with a surprising delicacy as he honed the edge of his tool.

Finn looked up, his expression serious. "Will do, Kiley. I'll take the surveyors with me. We'll check the foundation and the main support columns."

"And make sure they're using the sonic scanners," Kiley added, her voice firm. "We need to detect any internal fractures that aren't visible on the surface. We can't afford any surprises with that structure."

Her foresight was a crucial element in their collective survival. She understood that proactive maintenance and early detection of problems were far more efficient and less costly than reactive repairs after a disaster had struck. This was a lesson learned from the harsh realities of their post-apocalyptic existence. The Sky Falling had taught them all the brutal consequences of neglect.

As she navigated through a particularly dense section of debris, Kiley encountered a small group of children, their faces smudged with dirt, their eyes wide with a mixture of curiosity and apprehension. They were playing near a partially collapsed section of a building, their game a precarious dance around the dangerous ruins.

"Hey!" Kiley called out, her tone firm but not unkind. "Come away from there, you lot. That section looks unstable. Wouldn't want anyone getting hurt."

The children scattered, a few offering nervous smiles as they retreated to a safer distance. Kiley watched them for a moment, a flicker of maternal concern softening her features. These children represented the future, and it was her responsibility, along with everyone else in the settlement, to ensure that future had a solid foundation, both literally and figuratively.

"You know," said a voice from beside her, a voice that always carried a hint of amusement, "you have a way of making even the most dangerous ruins sound like a construction site needing a supervisor."

It was Marcus, his frame lean and his smile easy. He was a skilled scavenger, his knowledge of the surrounding territories unmatched. He often worked alongside Kiley, his ability to procure rare materials complementing her organizational skills.

Kiley grinned, a genuine, unguarded expression that rarely surfaced during her work. "Someone has to. Can't let them run wild, can we? Besides, a little bit of structure keeps the chaos from swallowing us whole."

Marcus leaned against a toppled signpost, its weathered letters barely decipherable. "You do a remarkable job, Kiley. Especially... given the circumstances." He paused, a flicker of something unreadable in his eyes, before continuing, "I saw the blueprints you drafted for the new filtration system. Ingenious. Truly."

Kiley's cheeks flushed slightly. She was used to praise for her practical skills, but Marcus's acknowledgement of her design work, her more abstract contributions, always struck a deeper chord. "It's just putting pieces together, Marcus. Like you do with your scavenging runs. We're all just trying to make do with what we have."

"But you do it with such... vision," Marcus countered. "You see beyond the immediate. You plan for the future, for the *next* problem. That's rare, Kiley. Especially when most people are just focused on getting through the day." He pushed off the signpost, his gaze sweeping across the ruined marketplace. "The western perimeter fence needs a significant overhaul. I found a cache of usable metal plating near the old highway overpass. Enough to reinforce a good section of it."

"Excellent," Kiley responded, her focus immediately shifting back to the task at hand. "We'll need to organize a transport team. And we'll need to assess the gate mechanisms. If we're reinforcing the fence, we need to ensure the entry points are just as secure. Have you had a chance to look at the hinges on the main gate?"

"I have," Marcus confirmed. "They're rusted through. We'll need to replace them entirely. And we'll need more of that high-tensile wire you sourced last month. The kind that doesn't snap when you look at it funny."

Kiley made another mental note. "I'll put in a request for the wire. And for the hinges, we'll need to see what we can salvage from the industrial district. There's an old factory complex there that might have what we need. I'll scout it out myself next week, if necessary. Bring the cutting gear and the heavy-duty winch."

Her wheelchair glided forward, her movements purposeful. She paused at the edge of a partially collapsed structure, peering into the gloom. "This building... the foundation looks compromised. It's leaning precariously. We'll need to cordon it off completely. And I want a full structural assessment before we even consider salvaging anything from inside. It's not worth risking lives for potentially damaged materials."

Her commitment to safety was unwavering. She understood that the pursuit of resources could not come at the cost of human lives. Her own experiences had instilled in her a profound respect for the fragility of life and the unforgiving nature of their world. She would often spend hours meticulously planning salvage operations, calculating risks, and implementing safety protocols, ensuring that every member of the team returned home safely.

Later that day, as the sun began its slow descent, casting long shadows across the devastated landscape, Kiley found herself near the settlement's medical bay. She saw Anya, the settlement's primary medic, tending to a young man whose arm was bandaged and splinted.

"How's he doing?" Kiley asked, her voice soft.

Anya looked up, her brow furrowed with a mixture of fatigue and concern. "He'll be alright. Just a bad sprain from a fall. But Kiley, we're running low on antiseptic solutions. And our supply of pain relievers is dwindling fast."

Kiley's jaw tightened. This was the constant, gnawing challenge of their existence: the scarcity of essential resources. "I know. I've been trying to find alternative sources. We've experimented with some of the local herbs, but their efficacy is... inconsistent." She gestured towards her wheelchair, a subtle but clear indication of her own reliance on medical supplies. "I'll make a priority of scouting the old pharmacy district tomorrow. It's a risk, I know, but we might find something usable."

Anya nodded, her gaze appreciative. "I trust your judgment, Kiley. You always find a way."

As Kiley prepared to leave, she noticed a young boy, no older than eight, sitting near the medical bay, his face pale and drawn. He clutched a crudely made wooden toy soldier.

"Hey there," Kiley said, her voice gentle. "Are you feeling alright?"

The boy nodded, but his eyes were downcast.

"You look a little under the weather," Kiley continued, wheeling closer. "Is your leg bothering you?"

He nodded again, a tear tracing a path through the grime on his cheek. "It aches, ma'am."

Kiley's heart ached. She remembered being that young, that vulnerable, that dependent on the kindness and ingenuity of others. "Don't worry," she said, offering him a reassuring smile. "Anya's the best at making things feel better. And if that doesn't work, I know where we can find some of those special soothing poultices. They smell a bit funny, but they work wonders."

She stayed with him for a few more minutes, talking about the games she used to play as a child, about the stories she'd heard from her grandmother, anything to distract him from his discomfort. It was this quiet empathy, this refusal to let the harshness of their world extinguish her compassion, that truly defined Kiley. She was a force of nature, not because she was immune to hardship, but because she refused to be defined by it. Her willpower wasn't just about fixing things; it was about holding onto the very essence of what it meant to be human in a world that constantly threatened to strip them of their humanity. Her wheelchair was merely her chariot, carrying her forward, always forward, towards a brighter, more secure future for her people. Her unwavering resolve was a silent, but powerful, testament to the enduring strength of the human spirit, a spirit that, like the whispered soil in Luis's greenhouse, found ways to grow, adapt, and thrive, even in the most desolate of landscapes. She was the architect of their resilience, the pragmatic guardian of their hope, and her unwavering will was the foundation upon which their future was being built, one salvaged beam, one repaired pipe, one secured fence at a time.

Jax moved through the skeletal remains of the city with a practiced stealth, the worn leather of his camera bag a familiar weight against his shoulder. His eyes, accustomed to the muted palette of their post-Sky Dark world, constantly scanned his surroundings, not for threats in the immediate sense – those were often too obvious to require such delicate observation – but for the stories etched into the very fabric of their existence. His camera, a relic salvaged from a time when capturing moments was an art form rather than a desperate act of remembrance, felt like an extension of his own being. It was his lens, his voice, his way of bearing witness.

He paused near what had once been a vibrant park, now a desolate expanse of cracked concrete and skeletal trees clawing at the perpetually bruised sky. A young woman, no older than Kiley, was meticulously tending to a small patch of hardy, urban weeds, her movements slow and deliberate. Jax raised his camera, the gentle whir of the aperture a soft punctuation in the pervasive silence. He framed her, capturing the determined set of her jaw, the grime on her hands, the quiet defiance in her posture as she coaxed life from the barren earth. This was not just about documenting destruction; it was about celebrating the persistent, stubborn pulse of life that refused to be extinguished. He clicked the shutter, a silent promise to remember.

Later, he found himself on the periphery of the marketplace, a place Kiley kept meticulously organized, a hub of salvaged goods and nervous energy. He saw a group of children, their faces smudged with the ubiquitous dust, gathered around an elderly man who was skillfully carving a small wooden bird from a piece of scavenged driftwood. The children watched, mesmerized, their usual boisterous energy subdued by a shared focus. Jax crouched, lowering his camera to their eye level, a gesture of respect and inclusion. He captured the rapt expressions on their faces, the hopeful glint in their eyes as the bird began to take shape, a fragile symbol of flight and freedom in a world that had grounded them all. He knew that these moments, these small acts of creation and wonder, were just as vital to their survival as Kiley's structural reinforcements or Anya's dwindling medical supplies. They were the threads of joy, the whispers of a future that, while uncertain, was still worth imagining.

Jax's camera was more than a tool; it was his way of processing the overwhelming loss. He had been a boy when the Sky Dark descended, and the memory of vibrant colors, of clear blue skies, of the mundane beauty of a world taken for granted, was seared into his mind. He remembered the blinding flash, the deafening roar, and then the suffocating, perpetual twilight that had followed. His parents... they were gone, swallowed by the initial chaos, leaving him to navigate the ruins with a knot of grief that had never truly loosened. His camera became his confidante, his way of holding onto what had been, and his shield against the crushing weight of what now was. He found solace in the act of framing, of distilling the vastness of their tragedy into manageable, meaningful images.

He followed Kiley's wheelchair as she navigated a particularly treacherous section of collapsed roadway, her focus unwavering as she directed Jian and his team. Jax didn't interfere with her work; his role was to observe, not to direct. He captured the determined set of her shoulders, the way her brow furrowed in concentration as she assessed a particularly precarious pile of debris. He saw the glint of determination in her eyes, the sheer force of her will that seemed to radiate outward, a silent command to the world around her. He framed a shot that included Kiley, Jian, and the precarious structural support they were struggling to erect, a visual narrative of their struggle against entropy. He knew that these images, these frozen moments of effort and resilience, would tell a story long after the dust settled.

He spent time with Elara and the other women as they painstakingly sorted through piles of salvaged fabric, their hands moving with a practiced rhythm. Jax captured the fine lines etched around their eyes, the quiet camaraderie that passed between them with a shared glance or a soft sigh. He focused on their hands, gnarled and weathered, yet still capable of transforming tattered remnants into usable material, a testament to their enduring artistry and resourcefulness. He saw in their work a powerful metaphor for their community – taking the broken pieces of the past and weaving them into a functional, if imperfect, present. He photographed Elara's smile as she held up a particularly well-patched piece of cloth, a small victory in a world of constant defeats.

Jax's process was slow, deliberate. He didn't chase after dramatic moments of destruction or overt displays of suffering. Instead, he sought out the quieter narratives, the subtle acts of kindness, the glimmers of hope that flickered in the dim light of their world. He would spend hours observing a single interaction, waiting for the right expression, the right angle, the right confluence of light and shadow to capture the essence of the moment. He believed that the true story of their survival lay not in the grand gestures, but in the countless small acts of resilience that happened every day, often unnoticed.

He remembered photographing Luis, a man whose dedication to his small, makeshift greenhouse was a constant source of wonder. Jax had found him there, a sanctuary of vibrant green against the muted grays and browns of the outside world. Luis was carefully misting a fragile seedling, his face illuminated by the soft glow of the salvaged grow lights. Jax had captured the tender way Luis cradled a leaf, his hands stained with soil, his eyes filled with a gentle reverence for the burgeoning life. These images, of Luis's verdant haven, of the children's rapt faces, of Kiley's tireless leadership, of Elara's patient hands, were not just photographs; they were affirmations. They were proof that even in the face of profound loss, humanity's capacity for creation, for care, and for hope, persisted.

Jax's archive was growing, a vast collection of digital files stored on salvaged data drives, a meticulously organized testament to their struggle. He saw his role as that of an archivist, a storyteller for a future that might never fully understand the depth of their sacrifice, but deserved to know of their endurance. He envisioned a time, perhaps generations from now, when these images would be viewed, not as relics of despair, but as proof of their resilience, of their refusal to be defined by the Sky Dark. He saw himself as a guardian of memory, ensuring that the faces, the struggles, and the quiet triumphs of his community would not be lost to the encroaching oblivion.

One evening, as the faint glow of emergency lights flickered across the settlement, Jax found himself near the perimeter fence, watching Marcus and his team work to secure a section that had been damaged by a recent tremor. Marcus, his movements efficient and strong, was supervising the installation of new metal plating. Jax framed a shot that captured the raw power of their labor, the sweat beading on Marcus's brow, the glint of metal in the dim light, and the determined focus of the men working alongside him. He saw in this image the unyielding determination of their community, their constant, tireless effort to mend, to rebuild, to protect.

He then turned his lens towards the children again, who were being led inside by Anya for the night. They walked hand-in-hand, their small silhouettes stark against the darkening sky. Jax captured their tired, but still hopeful, faces, the faint smiles that touched their lips as they looked towards the warmth and safety of their communal living quarters. He knew that these children, so innocent and yet so resilient, represented the future he was working to document, the future his photographs were meant to honor.

Jax often found himself drawn to the edges of their settlement, to the points where the fragile order of their community met the chaotic vastness of the ruined world. He would stand for hours, his camera by his side, observing the subtle shifts in the light, the distant sounds of the wind whistling through broken structures, the quiet dignity of those who continued their daily tasks amidst the ruins. He wasn't a fighter, nor a builder, but he understood his own unique value. He was the chronicler, the one who would ensure that the story of their survival, the story of their enduring humanity, would not be lost to the shadows. His lens was a constant, quiet presence, capturing the unvarnished truth of their lives, a testament to their strength, their loss, and their unwavering hope for a brighter dawn. He understood that memory was a powerful weapon against despair, and his photographs were his contribution to that ongoing fight, his way of etching their story into the fabric of time, ensuring that the Sky Dark would never truly have the last word. He would capture the way Kiley's face lit up when a particularly difficult engineering problem was solved, the quiet pride in Anya's eyes when a patient recovered, the shared laughter that erupted unexpectedly during a communal meal. These were the moments that mattered, the moments that proved their spirit remained unbroken.

He remembered a particular day when a dust storm had threatened to overwhelm their defenses. He had been with Anya, helping her secure the medical bay's windows. The wind had howled like a banshee, and the dust had swirled with an almost malevolent intent. Yet, even in the midst of that chaos, he had seen Anya calmly reassure a frightened child, her voice a steady anchor in the storm. He had captured the soft glow of her lantern illuminating the child's face, a small pocket of peace within the tempest. That photograph, he felt, encapsulated the essence of their struggle – the relentless battle against the elements, the unwavering commitment to protect the vulnerable, and the quiet courage that sustained them.

Jax's collection was not just about preserving the past; it was about understanding the present and, in some small way, shaping the future. By documenting their resilience, he hoped to inspire it. By capturing their moments of joy, he hoped to create more of them. He was a silent observer, a patient witness, and his camera was the conduit through which their story would be told. He continued his work, day after day, click by click, frame by frame, adding to the burgeoning visual narrative of a community determined to survive, to rebuild, and to remember, long after the Sky Dark had faded into a distant, harrowing memory. He understood that the true measure of their survival would not be in the absence of scars, but in the strength and beauty they found in healing and in creating anew, a concept he strived to embody in every frame he captured.

Chapter Two
SEEDS OF HOPE

The remnants of the old world, so carefully cataloged by Jax, offered little in the way of established currency. The gleaming coins and crisp paper that had once dictated value were now mere historical curiosities, useless artifacts of a forgotten age. In their place, a more fundamental form of exchange had begun to bloom, an organic, often messy, manifestation of necessity and mutual need. It was the barter system, a testament to humanity's innate ability to adapt and innovate, even when faced with the bleakest of circumstances.

In the heart of what had once been a bustling marketplace, now a haphazard collection of makeshift stalls and huddled groups, the rhythm of this new economy pulsed. It wasn't dictated by the ticking of clocks or the pronouncements of distant authorities, but by the more primal urgencies of hunger, shelter, and survival. A farmer with a surplus of dried roots might trade with a scavenger who had managed to secure a spool of sturdy wire. A former mechanic, his hands still possessing a surprising dexterity despite the grime that coated them, could offer to mend a broken water pump in exchange for a week's worth of preserved rations.

Mika, with her sharp mind and even sharper fingers, found herself at the center of a peculiar niche within this burgeoning trade. Her understanding of the salvaged technological marvels that littered their landscape was invaluable. The flickering lights of their communal shelters, the temperamental generators that sputtered to life only with coaxing, the salvaged communication devices that sometimes, miraculously, crackled with faint, distant signals – these were her domain. She could coax life back into dead circuits, reroute power grids that had long since surrendered, and decipher the cryptic schematics that offered glimpses into the lost art of engineering.

Her skills were in high demand. A family struggling to keep their salvaged food synthesizer functioning, its monotonous hum now a precious sound, would offer her a portion of their precious harvest in return for her expertise. Luis, his hands perpetually stained with the rich earth he now cultivated, would often seek her out. His small, meticulously tended plots of resilient vegetables were a lifeline, and he understood the importance of preserving the bounty. "Mika," he'd say, his voice raspy but kind, holding out a basket of the first tender shoots of a hardy kale variant, "this generator is making a strange noise again. It sounds like it's about to cough its last breath."

Mika, wiping grease from her brow with the back of her hand, would nod. "Let me see, Luis. I think I know what it is. A loose coupling, perhaps. And in return," she'd add, a faint smile playing on her lips, "I'll need a double portion of those greens. My stomach has been rumbling like a distressed transformer all morning." Their exchanges were often accompanied by a quiet understanding, a mutual respect forged in the crucible of shared hardship. Luis, in turn, would sometimes find himself explaining the intricacies of crop rotation to Mika, his passion for the earth as evident as her passion for the machines. He'd teach her how to read the soil, how to coax life from barren ground, knowledge that was becoming increasingly vital as their reliance on salvaged rations dwindled.

Kiley, ever the pragmatist, played a crucial role in stabilizing these nascent economic interactions. Her understanding of their settlement's infrastructure, her ability to assess structural integrity and predict potential points of failure, made her an indispensable facilitator. She didn't directly trade in goods, but in services and in the vital infrastructure that allowed trade to occur. When a scavenger returned with a haul of useful materials – sturdy planks of salvaged metal, coils of insulated wire, functional gears from long-dead machinery – Kiley was often the first point of contact. She would assess their value, not in terms of pre-Collapse currency, but in terms of what they could be used for.

"These metal sheets are good," she'd declare, her voice carrying a no-nonsense authority as she ran a gloved hand over the cool, unyielding surface. "Strong enough to reinforce the eastern wall. We can offer you two days of guarded scavenging duty for this, or a share of the next grain harvest, processed and milled." She became a de facto arbiter, her judgment respected precisely because it was rooted in the practical needs of their survival. She also facilitated the exchange of repaired tools. If Jian's team managed to salvage and refurbish a set of spades or a functioning axe, Kiley would negotiate their distribution, ensuring they went to those who could most effectively utilize them, and in return, extract promises of labor or produce. She was the grease that smoothed the gears of their rudimentary market, ensuring that valuable resources were not hoarded but strategically deployed.

And then there was Jax. His camera, once a tool for artistic expression and documentation, had evolved into something more. In a world starving for connection and a sense of continuity, his photographs became a form of social currency. He didn't trade in tangible goods, but in captured moments, in visual narratives that reminded them of what they were fighting for, and what they had already achieved.

He would often spend his days observing the exchanges, the quiet negotiations, the small triumphs and inevitable frustrations. He'd photograph Mika working on a sputtering generator, her face illuminated by the harsh glow of a salvaged work lamp, the image conveying not just her technical skill, but the quiet desperation and hope that fueled their existence. He'd capture Luis, his hands buried in the earth, a picture of quiet dedication, the vibrant green of his fledgling crops a stark contrast to the muted tones of their world. He'd photograph Kiley, her brow furrowed in concentration as she directed a team reinforcing a crumbling wall, the image a testament to her leadership and the community's collective effort.

These photographs weren't just personal keepsakes; they became something of value in themselves. When resources were scarce, and a family needed an extra ration or a coveted tool, offering Jax a compelling story, a chance to capture a moment that truly represented their contribution or struggle, could sometimes sway the decision. He became a storyteller, and in their fractured world, stories held a potent, intangible power. He had once photographed an elderly woman, her name lost to the chaos, meticulously mending a child's worn-out shoe. The image, imbued with a profound sense of care and resilience, had been offered to the community council, and in return, the woman had been granted an extra portion of medicinal herbs for her persistent cough. Jax's documentation was a form of social capital, a way of acknowledging and validating the contributions of individuals, and in doing so, weaving a stronger social fabric. He wasn't just capturing images; he was reinforcing the bonds that held them together.

The challenges of this new economic order were, of course, numerous. Disputes arose over the perceived value of goods and services. A bushel of plump, sun-ripened tomatoes might seem like a king's ransom to a family that had subsisted on dried rations for months, but to Luis, who had painstakingly nurtured them, their value was tied to the labor, the water, and the precious sunlight required to produce them. Ensuring fairness was a constant negotiation. Kiley often found herself mediating these disagreements, her calm demeanor and logical approach a much-needed balm.

"This is not a fair trade," a man might grumble, holding up a handful of polished stones he had found near the old riverbed. "These are beautiful. They should be worth more than a single loaf of bread."

Kiley would patiently explain, "Those stones are beautiful, Silas, and I appreciate your effort in finding them. But this bread is made from grain that took weeks to mill, and the baker needs to eat too. And this loaf will feed a family for two meals. The stones, while lovely, do not sustain us. Perhaps if you found a dozen of them, or something that could be crafted into something useful, we could discuss a different exchange."

Her explanations were never dismissive, but always rooted in the practical realities of their survival. She understood that resentment and perceived unfairness could quickly erode the fragile trust that held their community together.

Jax, in his own quiet way, also contributed to this sense of fairness. By documenting the hard work of individuals – the long hours spent scavenging, the meticulous care given to crops, the painstaking repairs of vital equipment – he provided a visual record of effort and contribution. His photographs served as an objective, albeit artistic, testament to the labor involved, helping to temper disputes by reminding everyone of the tangible efforts behind every salvaged item and every cultivated harvest. When a debate arose over the value of a repaired tool, Jax's image of the mechanic painstakingly working on it, sweat beading on their brow, could often tip the scales towards a more equitable agreement.

Mika, too, faced her own ethical quandaries. As the sole person with the intricate knowledge to repair the salvaged water purification system, she held significant leverage. There were whispers, hushed conversations in shadowed corners, about her demanding exorbitant amounts for her services. But Mika, though pragmatic, had a deep-seated sense of community. She remembered the kindness shown to her when she first arrived, broken and alone. She had seen the devastation wrought by unchecked greed in the stories of the Collapse. And so, she tried to balance her needs with the needs of others. She would often ask for payment in terms of knowledge shared, in spare parts that could be used to train others, or in simple acts of kindness. She would accept extra food, yes, but she would also meticulously teach a willing apprentice the basics of her craft, ensuring that her unique skills would not die with her. This commitment to sharing her knowledge was its own form of social currency, building goodwill and investing in the long-term survival of the community.

Luis's agricultural skills, though nascent, were a vital contribution. He had a knack for coaxing life from the often-stubborn soil of their region. He experimented with different salvaged seeds, cross-referencing them with faded botanical guides he had found, meticulously recording their growth patterns. His small greenhouse, a patchwork of salvaged glass and plastic sheeting, was a testament to his dedication. He traded his produce cautiously, understanding its intrinsic value. He would offer a share of his harvest to those who helped him maintain the greenhouse – reinforcing its fragile structure, hauling water, or standing guard against opportunistic scavengers drawn by the promise of fresh food. He also traded with families who had specific dietary needs, understanding that a consistent supply of fresh vegetables was crucial for maintaining health. His exchanges were marked by a deep respect for the natural world and a recognition of the slow, patient work required to nurture life. He'd often speak of the interconnectedness of things, how the rain that nourished his crops also filled their water stores, how the earth that fed them also provided the materials for their homes. This philosophy permeated his trading, ensuring that his exchanges were not just transactional but symbiotic.

The barter system, therefore, was more than just a series of one-off trades. It was an evolving social contract. It fostered interdependence, forcing individuals to recognize their reliance on one another. The lone scavenger who managed to find a cache of perfectly preserved tools might be strong and resourceful, but without Mika's ability to repair their damaged equipment, their finds would be of limited use. The farmer with a thriving harvest, without Kiley's foresight in reinforcing their storage facilities, risked losing their precious bounty to decay or opportunistic raids.

Jax's camera served as a constant visual reminder of this interdependence. He would often photograph scenes of collaboration: Mika and Luis working together to troubleshoot a faulty irrigation system, Kiley overseeing a joint effort to repair a damaged marketplace stall, Jian's team working alongside scavengers to bring in essential building materials. These images, displayed in communal areas, served as subtle, yet powerful, reinforcements of their shared destiny. They illustrated the principle that their collective strength lay not just in individual prowess, but in their ability to cooperate and to pool their diverse talents.

The challenges, however, were far from over. As the community grew, so did the complexity of its needs. The initial, straightforward exchanges of food for labor or tools for services began to evolve. Disputes over quality and quantity became more frequent. The temptation to hoard, to exploit a momentary advantage, remained a constant threat to the fragile harmony. There were those who, remembering the excesses of the pre-Collapse world, sought to amass personal fortunes through shrewd, and sometimes ruthless, bartering. Kiley and the community council had to be vigilant, establishing clear guidelines and resolving conflicts with fairness and consistency.

One recurring issue involved the "luxury" items salvaged from the old world. A working music player, a collection of intact books, or a finely crafted piece of jewelry, while not essential for survival, held significant emotional and social value. Their exchange became a delicate balancing act. Should such items be traded for vital resources, or should they be preserved as reminders of a richer past? Jax, through his documentation, often provided a way to navigate these questions. He'd photograph a family sharing a salvaged book by the flickering light of a communal fire, capturing the joy and intellectual nourishment it provided. This visual narrative could then be used in discussions about the broader value of such items, pushing for exchanges that acknowledged not just material needs, but also the psychological and cultural sustenance that these relics offered.

Mika, too, faced a constant pressure to prioritize essential repairs over the more trivial requests that sometimes came her way. A plea to fix a child's salvaged toy might be met with a polite refusal, or a request for a more critical need in return. But she also understood the importance of morale. A small, working toy, a moment of childhood normalcy, could be as vital to a child's well-being as a functioning generator was to the community's infrastructure. These nuanced decisions, the constant weighing of immediate needs against long-term well-being, were a hallmark of the evolving leadership within their settlement.

Luis, while deeply committed to the practical aspects of agriculture, also recognized the symbolic power of his harvests. The first ripe tomato, offered as a gift rather than a trade, could signify goodwill and abundance. The sharing of seeds, not just for exchange but for the purpose of propagation, fostered a sense of shared ownership and future growth. His approach to trading was less about maximizing personal gain and more about cultivating a resilient ecosystem, both in the soil and within the community.

The barter system, in its nascent form, was a testament to human ingenuity. It was a messy, imperfect, but ultimately vital mechanism for survival. It highlighted the inherent desire for connection and cooperation that lay at the heart of human society. Jax's photographs, Mika's technical prowess, Luis's connection to the earth, and Kiley's pragmatic leadership – these were the threads that were slowly, tentatively, weaving a new social and economic tapestry from the tattered remnants of the old world. It was a system built not on abstract value, but on tangible needs, shared labor, and the dawning realization that their collective survival depended on their ability to rely on one another, to trade not just goods, but trust, knowledge, and hope. The marketplace, once a symbol of individual enterprise and profit, was slowly transforming into a crucible where community was forged, one carefully considered exchange at a time.

The ever-present haze, a constant reminder of the Collapse and the lingering poison in the air, was Mika's silent adversary. It wasn't just a visual blight; it was a tangible threat, a gritty veil that settled on everything, clinging to lungs and etching itself into the collective consciousness. While others focused on the immediate needs of food, water, and shelter, Mika's mind, always a few steps ahead, wrestled with the invisible enemy. The whispers of persistent coughs, the dull ache behind the eyes that never quite disappeared, the knowledge that every breath taken outside their meager shelters was a gamble – these fueled a quiet, gnawing anxiety within her. It was this pervasive unease, coupled with her insatiable curiosity about how things worked and how they could be *made* to work better, that spurred her most ambitious project yet.

Her small dwelling, a salvaged section of a pre-Collapse office building, offered a modicum of protection, but even here, the air felt thick, heavy. She'd spend hours staring out the grime-streaked window, watching the motes of dust dance in the weak sunlight, wondering what invisible particles they carried. The salvaged fans she'd managed to coax back to life offered some circulation, but they merely churned the existing air, pushing the same contaminants around. It wasn't enough. She craved something more, something that would actively cleanse, that would offer a true sanctuary from the pervasive toxicity.

The idea began as a flicker, an almost subconscious thought born from observing the remnants of the old world. She remembered seeing images of complex ventilation systems in industrial schematics, abstract diagrams that had once seemed impossibly intricate. Now, those same diagrams, once discarded as irrelevant relics, became her blueprints. Her workshop, a corner of her dwelling piled high with salvaged electronics and mechanical detritus, became a laboratory of innovation.

Her primary focus was on creating a functional air filter, a device that could actively scrub the air she breathed. It was a monumental task, requiring a blend of salvaged ingenuity and a deep understanding of basic physics. She started with the core components. The salvaged fans, small but surprisingly robust desk fans from defunct offices, were the obvious choice for air circulation. But simply blowing air wasn't the solution. She needed a filtration medium.

The old furnace filters, brittle and stained with decades of neglect, were her first significant find. They were designed for a different era, a different kind of air, but the principle was sound. She meticulously cleaned them, using precious water and a stiff brush, painstakingly removing the accumulated grime. Some were too far gone, disintegrating in her hands, but she managed to salvage enough intact sections to begin her work.

Layering became her new art form. She experimented with different fabrics, scavenged from old clothing, upholstery, even the tattered remnants of advertising banners. She discovered that tightly woven cotton provided a decent initial barrier, catching larger particles. Thinner, more permeable synthetics, when layered strategically, seemed to trap finer dust. She even found success with activated charcoal, a surprising find from a discarded aquarium filter, meticulously crushed and layered between fabric sheets. This, she theorized, would be crucial for absorbing some of the more volatile airborne compounds, the invisible toxins that worried her the most.

The process was painstaking. She'd spend days hunched over her makeshift workbench, carefully cutting, sewing, and assembling. Her fingers, usually nimble with wires and circuit boards, now worked with a different kind of precision, stitching seams to ensure no gaps remained, testing the airflow of each newly constructed filter element. She learned to feel the resistance, the subtle change in how the fan's motor labored as more layers were added. It was a delicate balance between effective filtration and maintaining sufficient airflow. Too much resistance, and the fan would overheat, burn out, or simply fail to move enough air. Too little, and the filtration would be inadequate.

She documented every step, her salvaged notepad filling with scrawled diagrams and observations. "Layer 1: Dense weave cotton, catches visible dust. Layer 2: Activated charcoal dust, bound with thin gauze. Layer 3: Finer weave synthetic, catches smaller particles. Layer 4: Another cotton layer for structural integrity." She tested the prototypes by holding them close to her face, taking deep breaths, trying to gauge the difference. The subtle shift, the slight reduction in that ever-present gritty sensation, was enough to keep her going.

One evening, after weeks of relentless work, she assembled her most promising prototype. It was an ungainly contraption, a salvaged desk fan bolted to a wooden frame, with a series of layered filter cartridges attached to its intake. She connected it to a salvaged power source, a small, hand-cranked generator she'd meticulously repaired, her heart pounding with a mixture of anticipation and dread. She began to crank, the generator groaning to life, and then, the fan whirred.

The sound was surprisingly gentle, a steady hum that filled her small dwelling. She held her breath and inhaled deeply, moving her head slowly, taking in the air from different parts of the room. It was...

different. Noticeably different. The oppressive weight seemed to have lifted. The subtle, metallic tang that usually lingered on her tongue was gone. She felt a lightness in her chest, a clean, crisp sensation she hadn't experienced in years.

A wide, unbidden smile spread across her face. It worked. Her chaotic, jury-rigged contraption, built from the discarded scraps of a dead world, was actually filtering the air. She sat there for a long time, simply breathing, reveling in the sensation of clean air filling her lungs. It was a profound relief, a physical manifestation of her ingenuity and her refusal to succumb to the environmental decay that had crippled so many others.

The implications were immediate. Her personal space, once a sanctuary only in its relative isolation, was now truly a haven. She could sleep better, her coughs lessening, her headaches subsiding. The constant anxiety that had accompanied every breath began to recede, replaced by a quiet sense of accomplishment. She had, in a small but significant way, reclaimed a piece of her own well-being from the clutches of the toxic environment.

But Mika's mind, even in moments of personal triumph, always looked beyond herself. She saw the weary faces of her neighbors, the children whose lungs were still developing in this poisoned atmosphere, the elders struggling with respiratory ailments. If she could create this for herself, couldn't she create it for them? The thought sparked a new wave of determination. This wasn't just a personal victory; it was a potential solution, a beacon of hope for others struggling with the invisible threat.

She began to refine her design, looking for ways to make it more efficient, more robust, and, eventually, more reproducible. She experimented with different fan speeds, different filter densities, and different housing materials. She realized that the charcoal layer was critical and began to stockpile any source she could find, even experimenting with burning and crushing wood in a controlled environment to create her own basic activated charcoal. The process was slow, requiring careful temperature regulation to avoid combustion, but the results were promising.

She also began to consider the practicalities of sharing her invention. Her initial prototype relied on a hand-cranked generator, a labor-intensive process. She explored ways to power multiple units, perhaps through a more robust, community-managed generator, or even by harnessing solar power if she could find enough intact solar panels and charge controllers. The challenges were immense, but the vision of clean air flowing through their communal shelters, of children being able to play outside without immediate respiratory distress, fueled her drive.

Mika's filtered breath was more than just a personal comfort; it was a tangible demonstration of what could be achieved with discarded materials and a determined mind. It was a subtle rebellion against the suffocating reality of their world, a quiet declaration that humanity's will to thrive, to seek comfort and health, was as resilient as the most stubborn weed pushing through cracked pavement. She had taken the remnants of what was broken and created something that not only functioned but offered a profound sense of relief and well-being. It was a seed of hope, carefully planted in the gritty soil of their existence, and she was determined to see it grow. Her workshop, once a place of solitary tinkering, was becoming a hub of quiet innovation, a testament to the power of a single, focused mind grappling with the environmental challenges of their new reality. She knew that replicating her device would require effort, resources, and cooperation, but the success of her personal filter had unlocked a new level of optimism within her, a belief that even the most insidious aspects of their fallen world could be countered, one carefully crafted breath at a time. She carefully logged the optimal layering sequence for the activated charcoal, noting the slightly rough texture of the crushed wood charcoal compared to the smoother, more uniform texture of the aquarium filter charcoal. The wood charcoal, while requiring more careful packing, seemed to offer a higher surface area for adsorption, a detail she meticulously recorded in her ever-growing technical journal. She also began to sketch out designs for a larger, more communal filtration unit, imagining a central hub that could service multiple dwellings, a network of clean air flowing through their settlement. The power source remained a significant hurdle, but she was confident that, with time and collaboration, a solution could be found. Perhaps Kiley could help assess the structural integrity of a larger housing unit, or perhaps Jax, with his keen eye for detail, could help document the process for wider dissemination, making it easier for others to understand and replicate. The possibilities, once confined by the limitations of her immediate surroundings, now seemed to stretch outwards, limited only by their collective will and ingenuity. Her filtered breath, once a personal victory, was slowly transforming into a blueprint for a healthier future.

The ache in Luis's back was a familiar companion, a dull throb that pulsed with every stoop and bend. For weeks, he'd been meticulously tending to the small patch of earth behind their dwelling, a sun-baked square that defied the usual barrenness of their settlement. It was an act of faith, a whispered prayer to the stubborn seeds his grandmother had pressed into his palm, each one a promise of sustenance from a world that seemed determined to deny it. She had spoken of the earth's resilience, of life's inherent drive to persist, even when scarred and poisoned. He hadn't fully understood then, but he felt it now, a nascent understanding blooming alongside the fragile shoots he'd nurtured.

His grandmother, Elena, had always possessed an uncanny connection to the land. Even in the twilight of her years, when the dust storms raged and the sky wept acid rain, she would speak of the earth's memory, of how it held the echoes of sun-drenched fields and the scent of rain on fertile soil. Her words, once dismissed by Luis as the ramblings of an old woman clinging to a lost past, now resonated with a profound truth. She had pointed to this specific patch, a slight depression where the wind seemed to carry less of the metallic tang, where the soil, though cracked and discolored, held a faint, earthy scent. "This is where the old roots still whisper, Luis," she'd told him, her voice raspy but firm. "Listen to them. They will guide you."

He had listened. He had watched the patterns of the meager sunlight, noting how it lingered longest on this particular plot. He had observed the subtle shifts in the soil's texture, feeling for the slightest hint of moisture after the infrequent, anemic showers. He had cleared away the brittle, inorganic debris, the ghosts of plastic and metal that littered the landscape, and carefully, almost reverently, turned the soil. The mutated earth was a strange substance – gritty in places, almost clay-like in others, with an unsettling undertone of chemical residue that pricked at his senses. Yet, he persisted, his hands raw and stained, his clothes perpetually dusted.

The seeds were a gamble. Most of the pre-Collapse seeds that had survived were sterile, or had been warped by the environmental cataclysm into something unrecognizable. But Elena had been a keeper of old ways, a hoarder of forgotten knowledge. She had a small, carefully guarded collection of heirloom seeds, kept in a cool, dark corner of their dwelling, protected from the pervasive damp and the ever-present dust. "These," she had explained, her fingers tracing the delicate contours of a dried bean, "these are strong. They remember what it is to grow."

Luis had planted them with a mixture of skepticism and desperate hope. He'd followed Elena's whispered instructions: plant them deep, give them what little precious water he could spare, and shield them from the harshest elements. He'd fashioned a makeshift cloche from a salvaged glass pane, propping it up with scavenged metal rods, creating a tiny greenhouse that offered a sliver of protection. He'd even mixed in some of the ash from their meager fires, a desperate attempt to introduce some semblance of organic matter into the depleted soil, remembering Elena's tales of ancient farmers enriching their fields.

And then, after what felt like an eternity of watching the barren earth, he saw it. A tiny, verdant shoot, impossibly green against the desolation, pushing its way towards the weak sunlight. It was a single sprout, barely a millimeter above the soil's surface, but to Luis, it was a beacon. He knelt, his breath catching in his throat, and traced its delicate form with a trembling finger. It was a radish, he thought, or something akin to it, its leaves small and serrated.

More shoots followed, a slow but steady emergence of life. He recognized the broad, sturdy leaves of what might be a bean plant, its stem already reaching upwards with a surprising vigor. And nestled amongst them, tiny, almost translucent leaves that hinted at a future harvest of something leafy and green, perhaps spinach or a hardy kale. They were few, these nascent plants, a mere handful against the vast emptiness, but their presence was a revolution.

He became a vigilant guardian. He chased away the scavengers – the mutated insects with their iridescent exoskeletons, the desperate rodents driven by hunger. He measured out his water with agonizing precision, each drop a sacrifice. He shielded them from the midday sun with fragments of salvaged cloth and defended them against the biting winds with makeshift windbreaks. His entire focus narrowed to this small, precious patch of earth, his days measured by the growth of these fragile lives.

The day of the first harvest arrived without fanfare, announced only by the deepening color of the radish leaves and the subtle swelling of the bean pods. Luis approached his garden with a mixture of reverence and anxiety. Had they grown? Had they managed to draw sustenance from this wounded soil? He gently loosened the earth around the base of the first radish. His fingers brushed against something firm, round. He tugged.

It came free with a soft resistance, a small, plump radish, its skin a mottled crimson and white, unlike any he had ever seen in the faded images from the old world. It was smaller than he imagined, not the perfectly formed spheres of storybooks, but undeniably a radish. Its roots, tangled and earthy, still clung to the soil. He held it in his palm, marveling at its weight, its solidity. It was real. It was food.

He harvested a few more radishes, each one a unique testament to resilience. Then, he carefully picked a handful of the young bean pods, still tender and green. The leafy greens, though sparse, were edible, offering a slight bitterness that was a welcome change from the bland rations they survived on.

He carried his meager bounty back to their dwelling, his heart thrumming with an unfamiliar excitement. He presented the vegetables to Mika, who was hunched over her latest air filtration prototype, her brow furrowed in concentration. She looked up, her eyes widening slightly as she took in the small pile of vegetables.

"Luis... where did you get these?" she asked, her voice hushed with surprise.

"From the garden," he replied, his voice thick with emotion. "My grandmother's seeds. They grew."

Mika set aside her tools, her usual scientific detachment giving way to a flicker of awe. She picked up a radish, turning it over in her fingers. "They're... different. Mutated, perhaps?"

"They're alive," Luis said simply. "And they're from our soil."

He watched as Mika carefully cleaned a radish, her movements precise and measured. He had never seen her so still, so focused on something so... organic. She took a bite, her eyes closed for a moment. When she opened them, there was a strange expression on her face.

"It's... earthy," she said, a hint of a smile touching her lips. "A little peppery. Not bad, Luis. Not bad at all."

He then prepared the beans, steaming them over a low flame, the small cooking pot barely containing their vibrant green. The leafy greens he added to a thin broth, a rare burst of color and flavor in their monotonous diet. They ate in near silence, savoring each bite. It wasn't a feast, not by any stretch of the imagination. It was a handful of vegetables, a testament to a few weeks of arduous work and unwavering hope. But it was more than just food. It was proof.

Proof that life could persist. Proof that the earth, even in its broken state, could still yield sustenance. Proof that their efforts, their struggles, were not in vain. This small harvest was a tangible victory against the encroaching desolation, a quiet rebellion against the forces that had sought to extinguish them. It was a symbol of what could be, a whisper of abundance in a world defined by scarcity.

Luis looked at the small pile of harvested vegetables, his mind already racing ahead. If these few seeds had managed to grow, what else could they cultivate? What other forgotten flavors, what other sources of nourishment, lay dormant beneath the surface, waiting for a guiding hand and a hopeful heart? The desolation was vast, the challenges immense, but in his hands, he held the nascent promise of a future where they might not just survive, but thrive. The act of sowing and reaping, of coaxing life from the very earth that had seemingly betrayed them, filled him with a profound sense of purpose. It was a connection to something ancient, something enduring, something that whispered of continuity in a world that felt irrevocably broken. He realized then that his grandmother's intuition, coupled with his own determined observations, had unlocked a door that many had long since given up on. The mutated soil was not just a wasteland; it was a canvas, waiting for the seeds of their resilience to be planted. He felt a new resolve harden within him, a quiet determination to continue this work, to expand this small patch of life, to bring more color, more flavor, more hope, back to their desolate existence. This was not just about survival; it was about rediscovery, about reclaiming a fundamental part of their humanity that had been eroded by the Collapse. The taste of the fresh radish, sharp and vital, lingered on his tongue, a potent reminder of the power of nature, even in its most altered forms, and the unyielding spirit of those who refused to let it be extinguished.

The success of Luis's small garden, though a triumph of personal perseverance, highlighted a growing logistical challenge within their settlement. As more individuals began to cultivate their own tiny plots or salvage useful materials, the efficient movement of goods and even people became increasingly difficult. The uneven terrain, littered with the debris of a fallen world, made even short distances arduous. This was particularly true for the older members of their community, whose joints ached with every step, and for those who managed to acquire larger or heavier items through the burgeoning barter system. Often, a successful trade for a crucial piece of equipment or a larger haul of salvaged metal would be rendered almost pointless by the sheer difficulty of transporting it back to its intended destination. The settlement, once a tightly knit cluster of dwellings, felt increasingly fragmented by the physical barriers that nature and neglect had imposed.

It was Kiley, with her perpetually smudged hands and an almost uncanny ability to see the potential in discarded junk, who recognized the need for a more robust solution. She had always been a tinkerer, drawn to the intricate mechanics of things, and the limitations of their current transport methods – primarily just their own two arms and backs, or the occasional, precarious balance of a found plank – grated on her. Her mind, a whirlwind of gears and levers, began to conceptualize something that could traverse the broken landscape with greater ease. She spent days observing, sketching crude diagrams on scraps of salvaged paper, her brow furrowed in concentration as she watched scavengers struggle with bulky loads and elders falter on their slow journeys.

Her initial ideas involved reinforcing the existing handcarts, but she quickly realized their limitations. They were too narrow, too fragile, and their small, often uneven wheels simply bogged down in the rubble and dust. What they needed, she declared one evening, her voice buzzing with an infectious energy, was something more substantial. Something with a broader base, sturdier wheels, and a frame built to withstand the rigmarole of their environment.

The concept solidified: a cart, but not just any cart. It needed to be adaptable, capable of carrying a decent weight, and, crucially, manageable by a single person even when fully loaded. She envisioned a system that leveraged the few functional remnants of the old world's ingenuity. Bicycle parts. They were relatively common, lightweight, and designed for efficient movement. The sturdy frames, the durable wheels, the reliable bearings – these were the building blocks she needed.

Kiley didn't just dream; she acted. She began scouring the scrap heaps with a renewed fervor, her eyes scanning not just for materials, but for specific components. She unearthed a discarded child's bicycle, its frame bent but salvageable, its tires surprisingly intact. She found another, larger bike, missing its handlebars but possessing two robust wheels. She meticulously stripped them down, her fingers adept at prying apart rusted components and carefully cleaning each bearing. The process was painstaking, each salvaged part a tiny victory.

Her workshop, a corner of a partially collapsed warehouse that she had claimed and reinforced, became a hub of activity. The air was thick with the scent of hot metal and creaking wood. She scavenged planks from collapsed structures, choosing pieces that were still solid and relatively free from rot. She found lengths of thick, braided wire that could be used for bracing and reinforcement. And from a particularly fruitful scavenging run, she managed to acquire a few lengths of discarded metal piping, which she envisioned as the main structural supports for the cart's frame.

The construction itself was a testament to her resourcefulness and growing engineering acumen. She carefully cut and shaped the metal piping, creating a strong, rectangular base. The salvaged bicycle wheels were her key innovation. She adapted their mounting points, creating a sturdy axle system that allowed them to rotate freely, even over uneven ground. She reinforced the frame with the salvaged wire, lacing it through drilled holes to create a rigid, supportive structure.

For the carrying platform, she used the salvaged wooden planks, carefully measuring and fitting them to create a flat, sturdy surface. She even devised a simple latching mechanism, using a bent piece of metal and a salvaged spring, so that the sides of the platform could be lowered or raised, making it easier to load and unload goods. This was a crucial detail, designed to accommodate a wide range of items, from sacks of grain to bulky pieces of salvaged technology.

But Kiley's vision extended beyond mere utility. She understood that for the cart to be truly integrated into the community, it needed to be accessible to everyone. She observed the difficulties faced by the elderly, the infirm, and those with limited strength. So, she designed a system of handles that could be adjusted, allowing for different heights and grips. She also incorporated a simple braking mechanism, a lever that pressed a piece of salvaged rubber against the wheel, providing control on inclines.

The first finished cart was a marvel. It was not aesthetically pleasing by any pre-Collapse standard; it was a patchwork of salvaged materials, showing the scars of its past life. But it was undeniably functional. The two large bicycle wheels provided excellent traction, allowing it to roll smoothly over rubble and soft earth. The reinforced frame felt solid and stable, capable of bearing a significant load. The adjustable handles made it comfortable to push and steer, and the braking system offered a much-needed sense of security.

Kiley, with a proud smile that lit up her dirt-smudged face, wheeled the cart out into the settlement's central gathering area. Heads turned. People stopped their conversations, their eyes drawn to this strange, new contraption. Luis, still basking in the glow of his garden's success, was among the first to approach. He ran a hand over the rough-hewn wood, then examined the sturdy axle.

"Kiley, this is... remarkable," he said, genuine admiration in his voice.

Kiley beamed. "It took some doing, but I think it'll make a difference, Luis. No more struggling with every little thing. Imagine, you could haul a whole week's worth of water in this, or even one of those old generators if you can find one."

Mika, ever the pragmatist, was already assessing its potential. "The weight distribution seems good. And the wheel clearance is impressive. What did you use for the bearings?"

Kiley proudly pointed to a cluster of small, gleaming metal balls nestled within a greased housing. "Salvaged from a dismantled drone. They're tiny, but they were in perfect condition."

Word of Kiley's cart spread like wildfire. Soon, others were approaching her, not just with admiration, but with requests. An elderly woman named Elara, whose arthritis made it painful to carry even her meager rations, shyly asked if Kiley could build one for her. A group of scavengers, who often returned with heavier finds, pooled some of their precious resources to commission a larger, more robust version.

Kiley, energized by the demand and the palpable gratitude of those who benefited from her work, set about building more. She refined her techniques, learning from each build, optimizing the design for different needs. She discovered that by altering the length of the frame and the number of wheels (some later designs incorporated a third, smaller wheel at the front for added stability), she could create carts suited for different purposes. Some were narrow and agile, ideal for navigating tight spaces. Others were wider and lower, perfect for transporting larger, bulkier items.

The impact on the community was immediate and profound. The barter system, which had been hindered by the practicalities of exchange, suddenly became more fluid. It was no longer a question of whether one could physically transport the goods; it was about the value of the trade itself. People could now negotiate for larger quantities, for heavier tools, for more substantial supplies, knowing that Kiley's carts could bridge the distance.

For the elderly and infirm, the carts were a lifeline. Elara, who had once spent hours painstakingly making her way to the communal well, could now fill a large salvaged canister and wheel it back to her dwelling with relative ease. Children, too, found joy in using the smaller, lighter carts, helping their families with errands and deliveries, their laughter echoing through the dusty streets as they navigated their cargo. The carts became a common sight, a symbol of the community's adaptability and Kiley's innovative spirit. They weren't just tools; they were facilitators of connection, of commerce, and of compassion. They allowed the community to move, not just physically, but forward, a collective step taken on sturdy, salvaged wheels. Kiley's ingenuity, rooted in a deep understanding of practical needs and a compassionate heart, had built more than just carts; she had built pathways, both literal and metaphorical, that bound them closer together. The carts became a tangible representation of their collective will to overcome obstacles, a rolling testament to the power of applied engineering fueled by the desire to serve. The subtle creak of the wheels, the gentle rumble over the uneven ground, became the soundtrack to their evolving lives, a constant reminder of how a single idea, born from necessity and nurtured by skill, could transform the everyday realities of their existence. The resourcefulness that had gone into their creation – the salvaged bicycle parts, the repurposed wood, the carefully cleaned bearings – mirrored the very spirit of their community: making the most of what they had, and transforming the remnants of the past into the foundations of their future. Kiley's carts were a quiet revolution, moving them, quite literally, towards a more connected and sustainable way of life.

Jax had always seen the world through a lens, but it was a world fractured, a panorama of ruin and quiet desperation. His early photographs, taken in the raw aftermath of the Collapse, were stark, unforgiving portraits of the physical landscape – skeletal remains of skyscrapers piercing the bruised sky, vast stretches of choked highways, the desolate emptiness where bustling cities once stood. These images were necessary, a grim cataloging of their new reality, a way for him to process the sheer scale of their loss. But as time wore on, and the dust began to settle not just on the ruins but on the spirits of the survivors, Jax felt a shift. The external decay was undeniable, but it was the internal resilience, the flicker of life stubbornly refusing to be extinguished, that began to draw his focus.

He started with small acts of defiance against the overwhelming grey. A child's bright, hand-painted rock left on a windowsill. The shared warmth of a communal meal, faces lit by the flickering glow of salvaged lamps. The meticulous care given to a fledgling sprout pushing its way through cracked concrete. These were not grand gestures, not the headline-grabbing acts of heroism that might be found in the old-world stories. They were quieter, more intimate moments, the bedrock of everyday existence reasserting itself. And Jax, with his battered but still functional camera – a relic he had painstakingly repaired, its leather casing worn smooth by his touch – began to capture them.

His process evolved. He no longer just documented destruction; he sought out creation. He would spend hours observing, his gaze sweeping across the settlement, looking for the subtle cues of human spirit at play. He learned to recognize the tell-tale signs: the determined set of a jaw as someone hauled a heavy beam, the gentle curve of a hand offering a shared ration, the shared laughter that, against all odds, could still erupt in the face of such hardship. He would approach his subjects with a quiet humility, his movements slow and unthreatening. He didn't bark orders or pose his subjects artificially. Instead, he would often sit with them, observing their routine, waiting for the genuine moment to present itself. Sometimes, a simple nod, a shared glance, was all the invitation he needed. Other times, he would offer a few salvaged batteries, a carefully bartered item, as a token of respect for their time.

His portraits became narratives in themselves. There was Elara, her face a roadmap of a life lived through hardship, her hands gnarled and spotted, yet her eyes held a quiet strength as she meticulously mended a torn garment. Jax had captured her in the soft, diffused light of her small dwelling, the patched fabric a testament to her resourcefulness, the slight, almost imperceptible smile playing on her lips a silent declaration of her refusal to surrender. He hadn't asked her to smile; it had just happened, a spontaneous flicker of satisfaction at her own quiet act of preservation.

Then there was Mika, the pragmatist and builder, his arms thick with muscle earned from countless hours of labor. Jax had found him one afternoon wrestling with a particularly stubborn piece of salvaged machinery, sweat beading on his brow, his expression one of intense concentration. But in the frame, it wasn't just the physical struggle. Jax had managed to capture the moment Mika paused, his head tilted, listening to the rhythmic clang of Kiley's hammers from her workshop. There was a shared understanding in that stillness, a silent acknowledgment of their complementary efforts in rebuilding their world. Mika's portrait wasn't just about strength; it was about purpose.

Luis, the gardener, was another frequent subject. Jax had photographed him surrounded by the vibrant green of his meticulously tended plot, the very antithesis of the arid landscape that dominated their surroundings. In one particular portrait, Luis was holding up a single, perfect tomato, its redness a startling burst of color against the muted tones of his clothing and the earth. His face was alight with a joy that transcended their grim circumstances, a pure, unadulterated pride in his creation. It was a visual argument for hope, a tangible symbol of life's tenacious grip.

Jax's photographs were not about glorifying suffering. Far from it. They were about showcasing the quiet dignity, the inherent strength, and the enduring spirit of the people who refused to be defined by their losses. He wasn't just taking pictures; he was creating a visual chronicle of their collective will to survive and, more importantly, to *live*. He understood that in a world stripped bare of so much, the preservation of morale was as vital as the replenishment of resources. His images served as a constant reminder to the community that they were not merely existing; they were actively creating, rebuilding, and nurturing.

He began to display his photographs in the communal gathering space, tacking them up on salvaged boards and scraps of metal. At first, people would pause, a flicker of recognition, a moment of quiet contemplation. But as the collection grew, a subtle transformation occurred. The images became more than just records; they became focal points for conversation, for shared memories, and for renewed determination. When someone felt overwhelmed by the sheer scale of their challenges, they could look at Jax's portraits and see a reflection of their own inner strength, echoed in the faces and actions of their neighbors.

There were images of children, their faces smudged with dirt but their eyes bright with curiosity, engaged in games that repurposed discarded objects into playthings. There was a group huddled together, sharing stories around a meager fire, their silhouettes casting long, dancing shadows on a crumbling wall – a scene of shared humanity in the face of isolation. There was a woman carefully tending to an injured bird, her gentleness a stark contrast to the harshness of their environment. Each photograph was a testament, a visual anchor grounding them in the present while simultaneously offering a glimpse of a future built not on what was lost, but on what they could still create.

Jax's work was a subtle, yet powerful, form of resistance. It was an act of defiance against the narrative of despair that the Collapse had so effectively imposed. He was reminding them that even in the darkest of times, the human capacity for compassion, ingenuity, and hope remained. His lens became a tool for collective therapy, offering a mirror to their best selves, a visual affirmation that they were more than just survivors; they were builders, nurturers, and creators. His portraits were not just images of resilience; they were embodiments of it, captured and shared, a quiet but potent fuel for the enduring flame of their community. He was, in his own way, planting seeds of hope, not in the soil, but in the very hearts and minds of his people, one powerful image at a time. The weight of the world was immense, but Jax's photographs suggested, with irrefutable clarity, that their spirits were lighter, their resolve stronger, and their capacity for life far more enduring than the rubble that surrounded them. His art was the quiet hum beneath the noise of survival, the persistent beat of a heart that refused to stop.

CHAPTER THREE

THE LOOMING SHADOW

The dust hadn't even fully settled on their carefully rebuilt lives when the first whispers began. They started as faint rumors, carried on the wind from the North, tales of desperation and endless journeys. Then, the vehicles, or what remained of them, began to appear at the edge of their settlement – sputtering, coughing wrecks of metal held together by sheer willpower and desperation. They were a stark contrast to the functional, albeit weathered, transports the community had managed to maintain. These were not the organized convoys of the early days, the planned migrations to safer zones; these were the stragglers, the ones who had been pushed to the very fringes, their journeys a desperate, often brutal, gamble.

The initial arrivals were few, a trickle at first. A battered truck, its tires bald and its engine wheezing, carrying a handful of gaunt faces that spoke of days, perhaps weeks, of constant fear and hunger. They were met with a mixture of apprehension and a deeply ingrained sense of obligation. The community, having endured its own share of hardship, understood the language of desperation. Basic provisions were offered – water, a handful of dried rations, a warm blanket. But even in these early encounters, the unspoken question hung heavy in the air: how many more?

The trickle soon became a steady stream, and then, a torrent. The stories they carried were grim, painting a far darker picture of the world beyond their relatively protected valley. They spoke of cities that had been reduced to charnel houses, of vast swathes of land rendered uninhabitable by prolonged environmental collapse and the ensuing, brutal resource wars. They told of journeys where every mile was a battle for survival, against the elements, against desperate scavengers, and sometimes, against each other. These refugees, huddled together in their makeshift vehicles or on foot, were the living embodiment of devastation. Their clothes were tattered remnants, their faces etched with exhaustion, their eyes holding a profound, hollow sadness that spoke of unimaginable loss.

This influx, while a testament to the community's perceived safety and relative stability, began to strain their already stretched resources. The communal granaries, meticulously managed, felt their reserves dwindling faster than anticipated. The water purification systems, designed for their current population, worked overtime. Every extra mouth to feed, every additional body needing shelter, represented a quantifiable drain on their finite supplies. It wasn't just about material scarcity; it was about the psychological toll. The constant influx of new faces, each carrying their own trauma and their own urgent needs, created a palpable shift in the community's atmosphere. The quiet hum of their rebuilt life was increasingly punctuated by the anxious murmurs of newcomers, their pleas for help, their stories of woe.

The newcomers were not a monolithic group. They came from different backgrounds, different former lives, bringing with them a kaleidoscope of skills, experiences, and crucially, expectations. Some were farmers, their hands still calloused from tilling land that no longer existed. Others were mechanics, their knowledge of pre-Collapse technology a valuable, if sometimes obsolete, commodity. There were doctors, nurses, engineers – individuals whose expertise was desperately needed. But there were also those who had been defined by less tangible skills, those whose lives had revolved around commerce, or administration, or even the arts. Their former roles held little immediate practical value in this new, brutal reality, and their displacement was often accompanied by a deep-seated sense of loss and disorientation.

This diversity, while potentially enriching, also sowed the seeds of friction. The established residents, who had painstakingly built their current existence through years of hard work and difficult compromises, watched with a growing unease as these newcomers, fresh from their harrowing experiences, seemed to demand more than what was readily available. There were hushed conversations in the communal mess halls, sharp glances exchanged in the market squares. The newcomers, accustomed to the chaos and scarcity they had fled, often displayed a directness, a raw desperation that could be perceived as abrasive by those who had learned to temper their needs with patience and understanding.

One of the most immediate points of contention was housing. The settlement had a limited number of salvaged structures, each carefully allocated. While the community had initially opened its doors to everyone, the sheer volume of arrivals meant that many found themselves in temporary shelters – repurposed storage units, the partially repaired shells of old buildings, even tents erected on the outskirts. The newcomers, having endured so much, felt entitled to more, to the same comforts and security that the established residents enjoyed. This led to a palpable sense of resentment among some of the original inhabitants, who felt their own sacrifices were being overlooked in the rush to accommodate the new arrivals.

"They come here, with their stories of suffering, and expect us to just hand over what we've worked so hard for," grumbled Silas, a grizzled elder who had been one of the first to establish the settlement. He was speaking to a small group gathered near the communal water pump, his voice a low rumble of discontent. "We built this place, brick by painstaking brick. We rationed, we sweated, we bled. And now? Now we're expected to share every last scrap with people who just rolled in yesterday."

His words, though harsh, resonated with a segment of the population. They had witnessed the newcomers' arrival, seen the better condition of some of their salvaged vehicles, the slightly more intact clothing they wore, and a whisper of suspicion began to circulate: were these truly the most desperate? Or were they simply those who had managed to hold onto more before their journey, those who had perhaps engaged in less than scrupulous dealings to acquire what they needed to survive and escape?

Jax, ever the observer, saw this growing tension. His camera, which had become an extension of his being, was his primary tool for understanding the pulse of the community. He saw the strained smiles, the averted gazes, the subtle shifts in body language that spoke volumes about the undercurrent of anxiety and burgeoning conflict. He began to document these changes, not with judgment, but with a desire to understand. He captured the quiet frustration etched on the faces of those who felt their resources were being depleted, but he also captured the weary hope in the eyes of the newcomers, their desperate need for a safe haven.

He photographed Elara, the seamstress, trying to teach a group of refugee women the basics of mending. Their hands, unaccustomed to the fine needlework, fumbled with the thread, their frustration evident. Yet, Jax saw the flicker of determination, the shared laughter when a stitch went awry, the small victories celebrated with quiet nods of encouragement. It was a microcosm of the larger struggle: bridging divides, sharing knowledge, and finding common ground in the face of adversity.

He also captured the more confrontational moments. A terse exchange between a community elder and a newcomer over a ration parcel, the elder's face set in a mask of weary authority, the newcomer's posture a mixture of defiance and desperation. These images were not for public display, not yet. Jax understood the delicate balance he was navigating. His work had always been about fostering unity, about highlighting the shared humanity. These new images, while important for his own understanding, were raw, and exposing them prematurely could exacerbate the very tensions he sought to understand and, perhaps, alleviate.

The strain wasn't limited to material resources and social dynamics. The newcomers brought with them knowledge of the wider world, of the devastation that had unfolded beyond their valley. Their stories, while valuable warnings, also served to amplify the fear. They spoke of roving gangs, of collapsed infrastructure on a scale that dwarfed their current understanding, of communities that had turned on themselves in the face of starvation. These narratives, whispered around campfires and shared in hushed tones, chipped away at the sense of security the established residents had so carefully cultivated.

"They say the West Coast is completely gone," a woman named Anya, her voice trembling, recounted one evening. "Cities swallowed by the sea, others just... ash. And the inland, it's all dust. Nothing grows. People are fighting over puddles of water." Her audience, a mix of old and new residents, listened with a chilling quietness, the horror in her words a stark contrast to the relative peace of their valley.

This constant exposure to amplified tales of woe began to wear down the community's collective spirit. The optimism that Jax's photographs had so carefully nurtured seemed to be challenged by the sheer, relentless weight of the outside world's misery. Some began to question the wisdom of their isolated existence. Was it a temporary reprieve, or simply a delay of the inevitable? The fear, once a distant shadow, now felt like a tangible presence, creeping into their daily lives.

The leadership of the settlement, a council of elders including individuals like Silas and more pragmatic figures like Mika, found themselves facing an unprecedented challenge. Their established protocols, designed for a stable and predictable community, were ill-equipped to handle such a rapid and overwhelming influx. Debates raged within the council. Some argued for stricter controls, for a more selective intake of refugees, based on their skills and potential contribution. Others, driven by a more humanitarian impulse, advocated for open arms, for upholding the principle of shared humanity, regardless of the cost.

Mika, who had seen firsthand the desperation that drove people to flee, argued for a balanced approach. "We cannot afford to turn them away," he stated firmly at one council meeting, his voice resonating with his usual calm authority. "But we also cannot deplete our own reserves to the point of self-destruction. We need to integrate them, not just accommodate them. We need to find ways for them to contribute, to become part of our effort, not just passive recipients."

His words were met with nods from some, but Silas remained skeptical. "Integrate them? How do you integrate desperation, Mika? How do you integrate fear? These people are like a flood. You can try to channel it, but if you're not careful, it will drown you."

The arrival of the refugees also brought with it the potential for new social structures and power dynamics. As the established community struggled to cope, some of the more assertive newcomers began to assert themselves, their survival instincts honed by years of hardship. They organized themselves into informal groups, looking out for their own, pooling their resources, and in some instances, challenging the authority of the settlement's leadership. This was not overt rebellion, but a subtle shift, a quiet assertion of their own agency in a situation where they felt their needs were not being adequately met.

Jax observed these dynamics with his usual keen eye. He saw the burgeoning leadership within the refugee groups, the quiet determination of individuals who had emerged as de facto spokespeople for their respective factions. He photographed a group of men, newly arrived, working together to reinforce a damaged section of the settlement's perimeter wall, their movements efficient and coordinated, a silent demonstration of their collective capability. He saw a woman, Anya, who had been vocal about the dangers outside, now organizing a group to share their limited medical supplies, her previous fear transmuted into a proactive desire to help.

The challenge was immense. The community had to find a way to absorb this influx without compromising its own survival. It required a delicate balancing act – extending compassion without succumbing to unsustainable demands, fostering unity without ignoring the legitimate concerns of its existing members, and maintaining a sense of hope in the face of overwhelming evidence of the world's suffering. The loom of the future, once a steady and predictable weave, now seemed to be threaded with the chaotic, unpredictable strands of a desperate tide. The shadow of the looming crisis was no longer a distant threat; it was at their doorstep, demanding to be acknowledged, demanding to be addressed. The true test of their resilience, of their humanity, was just beginning.

The relentless passage of time, marked not by calendars but by the changing hues of the perpetual twilight sky and the diminishing contents of communal stores, began to etch a new kind of fear into the fabric of their lives. What had started as a manageable strain on their resources had, over the span of mere months, transformed into a gnawing, pervasive anxiety. The carefully curated caches of preserved foods, once a source of comforting security, were now visibly depleted. The shelves in the communal pantry, which had once groaned under the weight of meticulously labeled jars and vacuum-sealed packets, now bore empty spaces like missing teeth. The bounty of the early harvest, so vital in replenishing their stocks, felt like a distant, almost mythical memory. The sweet tang of preserved berries, the hearty starchiness of dried tubers – these were no longer everyday staples but precious commodities, rationed out in minuscule portions that did little to quell the persistent hunger pangs.

The fuel situation was even more dire. The generators, the lifeblood of their modest technological infrastructure, sputtered and coughed with increasing frequency. The precious reserves of bio-diesel, painstakingly synthesized and meticulously hoarded, were dwindling at an alarming rate. The lorries that brought in vital supplies from salvage expeditions, once a reassuring sight, now ventured out less and less frequently, their journeys more perilous and their returns laden with less. The hum of essential machinery, the soft glow of internal lighting that had become a symbol of their reclaimed normalcy, was gradually being replaced by the flickering shadows of oil lamps and the eerie silence of powered-down systems. Every flick of a light switch, every whir of a pump, was now a conscious, calculated decision, a weighing of necessity against the ever-present specter of depletion.

Even the simplest of necessities had become objects of intense focus and subtle competition. Clean water, once a taken-for-granted abundance thanks to their advanced purification systems, now required more careful monitoring. The influx of new residents had placed an unforeseen burden on the filtration units, and while they still functioned, the margins of safety were narrowing. The communal laundries, once a hive of activity, now saw fewer loads, as conserving water became a paramount concern. The very air, once purified and circulated with a steady hum, now carried a faint undertone of dust and stale air in some of the less-ventilated communal areas, a subtle indicator of systems being pushed beyond their intended capacity.

This tangible scarcity was not merely an inconvenience; it was a psychological assault. The initial hope, the quiet triumph of having carved out a sanctuary from the wreckage of the old world, was being systematically eroded. The optimism that had fueled their early rebuilding efforts, the belief that with hard work and ingenuity they could not only survive but thrive, felt increasingly fragile. The constant, gnawing awareness of what they lacked began to overshadow the appreciation for what they still possessed. Every empty shelf, every sputtering generator, every rationed meal was a stark reminder of their precarious existence, a confirmation of the shadows that lurked just beyond their valley's perceived safety.

The newcomers, those who had arrived with tales of desperate journeys and shattered lives, now found themselves facing a different kind of hardship. Their initial relief at finding a safe haven was slowly being replaced by the stark reality of communal rationing. The meager portions, though still a lifeline, were a far cry from the abundance they might have imagined, or perhaps, the slightly more plentiful provisions some of them might have managed to retain from their previous lives. This led to a subtle shift in their demeanor. The wide-eyed gratitude, the palpable relief, began to be tinged with a quiet frustration, a low murmur of discontent that rippled through the temporary shelters and the less established living quarters.

"It's not what they promised," whispered a woman named Anya, her voice barely audible above the rustling of scavenged fabric that served as her tent's partition. She spoke to a small group of equally weary-looking individuals, their faces illuminated by the faint glow of a salvaged LED lantern. "They said it was a sanctuary. They said there was enough. But look at this. Barely enough to keep a child alive." Her words, though spoken in hushed tones, carried the weight of genuine despair. She had seen others, those who had arrived earlier, with better-maintained clothing and slightly less gaunt faces. A seed of suspicion had been sown in her mind: had those with more just managed to hold onto it, while the truly desperate were being short-changed?

This feeling of being short-changed, or at least of being perpetually on the edge of deprivation, began to manifest in subtle ways. The communal mess hall, once a place of shared meals and conversation, became an arena of quiet tension. Individuals would hover near the serving stations, their eyes fixed on the dwindling portions, their movements a little too quick, their greetings a little too strained. Jax, with his ever-present camera, documented these shifts with a somber diligence. He captured the furtive glances, the tight set of jaws, the way hands would instinctively clench when the server's ladle scraped against the bottom of a pot. These were not the dramatic confrontations of a breakdown, but the quiet, insidious erosion of trust and goodwill, the slow decay of communal harmony under the pressure of scarcity.

He photographed Elara, the seamstress, her brow furrowed with a new kind of worry. Her workshop, once bustling with the mending of clothes and the creation of new garments from salvaged materials, was now seeing a surge in requests for more substantial repairs. Patches were becoming larger, seams were being reinforced multiple times, and the very fabric of their clothing was beginning to show the strain of constant wear and tear. She spoke of the difficulty in finding durable thread, of the dwindling supply of good quality needles. "It's not just about looking presentable anymore," she confided to Jax, her voice laced with weariness. "It's about keeping out the cold, about having something sturdy enough to face the elements. And the materials... they're becoming so worn, so fragile. We're patching up ghosts of clothes."

The fuel shortage, in particular, cast a long shadow. The reliance on generators for light, heat, and the operation of vital machinery meant that every power outage was a stark reminder of their vulnerability. The silence that descended when the generators faltered was not just an absence of noise; it was an absence of progress, an absence of comfort, an absence of safety. During these periods, the community was plunged into an almost pre-industrial darkness, the flickering lamplight casting long, distorted shadows that amplified anxieties. Children, who had grown accustomed to the steady glow, would whimper, and adults would huddle closer, their voices hushed, their eyes wide, searching the encroaching gloom for any sign of threat.

Silas, the grizzled elder, became even more vocal in his concerns. His initial skepticism towards the newcomers had deepened into a pronounced distrust. He saw their presence not just as a drain on resources, but as a catalyst for this accelerated scarcity. "I told you," he would grumble to anyone who would listen, his voice a low rumble of vindication. "You can't just open the floodgates. These people... they don't understand conservation. They don't know what it means to truly economize. They've lived in the chaos, and they expect us to be the ones to suffer for it." He would point to the slightly more intact vehicles that some of the later arrivals had managed to pilot into the settlement, to the less threadbare quality of certain items they carried, fueling the whispers that perhaps not all who arrived were equally deserving of compassion.

The council, which had previously focused on the logistics of integration and resource management, found itself increasingly grappling with the emotional fallout of scarcity. Mika, ever the pragmatist, tried to maintain a sense of order and fairness. He implemented stricter rationing protocols, clearly outlining the dwindling reserves and the rationale behind each decision. He organized work details specifically focused on salvaging for fuel and food, expanding the search radius and increasing the risk for the brave few who undertook these perilous expeditions. He also initiated community-wide discussions, attempting to foster a sense of shared responsibility and to discourage the burgeoning us-versus-them mentality.

"This is not about blame," Mika stated at a tense council meeting, his gaze sweeping across the faces of his fellow leaders. "It is about reality. Our reserves are finite. The world outside is unforgiving. We are facing a challenge that demands our collective ingenuity and our collective sacrifice. We need to ensure that every member of this community, old and new, understands the gravity of our situation and contributes to finding a solution. Turning on each other will only hasten our demise."

However, his words, though well-intentioned, struggled to penetrate the growing fog of fear and suspicion. The newcomers, their initial hopes dashed by the persistent reality of insufficient provisions, began to organize themselves more cohesively. They formed small, informal councils within their own groups, pooling their remaining resources and looking out for their own members. This was not a deliberate act of defiance, but a natural response to perceived neglect and a deep-seated instinct for self-preservation. They began to voice their needs more assertively, their pleas for a fairer share of resources becoming more frequent and more insistent.

Jax documented these shifts with a growing sense of unease. He saw the subtle formations of these new allegiances, the quiet huddles in corners of the settlement, the sharing of scarce items that bypassed official channels. He photographed Anya, no longer just a victim of circumstance, but a figure of quiet authority among a group of newly arrived women. She was teaching them how to identify edible wild plants, a skill she had learned during her harrowing journey, transforming her fear into a proactive, albeit precarious, form of sustenance. He captured the determined set of her jaw, the focused intensity in her eyes as she explained the difference between a nourishing root and a poisonous one, her hands gesturing with a practiced ease.

The scarcity was a breeding ground for new anxieties. The whispers of dwindling food and fuel were soon joined by hushed rumors of discontent bubbling within the refugee camps. Tales of minor disputes over rations, of individuals hoarding small quantities of food, of a general weariness that threatened to tip into open resentment, began to circulate. These whispers, amplified by fear and uncertainty, painted a picture of a community teetering on the brink, its carefully constructed facade of unity cracking under the immense pressure of deprivation. The once-welcoming atmosphere was now tinged with an undercurrent of apprehension, a palpable sense of unease that permeated every interaction. The simple act of sharing a communal meal, once a symbol of their shared humanity, was becoming a silent, tense negotiation, each person acutely aware of the dwindling portions and the unspoken needs of those around them. The shadow of scarcity was no longer looming; it had arrived, and its chill was seeping into the very core of their lives.

The hum of the air filtration system, usually a comforting thrum that underscored the settlement's technological prowess, now grated on Mika's nerves. It was a constant reminder of the precarious balance they maintained, a sound that spoke not of abundance, but of a desperate clinging to what little control they had. Even with the best efforts of her engineering team, the air in the more densely populated sectors still carried a faint, almost imperceptible staleness. It was the ghost of dust motes, of recycled breath, a subtle testament to the strain on systems designed for a smaller, less desperate populace. Each breath she took felt heavy, laden with the unspoken anxieties of a community stretched too thin. This persistent concern about air quality, a seemingly minor issue in the grand scheme of survival, gnawed at her. It was a tangible problem with no easy solution, a leak in their carefully constructed dam that threatened to widen with every new arrival. She found herself constantly poring over schematics, re-calculating energy outputs, and sketching out modifications to the purifiers, her fingers smudged with graphite and grease. The urgency of finding a truly sustainable, self-replicating solution, one that didn't rely on dwindling salvaged components, became an obsession. It wasn't just about comfort anymore; it was about fundamental health, about ensuring that the air they breathed didn't become another silent enemy.

The influx of refugees, while a moral imperative and a testament to their haven's reputation, had amplified Mika's anxieties tenfold. The initial joy of seeing more faces, of hearing more stories of survival, had quickly been overshadowed by the stark reality of resource allocation. Every new mouth to feed, every new body to house and clothe, every new demand on their already strained power grid, sent a fresh wave of unease through her. She saw it in the hushed conversations at the communal mess hall, in the increasingly sharp exchanges during council meetings, and in the subtle but undeniable shift in the mood of the settlement. The initial solidarity, the shared purpose that had bound them together in the early days, was beginning to fray at the edges, strained by the weight of competing needs. Mika, always the pragmatist, understood the logic of self-preservation. She also understood that in a community like theirs, such instincts, if left unchecked, could be the very thing that tore them apart. Her days were consumed by the endless task of trying to stretch their finite resources, of devising fair distribution methods, and of mediating disputes that threatened to erupt over a handful of preserved rations or a few extra hours of generator power. The pressure was immense, a constant, invisible weight pressing down on her shoulders.

Her workshop, a space that had once been a sanctuary for her creativity and problem-solving, now felt like a battlefield. The organized chaos of tools, salvaged electronics, and half-finished prototypes had taken on a frenetic edge. Her tinkering, once a methodical process of innovation, had become a desperate race against time. She worked long into the cycles of dim light, her focus narrowed to the intricate circuitry and the complex algorithms that governed their life support systems. Each success, like the improved efficiency of a solar array or the more robust design of a water purification unit, brought a fleeting sense of relief, quickly followed by the chilling realization of how much more needed to be done. It was a treadmill of innovation, where every step forward only revealed a longer, more daunting path ahead. This escalating effort was fueled by more than just her ingrained desire to improve their lives; it was driven by a deep-seated fear, a gnawing dread that no matter how ingenious her solutions, how relentless her efforts, they might still not be enough. The sheer scale of their vulnerability, the fragility of their existence against the backdrop of a hostile world, weighed heavily on her. She saw the potential for cascading failures, for one small problem to snowball into an insurmountable crisis, and the responsibility to prevent that felt like a crushing burden. The metallic tang of ozone from overworked equipment was a constant olfactory reminder of the strain, a subtle scent of desperation clinging to the air she breathed, mirroring the ever-present unease that had become her constant companion.

She found herself scrutinizing the newcomers with a more critical eye, a departure from her usual open-hearted empathy. It wasn't that she distrusted them, not entirely, but she saw them as a variable she couldn't fully control, a factor that could tip the delicate scales of their survival. She watched them adapt, or sometimes, fail to adapt, to the strictures of their community. Some embraced the shared responsibility with a quiet dignity, while others, accustomed to the more individualistic survival strategies of the Wastes, struggled with the concept of communal sacrifice. She saw a few, their faces etched with hardship but their eyes sharp with resourcefulness, already beginning to forge their own networks, sharing skills and meager possessions in ways that bypassed the official channels. While she recognized the instinct for self-preservation, it also represented a fragmentation of their collective effort, a potential for the very divisions she worked so hard to prevent. She imagined these independent networks growing, becoming insular, eventually leading to a breakdown of the trust that was so vital to their continued existence. The idea of factions forming, of "us" and "them" solidifying within their walls, sent a shiver down her spine.

The settlement's rudimentary communication system, an essential tool for coordination and information dissemination, also became a source of Mika's growing unease. The salvaged radios, prone to static and interference, were a constant source of frustration. During periods of low solar power, or when atmospheric conditions were unfavorable, their communication channels would go silent, leaving a void filled with speculation and fear. She had dedicated a significant portion of her limited workshop time to improving their communication infrastructure, to creating more robust and reliable ways to transmit information, but the scarcity of specialized components was a constant impediment. She yearned for the days when she could simply order what she needed, when the theoretical could be so readily translated into practical application. Now, every wire, every capacitor, every circuit board was a precious resource, hard-won from dangerous salvage expeditions or painstakingly replicated with her limited fabrication tools. The thought of a critical warning failing to reach its destination, of an emergency response being delayed due to a faulty radio signal, was a recurring nightmare. She saw the potential for a localized crisis to escalate into a full-blown disaster simply because the necessary information couldn't be transmitted in time. This reliance on temperamental technology, this constant vulnerability, was a persistent thorn in her side.

Her sleep offered little respite. The dreams were often vivid, a jumble of fragmented images: the oppressive twilight sky, the gnawing hunger of her own childhood in the Wastes, the faces of the refugees etched with a desperate hope that she feared they couldn't fully fulfill. Sometimes, she would dream of the generators failing entirely, plunging the entire settlement into darkness, the only sound the panicked cries of children and the rasping breaths of the elders. These nightmares left her waking with a racing heart, the cold sweat of fear clinging to her skin, and the tangible reality of their precarious situation weighing even heavier. She would often lie there in the dim light of her personal dwelling, the soft glow of her energy-efficient lamp barely pushing back the shadows, and listen to the muted sounds of the settlement – the distant clatter of a tool, the hushed murmur of conversation, the omnipresent hum of the life support systems. Each sound was a reminder of their ongoing struggle, of the constant, relentless effort required to simply exist.

The pressure to find a truly permanent solution, something beyond the makeshift repairs and salvaged components, was becoming overwhelming. Mika felt a responsibility not just to survive, but to build something lasting, something that could withstand the inevitable challenges the future held. She envisioned a system that was entirely self-sustaining, drawing power from renewable sources, recycling all its waste, and producing enough food and clean water for everyone, with a surplus. But the Wastes offered few answers, and the remnants of the old world were increasingly depleted and unreliable. Her work became more than just an intellectual puzzle; it was a desperate plea to the universe, a testament to her belief in humanity's ability to overcome even the most dire circumstances.

Yet, with each passing day, as the resources dwindled and the demands grew, the fear that her efforts might not be enough, that she might be fighting a losing battle, became a more potent and pervasive force. It was a fear that gnawed at the edges of her resolve, a shadow that lengthened with every flicker of the lights, every dip in the power grid, every empty space on the communal larder shelves. The weight of the world, or at least this fragile fragment of it, rested heavily on her shoulders, and the growing unease in her heart was a constant, unwelcome companion.

The sun, a muted disc behind a perpetual haze, offered scant warmth to the small patch of ground Luis tended. It was less a garden and more a defiant experiment, a fragile sanctuary carved out of the scarred earth on the settlement's periphery. Each seedling, painstakingly nurtured from salvaged seeds, represented a gamble, a small act of faith against the overwhelming evidence of the Wastes. He'd coaxed life from soil that whispered of ancient poisons and unnatural mutations, a process that felt less like cultivation and more like a desperate negotiation with a capricious, dying planet.

The initial promise had been intoxicating. A few stubborn shoots had broken through the ochre-colored dirt, their vibrant green a shocking contrast to the muted palette of their surroundings. Luis had watched them, a lump in his throat, feeling a profound connection to the primal act of growth. He had seen them as a symbol, a testament to the enduring power of life, a tangible counterpoint to the pervasive despair that clung to the settlement like the omnipresent dust. He imagined rows upon rows of nutrient-rich vegetables, a vibrant tapestry that could supplement their meager rations, a source of hope that could be tasted and felt. His heart had soared with the possibilities, envisioning a future where hunger was not a constant, gnawing presence.

But the Wastes were not easily tamed. The soil, while showing signs of amendment thanks to Mika's chemical treatments and Luis's own organic compost, remained stubbornly unpredictable. One day, a row of burgeoning bean plants would stand tall and proud, their leaves unfurling with vigor. The next, they might be withered and blackened, their very essence seemingly leached away by an unseen force. Luis would kneel, sifting the soil through his calloused fingers, searching for answers. Was it a sudden spike in heavy metals? A deficiency in a crucial trace element? Or something more insidious, a lingering toxicity that resurfaced with the slightest imbalance? The questions multiplied, each one a small splinter lodging itself in his resolve.

The atmospheric conditions, another constant source of anxiety for Mika and the settlement at large, directly impacted Luis's delicate ecosystem. The unpredictable shifts in air pressure, the sudden lurches in temperature, the infrequent but violent dust storms – each played havoc with his nascent crops. A gentle rain, when it came, was a blessing, but it could quickly turn into a torrential downpour that threatened to wash away his carefully constructed irrigation channels. The filtered sunlight, crucial for photosynthesis, was often insufficient, leaving his plants pale and leggy. He'd rigged up makeshift shade cloths and rudimentary windbreaks, but they were often no match for the Wastes' volatile temperament. It was a constant battle against the elements, a Sisyphean task of trying to create a microclimate of stability within a macrocosm of chaos.

The increased demand for resources within the settlement added another layer of pressure. Every drop of water, every watt of energy, was meticulously accounted for. Luis's irrigation system, a network of recycled pipes and repurposed pumps, drew from the settlement's precious water reserves. He was acutely aware of the strain this placed on Mika's already overstretched systems. He'd tried to be as efficient as possible, implementing a drip irrigation method that minimized waste, but the sheer volume of water required to sustain his experimental plot was significant. He often found himself scrutinizing the communal water allocation reports, his stomach clenching with guilt whenever he saw the figures associated with his garden. He knew the need was great, that every drop counted for drinking, for hygiene, for the air purifiers, but his crops were hungry. They demanded hydration, and he, in turn, demanded it from the settlement's finite supply.

Nutrient depletion was another specter haunting his garden. While his compost provided a baseline of sustenance, the mutated soil seemed to possess an insatiable appetite. Even with regular additions of organic matter, he noticed signs of deficiency in some of his crops. The leaves of his kale, once a deep, healthy green, began to show yellowing edges. His small potato plants, which had initially promised a decent yield, were producing smaller, less vigorous tubers than he had hoped. He'd experimented with different compost blends, trying to incorporate micronutrients salvaged from old industrial sites – iron filings, trace minerals from discarded batteries – but it was a delicate art, and the risk of introducing new toxins was ever-present. He was working blind, trying to balance a complex equation with too many unknown variables.

Then there were the pests. The Wastes teemed with them, creatures that had adapted to the harsh environment with a terrifying resilience. Small, scuttling insects with exoskeletons like chipped obsidian burrowed into the roots of his carrots. Tiny, iridescent flies, seemingly impervious to the smoke from his meager deterrent fires, laid their eggs on the tender shoots of his radishes. He'd tried to be judicious in his use of any available pesticides, preferring a more organic approach, but the sheer numbers and the tenacity of these new forms of life were overwhelming. He found himself spending hours each day meticulously inspecting each leaf, each stem, for any sign of infestation, his heart sinking with every discovery. He waged a constant, often losing, war against these tiny invaders, each infestation a personal defeat.

The scale of the need was a weight that pressed down on him with an almost physical force. He looked at the faces of the settlement's inhabitants, at the children with their hollow eyes, at the elders with their stooped shoulders, and he felt the crushing responsibility of his endeavor. His small patch of land, his handful of struggling vegetables, felt utterly inadequate. He yearned to produce enough to make a real difference, to significantly supplement their diet, to alleviate the constant worry about food scarcity. But the reality was stark: his garden was a drop in the ocean of their need. It was a fragile symbol of hope, but a symbol nonetheless, and he worried that its very fragility would become a source of despair.

He imagined a blight, a sudden, catastrophic infestation, or a prolonged period of adverse weather, and his entire harvest, all his hard work, would be wiped out. The thought sent a chill down his spine. He was building their hope on a foundation of soil that was still fundamentally unstable, on plants that were still at the mercy of forces beyond his control. It was a precarious existence, not just for his crops, but for the fragile optimism they represented. He would meticulously record his findings in his weathered notebook, the pages filled with precise measurements, chemical analyses, and hurried sketches of insect anatomy. But the data, however detailed, couldn't mask the underlying uncertainty. He was a gardener in a land that seemed determined to remain barren, a farmer facing an uncertain harvest, a man trying to nurture life in the shadow of impending scarcity. Each day, as he walked the rows, tending to his plants with a mixture of hope and dread, Luis felt the precariousness of his garden, and by extension, the precariousness of their newfound sustenance, weighing heavily on his soul. It was a constant, quiet anxiety, a counterpoint to the faint hum of the life support systems that kept them all alive, a reminder that survival was a delicate, ever-shifting balance. He would often pause, the scent of damp earth and nascent greenery filling his nostrils, and look back towards the settlement, a knot of worry tightening in his chest. What if his experiment failed? What if this promising new source of sustenance proved to be as fleeting as a desert mirage? The questions lingered, unanswered, in the hazy, uncertain air.

The metallic click of Jax's camera shutter had become a familiar sound in the settlement, a rhythmic counterpoint to the low hum of the air scrubbers and the distant, mournful cry of the wind outside. It had once been a sound of progress, of documenting their nascent community's struggle and triumphs. Now, however, the clicks felt heavier, each one a captured moment of burgeoning unease. Jax had started his project with an almost messianic zeal, a conviction that the resilience of the human spirit, even in the face of the Wastes, was a story worth telling, a beacon of hope for anyone who might one day stumble upon their forgotten corner of the world. His early portraits were filled with a raw, unvarnished optimism. He'd captured the determined set of Mika's jaw as she wrestled with a failing water purifier, the defiant glint in Luis's eyes as he surveyed his struggling crops, the shared laughter of children playing with scavenged toys under the artificial glow of the settlement's lamps. These were images of people refusing to be defined by their circumstances, individuals who, despite the looming shadow of scarcity and the ever-present threat of the Wastes, found ways to create beauty and connection.

But the Wastes, like a persistent stain, were beginning to seep into the fabric of their daily lives, and the faces Jax pointed his lens at were starting to change. The initial shock and awe of survival had given way to a grinding, everyday anxiety. The refugees, who had arrived with a desperate hope for sanctuary, now carried a weariness that went beyond physical exhaustion. Their eyes, once wide with a plea for help, now held a guardedness, a flicker of suspicion that Jax hadn't seen before. He'd begun photographing them in the communal mess hall, their meals a stark reminder of the meager rations. He'd tried to capture the quiet dignity with which they ate, but his lens kept straying to the subtle shifts in their posture, the way they instinctively huddled closer together, their gazes occasionally darting towards the settlement's long-term residents. It was in the nuances, the almost imperceptible tightening of a jaw, the way a hand would instinctively rest on a meager bundle of possessions, that Jax began to see the cracks forming in their unity.

He remembered a particular portrait of Elara, a young woman who had been one of the first refugees to arrive. In his earlier work, Elara had been a symbol of fragile hope, her smile tentative but genuine as she helped tend to Luis's garden. Jax had captured her profile against the muted hues of a dawn sky, her face etched with a quiet determination. He had seen her as a testament to the enduring power of life, a living embodiment of their collective effort. Now, a few months later, Elara's face told a different story. Jax had seen her arguing with one of the settlement's elders over a distribution of purified water. It wasn't a loud, explosive argument, but a hushed, intense exchange, their voices barely audible above the whir of the ventilation system. When he'd raised his camera, Elara had turned away, her shoulders slumping, a profound weariness radiating from her. The resulting photograph, when he later reviewed it, was stark.

Her features, once softened by hope, were now sharp, almost gaunt. Her eyes, which had once held a spark of optimism, were clouded with a deep, unsettling sadness. The lines around her mouth were no longer from laughter, but from worry, from the constant pressure of making do with less. It was a portrait of a spirit being slowly eroded, not by external threats, but by the internal erosion of trust and the gnawing fear of scarcity.

The long-term residents, too, were showing the strain. Jax had always admired their stoicism, their quiet resilience in the face of the Wastes' initial onslaught. They were the ones who had built this place, who had laid the foundations of their survival. But even their faces, once etched with the hardships of building, were now showing the subtle signs of defensiveness. He'd photographed a gathering in the central plaza, a rare moment where the community was supposed to come together for a shared meal. Instead, he'd seen subtle divisions forming. The long-term residents, a group he'd always seen as a cohesive unit, were now clustered together, their conversations more animated amongst themselves, their smiles less readily offered to the newcomers. The refugees, by contrast, occupied a separate, more isolated space, their expressions a mixture of polite deference and simmering resentment. Jax's camera had captured it all: the averted gazes, the forced pleasantries, the unspoken tensions that hung in the air like the ever-present dust. He'd tried to frame it as a snapshot of a community in transition, but the reality felt more divisive. He'd zoomed in on the hands of a long-term resident, his fingers laced possessively around his ration pack, while across the plaza, a refugee woman clutched her child's hand a little tighter, her knuckles white. It was a visual shorthand for the growing chasm, a silent testament to the fear that was beginning to override their shared humanity.

Jax found himself wrestling with his role as a documentarian. He had set out to capture the triumph of the human spirit, the indomitable will to survive and thrive against all odds. But the Wastes were not a romantic backdrop for heroic struggle; they were a relentless, grinding force that chipped away at people's resolve, exposing their baser instincts. He couldn't ignore the fear, the suspicion, the subtle but growing resentments that were fracturing their community. To present an idealized version of their lives would be a disservice, a lie. Yet, to fully capture the darker aspects of their existence felt like a betrayal of the very people he had come to document, a judgment he was not qualified to make.

He started to experiment with his framing, using the stark, utilitarian architecture of the settlement to emphasize the isolation and confinement. He'd photograph individuals against the blank, unyielding walls of their living quarters, the harsh lines of the structures mirroring the harshness of their circumstances. In one striking portrait, he captured a group of children playing a game that involved kicking a deflated synthetic ball. Their laughter, though genuine, was tinged with a desperate energy, a frantic attempt to create normalcy in an abnormal world. But Jax focused on their bare feet, calloused and stained with the ubiquitous dust, and the way their eyes, even in play, held a certain wariness, a maturity that children should never possess. The background was deliberately blurred, drawing all attention to the small, fragile bubble of their innocence being buffeted by the harsh realities of their environment.

The increasing scarcity of resources was a constant undercurrent, and Jax felt compelled to document its impact. He'd spent hours observing the rationing process, the meticulous weighing and distributing of food, water, and energy credits. His camera captured the guarded expressions of those receiving their meager portions, the subtle disappointment in their eyes when a particular item was in short supply. He remembered a scene where a family received their water allocation. The youngest child, a girl no older than six, reached out a small, grimy hand, her fingers spread wide, as if expecting a cascade. Her mother gently pulled her hand back, her own face a mask of quiet stoicism, but her eyes, when they met Jax's, conveyed a world of unspoken apology and regret. Jax had captured the moment, the stark contrast between the child's hopeful expectation and the mother's resigned acceptance. It was a powerful, heartbreaking image, and it haunted him.

He found himself increasingly drawn to the faces of those who were struggling the most, the ones whose optimism was visibly fraying. He'd noticed a man named Silas, one of the settlement's mechanics, who had always been a source of wry humor and practical solutions. Silas had a knack for coaxing life out of broken machinery, his hands perpetually stained with grease, his laughter deep and resonant. But Jax had seen Silas lately, hunched over a malfunctioning air filtration unit, his usual jovial demeanor replaced by a grim frustration. His brow was furrowed, his lips pressed into a thin line, and his eyes, usually so full of spark, were dulled with exhaustion and despair. Jax had taken a series of shots, capturing the moment Silas slammed his wrench down on the metal casing of the unit in a burst of pent-up frustration, a sound that echoed jarringly in the otherwise quiet workshop. The resulting portrait was of a man pushed to his limit, his resilience worn thin by the relentless demands of their precarious existence. It was a portrait of quiet desperation, of a man who, for the first time, seemed to doubt his own ability to fix what was broken.

Jax also began to document the subtle ways people were starting to withdraw, to build their own internal walls against the growing pressures. He'd photographed a communal storytelling session, an event that had once been a vibrant exchange of shared experiences and hopes. Now, the stories were shorter, more hesitant, punctuated by awkward silences. People seemed more reluctant to share personal details, their words carefully chosen, their emotions guarded. He noticed how individuals would often break away from the group, seeking the solitude of their cramped living quarters, or finding solace in repetitive, solitary tasks. He'd captured a woman meticulously mending a tattered piece of fabric, her focus so intense it seemed she was trying to mend not just the garment, but the unraveling fabric of her own hope. Her face, illuminated by the dim glow of a desk lamp, was a study in quiet determination, but beneath the surface, Jax could sense a deep well of unspoken sorrow.

The fear of the unknown was a palpable presence, and Jax felt it creeping into his work. The Wastes were an ever-present threat, a vast, untamed wilderness that held untold dangers. The rare encounters with mutated fauna, the sudden shifts in atmospheric conditions, the unsettling silence that sometimes descended – all contributed to a pervasive sense of vulnerability. He'd photographed a group of scouts returning from a patrol, their faces grim, their movements slow and weary. Their gear was scuffed, their expressions etched with a weariness that spoke of more than just physical exertion. One of the scouts, a young man named Finn, who had always been eager and adventurous, now had a haunted look in his eyes. Jax had captured Finn staring out into the hazy distance, his gaze fixed on something unseen, his knuckles white as he gripped the strap of his rifle. It was a portrait of a man who had glimpsed something that had irrevocably changed him, a man forever marked by the lurking dangers of the Wastes.

Jax grappled with the ethical implications of his work. He was capturing these moments of vulnerability, of fear, of quiet desperation. Was he exploiting their pain for the sake of a compelling narrative? He found himself constantly questioning his motives, trying to find a balance between documenting the unvarnished truth and maintaining a sense of empathy and respect. He realized that his early optimism, while genuine, had been naive. He had focused on the resilience, but had perhaps overlooked the toll that resilience took. He had seen the strength, but had failed to fully acknowledge the weariness that lay beneath.

He began to incorporate more abstract elements into his photography, using light and shadow to convey the emotional landscape of the settlement. He'd photograph individuals partially obscured by shadow, their features indistinct, suggesting the anonymity and isolation that many felt. He'd use harsh, unforgiving light to highlight the lines of fatigue on people's faces, the worn textures of their clothing, the stark realities of their meager possessions. He was no longer just documenting their lives; he was trying to convey the *feeling* of their lives, the weight of their struggles, the quiet anxieties that permeated their days.

One evening, while reviewing his recent shots, Jax came across a series he'd taken of the settlement's older children helping with the energy distribution. They were diligently plugging in power cells, their faces serious and focused. But in one frame, he'd captured a brief, unguarded moment. A young girl, no older than ten, paused in her task, her eyes drifting towards a flickering holographic image displayed on a communal screen – a faded advertisement for a product that no longer existed, a relic of a world long gone. Her expression was a complex mix of curiosity, longing, and a profound sadness, as if she were glimpsing a dream she could never fully comprehend. It was a powerful image, a testament to the lost world and the uncertain future they inhabited. Jax knew that this was the kind of story he needed to tell now – not just the triumph of survival, but the cost of it, the quiet sacrifices, the lingering shadows of what was lost, and the ever-present uncertainty of what was to come. His portraits, once a celebration of hope, were now becoming a more complex tapestry, woven with threads of fear, resilience, and the enduring, yet fragile, human spirit. The looming shadow was not just an external threat; it was an internal one, and his camera was now capturing its subtle, yet profound, impact.

CHAPTER FOUR

THE INVASIVE BLOOM

The air hung thick and heavy, a cloying miasma of sulfur and decay that clung to their suits like a second skin. Even through the reinforced filters, the acrid tang of the mire managed to seep in, a constant, unsettling reminder of the desolation they traversed. Jax adjusted the strap of his pack, the worn canvas digging into his shoulder. His camera, a bulky, state-of-the-art device that had once been a symbol of his optimistic endeavors to document humanity's resilience, now felt like an extension of his own growing apprehension. The Wastes, with their unpredictable toxins and mutated lifeforms, offered little in the way of solace, and every scouting mission was a gamble, a desperate search for resources that grew scarcer with each passing cycle.

Mika, ever the pragmatist, led the way, her movements precise and economical as she navigated the treacherous terrain. Her environmental scanner, a sophisticated piece of tech that could detect minute traces of airborne pathogens and ground contamination, chirped a constant stream of data, a digital heartbeat in the otherwise dead landscape. Beside her, Luis, his face etched with a familiar blend of determination and worry, scanned the horizon with an experienced eye, his hand resting on the worn grip of his pulse rifle. The younger members of their party, Anya and Ren, followed close behind, their youthful faces a stark contrast to the seasoned veterans, yet their eyes held a similar, watchful tension. They were tasked with collecting samples, a crucial role that demanded both caution and a keen eye for anything out of the ordinary.

They had ventured further than usual, drawn by a faint, anomalous energy signature detected by Mika's long-range sensors. It was a gamble, but their own settlement's resource reserves were dwindling, the hydroponic farms struggling, and the water purifiers working overtime with diminishing returns. The signature suggested a pocket of unusual geological activity, perhaps even a hidden geothermal vent that could provide much-needed energy, or, at the very least, a source of rare minerals. The low-lying region they now entered was known for its toxic marshes, a treacherous expanse where the very air seemed to hum with danger. The ground underfoot was a treacherous, viscous muck, bubbling with noxious gases, and the skeletal remains of long-dead flora jutted out like accusations from the suffocating earth.

"Readings are... strange," Mika murmured, her voice slightly muffled by her helmet. She gestured towards her scanner. "There's a significant concentration of bio-activity here, far more than should be possible in this environment. And it's... pulsing."

Jax felt a prickle of unease. "Pulsing? What kind of bio-activity?"

"That's the odd part," she replied, frowning. "It doesn't match any known terrestrial or even mutated flora in the database. The energy output is also surprisingly high, almost like a localized, contained power source."

Luis squinted, his gaze sweeping across the seemingly barren marsh. "I don't see anything. Just mud and dead trees. Are you sure it's not a faulty reading, Mika?"

"The scanner's been calibrated twice since we left the settlement," Mika said firmly. "The readings are consistent across multiple sensors. Whatever it is, it's generating a significant amount of life-sustaining energy, enough to thrive in... this." She gestured to the toxic landscape around them, the air shimmering with heat and chemical fumes.

Anya, who had been cautiously probing the ground with a long, insulated rod, suddenly called out, her voice sharp with surprise. "Captain! Over here! Look!"

They moved towards her, their boots sinking into the thick, muddy substrate with a disconcerting squelch. Anya pointed to a patch of ground a few meters away. At first glance, it appeared as barren and desolate as the rest of the marsh. But as they drew closer, they began to notice something subtle, something that defied the pervasive decay.

Nestled within a particularly stagnant pool of iridescent green water, where the skeletal branches of dead trees reached out like grasping claws, was a plant. It was unlike anything any of them had ever seen. It stood about waist-high, its form both elegant and alien. Its stalk was a deep, iridescent violet, smooth and almost metallic in its sheen, and it pulsed with a soft, internal light, a gentle ebb and flow of luminescence that seemed to emanate from within its very core. The leaves were broad and elongated, a deep emerald hue that seemed to absorb the dim, filtered light of the Wastes and reflect it back with an almost ethereal glow. But the most striking feature was its bloom.

Atop the stalk sat a cluster of large, bell-shaped flowers, their petals a vibrant, incandescent blue. They glowed with an intense, almost otherworldly light, casting an ethereal luminescence that cut through the oppressive gloom of the marsh. The light wasn't harsh; it was soft, inviting, a beacon in the desolation.

"By the Founders..." Ren breathed, his eyes wide with wonder. "What is that?"

Jax felt his photographer's instinct surge, overriding his apprehension. He fumbled for his camera, the familiar weight a comforting presence in his hands. This was it. This was the story he had been searching for – a testament to life's unyielding persistence, a miracle blooming in the heart of desolation.

Mika approached cautiously, her scanner held steady. "Incredible," she whispered, her gaze fixed on the luminescent plant. "The bio-activity readings are off the charts, originating entirely from this single organism. It's... thriving. In pure toxin."

Luis, ever the pragmatist and a seasoned farmer, was equally astonished. "I've never seen anything like it. Not in any seed bank, not in any historical record. It's impossible. This soil is toxic, the air is corrosive. Nothing should be able to grow here."

Anya, the youngest and perhaps the most impressionable, reached out a gloved hand towards the plant, her fingers hovering just above the glowing petals. "It's so beautiful," she murmured. "It's like... a star fell into the marsh."

Jax began to photograph, his lens capturing the vibrant hues, the soft luminescence, the impossible bloom against the backdrop of death. He focused on the details: the delicate veins on the leaves, the subtle shimmer of the stalk, the almost hypnotic pulse of light within the plant. He framed shots that emphasized its isolation, its defiant existence in the face of overwhelming odds. He captured the contrast between the plant's vibrant life and the skeletal decay that surrounded it.

"It's not just surviving," Mika said, her voice laced with awe. "It's flourishing. The light it's emitting isn't just for show; it's a byproduct of a highly efficient photosynthetic process, one that's somehow adapted to break down and utilize these toxins as a primary energy source. It's metabolizing the very poisons that would kill us."

Ren, meanwhile, was carefully collecting a soil sample near the plant's base, his movements precise and deliberate. "The soil here is incredibly rich in heavy metals and corrosive compounds," he reported, his voice tense. "But right around the plant... it's different. Almost... purified. As if the plant is actively altering its immediate environment."

Jax zoomed in on the plant's roots, which were partially exposed by the churned-up mud. They were thick and fibrous, a deep, almost blackish hue, and they seemed to weave through the toxic soil with an unnatural ease. The luminescence appeared to be strongest at the points where the roots met the soil, as if the plant was drawing energy directly from the poisoned earth.

"This is beyond anything we've ever encountered," Luis said, his initial skepticism replaced by a profound sense of wonder and a touch of apprehension. "If this plant can thrive in such an environment, if it can break down these toxins... what else could it do? What other applications could it have?"

Mika was already running more complex analyses. "The cellular structure is unlike anything in our database. It's incredibly resilient, capable of repairing damage at an astonishing rate. And the bioluminescence... it's not just light; it's a complex bio-energy emission. It's generating its own energy field. This plant is a self-sustaining ecosystem unto itself."

Jax continued to shoot, his focus sharpening. He captured the way the light from the flowers cast an ethereal glow on the surrounding water, making the stagnant pools shimmer with an unnatural beauty. He noticed small, iridescent insects, unlike any he had seen before, flitting around the blooms, their wings catching the light like tiny jewels. They seemed unaffected by the toxic environment, drawn to the plant's radiant energy.

"There are other, smaller ones," Anya said, pointing further into the marsh. "Dozens of them, scattered around. They're not as bright as this one, but they're definitely the same species."

Indeed, as they looked more closely, they began to see them – smaller, less developed specimens of the same luminous flora, peeking out from the muck and mire, each a tiny beacon of life in the desolate expanse. The discovery was no longer a single anomaly; it was an emergent phenomenon, a species actively colonizing a hostile environment.

"This changes everything," Luis said, his voice hushed. "If we can understand this plant, its properties... it could revolutionize our efforts. Imagine, a way to purify contaminated land, to generate clean energy, to create new food sources." The farmer in him was captivated by the potential for abundance.

Jax, however, felt a familiar unease begin to surface. He had seen too many desperate attempts to harness the Wastes' power backfire, too many hopeful discoveries turn into unforeseen disasters. The Wastes were a place of extreme adaptation, of ruthless survival. Life here was not gentle; it was fierce, primal, and often, dangerous. This plant, so beautiful and radiant, was a product of this brutal world. Its very existence was a testament to its ability to overcome unimaginable adversity. But what was the cost of that adaptation?

He zoomed in on the flowers again. The petals seemed almost too perfect, their luminescence a little too intense. There was an unnatural quality to their vibrant health. He noticed that where the plant's roots extended into the mud, the surrounding water seemed to boil with a faint, almost imperceptible heat, and the mud itself began to take on a greyish, chalky texture, a sign of intense chemical breakdown.

"It's incredibly efficient," Mika confirmed, her brow furrowed as she studied her readings. "But there's a... significant byproduct. The plant is not just breaking down toxins; it's re-processing them into highly concentrated forms of energy. And some of that energy is being released as heat. This entire area is warmer than it should be. And look at the water composition around the root system." She pointed to a section of her display. "It's becoming increasingly alkaline. Extremely so. Enough to be corrosive to organic tissue over prolonged exposure."

Jax felt a chill, despite the ambient warmth of the marsh. This beautiful, glowing plant was not a gift from the Wastes; it was a predator, a life form that had evolved to consume and transform its environment with a ferocity that mirrored the Wastes themselves. Its beauty was a lure, its luminescence a siren song.

"So, it cleans the land, but it makes the soil deadly in a different way?" Ren asked, his initial excitement tempered by Mika's findings.

"Essentially," Mika confirmed. "It's a highly specialized organism. It can thrive where others can't, but its process has a... side effect. It's a potent terraforming agent, but not necessarily in a way that would be beneficial for us, or for other life forms we might want to cultivate."

Luis looked at the plant with a mixture of awe and apprehension. "So, it's a miracle... and a warning. Like so many things out here."

Jax lowered his camera for a moment, taking in the scene with his own eyes. The plant pulsed with life, a vibrant splash of impossible color in a world of muted decay. The light it cast was mesmerizing, drawing them in, promising salvation. But beneath the surface, the Wastes' brutal logic was at play. Life here found a way, but it was a way that often came with a terrible price. This was not just a discovery; it was a revelation about the nature of the Wastes themselves. Life, in its most desperate and adaptive forms, could be as dangerous as it was miraculous. The invasive bloom was a beautiful, terrifying testament to that truth. He raised his camera again, the clicks of the shutter now carrying a heavier resonance, documenting not just a discovery, but a profound and unsettling truth about the world they inhabited. This plant, born from the heart of poison, was a potent symbol of the Wastes' dual nature: the ever-present threat, and the equally potent, albeit dangerous, promise of renewal. He captured the details of the iridescent insects that danced around the luminescent blossoms, their delicate forms a stark contrast to the harsh, toxic environment. He noted the way the light seemed to refract through the water droplets clinging to the petals, creating miniature rainbows that shimmered with an almost hypnotic beauty. He focused his lens on the intricate patterns of the plant's vascular system, visible beneath the translucent violet stalk, each line a testament to its incredible efficiency. He documented the subtle variations in the plant's glow, a slow, rhythmic pulsing that seemed to sync with the distant thrum of geothermal activity deep beneath the marsh. He zoomed in on the edge of the bloom, where the blue petals met the vibrant green leaves, the transition a seamless blend of impossible hues. He tried to capture the subtle scent that now permeated the air, a faint, sweet perfume overlaid with the metallic tang of the Wastes, a contradiction that spoke volumes about the plant's nature.

The longer they observed, the more they noticed the subtle interactions between the plant and its environment. Tiny, almost microscopic organisms swarmed around the base of the stalk, seemingly feeding off the waste byproducts of the plant's metabolic process. The mud immediately surrounding the roots was a different texture, more granular, almost sandy, as if the plant was actively breaking down the dense, viscous muck into something more manageable. Jax captured close-ups of this altered soil, the fine particles clinging to the roots, hinting at a complex chemical transformation occurring at a microscopic level.

"It's not just metabolizing toxins; it's actively reconstructing the soil," Mika mused, her eyes glued to the data streaming from her scanner. "It's creating a niche for itself, a pocket of habitable space within this otherwise lethal environment. The process is incredibly precise, incredibly efficient." She paused, then added, "And incredibly energetic. The sheer output of this one organism is astounding. If we could replicate this... the implications are enormous."

Luis, the farmer, was captivated. "Imagine being able to 'reclaim' land like this. To turn contaminated zones into something that could sustain life. We could grow food again, not just in sterile hydroponics, but on actual soil." His voice held a note of longing that resonated with everyone.

Anya, her initial awe now mixed with a scientific curiosity, carefully collected a small sample of the altered soil using a sterilized scoop. "It feels different too," she commented, her gloved fingers probing the grainy texture. "Less... sticky. Almost dry, despite being in the middle of the marsh."

Jax photographed her as she worked, the stark contrast between her clean, white suit and the alien soil a visual metaphor for their intrusion into this unknown ecosystem. He captured the way her face, even through the helmet's visor, was etched with concentration and a budding sense of discovery.

"But what about the heat?" Ren asked, bringing them back to a more grounded concern. "And the alkalinity? That's a major drawback."

"Indeed," Mika replied, her gaze sweeping over the surrounding marsh. "This plant creates its own microclimate. The heat it dissipates is significant, and the alkalinity is a powerful deterrent to most other life forms. It's a closed loop, a highly specialized adaptation. It thrives, but it also isolates itself, and potentially, poisons its surroundings in a different way."

Jax shifted his focus, capturing a wider view of the marsh. He noticed that the areas immediately surrounding the larger blooms seemed to shimmer with a slight distortion, a visual anomaly caused by the heat radiating from the plants. The very air above them seemed to warp, creating a mirage-like effect. He zoomed in on the water's surface, noting the tiny bubbles of gas that were constantly rising from the mud near the plant's base, a visual indication of the intense chemical reactions occurring beneath.

"It's a double-edged sword, then," Luis said, his voice laced with a familiar post-apocalyptic pragmatism. "A miracle that could be a curse. We've seen it before. The Wastes don't give gifts; they offer bargains, and the price is always steep."

Jax felt a surge of creative energy. He began to experiment with his camera settings, trying to capture the ethereal quality of the plant's luminescence. He used longer exposures, allowing the subtle pulsing of light to create streaks and trails in his images, transforming the static plant into something dynamic and alive. He played with different focal lengths, capturing both the intimate details of the bloom and the grand scale of its improbable existence within the desolate marsh. He tried to convey not just the visual beauty, but the underlying power and potential danger. He focused on the interplay of light and shadow, using the harsh Wastes' light to sculpt the plant's form, highlighting its alien contours. He captured the droplets of condensed moisture that clung to the leaves, each one acting as a tiny lens, reflecting the plant's inner glow.

"We need samples," Mika stated, her scientific drive overriding any immediate apprehension. "Multiple samples. Soil, water, plant tissue. We need to understand the exact biochemical processes at play. If we can isolate the enzymes responsible for breaking down these toxins, or the mechanism behind its energy generation..." Her voice trailed off, filled with the vast possibilities.

"And we need to be careful," Luis added, his hand instinctively tightening on his rifle. "This isn't a greenhouse back at the settlement.

This is the Wastes. Anything this vibrant, this powerful, could have defenses we can't even imagine."

Jax continued to photograph, his lens a silent observer of this extraordinary moment. He captured the team at work, their caution, their fascination, their quiet determination. He framed Mika as she carefully collected a tissue sample, her movements precise and sterile, a stark contrast to the wild, untamed nature of the plant. He photographed Ren as he meticulously bagged the soil and water samples, his brow furrowed in concentration. He caught Anya's wide-eyed gaze as she observed a particularly large bloom, her wonder evident even through her visor. He even managed to capture a fleeting shot of Luis, his usual gruff exterior softening as he gazed at the impossible flora, a flicker of something akin to hope in his eyes.

As they prepared to extract a larger section of the plant for more detailed study, a subtle shift occurred. The rhythmic pulsing of the plant's light intensified, becoming more rapid, more urgent. The air around it grew perceptibly warmer, and the rising bubbles from the mud increased in frequency. The iridescent insects that had been flitting around the blooms suddenly dispersed, vanishing into the haze of the marsh.

"It's reacting," Mika said, her voice sharp with alarm. "It's sensing our intrusion. The energy output is spiking."

Jax instinctively zoomed in on the central bloom. The blue petals, which had been gently unfurled, began to draw inward, contracting as if recoiling. The luminescence intensified to a blinding degree, casting sharp, stark shadows across the marsh. A low hum, almost a vibration, emanated from the plant, a sound that seemed to resonate deep within their chests.

"Pull back!" Luis commanded, his voice cutting through the rising tension. "Now!"

They retreated, their movements hurried but controlled. Jax, still snapping photos, managed to capture the moment the plant's luminescence reached its peak, a blinding flash of blue that momentarily washed out the muted colors of the Wastes. Then, with a soft, almost inaudible sigh, the light receded, the pulsing slowed, and the plant returned to its gentle, rhythmic glow, though it seemed somehow more guarded, more watchful.

The air, however, remained charged with a subtle energy, and the faint scent of ozone hung heavy in the miasma. They had discovered a miracle, a testament to life's tenacious will. But they had also touched upon something primal, something powerful, something that clearly did not wish to be disturbed. The invasive bloom, born of poison and thriving in desolation, was not merely a botanical curiosity; it was a living entity, a formidable force of nature that demanded respect, and perhaps, a healthy dose of fear. Jax knew, as he lowered his camera, that this was only the beginning of understanding this extraordinary, and potentially perilous, new life. The secrets held within that luminous blossom were far deeper, and far more complex, than he had initially imagined. He reviewed the last few frames on his camera's small screen, the blinding flash of blue a stark reminder of the plant's potent defense mechanism. It was a beautiful, terrifying image, a testament to the Wastes' ability to create life that was as dangerous as it was awe-inspiring. He felt a strange mix of exhilaration and trepidation. They had found something remarkable, something that could change their world, but they had also glimpsed its power, its unwillingness to be simply harvested. The Wastes were always a lesson in humility, and this invasive bloom was the latest, most vibrant, and perhaps the most dangerous, instructor.

The metallic tang of the settlement's filtered air was a stark contrast to the acrid, yet somehow vital, atmosphere of the marsh. Back within the relative safety of Haven, the discovery of the luminescent flora was met not with universal acclaim, but with a swirling eddy of opinion, a microcosm of the conflicting desires and anxieties that defined their precarious existence. Jax found himself at the epicenter of this burgeoning debate, his camera, ever the impartial witness, documenting the passionate arguments that echoed through the communal hall.

Luis, his face still etched with the awe he'd felt amidst the toxic bloom, was the first to articulate the immense promise. He stood before a projected image of the plant, its ethereal blue glow a stark contrast to the utilitarian grey of the hall. "Look at it," he urged, his voice resonating with a farmer's deep-seated reverence for life. "It thrives in poison. It metabolizes what kills us. Think of the applications! If we can understand its bio-chemistry, its ability to neutralize toxins... we could reclaim land. Land that's been dead for generations. We could grow crops again, real food, not just the nutrient paste from the hydroponics. And medicine! What if its properties extend beyond soil purification? What if it holds the key to healing some of the diseases that plague us, diseases born from generations of exposure to the Wastes?" His eyes, usually steady and practical, now gleamed with the vision of a world reborn, of fertile fields pushing back the encroaching desolation. He saw not just a plant, but a potential lifeline, a botanical savior in a world starved of hope. He spoke of the possibility of cultivating it, of creating sterile nurseries within the settlement walls, meticulously studying its root systems, its cellular structure, its unique energy output. He imagined the day they could introduce it to the perimeter of Haven, a living, breathing defense against the toxic air, slowly but surely expanding their habitable zone. He even mused about the potential for creating new, hardy strains of food, genetically modified using the plant's inherent resilience, crops that could withstand the harsh realities of their environment. For Luis, this was not just a scientific curiosity; it was a tangible dream of abundance and a return to a more natural, sustainable way of life.

Mika, however, stood in stark opposition, her scientific rigor a formidable bulwark against the tide of optimism. She held a data tablet, her fingers rapidly scrolling through complex molecular diagrams and environmental impact assessments. "Luis, I understand your enthusiasm, truly. But we cannot afford to be blinded by its beauty or its apparent utility. 'Thrives in poison' is accurate, but so is 'repurposes poison into something equally potent, if not more so.' We saw the alkalinity of the soil around its roots. We felt the heat radiating from it. This is not a benevolent gardener; it is a supremely adapted predator. Its ability to break down toxins is undeniable, but its byproducts are also extreme. Introducing it carelessly could create localized pockets of intense chemical imbalance, rendering the land sterile in a different, perhaps even more insidious, way. And that's before we even consider its potential for uncontrolled growth. What if it's not just invasive, but aggressively so? What if its resilience means it outcompetes everything, including our own hard-won crops and the few remaining native species we're trying to protect?" Her tone was calm, almost dispassionate, but the underlying concern was palpable. She presented data projections, hypothetical scenarios of ecological collapse if this organism were to spread unchecked. She spoke of the delicate balance of even the Wastes' harsh ecosystem, and how such a powerful, alien force could shatter it irrevocably. She detailed the extensive research that would be required – months, perhaps years, of contained study in high-security bio-labs, isolating its genetic code, understanding its reproductive mechanisms, and rigorously testing its effects on every conceivable form of life. The resources required, she argued, were substantial, diverting attention and vital personnel from more immediate survival needs. Jax observed the subtle tightening of her jaw as she spoke, a sign of the deep-seated caution that years of studying ecological disasters had instilled in her. She was not dismissing the plant; she was demanding a thorough, unbiased, and utterly rigorous scientific evaluation before any further steps were taken.

Kiley, the settlement's chief resource manager, chimed in with a more pragmatic, almost cynical, perspective. He gestured dismissively at the projected image. "Let's talk brass tacks, shall we? This thing glows. Great. It eats poison. Even better. But what's the *cost* of all this? Mika's right about the research. It'll take labs, containment units, specialized personnel, not to mention the risk of accidental release. Luis, you talk about reclaiming land for farming. How long will that take? Years of careful cultivation, of monitoring, of potential crop failure. And what if it turns out to be too volatile, too dangerous to ever be safely integrated? We have limited power reserves, limited personnel, limited clean water. Is studying a pretty, glowing plant really the best use of those resources right now, when our water purifiers are struggling and our air filters need constant recalibration?" Kiley's concern was not with the potential of the plant itself, but with the practical allocation of their scarce resources. He saw the discovery as a potential drain, a seductive distraction from the day-to-day fight for survival. He spoke of the allocation of power that would be needed to run the specialized containment labs, the personnel that would have to be diverted from essential tasks like scavenging and defense, the sheer logistical nightmare of transporting and storing potentially hazardous biological material. He posed hypothetical scenarios of what could go wrong – a breach in containment, an accidental contamination of the settlement's water supply, a failure of the power grid that left the containment labs vulnerable. For Kiley, every decision was a calculation of risk versus reward, and in this instance, the risks seemed to outweigh the tangible, immediate benefits. He was a man who dealt with budgets and resource allocation, and the glowing plant represented an unknown variable that could destabilize his carefully managed equilibrium.

Jax, his camera clicking softly, captured the scene. Luis, the farmer, the nurturer, representing the yearning for abundance and a return to nature. Mika, the scientist, the protector, embodying the cautious pragmatism of survival and the fear of unforeseen consequences. Kiley, the pragmatist, the guardian of dwindling resources, highlighting the stark realities of their daily struggle. The debate was not merely about a plant; it was a reflection of their fractured society, a society grappling with the fundamental question of how to move forward: with bold, hopeful leaps into the unknown, or with measured, cautious steps rooted in the hard-won lessons of the past. He zoomed in on Luis's hands, calloused and strong, the hands of a man who understood growth and sustenance, his fingers now gesturing with an almost evangelistic fervor. Then he panned to Mika, her posture rigid, her gaze sharp and analytical, her expression conveying a deep-seated skepticism born from a thousand failed experiments and ecological collapses. Finally, he captured Kiley, his arms crossed, his expression a mask of weary pragmatism, the weight of their entire settlement's survival resting on his shoulders. Jax felt a profound sense of the symbolic weight of the moment. This invasive bloom, this anomaly of nature, had become a potent metaphor for their own internal divisions, a living embodiment of the eternal tension between hope and caution, opportunity and danger. It was the very essence of their struggle, laid bare in the heart of their sterile, controlled environment. He moved through the hall, his lens capturing the subtle shifts in expression, the furrowed brows of concern, the bright sparks of excitement, the tight-lipped reservations. He documented the quiet hum of the air recyclers, a constant reminder of their artificiality, a stark contrast to the raw, potent life that had been unearthed in the Wastes. He focused on the way the projected light of the plant seemed to cast an almost magical glow on the faces of those who were captivated by its promise, while simultaneously casting long, ominous shadows for those who saw only peril. He even managed to capture the fleeting glances exchanged between the opposing factions, a silent language of conviction and doubt. This was more than just a debate; it was a philosophical battle for the soul of Haven, a struggle to define their future in the face of an extraordinary discovery. The luminescence of the plant, once a beacon of hope, now illuminated the deep fissures within their community, forcing them to confront not only the unknown dangers of the Wastes, but also the equally challenging terrain of their own conflicting desires. He knew his role was not to take sides, but to record the truth of their response, to etch into his digital archive the raw, unvarnished spectrum of human reaction to the sublime and the terrifying. He continued to shoot, his focus unwavering, capturing the vibrant clash of ideologies that the invasive bloom had so unexpectedly ignited. He saw the potential for scientific breakthroughs, for a new era of sustainable living, but he also saw the specter of ecological disaster, of wasted resources, of heightened division. The plant, in its alien beauty, was a mirror, reflecting back the best and worst of their collective aspirations and their deepest fears. He captured the subtle nods of agreement, the sharp shakes of heads, the hushed whispers that punctuated the formal arguments. He saw how some were already sketching designs for containment units, their eyes alight with the thrill of innovation, while others were poring over old contingency plans, their faces etched with the grim determination of those who expected the worst. The very air in the hall seemed to crackle with the intensity of their diverging viewpoints. Jax felt a growing sense of urgency, not just to document, but to understand. This plant, this "treasure" or "threat," was forcing Haven to define itself, to articulate its values, to decide what kind of future it truly sought, even if that future was fraught with uncertainty. He continued to photograph, determined to capture every nuance of this critical juncture, the moment when a single, extraordinary bloom threatened to unravel the delicate fabric of their survival, or to weave it into something stronger, something more resilient, than they had ever dared to imagine. He captured a wide shot of the hall, the assembled faces a mosaic of hope, fear, and relentless pragmatism, all bathed in the ghostly luminescence of the alien flora. It was a moment pregnant with possibility, a turning point in their long and arduous journey through the Wastes, and Jax was there to bear witness, his camera a silent, unflinching chronicler of their collective destiny.

Mika's makeshift laboratory, cobbled together from salvaged medical equipment and jury-rigged power conduits, hummed with a low, persistent energy. The air, thick with the scent of ozone and sterile alcohol, was a stark contrast to the earthy, vital musk of the marsh she had recently left. Here, amidst the flickering glow of her diagnostic arrays and the sterile gleam of repurposed surgical steel, Mika began her meticulous examination of the luminescent flora. She worked with a focused intensity, her movements precise and economical, each action born from years of rigorous scientific training and a deep-seated instinct for self-preservation. The samples, carefully sealed in containment vials, lay before her, their faint, ethereal glow a constant, almost hypnotic presence. She treated them with the reverence due to any unknown entity, yet beneath the scientific detachment lay a palpable current of apprehension. This was not merely an academic exercise; it was a critical assessment of a potential threat, a potential salvation, and the lines between the two felt impossibly blurred.

Her primary objective was to understand the fundamental nature of the organism. She began with microscopic observation, her salvaged electron microscope, a marvel of resurrected technology, revealing a cellular structure unlike anything cataloged in her extensive databases. The cells were dense, almost crystalline, with an unusually robust cell wall that seemed to resist her initial attempts at lysis. "Remarkable resilience," she murmured, her voice barely audible above the hum of the equipment. "Even at a cellular level, it's built for survival." The chloroplasts, or what appeared to be their equivalent, pulsed with an internal light, a vibrant, almost aggressive energy that seemed to fuel the plant's luminescent property. She noted the unusual density of mitochondria, suggesting an extraordinarily high metabolic rate, capable of processing vast quantities of energy. The cytoplasm itself appeared to be a viscous, almost gel-like substance, infused with a complex network of what her preliminary spectral analysis identified as highly concentrated metallo-organic compounds. These compounds, she suspected, were key to its ability to metabolize toxins.

She carefully extracted a small tissue sample, meticulously teasing apart the cellular matrix with micro-dissection tools. The process was painstaking, each movement designed to preserve the integrity of the sample while allowing for a deeper examination of its biochemical makeup. Her spectral analyzer, calibrated to detect a wide range of organic and inorganic signatures, began its slow, deliberate scan. The results began to populate her data tablet, a cascade of readouts and graphical representations that Mika interpreted with practiced ease. The presence of heavy metal ions, particularly cadmium and lead, was significantly higher than would be considered survivable for most terrestrial life. Yet, the plant not only tolerated these elements but seemed to actively incorporate them into its cellular structure. "It's not just absorbing them," she explained to the silent, observant lenses of Jax's camera, which had been strategically placed to document her work. "It's integrating them. Binding them. Reorganizing them. This isn't passive resistance; it's active biochemical engineering."

The luminescent quality, she theorized, was a byproduct of this detoxification process, an energy release as the plant converted harmful compounds into less reactive forms. The spectral analysis confirmed a unique bio-luminescent pathway, distinct from any known phosphorescent or fluorescent mechanisms. It was as if the plant itself was a living battery, perpetually recharging by consuming the poisons that had rendered the Wastes so deadly. This discovery sent a ripple of excitement through her, a scientist's thrill at unraveling a profound mystery. But it was immediately tempered by the sheer alienness of it all. "The efficiency is... unsettling," she admitted, her brow furrowed. "It suggests a pathway that bypasses many of the energy limitations we see in conventional biological systems. Where does that extra energy go? What else is it capable of?"

Her attention then shifted to the reproductive mechanisms. Using a high-magnification scanner, she examined the spores, or what appeared to be reproductive propagules, nestled within specialized structures on the plant's leaves. They were incredibly small, almost dust-like, and possessed an outer casing that was astonishingly durable. She subjected a sample to a simulated atmospheric exposure, mimicking the harsh conditions of the Wastes. The spores remained viable, their genetic material protected by the resilient shell. "The reproductive cycle is incredibly rapid," she reported, her voice taut with concern. "And the dissemination mechanism... it's designed for widespread dispersal. These spores can travel long distances, carried by the wind, adhering to surfaces, surviving conditions that would obliterate most known seeds." She showed data visualizations depicting the exponential growth potential, a terrifying projection of how quickly the plant could colonize new territory. One simulation showed a single patch of the flora spreading to encompass acres within a matter of weeks, outcompeting any existing vegetation and altering the soil chemistry in its wake.

The alkalinity of the soil around the root systems was another critical observation. Her pH meter registered readings that would be corrosive to most plant life. "It's not just detoxifying the soil," Mika explained, gesturing to a series of soil samples arranged on her workbench, each meticulously labeled with its origin point. "It's fundamentally changing its composition. The byproduct of its metabolic processes appears to be a highly alkaline residue. While this might neutralize certain acidic toxins, it creates a completely different set of challenges for other organisms. It could render the soil sterile for conventional agriculture, even if it does absorb the heavy metals." She held up a small pot containing a few struggling shoots of a hardy, genetically modified grain variety, a staple of their diet. They had been exposed to the soil from the plant's vicinity for just a few days, and their leaves had already begun to yellow and curl. "This," she stated, her voice grave, "is not a friendly neighbor."

She ran tests for radiation resistance, a crucial parameter in their world. The plant's cellular structure exhibited an uncanny ability to repair radiation-induced damage, its genetic material seemingly self-correcting at an astonishing rate. This was a double-edged sword: a potential shield against the pervasive radiation of the Wastes, but also a testament to its near-indestructibility. "It's like a biological Teflon coating," she mused darkly. "Radiation, toxins, extreme pH... it shrugs them off. This resilience is precisely what makes it so potentially dangerous if we lose control."

Mika documented her findings meticulously. She recorded the spectral signatures of the plant's unique bio-luminescent compounds, the detailed cellular morphology, and the alarming growth rate projections. She generated comparative analyses, pitting the plant's known properties against established ecological models, all of which screamed of potential disruption. Her data painted a picture of an organism of extraordinary adaptability and resilience, a biological marvel that could, under the right circumstances, rewrite the rules of survival in the Wastes. But it was a narrative punctuated by stark warnings, by the chilling potential for unintended consequences. The very traits that made it so attractive – its ability to thrive in poison, its rapid reproduction, its resilience – were also the characteristics that made it a formidable threat.

She ran simulations on potential interactions with other species. Even the hardy scrub weeds that managed to eke out an existence at the fringes of Haven's perimeter showed signs of distress when exposed to the plant's influence. The delicate symbiotic relationships that existed, however fragile, were demonstrably disrupted. Her models predicted that if introduced into a balanced ecosystem, the plant would likely become an apex competitor, its aggressive growth and resource acquisition overwhelming native species. The glowing bloom, so beautiful and alluring, was also a biological bulldozer, capable of flattening the existing landscape and reshaping it in its own image.

Her analysis confirmed Luis's observations about its toxin-metabolizing capabilities, providing concrete biochemical pathways that supported his claims of potential reclamation. But her findings also validated Kiley's concerns about resource allocation. The containment protocols required for such an organism were extensive and costly, demanding specialized equipment, constant monitoring, and highly trained personnel – resources that were already stretched thin within Haven. The risk of an accidental release, she calculated, was non-negligible, and the potential consequences catastrophic. Even with the most stringent containment, the sheer abundance of its spores and its inherent hardiness presented an ongoing challenge.

Mika paused, rubbing her tired eyes. The data was complex, multifaceted, and offered no easy answers. It was a testament to the intricate beauty and brutal pragmatism of nature, even a nature twisted and mutated by centuries of human folly. The plant was a paradox: a potential cure that could also be a plague, a symbol of hope that harbored the seeds of destruction. Her preliminary analysis had not resolved the debate; it had, in fact, amplified it, providing scientific weight to both sides of the argument while simultaneously introducing a host of new, terrifying unknowns. The glow of the samples seemed to intensify in the dim light of the lab, a silent, radiant testament to the profound questions it posed. She knew that her work was far from over. This was just the beginning of understanding the invasive bloom, and the deeper she delved, the more complex and perilous the journey appeared to become. The data she had collected was a powerful tool, but it was a tool that demanded wisdom and caution in its application. And in the heart of Haven, those were commodities as scarce as clean water. She saved her findings, a digital record of the organism's astonishing capabilities and its equally astonishing dangers, a ledger of potential and peril that would undoubtedly fuel the ongoing debate, and perhaps, dictate their very survival.

The air in Luis's small, salvaged greenhouse, tucked away behind the hydroponic nutrient tanks, was a world apart from the sterile chill of Mika's lab. Here, the atmosphere was thick with the damp, earthy scent of growing things, a primal perfume that spoke of life's enduring tenacity. Sunlight, filtered through the grimy panes of repurposed plexiglass, cast dappled patterns on the makeshift workbench. Luis, his hands perpetually stained with the rich, dark soil he so lovingly coaxed into yielding, hummed a tuneless melody as he worked. His movements were slow, deliberate, each gesture imbued with a tenderness that bordered on reverence. He was coaxing a miracle from the wreckage, and he knew it.

He had started with a single, precious sample, a small cluster of the luminescent flora he'd carefully extracted from the fringes of the toxic marsh. The others, including Mika, saw it as a harbinger of doom, an aggressive invader whose very existence threatened the delicate balance of their fragile ecosystem. But Luis saw something else. He saw a stubborn, defiant spark of life that refused to be extinguished by the poisoned earth. He saw a whisper of hope in a world drowning in despair. His belief in nature's inherent ability to heal, to adapt, and to reclaim, burned brighter than any skepticism the community could muster.

His cultivation setup was rudimentary, born of necessity and ingenuity. He'd lined a discarded industrial container with layers of scavenged bio-plastic, creating a sealed environment. The substrate was a carefully balanced mixture, a blend of the nutrient-poor soil from their immediate vicinity and a generous infusion of the richer, albeit still contaminated, marsh mud. He'd even managed to rig a low-power grow lamp, salvaged from a defunct agricultural drone, to supplement the meager sunlight. It was a far cry from Mika's sophisticated equipment, but it was his. And he poured every ounce of his faith and determination into it.

He observed the specimen with an almost paternalistic gaze. Unlike the aggressive, rapidly spreading tendrils Mika had documented in her simulations, Luis's specimen seemed to exhibit a placid, almost passive nature. It pulsed with a soft, internal light, a gentle emanation that seemed to soothe rather than alarm. Its leaves, a deep, iridescent green, unfurled slowly, deliberately, reaching towards the light like thirsty newborns. He marveled at its resilience. Even in the harsh, nutrient-starved soil, it thrived, its root system, visible through the translucent lining of the container, a delicate network of fine filaments drawing sustenance from what others deemed uninhabitable.

"You're stronger than they think, aren't you?" he'd murmur, his voice a low rumble of encouragement. He would spend hours just watching, meticulously recording every subtle change. He noted the slight variations in luminescence, the way the light seemed to ebb and flow with the rhythm of the artificial day. He observed how the plant seemed to draw moisture directly from the air, its waxy cuticle shimmering with condensation. There were no visible signs of aggression, no outward manifestations of the invasive potential Mika's data suggested. It simply *was*, a testament to the quiet persistence of life.

Luis believed, with an unshakeable conviction, that the plant's ability to detoxify the soil was its greatest gift, not its greatest threat. He'd seen firsthand how the Wastes had stripped the land bare, how the lingering toxins made even the most basic agriculture a near-impossible endeavor. The genetic modifications that had once allowed their crops to survive were now failing, the poisons adapting, evolving, always one step ahead. But this plant... this plant seemed to possess a natural solution, a biological alchemy that could, perhaps, reverse the damage. He imagined fields of it, a glowing carpet spreading across the poisoned plains, slowly, patiently, transforming the dead earth back into something fertile, something alive.

He meticulously monitored the soil around his cultivated specimen. Using a handheld pH meter, a device he'd meticulously repaired himself, he charted the gradual shift in alkalinity. It was true, the soil was becoming more alkaline, a byproduct of the plant's metabolic processes, as Mika's data had confirmed. But Luis saw not sterility, but a different kind of balance. He believed that with careful management, this alkaline shift could be managed, even harnessed. Perhaps, he mused, certain native, alkali-tolerant species could be introduced, their growth encouraged by the very conditions that would have previously been toxic. It was a complex dance, a delicate negotiation with the plant's inherent nature, but he felt a burgeoning confidence that it was a dance they could learn.

His secret cultivation wasn't an act of defiance against Mika or the council, but rather an act of faith. He understood their fear; the Wastes had taught them caution, had etched the scars of past mistakes onto their collective consciousness. But sometimes, he felt, fear blinded them to possibility. He wanted to gather more data, irrefutable proof of the plant's benevolent potential, before he presented it again. He wanted to show them not just theoretical projections, but a living, breathing testament to his belief.

He introduced a small, hardy variety of scrub weed into the container with the main specimen, a plant known for its ability to tolerate even the most degraded soil. To his immense satisfaction, the scrub weed, instead of wilting, seemed to perk up. Its leaves, which had been a dull, dusty green, now exhibited a faint, healthy sheen. The luminescent plant didn't appear to consume the resources of its companion; instead, it seemed to create an environment where it could flourish. It was subtle, almost imperceptible, but to Luis, it was a revelation. It suggested that the plant's primary function was not to dominate, but to remediate. It was not an aggressor, but a gardener.

He carefully collected samples of the runoff water from his cultivated environment. He analyzed its chemical composition, comparing it to the untreated marsh water. The results were subtle but significant. The concentration of certain heavy metals had decreased, while the overall pH had increased, as expected. But more importantly, there was a discernible increase in dissolved oxygen and a reduction in the overall toxicity markers. It was a small step, a tiny microcosm of what could be achieved on a larger scale, but it was a step nonetheless. It was the sound of the Wastes whispering its surrender, the first quiet notes of a healing symphony.

Luis continued his meticulous work, his belief in the plant's potential growing with each passing day. He saw its luminescence not as an eerie glow of alienness, but as the soft light of a beacon, guiding them towards a future where the Wastes were no longer a death sentence, but a canvas for renewal. He nurtured his small, glowing hope in the quiet sanctuary of his greenhouse, waiting for the day when the skepticism of his community would finally yield to the undeniable evidence of life's persistent, gentle, and ultimately triumphant cultivation. He was not just growing a plant; he was growing a future. And in his hands, with his unwavering faith, that future felt not just possible, but inevitable. The very act of tending to it, of providing it with the care and attention it needed to thrive, was a profound statement of his belief in the restorative power of nature, a power that had been so brutally suppressed for so long. He knew that his efforts were a gamble, a deviation from the rigid protocols that governed Haven's survival. But he also knew that sometimes, the greatest leaps forward required stepping outside the lines, trusting in a vision that others could not yet see. He was playing the long game, cultivating not just a specimen, but a paradigm shift, one gentle, glowing leaf at a time.

The subtle shifts in the ecosystem within the greenhouse were a constant source of fascination for Luis. He noticed how the microscopic organisms in the soil seemed to change in character, becoming more robust, more active. He collected soil samples from different depths within the container, observing the increased microbial diversity under his simple microscope. It was as if the plant was not only neutralizing toxins but also actively fostering a new, healthier soil biome. This was more than just a chemical reaction; it was a biological resuscitation. He imagined the potential for this on a larger scale – not just cleaning the soil, but reawakening it, bringing back the complex web of life that had been so thoroughly decimated.

He also began to experiment with introducing different nutrient solutions, carefully measuring their impact on the plant's growth and luminescence. He found that while the plant was incredibly efficient at drawing sustenance from the contaminated soil, it also responded positively to enriched environments. This suggested a potential for accelerated growth and enhanced detoxification if they could develop targeted nutrient delivery systems. He sketched out diagrams in his worn notebook, ideas for automated irrigation and nutrient dispersal, visualizing a future where these glowing plants could be strategically deployed across the Wastes, transforming them into self-sustaining oases of life.

His quiet work continued, fueled by a persistent, almost stubborn optimism. He knew that Mika's findings, with their emphasis on the plant's resilience and rapid reproductive potential, were valid. He didn't discount the risks. But he believed that with careful understanding and deliberate stewardship, those risks could be mitigated. The key, he felt, lay not in eradication or containment, but in integration. He envisioned a symbiotic relationship, where humanity and this extraordinary flora could co-exist, each benefiting from the other. It was a vision that stood in stark contrast to the prevailing narrative of fear and control, a narrative that had kept them trapped in a cycle of scarcity and survival.

He would often look at the glowing plant, its light pulsing softly in the dim confines of his greenhouse, and feel a profound sense of connection. It was more than just a botanical specimen; it was a symbol of nature's indomitable spirit, a testament to the fact that even in the most inhospitable conditions, life finds a way. And in that resilience, Luis found his own strength, his own resolve to continue believing in a brighter future, a future where the Wastes would bloom once more, not with the toxic hues of contamination, but with the gentle, life-affirming glow of a world reborn. His hands, calloused and stained, were not just tending to a plant; they were gently, patiently, coaxing hope from the very earth that had been declared dead. He was cultivating possibility, and in the quiet hum of his makeshift greenhouse, that possibility felt as tangible as the soil beneath his fingernails.

The metallic tang of ozone hung heavy in the air, a stark contrast to the earthy scent Luis cultivated in his sanctuary. Jax, hunched over his portable imaging unit, felt the familiar prickle of apprehension mixed with an artist's thrill. He'd ventured beyond the immediate perimeter of Haven, into the skeletal remains of what was once a forest, now a desolate tableau of petrified trees and ash-choked earth. Here, under a sky the colour of old bruises, the invasive bloom thrived.

He'd spotted it first as a whisper of impossible colour against the monochromatic desolation. Now, a few weeks later, it was an undeniable presence. Jax knelt, his breath misting in the cool, sterile air, and carefully adjusted the macro lens. The plant before him was a marvel of alien biology, its tendrils a deep, pulsating violet, tipped with bioluminescent nodes that pulsed with a rhythm unsettlingly akin to a heartbeat. Its leaves, broad and leathery, were streaked with veins that glowed with an internal emerald light, casting an ethereal aura onto the surrounding grey ash. He framed the shot, focusing on the way the plant seemed to drink in the meagre light, its luminescence a defiant counterpoint to the oppressive gloom. He wanted to capture that inherent contradiction: beauty born from devastation. He imagined the townsfolk, accustomed to the muted palette of their existence, recoiling from or being mesmerized by this vibrant intruder. His photographs were intended to be an honest reflection, not a propaganda piece, a visual dialogue that bypassed the spoken fear and presented the plant's undeniable existence.

He spent hours in that desolate landscape, moving with a practiced stillness that came from years of observing and documenting the subtle shifts in a dying world. He captured the plant's tenacity, its root systems, thick and sinewy, burrowing deep into the poisoned earth as if drawing strength from its very toxicity. He photographed the way it clustered, forming vibrant, almost iridescent carpets that seemed to push back against the encroaching grey. There was a stark beauty to it, a raw, untamed vitality that spoke of a primal will to survive. He used a low-angle shot to emphasize the towering, skeletal trees that loomed over the bloom, creating a sense of awe and insignificance, highlighting how this new life dwarfed the remnants of the old. He also experimented with long exposures, capturing the slow, deliberate pulse of its luminescence against the twilight sky, transforming the plant into a celestial entity, a visitor from another realm. He was acutely aware of the fear the plant invoked, the whispers of contamination and uncontrolled growth. His photographs, he hoped, would offer a different perspective, one that acknowledged the plant's alien nature but also its inherent vibrancy. He was not trying to win hearts and minds, but to present a visual record, an objective yet evocative portrayal of this new reality.

His work continued in the sterile confines of Mika's laboratory. The air here was sharp with the scent of disinfectant and something else, something metallic and sterile that hinted at the advanced, yet ultimately limited, technology at their disposal. Jax found himself drawn to the contrast between the plant's wild origin and its controlled environment. He set up his equipment beside Mika's gleaming consoles, capturing the sterile precision of her containment units. Here, the plant was a specimen, a subject of rigorous study. He focused on the subtle details of its cellular structure, magnified to an almost terrifying degree, the intricate patterns of its glowing veins laid bare under the harsh laboratory lights. He photographed Mika herself, her face a mask of focused concentration as she manipulated the plant with gloved hands, her movements precise and economical. He wanted to capture the tension between her scientific objectivity and the undeniable, almost beguiling, allure of the organism she studied. He contrasted the cold, clinical gleam of her instruments with the soft, pulsating light of the plant's bioluminescence, a visual metaphor for their struggle to understand and control the unknown.

He then moved to Luis's makeshift greenhouse, a pocket of vibrant green within the grey austerity of Haven. The air here was warm and humid, thick with the scent of living soil and damp leaves. Luis, his face creased with a gentle smile, moved among his carefully tended plants. Jax framed shots that highlighted the symbiotic relationship Luis was fostering, the glowing tendrils of the invasive bloom intertwining with the roots of more conventional flora, its luminescence casting a soft glow on the surrounding greenery. He captured Luis's hands, stained with soil and nurturing a small, glowing specimen, as if it were a fragile newborn. He juxtaposed the raw, untamed beauty of the plant in its natural habitat with its more serene, integrated presence in Luis's care. The photographs from the marsh, stark and almost menacing, stood in direct contrast to the gentle, hopeful glow emanating from Luis's carefully cultivated specimens. He wanted to show the spectrum of its existence, from wild defiance to potential integration. He even managed to capture a shot of Luis's prized scrub weed, its dull green leaves now exhibiting a faint, healthy sheen, bathed in the soft light of the invasive plant. This visual narrative was about showing, not telling, the plant's complex nature.

Back in his small studio, a converted storage unit filled with salvaged equipment and the comforting clutter of creative chaos, Jax began the meticulous process of selecting and editing his images. He projected them onto the bare concrete wall, a silent, evolving exhibition. The stark, ash-covered landscape shots were powerful, emphasizing the plant's alienness and the precariousness of its existence. He paired these with images from Mika's lab, where the plant's bioluminescence seemed almost too bright, too artificial under the sterile lights, highlighting the questions of control and manipulation. Then came the images from Luis's greenhouse, bathed in a warm, inviting light, suggesting a different path, one of co-existence and integration.

He deliberately avoided any single narrative. His intention was not to declare the plant a menace or a miracle, but to present its multifaceted reality. He captured a close-up of a dewdrop clinging to a violet tendril, reflecting the desolation of the Wastes in its tiny, curved surface. This image, he felt, encapsulated the plant's very essence: beauty found in the most desolate of places, a captured fragment of a harsh world, magnified and made wondrous. He also focused on the interactions, or lack thereof, between the plant and its environment. He had a series of shots where the ash seemed to cling to the plant's leaves, only to be shed in slow, deliberate movements, as if the plant actively rejected the contamination. This suggested a natural defense mechanism, a form of self-cleaning that Mika had yet to fully quantify.

He then turned his attention to the townsfolk themselves. He began discreetly photographing them as they reacted to the news, their faces etched with a mixture of fear, curiosity, and suspicion. He captured a group of children, their eyes wide with wonder, pointing at a smuggled sprig of the glowing flora, a forbidden fruit brought back by a cautious scout. He also documented the hushed conversations, the worried glances exchanged in the marketplace, the palpable tension that permeated Haven. He framed these images to show the human element, the emotional response to the ecological shift. One powerful diptych showed a weathered hand reaching out tentatively towards a glowing leaf, the skin worn and calloused, a stark contrast to the vibrant, smooth surface of the plant. It was a visual question: a gesture of fear or fascination?

Jax continued to expand his visual narrative, focusing on the subtle nuances that spoke volumes. He found a patch of the invasive bloom growing precariously close to a water purification unit, its tendrils reaching out like inquisitive fingers. He photographed this with a telephoto lens, compressing the perspective to make the plant seem larger, more threatening, its glow an ominous warning against the metallic gleam of the machinery. He then juxtaposed this with a shot he'd managed to capture of the plant growing around the base of a weathered signpost, its lettering almost completely eroded by the elements. The vibrant violet against the faded grey offered a sense of history, of an ancient cycle of life and decay being reasserted, with this new bloom as its latest manifestation.

He also sought out the few individuals who dared to express a different sentiment, those who, like Luis, saw something beyond the immediate threat. He spent an afternoon with Elara, the community's elder botanist, a woman whose knowledge of pre-Collapse flora was legendary. He photographed her examining a wilting, native plant, her brow furrowed with concern, and then immediately followed with a shot of her holding a glowing leaf from the invasive bloom, a hint of something akin to respect in her ancient eyes. It was a silent acknowledgement that nature, in its infinite capacity for adaptation, often defied simple categorization. He wanted to illustrate that not everyone viewed the bloom through a lens of pure fear; there were those who approached it with a more complex, nuanced understanding.

His work was becoming a silent debate, played out on screens and printouts scattered across his studio. He meticulously crafted pairings, forcing the viewer to confront the contradictions. A shot of the plant's spores, microscopic and airborne, hinting at its insidious spread, was placed next to an image of a child's drawing, depicting a vibrant, glowing flower, a testament to the plant's ability to inspire wonder even in the young. He captured a discarded nutrient pack from Mika's lab, its contents analyzed and deemed inert, lying in the ash near a cluster of the invasive bloom. It was a visual question about cause and effect, about the legacy of their past actions.

Jax also began to photograph the very act of fear. He captured the averted gazes, the tightened grips on tools and weapons, the hurried steps taken to avoid passing too close to a discovered patch of the bloom. He focused on the shadows it cast, long and distorted in the dim light of Haven's alleys, making the plant seem even more imposing and mysterious. He then countered these with images of quiet observation, of individuals, their faces hidden in shadow, simply watching the plant's gentle, rhythmic pulse, as if mesmerized by its alien rhythm. He was attempting to capture the internal struggle of the community, the war being waged between instinctual fear and the innate human drive for understanding.

He even managed to procure a small, wilting sample of a native lichen, a species that had once been common before the Blight. He placed it carefully on a sterile tray, its grey-green hue a faded echo of lost vibrancy. He then placed a single, luminous tendril from the invasive bloom beside it. The contrast was stark and profound. The lichen seemed to shrink from the alien glow, a visual representation of the old succumbing to the new. But then, in a twist that surprised even Jax, he noticed a faint, almost imperceptible luminescence begin to appear along the edges of the lichen, as if it were tentatively responding to the invasive plant's energetic aura. He knew this was likely an anomaly, a trick of the light, but he captured it nonetheless.

It was a visual whisper of the possibility that this was not simply an invasion, but a transformation, a reawakening of dormant potentials.

His photographic journal became a testament to the plant's pervasive influence, not just on the environment, but on the psyche of Haven's inhabitants. He documented the subtle shifts in their behaviour, the way they spoke in hushed tones about the "glowing marsh," the furtive glances cast towards the outer perimeter. He captured a moment of collective unease as a distant, faint pulse of light was seen on the horizon, a silent, bioluminescent rumour spreading across the Wastes. Jax's work was not about providing answers; it was about deepening the questions. He wanted his images to spark conversations, to challenge assumptions, and to force the people of Haven to confront the complex, unsettling beauty of the world that was slowly, irrevocably, returning. He was the visual storyteller of their uncertain future, his camera an extension of their collective gaze, capturing the profound and the unsettling in equal measure.

CHAPTER FIVE

THE ACID DOWNPOUR

The oppressive, perpetual twilight that had become the norm in Haven was shattered, not by the hesitant return of sunlight, but by an unsettling, phosphorescent stain spreading across the bruised canvas of the sky. It began as a subtle discoloration, a faint, sickly green seeping into the prevailing greys and violets, like a wound festering. Initially, it was easily dismissed as another anomaly of the Blighted atmosphere, another trick of light in a world starved of clarity. But then, the hue deepened, intensifying to an almost bilious emerald, pulsating with an unnatural energy. The air, already a cocktail of ozone and dust, thickened. It became viscous, clinging to the lungs with a new, acrid bite. The faint, metallic tang of ozone was drowned out by a more potent, more visceral aroma – the unmistakable stench of sulfur, sharp and biting, overlaid with a cloying sweetness that hinted at decay, at something putrid and rotten.

A collective unease rippled through Haven. The children, those who were not already huddled in the safety of their homes, stopped their games. Their heads tilted back, small faces etched with a primal, uncomprehending fear. The adults, their weathered faces perpetually etched with worry, exchanged furtive glances. The erratic weather patterns, a constant source of anxiety since the cataclysmic eruption that had reshaped their world, had always been unpredictable, but this felt different. This felt... deliberate. The sky, usually a muted tapestry of atmospheric fallout, was now a churning, vibrant spectacle of dread. The deepening green was not the gentle verdancy of life, but the lurid glow of corruption, a harbinger of something truly foul. It spread with a terrifying speed, consuming the familiar gloom and replacing it with an alien, glowing menace. The wind, which usually carried the dry whisper of ash, began to stir with a heavy, languid movement, as if the very air was becoming too dense to flow freely. It carried with it the acrid scent, a constant, unwelcome reminder of the atmospheric shift. From his studio, Jax watched through his reinforced window, the scene outside a surreal tableau. The usual muted tones of Haven – the muted greys of the repurposed buildings, the dull browns of the scavenged fabrics worn by the townsfolk – were now cast in this ghastly, emerald light. It lent an almost infernal glow to the familiar, making even the most mundane structures appear monstrous. He instinctively reached for his camera, the urge to document this unfolding horror overriding the creeping dread in his own gut. This was more than just weather; this was a transformation, a terrifying overture to an unknown act. He thought of Mika's meticulous readings, of the atmospheric sensors scattered across the Wastes, their data streams often a jumble of incoherent spikes and dips. What would they be reporting now? What unimaginable compounds were being churned and brewed in the upper atmosphere? He imagined the readings, numbers spiraling out of control, alarms blaring in the sterile confines of her lab, a frantic dance of data that would do little to prepare them for what was coming. The luminescence of the sky seemed to seep into the very walls of Haven, making the shadows writhe with an unwholesome energy. It was a light that offered no warmth, no hope, only a stark, terrifying illumination of their precarious existence. The sulfurous stench intensified, prickling at the back of his throat, a physical manifestation of the atmospheric poison that was gathering strength. He could almost taste it, a sharp, metallic bitterness that spoke of a world irrevocably altered.

The change was palpable, a heavy blanket descending upon Haven, pressing down on the collective spirit of its inhabitants. The air, already a harsh reminder of their fallen world, now turned traitorous. It grew thick, humid, and laden with a suffocating weight that made each breath a conscious effort. The characteristic ozone tang, usually a sharp, almost clean scent, was now drowned out by a more noxious perfume, a noxious blend that whispered of decay and a deeply unnatural chemical reaction. It was the smell of a planetary sickness, a miasma born from the ravaged earth and the poisoned skies. The sulfur was the most dominant note, sharp and metallic, but beneath it lay a sickly sweet undertone, like overripe fruit left to rot, or the faint, unsettling odour of a charnel house. This was not the scent of rain, nor of any natural phenomenon they had ever known. It was the aroma of impending doom, a sensory alarm that screamed of an atmospheric event of unprecedented danger.

Whispers, quick and hushed, flitted through the narrow streets and communal spaces of Haven. The elders, their faces lined with the wisdom of survival, spoke of ancient prophecies, of skies turning venomous, of the earth weeping tears of fire. The younger generations, born into a world already scarred, listened with wide, fearful eyes, their imaginations painting vivid, terrifying pictures of what these omens portended. The already erratic weather, a constant source of anxiety since the Great Eruption, had always been a capricious dance of dust storms, unpredictable temperature shifts, and the occasional, meagre rainfall. But this was different. This was a deliberate darkening, a menacing intensification of the sky's grim palette. The usual muted greys and somber violets were being consumed by a virulent, unnatural green, a hue that spoke not of life, but of corruption. It pulsed with an inner light, a sickly luminescence that seemed to emanate from the very fabric of the atmosphere. It was a light that promised no warmth, no respite, only a stark, chilling illumination of their vulnerability.

Jax, from the relative safety of his studio, felt the change most acutely. His reinforced windows, usually offering a muted view of the desolate landscape, now seemed to amplify the growing terror. The emerald glow outside painted the familiar, repurposed structures of Haven in an eerie, almost infernal light. The dust that perpetually coated everything, usually a dull grey, now shimmered with an unwholesome iridescence under the alien sky. He found himself instinctively reaching for his camera, the artist's imperative to document warring with a primal urge to seek shelter. This was a spectacle of destruction, a terrifying beauty that demanded to be witnessed, to be recorded, even as it threatened to overwhelm. He imagined Mika, hunched over her consoles in the sterile hum of her laboratory, the readouts on her screens likely behaving like a frantic, chaotic heartbeat. Her sensors, scattered across the vast expanse of the Wastes, would be screaming warnings, their data streams a cascade of incomprehensible spikes and faltering signals. What compounds, what unknown energies, were being forged in the upper reaches of their atmosphere? The sheer density of the air was becoming noticeable, each breath a conscious, heavy intake. It felt as if the sky itself was weeping, not water, but a viscous, chemical tears that would scar and corrode. The sulfurous stench intensified, a constant, sharp prickle at the back of his throat, a physical testament to the atmospheric poison that was steadily accumulating, gathering its strength for a devastating descent. He could almost taste the bitterness, a metallic tang that spoke of a world undergoing a catastrophic transformation, a visceral warning of the inevitable.

The dread was no longer a subtle undercurrent; it was a palpable presence, settling over Haven like a shroud. The townsfolk, their faces etched with a familiar blend of weariness and resilience, moved with a heightened sense of urgency. Their usual stoic demeanor was replaced by a nervous tension, a shared awareness that something profound and terrible was unfolding above them. Children were hurried indoors, their playful shouts replaced by hushed cries and the anxious murmurs of their parents. The air, which had been merely unpleasant, now felt actively hostile, each gust of wind carrying a heavier burden of acrid scent and unseen particulate matter. The sickly green hue of the sky intensified, shifting from a hazy veil to a churning, almost liquid expanse of toxic luminescence. It pulsed with an irregular rhythm, as if the sky itself were drawing a ragged, agonizing breath. Shadows, usually softened by the perpetual twilight, now seemed to deepen and writhe, imbued with the unholy glow from above. The visual distortion was unsettling, familiar shapes taking on monstrous outlines under the unnatural light.

Mika's sensors, Jax knew, would be struggling to make sense of the onslaught of data. Their sophisticated algorithms, designed to interpret the relatively stable chaos of the post-eruption atmosphere, were likely being overwhelmed by this unprecedented anomaly. He pictured her, her brow furrowed in concentration, her fingers flying across the holographic interfaces, trying to isolate the source of the escalating readings. Was it a new form of atmospheric fallout, a chemical cocktail of unimaginable toxicity? Or was it something more... volatile? The sulfurous smell was becoming overpowering, a constant, burning sensation in the nostrils that hinted at the corrosive nature of the impending event. It was a smell that spoke of burning flesh, of metal dissolving, of lungs filling with poison.

Luis, in his sanctuary of burgeoning life, would be feeling the subtle shifts even more keenly. His connection to the earth, to the nascent life he painstakingly cultivated, would make him exquisitely sensitive to any disturbance in the natural order. Jax imagined him looking up from his precious scrub weed and glowing flora, his eyes wide with a dawning comprehension of the peril that was gathering strength above his small haven of hope. He wondered if the invasive bloom itself would react, if its bioluminescence would surge or dim in response to the atmospheric onslaught. Was it a harbinger, or a victim? The questions swirled in Jax's mind, each one more urgent than the last. He tightened his grip on his camera, the cool metal a small comfort against the rising tide of fear. The world outside his window was transforming, shedding its familiar desolation for a terrifying, alien beauty. This was not just a storm; it was an announcement, a declaration that the Wastes, in their infinite and terrifying capacity for change, were preparing to unleash something new, something that would test the very limits of Haven's endurance. The unnatural green light painted the faces of the few remaining figures in the street, transforming their worried expressions into gaunt masks of apprehension. The wind picked up, no longer a gentle caress but a sharp, biting force, carrying with it the stinging sensation of unseen particles. It whipped at cloaks and hair, a physical manifestation of the atmosphere's growing hostility. The acrid scent grew more potent, making the eyes water and the throat constrict. It was the smell of chemical warfare, waged not by any human hand, but by the very elements that had once sustained life. This was no ordinary weather event; it was a descent into an atmospheric abyss, a terrifying prelude to the unknown.

The sky had not simply darkened; it had curdled. The sickly, virulent green that had begun as a faint stain had intensified, blooming into an opaque, phosphorescent canopy that pressed down on Haven with suffocating weight. It wasn't merely a change in hue; it was a palpable transformation of the atmosphere, a thickening that made the very air feel viscous, clinging to exposed skin with an unsettling, oily sheen. The acrid, sulfurous stench, once a mere prickle at the back of the throat, now burned with an insistent fury, a chemical assault that stole the breath and stung the eyes. This was not the gentle herald of a storm; it was a pronouncement of planetary vengeance.

Then, it began. Not with a rumble of thunder or a flash of lightning, but with a soft, insidious hiss, like a thousand vipers exhaling. Droplets, not of water, but of something far more sinister, began to fall. They were large, viscous, and tinted with the same malevolent green as the sky. The first few splatters landed on the metal plating of the communal shelter, and where they struck, they did not simply wet the surface – they ate into it. A faint, bubbling sizzle accompanied each impact, a tiny plume of noxious vapor rising from the dissolving metal. Panic, a cold, sharp shard, pierced through the anxious murmurs that had been circulating for hours. The makeshift shelters, the proud bastions of their survival, the cobbled-together collections of scavenged corrugated iron, reinforced tarpaulin, and reclaimed plastic sheeting, were about to face their ultimate test.

Jax watched from his studio window, his camera forgotten, his hands clenched into fists. The view was nightmarish. The familiar, utilitarian structures that dotted Haven, normally a testament to their ingenuity and desperation, were now being systematically dismantled by the sky. The acid, thick and unnervingly viscous, clung to surfaces, its corrosive touch a visible blight. Sheets of metal, painstakingly salvaged and hammered into place, began to warp and buckle, their surfaces pockmarked with bubbling craters. The reinforced plastic sheeting, designed to withstand the abrasive dust storms, sagged and dissolved, revealing the terrified faces of those huddled within. The communal hall, the largest and most robust of their shelters, groaned under the onslaught. Rivulets of green fluid, thick as syrup, streamed down its walls, pooling on the ground in shimmering, toxic puddles. The air within the hall, already thick with the fear of its inhabitants, was now becoming heavy with the metallic tang of corroding materials and the sharp, biting scent of the acid itself.

"Mika!" Jax yelled into his comm, his voice hoarse. "Are you getting anything? What is this stuff?"

Static crackled in response, then Mika's strained voice, laced with a desperate urgency, broke through. "Jax, it's... it's off the charts. The atmospheric composition... it's a cocktail of concentrated sulfuric and nitric acids, Jax, suspended in a highly volatile organic compound. The readings are spiking faster than I can log them. The humidity levels are climbing, but it's not water vapor. It's... it's the acid itself condensing." Her voice hitched. "The dispersal pattern is almost... deliberate. It's targeting areas with higher concentrations of metal and certain polymers. It's like the atmosphere is actively... fighting back."

Fighting back. The words echoed in Jax's mind, a chilling confirmation of the primal fear that had gripped him since the sky had begun to bleed its toxic green. He saw Elara, her small frame dwarfed by the oversized protective gear she wore, desperately hammering salvaged metal scraps onto the failing seams of a smaller dwelling. Her movements were frantic, her breath coming in ragged gasps, the acid already beginning to eat through the thin, synthetic fabric of her mask. The smell was getting worse, so potent now that it felt like swallowing shards of glass. Children, their faces pressed against the reinforced glass of their homes, let out terrified whimpers as the alien rain ate at the world outside.

The communal shelter, built from the largest salvaged pieces of what Jax vaguely remembered as an ancient transportation hub, was taking a beating. Its primary walls, thick sheets of a composite material that had once been impossibly durable, were now weeping green streaks. The metal reinforcement bars, the very skeleton of their collective safety, were visibly corroding, the rust blooming not in reddish-brown, but in a sickly, iridescent green. The sound inside was a cacophony of panicked shouts, the relentless hiss of the downpour, and the sickening groans of stressed materials. Children cried, their voices thin and reedy against the backdrop of the storm. Elders, their faces etched with a grim resignation, tried to soothe them, their own hands trembling as they reinforced sagging tarpaulin roofs with desperate haste.

"We need more sealant!" a man shouted from within the communal hall, his voice strained. "The seams are giving! It's coming through!"

The "sealant" was a crude mixture of melted plastics and scavenged resins, a desperate attempt to patch the inevitable. It was a temporary fix at best, and the acid seemed to have a particular appetite for it. Jax saw a section of the tarpaulin, painstakingly patched just minutes before, begin to sag and tear, the corrosive liquid seeping through like a slow-motion disaster. A woman shrieked as a droplet landed on her outstretched arm, leaving a raw, blistering mark almost instantly. The protective gear they wore, the repurposed industrial suits and makeshift respirators, were designed for dust and minor chemical exposure, not for this relentless, concentrated assault.

Luis, Jax knew, would be in his underground hydroponics bay, a space he had meticulously constructed to be as sealed and inert as possible. But even underground, the corrosive vapors would eventually find their way in. His precious plants, the fragile shoots of new life he had so painstakingly nurtured, were their future. The thought of that future being dissolved by this airborne poison was almost unbearable. Jax imagined Luis, his usually serene face a mask of intense worry, checking his air scrubbers, his bio-filters, his every instinct screaming at the unnatural intrusion of this chemical rain. Would the plants wilt, their leaves dissolving like tissue paper? Would the very soil, or the nutrient paste Luis used, become contaminated?

The relentless downpour continued, each drop a tiny act of annihilation. The ground around the shelters turned into a treacherous mire of dissolved debris and acidic puddles. The air was thick with a chemical fog, stinging the eyes and lungs. Jax watched a discarded metal tool, left too close to the edge of the shelter's overhang, begin to disintegrate, its form blurring and dissolving until only a shimmering, acidic stain remained. This was not just a storm; it was an environmental purge, a violent cleansing by a planet pushed beyond its limits.

The thought struck Jax with the force of a physical blow: their shelters, their meticulously constructed havens, were not designed for this. They were built to withstand the dust, the wind, the occasional extreme temperature fluctuations. They were built for a world that was harsh, but fundamentally

stable. This... this was an active, aggressive attack. The materials they relied on for survival – metal, plastic, treated fabrics – were precisely the things this acid seemed most eager to consume. Their ingenuity, their resilience, their very methods of survival were being turned against them by the very elements they sought to control.

He saw a group of residents, armed with buckets and salvaged sponges, attempting to push back the pooling acid from the base of the communal shelter. Their movements were slow, hampered by the bulky protective gear and the pervasive stench. Each splash of their makeshift cleaning solutions seemed to only exacerbate the problem, creating new chemical reactions, new plumes of noxious fumes. It was a losing battle, a desperate, futile gesture against an overwhelming force. The acid was not just falling; it was spreading, pooling, and creating a toxic environment that threatened to engulf them all.

Jax felt a surge of helplessness wash over him. He was an observer, a documentarian, but in this moment, his camera felt like a useless artifact. What good was recording this horror if they couldn't stop it? He looked at the sky, the oppressive, glowing green, and felt a profound sense of being utterly outmatched. The planet was not merely indifferent; it was actively hostile. It was reasserting its dominance in the most brutal, unforgiving way imaginable.

A sudden, deafening screech tore through the air, followed by a violent shudder that ran through the entire structure of the communal shelter. Jax's heart leaped into his throat. A large section of the roof, near the main entrance, had collapsed inwards, the acid-soaked metal and torn tarpaulin creating a gaping maw. Screams erupted from within, a chilling symphony of terror and pain. The acid, no longer held at bay, poured in with renewed ferocity, its hiss and sizzle amplified in the confined space. Dust, mingled with the corrosive spray, billowed outwards, catching the lurid green light.

"No!" Jax yelled, scrambling for his comm again. "Mika! The communal hall! It's... it's breached! We have casualties!"

Mika's voice, when it finally came, was even more frantic. "Jax, I'm losing sensors around the main settlement. The corrosive elements are degrading them at an alarming rate. I... I can't get a clear picture of what's happening. Just... hold on. Try to reinforce your own position."

"My own position?" Jax scoffed, a bitter laugh escaping his lips. His studio, while built with reinforced glass and more robust materials than the communal shelters, was still just a studio. It was not a bunker. The acid would eventually find its way through. He glanced at his own walls, already streaked with the vile green fluid. The windowpanes were clouded, the seals starting to hiss ominously.

He saw a figure emerge from the chaos of the breached shelter, staggering into the open. It was Anya, her face streaked with tears and grime, her arm held at an unnatural angle. She was shouting, her voice barely audible above the storm, "They're trapped! Inside! The roof... it's still unstable!"

Jax knew he couldn't just stand there. His training, his instincts, his very humanity screamed at him to act. He grabbed a thick, salvaged metal pipe, its surface already beginning to develop a faint green sheen, and bolted for the door. The outside air hit him like a physical blow, the stench of sulfur and acid so thick it made his eyes water uncontrollably. Each breath was a searing agony. He could feel the corrosive droplets landing on his exposed skin, a burning sensation that spread rapidly. He pulled the hood of his protective cloak tighter, cinched the mask around his face, but he knew it was a futile gesture against this relentless assault.

As he ran towards the communal shelter, the ground beneath his feet felt slick and treacherous. The pooled acid was everywhere, reflecting the unholy green light of the sky, transforming the familiar pathways of Haven into a deadly, chemical maze. He saw another resident collapse, their protective suit dissolving around them, their cries cut short by a horrifying gurgle. The sight fueled his desperate urgency. He had to reach Anya, had to help. Their shelters, their supposed sanctuaries, were failing. And the sky, that once distant, often indifferent entity, had become their most terrifying enemy. The acid rain was not just a weather event; it was a siege, and Haven was under siege. The fight for survival had just entered its most desperate, corrosive phase. The very foundations of their existence were being eaten away, drop by agonizing drop. The hiss of the rain was the sound of their world dissolving.

The infernal hiss of the acid rain was a constant, maddening symphony that permeated every corner of Mika's small, self-contained laboratory. It was no longer a distant threat, but an immediate, invasive enemy. The air scrubbers, her pride and joy, designed to filter out the worst of the lingering dust and residual toxins from the old world, were groaning under the unprecedented chemical assault. She'd sealed every conceivable joint, every ventilation shaft, every minute gap with the industrial-grade polymers she'd salvaged, but the atmosphere itself seemed to sweat the corrosive compound. She watched, her heart a cold, heavy stone in her chest, as faint green rivulets began to snake their way down the exterior of her primary filtration unit, a grim testament to the futility of her initial efforts. The advanced nano-filters, meticulously crafted to capture microscopic particulates, were being dissolved, rendered useless by the sheer, unadulterated corrosiveness of the falling deluge.

"This isn't just rain," she muttered, her voice raspy, amplified by the mask she still wore, more out of habit and a desperate clinging to perceived safety than any genuine belief in its efficacy against this onslaught. "It's... it's a chemical solvent. A planetary-scale acid bath." Her fingers, encased in thick, reinforced gloves that were already starting to feel uncomfortably warm and slightly sticky, flew across the diagnostic panel of her central environmental control system. The readings were a terrifying kaleidoscope of red and amber, alarms blinking insistently. The internal atmospheric pressure was dropping, not because of a leak in the conventional sense, but because the very air molecules were being... eaten.

She needed to reinforce, to innovate. Her mind, usually a placid lake of logic and calculation, was now a churning tempest of panicked creativity. The salvaged polymer sealant, while robust, was clearly insufficient. It offered a temporary reprieve, a few precious minutes, but the acid was relentless, its chemical hunger insatiable. She needed something that would not just resist the acid, but perhaps even neutralize it. A wild thought, bordering on desperation, flickered through her mind: could she create a counter-agent? A chemical balm for the wounded atmosphere?

Her gaze fell upon the emergency stores, a meticulously organized collection of rare earth elements, catalytic converters, and specialized chemical compounds that she had hoarded for years, anticipating various environmental collapse scenarios, but never anything like this. This was an extinction-level event unfolding in real-time, a testament to humanity's catastrophic mismanagement of its own cradle. She grabbed a dense canister labeled 'Zeolite Composite – High Reactivity.' It was primarily used in industrial waste neutralization, designed to absorb and bind with volatile compounds. If she could somehow combine it with a stabilizing agent, perhaps a calcium carbonate slurry... it might, just might, provide a temporary shield.

Working with a feverish intensity that bordered on manic, Mika began to concoct her desperate brew. She poured the granular zeolite into a repurposed mixing vat, the sickly green light of the sky reflecting in the metallic sheen of the vessel. Then came the calcium carbonate, a fine white powder that was supposed to buffer the reaction. She activated the sonic mixer, its low hum a counterpoint to the incessant hiss outside. The mixture churned, a thick, grey paste forming at the bottom. She knew the risks. Uncontrolled reactions could be catastrophic. But inaction was a guaranteed death sentence.

Meanwhile, the tremors from the communal shelter's partial collapse had sent a fresh wave of fear through the small settlement. Mika's comm unit crackled to life, Jax's voice, raw and strained, cutting through the din. "Mika! We've got people trapped! The roof... it's completely gone in sections. The acid's pouring in. We need... we need something! Anything!"

"Jax, I'm working on it!" Mika shouted back, her voice tight with a mixture of urgency and burgeoning dread. "I'm... I'm trying to develop a localized neutralization agent. But it's experimental. And I'm already fighting breaches in my own filters. The air scrubbers are failing. I can't maintain internal atmospheric integrity for long if the external environment keeps degrading my systems." She didn't want to admit how dire her own situation was becoming. The secondary seals on her airlock were already showing signs of delamination, the formerly pliable rubber hardening and cracking under the relentless chemical attack. A thin, acrid mist, smelling faintly of burnt metal and vinegar, was beginning to seep into her personal quarters.

She needed to distribute her concoction. But how? The small, personal drones she used for external surveys were too fragile, their delicate components unable to withstand the corrosive rain. She would have to venture out. The thought sent a fresh wave of cold dread through her. She was a scientist, an engineer, not a survivalist. Her protective gear, while advanced for laboratory work, was not designed for sustained exposure to this level of atmospheric toxicity.

"Hold on, Jax," she said, her voice trembling slightly. "I'm going to try and reinforce your shelter's ventilation intake. I can't guarantee it, but I'll bring what I have. Just... try to keep everyone calm. And away from the breaches."

Slipping into her most robust environmental suit, a bulky, multi-layered affair designed for extreme hazard environments, Mika felt a profound sense of unease. The helmet sealed with a heavy thud, and the internal HUD flickered to life, displaying atmospheric readings that made her stomach clench. Even within the suit, the air she breathed was heavily filtered and recirculated. She checked the integrity of the seals for the tenth time, her gloved fingers fumbling slightly with the pressure clasps.

She donned the large, wheeled cart that held her precious zeolite mixture, its containment vat sealed with a heavy-duty locking mechanism. Each movement felt sluggish, the suit restrictive, a constant reminder of her vulnerability. The airlock hissed open, and the full horror of the acid downpour slammed into her senses.

It was worse than she could have imagined. The green sky was a solid, suffocating mass, devoid of any discernible light source, yet illuminating the devastated landscape with an eerie, phosphorescent glow. The acid was not falling in discrete drops anymore; it was a viscous sheet, a relentless curtain of corrosive liquid. The air was thick with it, a choking, burning miasma that stung her eyes even through the reinforced visor. The ground was a shimmering, toxic swamp, the metallic tang of corroding infrastructure overpowering even the acrid stench.

She could see the communal shelter in the distance, a silhouette against the unnatural green. Even from this distance, she could see the damage. Sections of its roof were gone, gaping holes from which tendrils of green mist curled outwards. The walls, once a patchwork of salvaged metal and reinforced sheeting, were now a weeping mosaic of dissolving material. The sound was an all-encompassing roar – the relentless hiss of the acid, punctuated by the groans of stressed metal and the distant, muffled cries of the trapped.

Pushing the heavy cart forward was an agonizing struggle. The wheels sank into the corrosive sludge that had once been earth and pathways. Each rotation required immense effort, the cart's weight amplified by the increasingly viscous terrain. The acid splattered against her suit, and she watched with a detached horror as the outer layers began to subtly change color, the protective material showing the first signs of degradation. The suit's internal temperature began to climb, the cooling system struggling valiantly against the external onslaught.

She passed smaller, individual shelters, their occupants huddled within, their faces pressed against windows that were rapidly becoming opaque and pitted. Some had tried to erect makeshift awnings from salvaged tarpaulin, but these were melting and tearing within minutes, offering no protection. One shelter, smaller and more crudely constructed, had completely collapsed, a twisted wreck of warped metal and dissolving plastic, its occupants nowhere to be seen. The sight fueled Mika's urgency, a desperate race against the inevitable.

As she neared the communal shelter, the scale of the devastation became horrifyingly clear. The main entrance was a scene of utter chaos. People, some in makeshift protective gear, others seemingly with nothing but a desperate hope, were attempting to reach those still trapped inside the ravaged sections. The air around the breaches was thick with a choking cloud of corrosive vapor, so dense that it was difficult to see more than a few feet. The sound of weeping and panicked shouts was almost unbearable, a raw testament to human suffering.

Jax emerged from the gloom, his face a mask of grime and sweat, his eyes wide with a terror that Mika had rarely seen in him. He was dragging a struggling form, a woman whose protective suit was visibly dissolving around her arm, leaving angry red welts where exposed skin met the chemical rain.

"Mika!" Jax yelled, his voice hoarse and distorted by the wind and the storm's roar. "Thank God! The intake... can you do something?"

Mika grunted, straining to push the cart the last few yards. "I have... a neutralizer. Zeolite composite. It's experimental. I need to get it to your main ventilation intake. It's our best shot at... at buying time." She gestured towards a large, reinforced grille on the side of the shelter, a critical component designed to draw in fresh air for their filtered breathing system. It was already heavily corroded, streaks of green weeping down its surface.

"The intake is partially blocked," Jax explained, his breath coming in ragged gasps. "The debris from the collapse... and the acid is eating at the mesh. We can't clear it without exposure."

Mika knew what she had to do. The cart was too heavy to maneuver into the confined space of the intake. She would have to brave the direct exposure. "Jax, cover me. Keep everyone back from the intake. I'm going to try and inject the mixture directly."

She unlatched the containment vat, her gloved hands surprisingly steady despite the tremors wracking her body. She activated the high-pressure dispenser, a nozzle designed for precise chemical application. Taking a deep, shuddering breath, she plunged her arm, then her entire upper body, into the swirling vortex of acid surrounding the ventilation grille.

The pain was immediate and searing. Even through the thick layers of her suit, she could feel the heat, the biting sensation of the acid attempting to breach her defenses. The HUD on her helmet flared red, warning of critical external temperature spikes and minor suit integrity breaches. She ignored it, focusing all her energy on the task. The zeolite mixture hissed as it met the corrosive rain, a violent, immediate reaction that sent plumes of steam and noxious fumes billowing outwards. She could feel the mesh of the grille beginning to soften and warp under the combined assault of the acid and her hastily concocted antidote.

She forced the dispenser into the opening, aiming for the internal workings of the ventilation system. The sound of the acid hitting the zeolite was a sharp, spitting hiss, a momentary reprieve from the relentless drumming of the rain. She squeezed the trigger, the thick grey paste being forced into the heart of the intake. She could feel the resistance lessening slightly, the chemical battle raging within the grille.

Suddenly, a sickening screech echoed from above. A section of the damaged roof, weakened by the acid and the structural stress, groaned and shifted. A cascade of molten metal and dissolving sheeting rained down towards Mika and the intake.

"Mika, get back!" Jax screamed, lunging forward, pulling the woman he was helping with him.

Mika reacted instinctively. She wrenched herself backwards, the dispenser still clutched in her hand. A heavy piece of warped metal struck the containment cart, sending it toppling. The vat of zeolite mixture shattered, its contents spilling out onto the corrosive ground, where it hissed and frothed violently, creating a localized zone of intense chemical reaction.

She stumbled backwards, her suit taking the brunt of the falling debris. The impact sent a jolt through her entire body. For a terrifying moment, she was engulfed in a cloud of steam and acrid fumes. When it cleared, she was on her knees, coughing violently. The intake grille was still partially intact, but the majority of her precious neutralizing agent had been lost. Her suit was smeared with the grey paste, and the material where it had contacted the acid was bubbling and discolored.

Jax was by her side in an instant, his face a mixture of relief and despair. "Are you alright? Mika, you have to get out of here! Your suit... it's compromised."

Mika coughed again, the air in her helmet suddenly feeling thin and strangely sweet. A wave of nausea washed over her. She looked at the ground, at the ruined cart, the spilled mixture, the weeping, dissolving shelter. Despair, cold and absolute, threatened to engulf her. All her planning, her years of research, her desperate gamble... it had all amounted to so little. The planet, it seemed, was determined to purge itself, and no amount of human ingenuity could stand against its fury.

"It's... it's not enough," she whispered, her voice barely audible. The realization settled upon her like a shroud. The acid was too pervasive, too potent. Her defenses, her carefully constructed sanctuary, were being systematically dismantled. The very air she breathed was becoming a poison. A single, large droplet of acid splattered directly onto her helmet visor, right in front of her eyes. It didn't simply wet the surface; it began to eat, a tiny, swirling hole appearing in the reinforced polycarbonate.

Panic, a primal, unreasoning force, finally seized her. She scrambled to her feet, ignoring Jax's shouts. "I... I have to get back. My lab... the main systems... I can't lose everything."

She turned and fled, leaving Jax to survey the scene of devastation. The cart was a twisted wreck, the zeolite mixture a toxic puddle. She ran through the increasingly treacherous landscape, her movements clumsy and desperate. The suit was failing. She could feel the burning sensation spreading across her skin, no longer confined to the points of impact, but a generalized heat that spoke of widespread breach. The air she was breathing felt heavy, metallic.

She had to reach her lab. She had to find another way. There had to be something else. A desperate hope, fragile and flickering, was all she had left. She would not surrender. Not yet. Not while there was still breath in her lungs, however chemically tainted it might be. The acid rain continued to fall, a relentless, unforgiving downpour, and Mika, a lone figure in a failing suit, ran towards the faint hope of her sanctuary, pursued by the wrath of a dying world.

The relentless drumming of the acid rain against the reinforced transparisteel of his makeshift greenhouse was a sound that had become the soundtrack to Luis's existence. Each drop, a tiny, chemical dagger, striking against the barrier that separated him from the poisoned world outside. He'd reinforced the seams with every scrap of salvaged sealant he possessed, the thick, grey polymer a testament to his desperation, but the constant battering was a reminder of its inherent fragility. The world had turned into a chemical bath, and his small sanctuary was a fragile island in a sea of corrosion. He watched, his breath misting the inside of the transparisteel, as the streaks of viridian fluid snaked down the exterior, etching deeper lines into the already scarred surface. It was a visual representation of the planet's agonizing decay, a slow, deliberate unraveling.

He'd been tending to his small patch of green, a defiant act of life in a world determined to extinguish it, when the storm had intensified. The invasive 'Veridian Vine,' a species that had proven alarmingly resilient to the initial toxic fallout and the subsequent environmental collapse, had been a constant source of worry. He'd managed to transplant a small cutting into his greenhouse just before the worst of the acid storms began, a gamble he'd almost regretted. It was a plant that thrived on decay, its tendrils reaching for any nutrient-rich surface, and he feared it would somehow exacerbate the situation, drawing in or reacting with the poisonous atmosphere.

But as he watched the acidic downpour intensify, a flicker of disbelief, then profound astonishment, began to dawn on him. The Veridian Vine, its broad, waxy leaves glistening under the eerie green light, seemed... untouched. The acid rain, which had turned the metal structures outside into weeping sores and corroded the very earth into a toxic sludge, seemed to slide off its surface as if it were merely water. Not only that, but the small pool of collected rainwater that had gathered at the base of the pot, water that had clearly come into contact with the acidic atmosphere and then dripped from the vine's leaves, appeared noticeably clearer than the rain falling outside.

Luis leaned closer, his nose almost pressing against the cool, reinforced glass. He carefully reached for a small, sterilized collection tube he kept for water samples. With a steady hand, he unlatched a small, sealed access port and carefully maneuvered the tube, catching a few precious drops of the water that had pooled around the plant's roots. He then collected a sample of the ambient rainwater that had managed to seep through a minuscule, near-invisible crack in the transparisteel, a crack he hadn't been able to seal completely. The difference was stark. The sample from the plant's base was a pale, almost neutral hue, while the ambient rainwater was a sickly, greenish-yellow, its corrosive nature palpable even from its appearance.

A radical thought, born of pure desperation and a scientist's ingrained curiosity, began to take root in Luis's mind. What if the Veridian Vine wasn't just resilient? What if it was... actively doing something? What if its waxy coating, its very cellular structure, possessed properties that could neutralize or at least significantly mitigate the effects of the acid rain? He had always considered the vine an unwelcome invader, a symbol of nature's chaotic, destructive adaptation. But what if it was something more? What if it was a key?

His mind, usually a methodical engine of calculations and environmental assessments, began to race, fueled by this unexpected observation. He recalled the initial reports about the vine's rapid proliferation after the 'Great Collapse,' its ability to grow in seemingly barren, toxic soil. Scientists at the time had attributed it to a hyper-efficient nutrient absorption system, a biological mechanism for extracting sustenance from even the most degraded environments. But this... this was different. This suggested an active defense, a proactive adaptation that went beyond mere survival.

He remembered the stories, the hushed whispers in the pre-collapse era about genetically modified crops, about engineered solutions to environmental problems that had backfired spectacularly. Could this invasive species be a relic of such an era? A plant designed, perhaps, for atmospheric remediation, a biological filter that had, ironically, become a pest when its intended purpose was rendered obsolete by the sheer scale of humanity's environmental vandalism?

Luis's heart began to pound, a frantic rhythm against the steady drone of the rain. This was more than just an interesting botanical anomaly; it was a potential lifeline. If he could understand *how* the Veridian Vine was neutralizing the acid, if he could isolate the mechanism, he might be able to replicate it. Or, at the very least, find a way to harness the plant itself.

He carefully picked up the pot, its weight surprisingly light. The soil within, a mixture of salvaged compost and his own carefully managed nutrient solutions, seemed rich and dark, utterly unaffected by the corrosive atmosphere outside. The vine's roots, thick and fibrous, were spread throughout the soil, their pale tendrils reaching out, searching. He gently touched one of the leaves, its surface cool and smooth beneath his gloved finger. He felt no stickiness, no hint of degradation. It was as if the rain simply couldn't adhere to it.

He needed to get a closer look, to perform more rigorous tests, but his small greenhouse offered limited resources. He had basic analytical tools, a rudimentary microscope, and a small collection of chemical reagents, but nothing to truly dissect the complex biological and chemical processes he suspected were at play. His mind immediately went to the old research facilities, the abandoned labs that dotted the periphery of the settlement, places usually deemed too dangerous or too depleted to be worth scavenging. He had always avoided them, preferring the relative safety of known, contained environments. But this... this changed everything.

He looked out at the storm, the green haze obscuring everything beyond a few hundred yards. The communal shelter, a stark reminder of the fragile interconnectedness of their small community, was barely visible. He knew that Mika was likely working tirelessly, her own genius a beacon of hope in this desolate landscape. He'd heard fragmented reports of her work, her attempts to create atmospheric scrubbers and protective sealants. But his discovery offered a different path, a natural, biological solution, something that might be far more sustainable than manufactured chemicals.

Luis carefully placed the pot back in its designated spot, a small oasis of life in his otherwise sterile environment. He knew he couldn't keep this discovery to himself, not in a world teetering on the brink of complete annihilation. The Veridian Vine, the plant he had so readily dismissed as a nuisance, might hold the key to their survival. It was a humbling, almost absurd realization. The solution wasn't in advanced technology, but in a tenacious, invasive weed.

He pulled out his comm unit, its casing scarred and worn. The battery life was precarious, and communication was often unreliable, but he had to try. He thought of Mika, of Jax, of the others huddled in the communal shelter, all struggling against the relentless onslaught.

"Mika? Jax? Can anyone hear me?" His voice, usually calm and measured, was tinged with an urgency he rarely allowed himself. "This is Luis. I... I think I've found something. Something important." He paused, the sound of the acid rain drumming a constant, insistent rhythm in the background. "It's about the Veridian Vine. It... it seems to be resistant to the acid. More than resistant. I think it's... neutralizing it."

He waited, the silence on the other end stretching, punctuated only by the infernal hiss of the storm. He could imagine Mika's brow furrowing, her analytical mind already sifting through the implications. Jax, ever the pragmatist, might be skeptical, or perhaps, like Luis, he would see the glint of hope in this unexpected revelation.

Then, Mika's voice, crackling but clear, responded, "Luis? Are you sure? Neutralizing it? How?"

Luis took a deep breath, the recycled air in his greenhouse feeling suddenly precious. "I'm not entirely sure

how yet. But the water pooling around the plant is significantly less acidic. The leaves themselves... they seem to repel it. It's like a natural barrier. I've collected samples. If I can get them to you, or if you can analyze them... we might be able to understand what's happening."

He could sense Mika's mind working at a thousand miles an hour. This was the kind of curveball that forced adaptation, the kind of unexpected discovery that could shift the entire paradigm of their fight for survival. The implications were vast. If the vine could neutralize the acid, perhaps it could be cultivated, its properties harnessed to create localized safe zones, or even larger-scale atmospheric purifiers. It was a long shot, a desperate gamble, but it was more than they had a moment ago.

"Luis, that's… remarkable," Mika said, her voice filled with a renewed, if cautious, hope. "I'm dealing with critical failures in my primary filtration systems. The acid is bypassing some of my best defenses. If your observation is correct, it could be a game-changer. I'm trying to synthesize a counter-agent myself, but it's slow, and the materials are scarce. A biological solution… that's a different approach entirely."

"I understand," Luis replied, his own hope surging. "But I can't analyze it properly here. I'll need to get to a more advanced lab. If there's any chance of getting out there, of reaching one of the old research outposts…"

A heavy silence followed, the weight of the impossibility of such a journey pressing down on them. The acid rain was a formidable barrier, a relentless enemy that made any movement outside a perilous undertaking. Even the most robust protective gear was proving insufficient against its corrosive fury.

"It's too dangerous, Luis," Jax's voice cut in, his tone grim. "The downpour is too heavy. Even with a suit, you wouldn't last long enough to reach anywhere. And we're barely holding our own here. We've had more breaches, and the acid is… it's eating through everything faster than Mika can repair it."

Luis's shoulders slumped. He had forgotten, for a brief, hopeful moment, the sheer, overwhelming power of the acid. He looked back at the Veridian Vine, its leaves a vibrant, defiant green against the suffocating grey-green of the storm. It was a paradox, a miracle born of destruction.

"What if... what if I could harvest some of the plant?" Luis asked, his voice barely a whisper. "Could we bring it to you? Even a small amount?"

"The transport would be the problem," Mika replied, her voice laced with frustration. "My drones are already failing. Anything I send out... it's unlikely to survive the journey. And bringing it here, through the acid... it would degrade the plant itself."

Luis fell silent, his gaze fixed on the thriving vine. The idea of a natural solution was so tantalizing, so close, yet so maddeningly out of reach. He was trapped, just like everyone else, with a potential key to their salvation just outside his door, a key he couldn't safely deliver. The irony was almost unbearable. He had cultivated a plant that could withstand the world's poison, only to be confined by the very poison that plant could defy.

He continued to study the vine, his scientific mind desperately seeking any clue, any detail that might offer a way forward. He noticed how the water droplets, after sliding off the waxy leaves, seemed to gather in tiny, concentrated beads before dripping to the soil. He wondered if there was a hydrophobic secretion, a natural oil or wax that was so potent it not only repelled the acid but somehow altered its chemical composition on contact.

He remembered a lecture, years ago, about extremophiles, organisms that thrived in environments that would kill most other life forms. Bacteria that could survive in boiling hot springs, in the crushing depths of the ocean, in highly acidic or alkaline conditions. Was the Veridian Vine one of these? Had it evolved, or been engineered, to become an extremophile of the highest order, specifically adapted to the toxic atmosphere of a dying planet?

Luis spent the next few hours meticulously observing the vine, cataloging every detail. He noted the subtle variations in leaf texture, the way the sunlight, or rather the dim, diffused green light, refracted through the waxy coating. He even carefully sniffed the air directly around the plant, trying to detect any subtle changes in scent, any olfactory clue to the chemical processes occurring. The air immediately around the vine smelled cleaner, fresher, a stark contrast to the acrid stench that permeated the rest of his greenhouse.

He began to sketch, filling the pages of his logbook with detailed drawings of the plant, annotating them with his observations. He was no longer just a gardener; he was a detective, piecing together clues to a devastating environmental crime. The Veridian Vine was his prime suspect, and its crime was potentially its salvation.

The communication crackled to life again, Mika's voice, sounding more strained than before. "Luis, we're experiencing a critical breach in the main filtration hub. The acid is getting through in significant quantities. I'm... I'm diverting all available power to containment, but it's not enough. We're running out of time."

Luis's heart sank. He knew the stakes were rising, not just for him, but for everyone. He looked at the Veridian Vine again, its resilience a silent, powerful statement against the encroaching doom. He couldn't get the plant to Mika, but perhaps... perhaps there was another way.

"Mika," he said, his voice firming with a new resolve. "I can't get the plant to you. But I might be able to bring a part of it. I can try to harvest some of the leaves, and maybe a bit of the root system, and encapsulate them. If I can get them into a sealed, reinforced container... maybe it can survive the journey if I can find a way to shield it."

He thought of the salvaged medical cryo-tubes he had in storage, designed to preserve biological samples for extended periods. If he could combine that with his strongest sealant, and perhaps a small internal humidifier, he might be able to create a viable transport vessel for a cutting or a root fragment. It was a long shot, a desperate improvisation, but it was something.

"It's risky, Luis," Mika warned, but there was a flicker of hope in her tone. "The journey... it's a death trap out there."

"I know," Luis replied, his gaze unwavering from the Veridian Vine. "But what choice do we have? If this plant can do what I think it can, it's worth the risk. I'll do it."

He began to gather his materials, his movements precise and deliberate. He would need his most robust environmental suit, the one designed for extreme hazard zones, even though he knew its limitations. He would need his tools, his sharpest cutting implements, and the cryo-tubes, along with the sealant and a small, portable atmospheric regulator he'd jury-rigged for emergencies.

As he prepared, he couldn't shake the image of the Veridian Vine, a testament to nature's relentless adaptability. It had taken root in the ruins of the old world, and now, it might just offer a path forward in the new, poisoned one. The acid rain continued its relentless assault, but within the small confines of his greenhouse, a fragile seed of hope had been planted, nurtured by the most unlikely of guardians. Luis, a solitary figure in a world of decay, was about to venture into the heart of the storm, carrying a tiny fragment of a miraculous plant, and with it, the possibility of a future.

The air in Jax's observation post, a reinforced alcove carved into the side of a crumbling overpass, tasted perpetually of dust and desperation. Even here, shielded by layers of salvaged plasteel and repurposed blast doors, the pervasive drumming of the acid rain was an inescapable presence. It wasn't a gentle patter; it was a percussive assault, each drop a tiny explosion against the warped metal and grimy transparisteel that formed his viewport. Jax, however, wasn't just listening; he was watching, his gaze fixed through the magnified lens of his camera, documenting the unraveling of their world, one corrosive droplet at a time.

His fingers, calloused and stained with a perpetual film of grime, moved with practiced efficiency, adjusting the focus, zooming in on the details that screamed of their precarious existence. Outside, the familiar, muted browns and greys of their urban wasteland were being leached away, replaced by a sickly, viridian hue. The rain, a relentless cascade of chemical fury, sluiced down the skeletal remains of skyscrapers, turning their metal skeletons into weeping sores and their concrete facades into pockmarked scars. Water, or what had once been water, pooled in the street below, not as a source of life, but as a viscous, acidic mire that glowed with an unholy luminescence. He zoomed in on a discarded ration pack, its plastic wrapping already beginning to blister and deform under the onslaught, a stark symbol of their dwindling supplies.

Through his lens, he saw figures darting between the skeletal remains of buildings, cloaked in hastily fashioned rain gear that offered little more than a futile symbolic gesture of protection. Their movements were jerky, desperate, a testament to the primal fear that gripped them. A child, no older than six, stumbled, her flimsy yellow poncho offering no defense against the stinging deluge. Her mother, a gaunt figure with terror etched onto her face, snatched her up, her own body shielding the child, a visceral, heartbreaking tableau of parental instinct against overwhelming environmental hostility. Jax's finger hovered over the shutter button, the weight of the moment pressing down on him. He captured the scene, a raw, unvarnished portrait of their vulnerability.

He panned his camera towards a makeshift barricade, cobbled together from rusted vehicles and scavenged metal sheets. A few figures, armed with salvaged pipe-rifles, stood guard, their faces grim, their stances taut with anticipation. The acid rain hammered against their flimsy defenses, a constant, insidious erosion. He focused on a seam where two sheets of metal met, watching as the viridian liquid found its way in, a slow, inexorable seep that promised to undermine their meager protection. He imagined the burning sensation, the creeping corrosion that would eventually render their defenses useless. He pressed the shutter, preserving the image of their defiance, their doomed struggle.

The landscape outside was a testament to nature's raw, untamed power, a power that humanity, in its hubris, had so carelessly unleashed. Jax had seen the initial reports, the frantic scientific analyses that had tried to explain the unexplainable. They spoke of atmospheric collapse, of runaway chemical reactions, of a planet pushed beyond its breaking point. But the dry, technical jargon of those reports did little to convey the visceral horror of witnessing it firsthand. His camera, however, did. It captured the sheer, overwhelming destructive force of the acid downpour, the way it etched away at the world, leaving behind only a residue of poison and decay.

He turned his lens towards a section of the overpass he called home. Even here, the signs of degradation were evident. The concrete was stained a deep, unsettling green, and faint fissures spiderwebbed across its surface. He zoomed in on a drip, a single, fat droplet of acidic rain that had somehow managed to bypass a weak point in his external sealant. It landed on a metal strut with a sharp hiss, a miniature volcanic eruption of corrosive spray. He watched as it ate away at the metal, a tiny, persistent destroyer. He had reinforced this section countless times, using every scrap of sealant he could find, but the rain was relentless, always finding a new weakness, a new way to intrude.

His work wasn't about beauty or art; it was about testimony. He was the archivist of their downfall, the recorder of nature's brutal retribution. His photographs would be the visual narrative for those who came after, a stark reminder of what had happened, of the world that had been lost. He hoped, with a desperate, fervent hope, that they would learn from it, that they would find a way to rebuild, to coexist with a planet that had shown them its terrifying, unyielding power.

He continued to shoot, his movements a silent ballet against the cacophony of the storm. He captured the eerie glow of the acidic pools, the distorted reflections of the broken world in their surface. He focused on the way the rain warped the remnants of old advertisements, their cheerful slogans dissolving into meaningless streaks of color, a mocking testament to a past that no longer existed. He documented the sheer, unadulterated power of the downpour, the way it flattened the sparse, struggling vegetation that dared to sprout in the poisoned soil, its leaves dissolving into a thin, acrid mist.

Jax's mind, usually a whirlwind of strategic planning and resource management, became a quiet observer. He let the camera lead him, letting the visual evidence speak for itself. He saw the slow, agonizing degradation of their meager shelters, the way the acid gnawed at the edges of their protective barriers, a constant, insidious threat. He captured the moments of despair, the hunched shoulders of individuals staring out at the relentless storm, their faces etched with weariness and resignation. But he also captured glimmers of defiance: a small, hardy weed pushing through a crack in the pavement, a lone bird, a creature of impossible resilience, sheltering in the lee of a crumbling statue.

He felt a profound sense of responsibility, a burden that settled heavy on his shoulders. These images, these frozen moments of chaos and despair, were his to bear. He had to ensure that the story of their struggle, the story of their fight for survival against the elements, was told. He thought of Luis and his quiet, scientific dedication, of Mika and her relentless pursuit of solutions, of the countless others who were fighting their own battles within the relative safety of the communal shelter. They were all part of this unfolding tragedy, and his photographs were a way of bearing witness to their collective suffering, their collective resilience.

He zoomed out, capturing a wider panorama of the devastated cityscape. The acid rain painted the sky in an unnatural, viridian hue, a suffocating blanket that pressed down on everything. The distant structures, once proud monuments to human achievement, now stood as skeletal warnings, their forms softened and blurred by the perpetual downpour. It was a world drowning in its own chemical tears, a world that had been irrevocably altered by the very forces it had sought to control.

Jax continued his work, his focus unwavering. He knew that these images would be more than just records; they would be a call to action, a testament to the destructive consequences of unchecked environmental exploitation. He would ensure that the world saw the terrifying beauty of nature's wrath, and the desperate courage of those who endured it. His lens was his weapon, his photographs his ammunition, and his aim was to preserve the memory of their fight, so that perhaps, just perhaps, a future could emerge from the ashes of their present. The drumming of the acid rain continued, a relentless, mournful dirge, but Jax kept shooting, capturing the harrowing truth, one frame at a time. He felt a flicker of hope, a faint whisper of defiance, each click of the shutter a small victory against the encroaching darkness, a testament to the enduring spirit of humanity, even in the face of utter annihilation. He was documenting the deluge, not just as a natural disaster, but as a profound existential crisis, a stark reminder of the delicate balance between humanity and the planet it called home. The acid rain, a monstrous force of nature, was a consequence, and his photographs were the evidence.

CHAPTER SIX

THE CLEANSING GREEN

The lab, a space carved out of what was once a gleaming corporate lobby, was a testament to their ingenuity. Scavenged beakers and centrifuges hummed alongside jury-rigged heating elements and jury-rigged atmospheric scrubbers. The air, though filtered, still carried the faintest metallic tang, a ghost of the world outside. Mika, her brow furrowed in concentration, meticulously arranged a series of petri dishes. Each contained a slurry of soil, a grim, greyish-brown concoction harvested from the polluted depths of the city's forgotten lower levels. Beside them, a row of vials held samples of the acid rain, its viridian luminescence stark and unsettling even in the controlled environment.

Luis, his movements economical and precise, carefully measured out a dose of nutrient solution. He was a quiet force, his scientific rigor a calming counterpoint to Mika's more dynamic approach. "Are you sure about this, Mika?" he asked, his voice low, a hint of the anxiety that always simmered beneath the surface of their collective efforts. "Introducing an unknown variable into already compromised samples..."

Mika met his gaze, her own eyes, usually alight with fierce intelligence, held a flicker of something akin to awe. "Luis, we've seen what this plant can do. The resilience, the way it thrives where nothing else can. It's more than just surviving. It's... changing." She gestured towards a corner of the lab where a cluster of the strange, iridescent flora grew, its leaves a vibrant emerald that seemed to pulse with an inner light. They had salvaged a few specimens, carefully cultivating them in a sealed environment, their curiosity piqued by their inexplicable hardiness.

Luis nodded, his scientific mind already cataloging the possibilities. "Resilience is one thing. Detoxification is another. If it truly possesses those properties, it could be... transformative." He carefully poured the nutrient solution into the soil samples, his hands steady.

Their experiments were designed with a stark simplicity born of necessity. They had divided the soil samples into four groups. The first, a control, would receive only filtered water. The second would be exposed to a controlled dose of the acidic rain. The third would be treated with a known contaminant, a simulated industrial waste product they had managed to synthesize from salvaged chemicals, a dark, viscous liquid that hissed ominously when disturbed. The fourth group, the crucial one, would be introduced to the invasive plant. Small cuttings, carefully pruned, were placed directly into the soil samples, their tendrils reaching out like hesitant fingers.

The acid rain samples underwent a similar stratification. One vial remained as a baseline, its acidic pH a terrifyingly stable number. Another would have a piece of the plant submerged within it. A third would be subjected to a high-frequency sonic treatment, an attempt to break down the molecular structure of the pollutants. And the fourth, a control group, would be left untouched, a grim benchmark of their current reality.

Days bled into nights. The hum of the lab equipment became a constant, droning lullaby. Mika and Luis alternated shifts, their sleep a fragmented, restless thing. They meticulously documented every change, every subtle shift in color, texture, and chemical composition. The control soil samples, as expected, remained inert, their greyish hue unchanged. The soil exposed to the acid rain began to show signs of distress, the fine particles clumping together, a thin, oily film forming on the surface. The simulated industrial waste, as predicted, was aggressively toxic, its presence rendering the soil inert and foul-smelling.

But the samples containing the plant... those were different.

The tendrils of the invasive flora, initially a pale, almost translucent green, began to deepen in color. They appeared to physically adhere to the soil particles, their microscopic structures seeming to weave themselves into the very fabric of the earth. And the soil itself began to change. The clumping lessened. The oily sheen on the surface of the acid rain-treated samples started to dissipate.

"Look," Mika whispered, her voice filled with a hushed excitement. She pointed to a petri dish containing the soil contaminated with the industrial waste. The plant cutting, which had initially looked somewhat wilted, was now exhibiting a vibrant, almost aggressive growth. More importantly, the dark, viscous liquid was receding, not evaporating, but seemingly being absorbed, its noxious odor diminishing.

Luis leaned closer, his magnifier pressed to the glass. "The cellular structure... it's actively engulfing the contaminant. It's not just absorbing it; it's breaking it down." He moved to the instrument panel, his fingers flying across the controls. He initiated a spectrographic analysis of the soil and the surrounding liquid. The readings that flashed onto the screen were astonishing. The levels of the primary industrial toxins were plummeting. New, simpler chemical compounds were appearing, compounds that were not only inert but, in some cases, appeared to be beneficial to plant life.

"The acid rain samples," Luis announced, his voice barely above a whisper. He gestured to the vial where the plant cutting had been submerged. The viridian luminescence had significantly faded. The water, once thick and viscous, was now clearer, its pH closer to neutral. "It's... neutralizing it. The acidic residue is being broken down. It's consuming the corrosive elements."

Mika's hands trembled slightly as she adjusted the microscope's focus on a cross-section of one of the plant's roots. "The root hairs... they're a different structure than anything I've ever cataloged. They're designed for absorption on an unprecedented scale. And within the cellular matrix... there are specialized organelles. I think they contain enzymes, potent catalysts that are specifically designed to break down these complex, harmful molecules."

They spent the next few days in a feverish state of confirmation. They replicated the experiments, varying the concentrations of contaminants, the types of toxins, and the exposure times. The results were consistently, overwhelmingly positive. The plant demonstrated an almost miraculous ability to cleanse. It didn't just tolerate the poisons; it actively sought them out, absorbed them, and transformed them. The acidic residue from the rain, a persistent threat that gnawed at their shelters and their very beings, was rendered inert. The toxic heavy metals and chemical sludge that leached into their water sources and poisoned their soil were broken down into harmless byproducts.

"It's a bio-remediation system," Luis stated, the scientific terminology a rare and welcome sound. He was looking at a complex chemical diagram he had sketched, his face alight with understanding. "Nature, in its infinite wisdom, has created a solution. This plant isn't just surviving the apocalypse; it's actively working to reverse it. It's a living, breathing detoxifier."

Mika traced the diagram with a finger. "But how? How did it evolve this ability? Was it a genetic mutation triggered by the environmental collapse? Or was it... engineered?" The question hung in the air, a tantalizing possibility that opened up a new, even more complex layer of inquiry.

"That's a question for later," Luis said, his gaze still fixed on the data. "Right now, what matters is what we have. This plant... it offers us a chance. Not just to survive, but to begin to heal."

They began to analyze the byproducts of the plant's detoxification process. The results were equally surprising. The "waste" material left behind after the plant had done its work was not inert sludge but a nutrient-rich substrate. In some cases, it was a fine, almost chalky powder that, when tested, showed a significantly reduced toxicity and a promising capacity to support microbial life. In other instances, the plant seemed to excrete simple organic compounds that could potentially be utilized as fertilizer.

"It's a closed-loop system," Mika marveled, her exhaustion momentarily forgotten. "It takes our poisons and turns them into something useful. It's the opposite of what humanity did. We took precious resources and turned them into waste. This plant... it's showing us a different way."

The implications were staggering. If they could cultivate this plant on a large scale, they could begin to reclaim the poisoned land. They could filter their water supplies, rendering the acidic rain a threat of the past. They could create pockets of habitable zones, areas where life could not only survive but thrive again.

Luis carefully collected samples of the byproduct material. "We need to test this further. Ensure there are no residual toxins, no unforeseen long-term effects. But the initial results are overwhelmingly positive. This could be the key to our survival, Mika. Not just our survival, but our recovery."

Mika picked up one of the larger leaves of the cultivated plant, its surface cool and slightly waxy. The iridescent sheen seemed to pulse faintly, a silent testament to its extraordinary capabilities. "We've spent so long fighting the fallout, Luis. Trying to build higher walls, to create better filters. We've been trying to shield ourselves from the damage. But this... this is about mending. It's about healing the wound."

The initial experiments, while groundbreaking, were just the beginning. They needed to understand the plant's optimal growing conditions, its propagation methods, and its limitations. Could it thrive in the harsh conditions outside? Could it be integrated into their existing infrastructure? The questions were endless, but for the first time in a long time, they were questions born not of despair, but of hope. The quiet hum of the lab seemed to take on a new resonance, a subtle undercurrent of optimism that had been absent for so long. The cleansing green, as Mika had begun to call it, held the promise of a new dawn.

The hum of the filtration units was a constant, low thrum against the silence of the reclaimed laboratory, a sound that had become as familiar to Kiley as her own heartbeat. It was a lullaby of survival, a testament to their persistent defiance against the poisoned world outside. Days had turned into weeks since Mika and Luis had shared their groundbreaking discovery, the implications of the 'cleansing green' weaving themselves into the fabric of Kiley's thoughts, transforming the grim landscape of their existence into something tentatively hopeful. The knowledge that a living entity possessed the ability not just to endure the toxins that plagued their lives but to actively dismantle them, to transmute the poison into potential, had ignited a spark within her. It was a spark that demanded action.

Kiley, with her inherent pragmatism and knack for engineering solutions, saw not just a scientific marvel but a tangible tool. The limited specimens they had managed to cultivate in the lab were a precious, fragile testament to this potential, but they were not enough. To truly begin the arduous process of reclamation, they needed more. They needed a viable population, a robust source from which to propagate and deploy. The marsh, a treacherous expanse of brackish water and skeletal remains of what was once a thriving wetland, was the only known source of this miraculous flora. It was also a place of profound danger, a labyrinth of treacherous footing, toxic fumes that clung to the stagnant air, and the ever-present threat of environmental hazards.

She presented her plan to the council, her voice steady and resolute, cutting through the usual murmur of anxieties and logistical hurdles. "We need to go back to the marsh," she stated, her gaze sweeping across the faces of the elders, each one etched with the weariness of years spent in a world that was actively trying to erase them. "We've analyzed the samples, we understand what the plant does. Now we need to secure a sustainable source."

There was a collective intake of breath, a palpable tension filling the small, dimly lit chamber. The marsh was spoken of in hushed tones, a place best avoided, a scar on the landscape that represented the worst of their current reality. But Kiley's conviction was unwavering. She had spent weeks poring over old geological surveys, cross-referencing them with their own observations of the plant's growth patterns and the peculiar, localized pockets of less-toxic soil she had noted on previous, less ambitious scouting missions. Her mind, a finely tuned instrument of logic and design, had already begun to formulate the strategies, the tools, the very methods by which they could venture into the heart of that desolation and return with the promise of a greener future.

"The risks are significant, Kiley," Elder Maris cautioned, her voice raspy, a testament to decades of breathing filtered air. "The marsh is unpredictable. The fumes can disorient, the ground can give way without warning. And we don't know what other... adaptations... might have occurred out there."

"Which is why we need to be prepared," Kiley countered, unrolling a series of meticulously drawn schematics onto the worn wooden table. "I've designed specialized containment units. They're sealed, lightweight, and equipped with an internal atmospheric scrubbing system, drawing on the same principles as our lab's filters. They'll keep the plants viable during transport and prevent any accidental release of airborne spores or toxins. I've also worked on improved respiratory filters, incorporating a new layer of charcoal composite that should offer better protection against the concentrated fumes."

She pointed to a section of her diagrams. "And for navigating the terrain, I've devised a series of deployable 'stepping stones.' They're a lightweight, reinforced polymer lattice that can be anchored to more stable ground, creating a temporary pathway across softer, more unstable areas. It's not foolproof, but it significantly reduces the risk of falling through."

Her words painted a vivid picture of meticulous planning, of a mind that saw challenges not as insurmountable obstacles but as problems to be solved. There was a quiet confidence in her demeanor that was infectious, a stark contrast to the usual expressions of apprehension. She wasn't just asking for permission; she was presenting a calculated solution to a desperate need.

"Who would go with you?" Maris asked, her eyes fixed on the diagrams, a flicker of reluctant admiration beginning to bloom amidst her concern.

"Myself, and two others," Kiley replied without hesitation. "Someone with expertise in botany, for identification and careful extraction – Mika, if she's willing. And someone with strong practical skills, someone who can handle the physical demands and assist with the deployment of the equipment – Jian. He's worked with the water purification systems, he understands filtration and containment."

The decision, when it finally came, was not one of unbridled enthusiasm, but of grim necessity. The council, recognizing the urgency of Kiley's proposition and the thoroughness of her preparations, agreed. The marsh expedition was sanctioned.

The day of departure dawned under a sky the color of weak tea, the air thick with the familiar, acrid scent of decay. Kiley, Mika, and

Jian stood at the edge of the settlement's fortified perimeter, the last vestiges of familiar safety. Kiley wore a reinforced, multi-layered suit, its seams sealed, its helmet providing a panoramic view of the desolate landscape. The new respiratory filters, bulkier than their standard issue, were already a comforting weight against her face. Strapped to her back was a pack containing the essential tools: the collapsible lattice stepping stones, a compact atmospheric sensor, a multi-tool, and, of course, the carefully designed containment units – sleek, cylindrical vessels with transparent panels, ready to cradle their precious cargo.

Mika, though less heavily armored, was equally prepared. She carried a robust sampling kit, a reinforced trowel, and a specialized magnifier. Her eyes, even behind the protective visor of her own helmet, held a keen, almost predatory focus, scanning the environment for the tell-tale signs of the plant. Jian, his frame sturdy and his movements economical, carried a larger pack containing spare filters, repair tools for the containment units, and additional anchoring equipment for the stepping stones.

"Remember the markers," Kiley said, her voice slightly distorted by the comms system within her helmet. "We're not just going in blind. I've mapped out the areas where we had the highest concentration of samples during the initial scouting. We'll stick to that general vicinity, work outwards methodically."

Their journey began. The ground immediately outside the settlement's perimeter was a patchwork of cracked earth and hardy, stunted vegetation, a testament to the ongoing efforts of the reclamation teams. But as they ventured further, the landscape began to transform. The air grew heavier, the scent of decay intensifying, underscored by a subtle, metallic tang that spoke of airborne pollutants. The sparse vegetation gave way to a landscape of mud, stagnant pools, and skeletal trees, their branches gnarled like arthritic fingers reaching towards the indifferent sky.

The marsh was a place that seemed to actively resist life, a testament to nature's brutal indifference when pushed to its limits. The silence here was different from the quietude of the settlement; it was an oppressive, suffocating absence of sound, broken only by the occasional, unsettling plop of something unseen disturbing the murky water, or the mournful creak of decaying wood.

"Atmospheric readings are stable, but elevated," Jian reported, his voice a steady presence in their comms. "Keep the filters engaged. We're approaching the first marker point."

They reached a patch of ground that, even from a distance, appeared slightly less desolate. It was a shallow depression, its edges marked by a cluster of half-submerged, waterlogged debris. Kiley deployed the first of the stepping stones. With practiced efficiency, she anchored the lattice sections, creating a surprisingly stable platform that extended towards a slightly firmer patch of mud a few meters away.

"This is where it gets tricky," she murmured, stepping onto the lattice. It held her weight, the polymer flexing slightly but remaining firm. Mika followed, her movements more cautious, her eyes already scanning the ground for any signs of the 'cleansing green.' Jian brought up the rear, ensuring the integrity of the path behind them.

The air here was noticeably thicker, a cloying miasma that seemed to press in on them. Kiley activated her helmet's external lights, their beams cutting through the gloom. The ground beneath the stepping stones was a viscous, dark mud, teeming with unseen life. And then, Mika pointed.

"There," she breathed, her voice tight with suppressed excitement.

Nestled amongst a clump of decaying reeds, its iridescent leaves catching the faint light, was a small cluster of the detoxifying plant. It was smaller than the cultivated specimens they had seen, its growth stunted by the harsh environment, but it was undeniably the same species. Its emerald hue was muted, almost an olive green in the dim light, but the subtle shimmer was unmistakable.

"Careful, Mika," Kiley cautioned, approaching slowly. She deployed a small, handheld atmospheric sensor near the plant. "Concentration of specific airborne toxins is significantly higher in this immediate vicinity. The plant seems to be creating a localized zone of relative purity around itself."

Mika nodded, her focus absolute. She carefully selected her tools, her movements deliberate and precise. Using a reinforced trowel, she began to gently loosen the soil around the plant, taking care not to disturb its delicate root structure. Kiley positioned herself to receive the plant, holding one of the containment units open.

"Once you have it, Mika, don't expose it to the open air longer than necessary," Kiley instructed. "Transfer it directly into the unit. Jian, be ready with the seal."

With a final, careful maneuver, Mika detached the plant from the marsh floor. It was smaller than she had hoped, its root ball compact, but the vibrancy within its leaves was still evident. She swiftly placed it into the containment unit. Kiley snapped the lid shut, activating the internal filtration system. A soft hum emanated from the unit, a miniature echo of the lab's life-sustaining machinery.

"First one secured," Kiley reported, a sense of accomplishment warming her despite the oppressive atmosphere. "Now, we move to the next marker."

The process was repeated, each extraction a tense, methodical dance between caution and urgency. They navigated treacherous terrain, Kiley's stepping stones proving invaluable. Jian's steady hand ensured the integrity of their path and the secure sealing of the harvested plants. Mika's keen eye and botanical knowledge allowed them to identify promising specimens, often hidden beneath layers of detritus or camouflaged by the surrounding decay.

At one point, as they were traversing a particularly unstable stretch of marshland, Jian's foot slipped. The lattice under him shifted violently. He let out a grunt of surprise, his body lurching towards the dark water.

"Jian!" Kiley yelled, reacting instantly. She lunged forward, her reinforced suit brushing against his, providing just enough counterweight to prevent him from toppling in. The lattice groaned under the strain, but held.

"Almost had me there," Jian grunted, regaining his footing. He paused for a moment, his breathing heavy. "This ground is... more unstable than the scans indicated."

"We're pushing the limits of what's possible out here," Kiley acknowledged, her heart pounding. "But we're doing it. We're getting what we need."

They found a larger, more established cluster of the plant near a partially submerged, rusted hulk of what might have been a transport vessel. This specimen was larger, its leaves a deeper, more vibrant emerald. As Mika began the extraction, she noticed something peculiar. The soil around this particular plant seemed less toxic, its texture richer, almost loamy.

"Kiley, look at this," Mika said, holding up a handful of the soil. "It's different. Less acidic, more organic matter. The plant... it's not just absorbing the toxins; it's actively improving the soil around it, even in these conditions."

Kiley leaned closer, her sensors picking up slightly different readings. "The soil's pH is indeed higher, and the concentration of heavy metals is significantly lower than in the surrounding area. It's creating a small, localized zone of improved fertility. This is... even better than we anticipated."

This discovery spurred them on. They began to actively seek out areas where the plant seemed to be thriving most robustly, suspecting that these were the most mature specimens, those that had been established for the longest period and had had the most significant impact on their immediate environment. The process was slow, painstaking, and fraught with minor peril. They encountered pockets of methane gas that Jian's sensors quickly detected, forcing them to reroute. They navigated through dense thickets of thorny, mutated scrub that snagged at their suits, requiring careful disentanglement.

As they worked, Kiley kept a close eye on their progress. They had managed to secure five containment units, each holding a healthy specimen. It was a promising start, but she knew they could do better. The goal was not just a few specimens; it was enough to establish a nursery, to begin propagation on a scale that could truly make a difference.

They pushed further into the marsh, the skeletal trees becoming more dense, the water deeper and more viscous. The air grew heavy with the scent of decay and something else, something faintly chemical that made the back of Kiley's throat itch.

"Readings are spiking," Jian announced, his voice tight. "High concentration of volatile organic compounds. We need to proceed with extreme caution."

Kiley scanned the area with her helmet's lights. The gloom was thick, almost impenetrable, but she could discern a denser patch of vegetation ahead, a hopeful anomaly in the pervasive decay. "There might be more there. A larger concentration. We push forward, but slowly. Stay vigilant."

They carefully advanced, each step measured, each breath a conscious act of filtering. Kiley deployed more of the stepping stones, creating a precarious pathway across a wider expanse of murky water. As they drew closer, the faint shimmer of the 'cleansing green' became more pronounced, a beacon in the oppressive darkness. They had found it – a dense thicket of the plants, far larger and more vibrant than any they had encountered before. The air around them, while still laden with pollutants, felt noticeably less oppressive, a testament to the collective power of the flora.

"This is it," Kiley whispered, a thrill of triumph running through her. "This is what we came for."

The extraction here was more involved. The plants were intertwined, their roots deeply embedded in the rich, though still somewhat compromised, soil. Mika worked with an almost reverent focus, carefully teasing apart the specimens, ensuring that each harvested plant retained as much of its root structure as possible. Jian assisted, his strength and dexterity proving invaluable in gently lifting the larger specimens from the earth. Kiley, meanwhile, managed the deployment of the containment units, ensuring a swift and secure transfer.

They worked for hours, the sun, a pale disc in the perpetually overcast sky, dipping lower. The process was exhausting, each movement requiring significant effort in the heavy suits. But the sight of the containment units filling, each one cradling a vibrant, living testament to nature's resilience, fueled their determination. They managed to secure three more specimens, bringing their total to eight. It was a significant haul, a substantial enough population to begin the vital work of propagation back at the settlement.

"That's it," Kiley finally declared, her voice hoarse with fatigue but filled with a deep satisfaction. "We have enough. We need to head back."

The return journey felt both longer and shorter than the outward trek. Longer, because of the sheer exhaustion that weighed on their limbs; shorter, because of the burgeoning sense of achievement that buoyed their spirits. They carefully retraced their steps, dismantling the stepping stone pathways as they went, leaving no trace of their passage except for the indelible mark of their purpose.

As they approached the settlement, the familiar silhouette of their fortified walls rising against the twilight sky, Kiley felt a surge of emotion. They had ventured into the heart of the blight, a place that had long been a symbol of their entrapment, and they had returned not with despair, but with hope. They had brought back the 'cleansing green,' a fragile promise of a future where the poisoned earth could begin to heal, a future where life, in its most tenacious and beautiful form, could once again reclaim its dominion. The mission had been a success, a daring reclamation project born of necessity and executed with skill, a testament to Kiley's leadership and the unwavering spirit of those who dared to dream of a world reborn. The weight on her back, the containment units cradling their precious cargo, felt not like a burden, but like the first seeds of a new beginning.

The hum of the newly installed bio-filtration units was a soft counterpoint to the persistent thrum of the main purification systems. It was a gentler sound, one that spoke of growth and adaptation, of a future Kiley had only dared to imagine a few weeks ago. Now, standing in the repurposed hydroponics bay, watching the emerald leaves of the *Chloris purificans* gently sway as water trickled through their root systems, that future felt palpably close. Mika, her brow furrowed in concentration, was meticulously adjusting a flow regulator, her movements precise and economical. The air in the bay was thick with the clean, earthy scent of the plants, a welcome change from the recycled, slightly metallic tang of their usual filtered atmosphere.

"The initial readings are promising, Kiley," Mika said, her voice a low murmur that carried easily over the gentle whirring of the pumps. She gestured towards a series of monitors displaying cascading graphs and fluctuating numerical values. "The *Chloris* is not only handling the suspended particulates with remarkable efficiency, but it's also actively breaking down certain complex organic compounds that our older mechanical filters struggled with. We're seeing a significant reduction in turbidity and, more importantly, a decrease in trace chemical contaminants."

Kiley nodded, a sense of awe settling deep in her chest. This was more than just a discovery; it was a revolution. The meticulous, painstaking work of extracting and cultivating the 'cleansing green' from the treacherous marsh had been worth every calculated risk. "And the water?" she asked, her gaze fixed on a clear stream of liquid emerging from the final stage of the filtration unit, a liquid so pure it seemed to shimmer.

"Potable," Mika confirmed, a rare smile gracing her lips. "Or at least, on its way to being perfectly potable. We're running parallel tests with a control group, of course, but the preliminary analysis suggests we're exceeding the purity standards set by the old world's water authorities, even with a simplified filtration process." She ran a gloved hand over the smooth, recycled plastic of the containment vessel, her touch almost reverent. "It's the roots, you see. They're not just acting as a physical barrier; they're secreting enzymes, complex biochemical agents that neutralize and break down a surprisingly broad spectrum of pollutants. It's like a living, breathing chemical processing plant, operating on a scale we could only dream of with our old technology."

The implications of Mika's work were staggering. For generations, survival had been a constant, uphill battle against the poisoned environment. Their water was carefully, laboriously filtered, each drop a testament to their struggle. Their arable land was virtually nonexistent, the soil leached and contaminated. The *Chloris purificans*, this unassuming organism, offered a pathway not just to survival, but to regeneration.

Mika explained, her voice gaining an excited cadence, how she had meticulously adapted the design of their existing water purification systems. The core principle remained – physical filtration and UV sterilization – but now, interspersed within the multi-stage process, were specially designed bio-reactors. These reactors, essentially transparent cylinders filled with nutrient-rich substrate, housed thriving colonies of the

Chloris. Water flowed through these chambers, the plant's root systems forming an intricate, living web that captured and neutralized toxins.

"We've observed that the plant's efficiency is directly proportional to its root density and the health of the microbial community it fosters," Mika continued, her eyes alight with intellectual fervor. "So, we're experimenting with different nutrient blends for the substrate, optimizing for enzyme production and root growth. We're also exploring ways to encourage the symbiotic relationship between the *Chloris* and certain beneficial bacteria that seem to thrive in its presence. It's a delicate balance, but the potential for enhanced purification is immense."

She pointed to another system, this one more rudimentary, a series of shallow trays filled with dark, rich soil. This was their soil remediation experiment. Small, carefully controlled plots of land, painstakingly cleared of debris and whatever stunted, mutated vegetation had managed to cling to existence, were being treated with a specially prepared compost infused with crushed *Chloris* rhizomes and actively growing plantlets.

"The acid rain has done irreparable damage," Mika said, her tone shifting to a more serious, almost somber note. "It's stripped the soil of essential nutrients, altered its pH to an extreme, and introduced heavy metals that are toxic to most known forms of plant life. Our conventional methods of soil amendment were slow, inefficient, and resource-intensive. But the *Chloris*... it's a game-changer."

She knelt down, scooping a handful of the treated soil. It was darker, less crumbly than the barren earth Kiley remembered from their initial reconnaissance missions. "The plant's enzymes don't just break down external pollutants," Mika explained, turning the soil over in her fingers. "They also seem to facilitate the breakdown of complex organic matter within the soil itself, releasing essential nutrients. We're observing a measurable increase in nitrogen and phosphorus levels, and the pH is gradually trending towards a more neutral range. It's a slow process, of course. We're talking months, perhaps even a year, before these plots are truly fertile enough for reliable food cultivation. But it's a process that requires minimal external input once established. It's sustainable."

Kiley watched, captivated. This was the long game. While the immediate benefit of clean drinking water was a monumental step, the prospect of reclaiming the earth itself, of transforming toxic wastelands back into arable land, was a vision of true rebirth. She imagined the day when they wouldn't have to rely solely on their carefully rationed hydroponic produce, when they could once again cultivate crops under an open sky.

"The containment units we brought back from the marsh were crucial," Kiley mused aloud, her mind already racing ahead, envisioning the future applications. "They're designed for transport and initial cultivation, but we'll need larger, more robust systems if we're going to scale this up. We'll need dedicated bio-reactors for water treatment, and larger nurseries for soil remediation."

"Exactly," Mika agreed, her eyes scanning the existing hydroponic bays, a familiar glint of innovation sparking within them. "We can adapt many of these structures. The existing hydroponic channels can be modified to house the water filtration systems. For soil remediation, we can create 'growth beds' – raised platforms where we can concentrate the enriched substrate and allow the

Chloris to establish a more extensive root network before introducing it to the broader environment. We'll need to harvest and process the plant material regularly to maintain optimal enzyme production in the remediation sites, but the energy expenditure for this is minimal compared to traditional methods."

The challenge, as always, was resources. Every new endeavor required materials, energy, and manpower. But Kiley had faith in their ingenuity, and in Mika's unparalleled talent. They had faced seemingly insurmountable odds before and emerged victorious. This was just another challenge, albeit one of a grander, more fundamental nature.

"We'll need to prioritize," Kiley said, her voice firm. "Clean water is the immediate necessity. The bio-filtration units for the settlement's main water supply need to be our first major project. Once that's stable, we can focus on expanding the soil remediation efforts. We can start with small, controlled 'test plots' outside the settlement's perimeter, areas that are already showing some marginal improvement, and gradually expand from there. We can monitor their progress using the atmospheric sensors and soil analysis kits we have."

"I've already begun drafting preliminary designs for scaled-up bio-reactors," Mika revealed, tapping a stylus against her datapad.

"They'll be modular, allowing us to connect multiple units for increased capacity. I'm also developing a cultivation guide for a dedicated

Chloris nursery. It will detail optimal light, nutrient, and humidity levels, as well as methods for encouraging rapid root growth and spore production. The more successfully we propagate the plant, the faster we can implement these systems across larger areas."

There was a palpable sense of excitement in the air, a shared vision of a world slowly, painstakingly, being made habitable again. The 'cleansing green' was not just a plant; it was a symbol of resilience, a testament to nature's enduring capacity for healing, even in the face of catastrophic destruction. It was a living embodiment of hope, a promise that the poison that had choked their world for so long could, with time and dedication, be transmuted into life.

Kiley looked at the rows of vibrant green plants, their leaves unfurling towards the artificial light, and felt a surge of profound gratitude. They had brought back not just specimens, but a solution. A sustainable, organic, living solution. The hum of the bio-filtration units seemed to resonate with a deeper truth, a quiet affirmation that life, in its most tenacious and beautiful forms, always finds a way to persist, to adapt, and ultimately, to cleanse. The task ahead was immense, the scars of the past deep, but for the first time in a long time, Kiley felt an unshakeable certainty. They would not just survive; they would thrive. They would reclaim their world, one cleansed drop of water, one revitalized plot of soil, at a time. And it would all begin with the quiet, persistent miracle of the

Chloris purificans, a testament to Mika's brilliance and the indomitable spirit of their people. The future, once a hazy, almost unattainable dream, was now taking root, nurtured by ingenuity and the unwavering power of life itself. The journey of reclamation had truly begun, not with brute force or complex machinery, but with the gentle, persistent work of a single, extraordinary organism, guided by the hands of those who dared to believe in a cleaner tomorrow. The subtle shimmer of the leaves seemed to hold the promise of that tomorrow, a verdant beacon in the long, arduous twilight of their existence.

The transformation of Luis's garden began not with a grand pronouncement, but with the quiet rustle of leaves and the soft whisper of water. For years, it had been a testament to stubborn hope, a small patch of reclaimed earth clinging to existence against the relentless blight of the poisoned world. Luis, his hands perpetually stained with the dark, recalcitrant soil, had coaxed reluctant life from it, his efforts a constant, weary struggle against the environmental decay that had consumed so much of their planet. His meager crops, stunted and often plagued by disease, were a daily reminder of how precarious their hold on sustenance truly was. But now, a new purpose was blooming within his small sanctuary, a purpose intertwined with Mika's groundbreaking work.

Mika had approached Luis with a proposition, a plea couched in scientific necessity. His garden, with its established soil and Kiley's careful monitoring of its meager output, was the ideal location to test the next phase of the *Chloris purificans* integration. Not just for water purification, but for its potential to revitalize the very earth that sustained them. Luis, his heart always open to the whisper of growing things, had readily agreed. He saw in Mika's careful explanations and the specimens she brought – vibrant, almost impossibly green tendrils and robust, deep-reaching roots – a potential that resonated with his own deep-seated desire to see life truly flourish again.

The process was methodical, almost ceremonial. Luis, guided by Mika's precise instructions, began to carefully introduce sections of the *Chloris purificans* into his existing garden beds. It wasn't a simple transplantation. Mika had stressed the importance of a symbiotic environment, of allowing the *Chloris* to integrate rather than overwhelm. Luis prepared the soil, not just turning it, but amending it with a specially prepared compost that Mika had provided, a dark, rich mixture infused with crushed *Chloris* rhizomes and nascent plantlets. He dug shallow trenches, carefully layering the *Chloris* root systems alongside the struggling roots of his own precious potato plants and hardy, nutrient-poor tubers. It felt like an act of faith, weaving this wild, potent new life into the familiar tapestry of his struggling farm.

He also adapted his watering system. The gentle, constant trickle of water was now routed through a rudimentary, yet effective, bio-filtration unit that Mika had helped him assemble from recycled materials. It was a scaled-down version of the systems being installed in the main settlement, a contained ecosystem designed to mimic the natural processes of the *Chloris*. Water from their cistern, still carrying a faint, metallic tang despite the initial purification, now flowed through a chamber filled with the *Chloris* roots. Luis watched, mesmerized, as the water seemed to clarify, to lose its residual harshness, as it passed through the living filtration. He would collect this purified water in separate containers, a precious, pristine resource, and then, with an almost reverent hand, he would administer it to his garden.

The change was not immediate, but it was undeniable. Within weeks, a subtle shift began to occur. The leaves of Luis's existing plants, once pale and prone to yellowing, deepened in color, taking on a richer, more vibrant hue. The wilting stalks of his meager tomato plants seemed to gain a new vigor, their branches reaching higher towards the filtered sunlight. The

Chloris itself, initially cautious, began to spread. Its sinuous vines, once confined to the areas Luis had designated, started to weave their way through the existing foliage, not aggressively, but in a graceful, supportive manner. Its tendrils curled around the stems of his beans, providing a natural support, while its roots, a network of fine, resilient fibers, intertwined with those of his root vegetables, creating a beneficial, shared rhizosphere.

Luis found himself spending more and more time in his garden, observing the intricate dance of life unfolding before him. He noticed how the *Chloris*, with its specialized root system, seemed to draw out impurities from the soil, leaving behind a more porous, nutrient-rich substrate. The slight acidity that had plagued his soil for so long was gradually diminishing, its pH trending towards a more neutral balance, thanks to the plant's enzymatic action. It was as if the *Chloris* was not just surviving in the soil, but actively tending to it, healing it from within. The water it filtered, imbued with the plant's own life-giving essence, further enhanced this restorative process, providing a pure, clean source of hydration that his struggling plants had long craved.

He began to experiment, subtly. He introduced small cuttings of *Chloris* into areas where his crops had consistently failed. He observed how the new plant would establish itself, and then, slowly but surely, the surrounding soil would begin to improve. Plants that had previously withered away would start to sprout, then grow, then thrive, their leaves unfurling with a newfound resilience. It was a testament to the *Chloris*'s remarkable ability to break down complex pollutants, to neutralize toxins, and to unlock essential nutrients that had been locked away in the corrupted earth.

One particularly stubborn patch of ground, near the edge of his garden, had always resisted his efforts. It was a barren expanse, the soil thin and depleted, riddled with microscopic fissures from years of toxic rain. Luis had tried everything – scavenged fertilizers, painstaking tilling, even carefully collected rainwater, which, though purified, still lacked the vital elements needed for robust growth. He had almost given up on it, marking it as lost territory. But now, he saw an opportunity. He carefully cleared away the sparse, mutated weeds that clung to it and then, with Mika's guidance, he prepared a concentrated substrate infused with *Chloris* rhizomes and beneficial microbes. He planted a dense cluster of the *Chloris* in this area, almost like a nursery, and began to irrigate it with the specially filtered water.

The results were astonishing. The *Chloris* took hold with incredible speed, its roots penetrating the recalcitrant soil with surprising ease. It seemed to draw sustenance not just from the prepared substrate, but from the very pollutants that had rendered the land infertile. As its root system expanded, it began to aerate the soil, break down heavy metal contaminants, and release bound-up minerals. Within a few months, the patch of ground was no longer barren. Small, vibrant green shoots began to emerge from the soil, not just *Chloris*, but also the hardy, nutrient-rich tubers that Luis had planted nearby. The soil itself had transformed, becoming darker, richer, and remarkably crumbly to the touch. He could feel the difference under his fingertips – a subtle springiness, a promise of fertility.

Luis's garden became a living, breathing demonstration of Mika's vision. It was no longer just a symbol of precarious hope, but a vibrant, thriving ecosystem. The

Chloris purificans, once a specimen brought back from the edge of annihilation, was now an integral part of his cultivated landscape, working in silent, profound harmony with the plants he had nurtured for so long. The formerly struggling plants, now nourished by purified water and revitalized soil, flourished with an abundance he hadn't seen in years. His potato plants yielded tubers larger and more numerous than he had ever dared to imagine. His hardy greens grew with a deep, satisfying crunch. Even the air in his garden seemed cleaner, fresher, imbued with the subtle, earthy fragrance of healthy growth.

He would often sit by his garden, particularly in the early mornings, when the rising sun cast long shadows and the dew clung to the leaves. He would watch the intricate network of roots, both his own and the *Chloris*, intertwining beneath the surface, a silent testament to their shared existence. He would observe the way the *Chloris* vines gently cradled his tomato plants, or how its broad leaves seemed to offer a natural shade to the more delicate seedlings. It was a symbiosis, a partnership, born of necessity but blossoming into something beautiful and profoundly effective.

The visual transformation was striking. Where once there had been patches of struggling, pale vegetation interspersed with barren earth, there was now a verdant tapestry of life. The *Chloris*, with its deep green, almost emerald foliage, created a vibrant understory, its tendrils weaving through the taller plants like living threads. It didn't compete, but rather complemented, enhancing the growth of the crops it integrated with. The very texture of the garden had changed;

the soil was no longer the dusty, lifeless substrate of the past, but a rich, dark loam, teeming with beneficial microbes and alive with the promise of sustained fertility.

Luis meticulously documented these changes. He kept detailed logs of his watering schedules, the nutrient content of the soil, the growth rates of his crops, and the visual progression of the *Chloris* integration. His observations, shared with Mika, provided invaluable data, confirming the plant's extraordinary adaptability and its profound capacity for environmental restoration. He discovered that the *Chloris* also seemed to deter certain pests. The insects that had once feasted on his precious crops now seemed to avoid the areas where the cleansing green had established itself, a natural form of pest control that eliminated the need for any artificial deterrents.

His garden became a beacon, a tangible representation of the hope that Mika's discovery offered. Neighbors, initially skeptical, would stop by, drawn by the unmistakable vibrancy radiating from Luis's small plot. They would marvel at the robust health of his plants, the deep color of his greens, and the size of his harvested produce. Luis, with quiet pride, would explain the role of the *Chloris purificans*, of the bio-filtration system, and of the revitalized soil. He would share cuttings of the plant, demonstrating how to introduce it into their own struggling gardens, passing on the knowledge and the hope that had transformed his own patch of earth.

The garden, once a symbol of his individual resilience, had become a shared resource, a growing testament to the collective potential of their community. It was proof that the blight that had gripped their world was not an insurmountable end, but a challenge that could be met, and overcome, with ingenuity, perseverance, and the remarkable, restorative power of life itself. Luis, his heart filled with a deep and abiding satisfaction, knew that his garden had become more than just a source of food; it had become a living laboratory, a promise of a greener, healthier future, nurtured by the quiet, persistent miracle of the *Chloris purificans*. The transformation was not just in the plants, but in the spirit of his small corner of the world, a spirit now watered by clean water and rooted in fertile ground.

Jax's camera had become an extension of his own vision, a tool for translating the silent resilience of their world into a language everyone could understand. He had spent so long documenting the stark realities of their existence – the skeletal remains of cities, the choked rivers, the pervasive grey that seemed to leach the very color from life. His early work had been a chronicle of loss, a stark and unvarnished testament to the consequences of humanity's hubris. But now, the narrative was shifting, and his lens was eager to follow. He found himself drawn to the fringes, to the places where life, against all odds, was beginning to assert itself.

His initial forays into documenting Mika's work had been tentative. He'd focused on the technical aspects – the gleaming, if utilitarian, filtration units Mika had overseen the construction of, the meticulous calibration of sensors, the sheer ingenuity of the recycled materials that formed the backbone of their nascent infrastructure. But the true magic, he realized, lay not just in the mechanics of purification, but in the tangible, undeniable results. And those results were most vividly displayed in the green that was beginning to reclaim their world.

He had first visited Luis's garden with a critical eye, expecting more of the same weary struggle he'd witnessed for years. He remembered the pale, sickly leaves, the stunted growth, the constant battle against pests and disease. But what he found was something entirely different. It was a riot of color and vitality, a vibrant splash against the muted backdrop of their scarred landscape. The potato plants, which had always yielded meager, often misshapen tubers, were now laden with heavy, dark earth, promising a bounty Luis hadn't seen in a decade. The hardy greens, once a testament to Luis's stubbornness, now unfurled with a deep, rich hue, their leaves almost glossy with health. And weaving through it all, a vibrant, almost alien green, was the *Chloris purificans*.

Jax spent days in Luis's garden, his fingers stained with ink from his worn notebook, his camera clicking incessantly. He captured the intricate dance of the *Chloris* tendrils, some gently curling around the stalks of tomato plants, others forming a living mulch around the base of burgeoning squash. He photographed the deep, probing roots of the *Chloris*, a stark contrast to the shallow, struggling roots of some of Luis's older crops, illustrating the plant's remarkable ability to break down compacted, toxin-laden soil. He even managed to capture close-ups of the microscopic life that was returning to the soil, a testament to its renewed health, a world invisible to the naked eye but profoundly significant in the grand scheme of recovery.

His photographs weren't just pretty pictures; they were data points, visual evidence of a paradigm shift. He contrasted images of the grey, barren earth that still dominated much of their settlement with the rich, dark loam of Luis's garden. He juxtaposed photos of the murky, oil-slicked water that still flowed in the distant river with shots of the crystal-clear water being collected from Mika's bio-filters, its purity almost luminous. He meticulously documented the growth rates, the yield increases, the sheer visual transformation. He wasn't a scientist, but he understood the power of a compelling image to convey complex truths.

He began to use his photography to document the progress of the water purification systems as well. He found himself drawn to the filtration units, their humble efficiency a stark contrast to the grand, failed technologies of the past. He photographed the water as it entered the chambers, often carrying a faint film of residual contaminants, and then again as it emerged, clear and pure. He captured the sheer volume of water being processed, a growing stream of life-giving resource, a stark reminder of what had been lost and what was now being painstakingly regained.

One particular series of photographs focused on a small, neglected patch of land on the outskirts of the settlement. It had been a dumping ground for years, a toxic scar on the landscape where nothing dared to grow. Jax had documented its desolation before Luis, with Mika's encouragement, had begun his work there. He then meticulously recorded the process: the initial planting of the

Chloris, the careful irrigation with filtered water, and the slow, almost imperceptible return of life. He captured the first hesitant green shoots of the *Chloris* pushing through the scarred earth, then the gradual improvement of the soil, its color deepening, its texture softening. Finally, he photographed the emergence of other, more familiar plants, drawn back by the improving conditions, creating a small but potent oasis of biodiversity.

The images were powerful, undeniable. They spoke of a world not merely surviving, but healing. They offered a tangible counterpoint to the pervasive narrative of despair, a visual argument for hope. Jax began to display his photographs in the communal gathering space, pinning them to the worn bulletin boards, projecting them onto any available wall. He arranged them thematically, creating visual narratives of recovery. One wall became a testament to the water –

before and after shots of filtration, images of the clean water flowing into communal tanks, children drinking from newly installed taps without fear. Another section focused on the soil, showcasing the transformation from barren dust to fertile earth, with Luis's garden as its crowning glory.

He saw the shift in people's faces as they studied his work. Skepticism gave way to curiosity, and curiosity to a dawning sense of possibility. They would gather in small groups, pointing, murmuring, their voices no longer filled with the weary resignation of the past, but with a hesitant excitement. Jax would often stand back, observing, letting the images speak for themselves. He saw a woman, her face etched with hardship, trace the vibrant green of a *Chloris* leaf on one of his prints, a small smile gracing her lips. He saw a group of children, their eyes wide, marveling at the size of the potatoes he had photographed, a stark contrast to the meager rations they were accustomed to.

He realized that his role was not just to document the *Chloris* and Mika's technology, but to capture the human response to it. He photographed the collaborative spirit that had emerged – people working together to build new filtration units, carefully tending to the expanding green spaces. He captured moments of shared joy: a successful harvest celebration in Luis's garden, a group of children laughing as they splashed in a newly cleaned communal fountain, its water purified by *Chloris*. These were the images that resonated most deeply, the ones that spoke of resilience and the enduring human capacity for hope.

Jax's artistic journey mirrored the larger transformation of their world. He moved from capturing the ashes of the past to celebrating the burgeoning life of the present. His camera, once a tool for documenting decay, had become an instrument of revelation, a beacon shining light on the path towards recovery. He understood that rebuilding their world was not just a matter of technology or science; it was also a matter of rekindling the spirit, of reminding people what was worth fighting for, what was worth cultivating.

He continued to expand his focus, venturing further out from the settlement, seeking out other pockets of *Chloris* integration. He found small, experimental plots where individuals were cautiously introducing the plant, their efforts mirroring Luis's initial struggles and subsequent triumphs. He photographed the challenges too – the occasional setbacks, the areas where the *Chloris* struggled to establish itself, the persistent toxins that still lingered in some of the soil. But even in these images, there was a sense of forward momentum, a testament to the perseverance of those who dared to hope.

His collection grew into a sprawling visual archive, a testament to the slow, persistent work of healing. It was a narrative of struggle and adaptation, of scientific innovation intertwined with ancient wisdom, and most importantly, of the indomitable power of life itself. Jax's hopeful exposures were more than just photographs; they were seeds of inspiration, planted in the minds and hearts of his community, promising a future where the grey would once again give way to the vibrant, life-affirming green. He saw his work as a crucial component of the cleansing, not just of the environment, but of the collective spirit, proving that even in the deepest desolation, beauty and renewal could still be found. He was a storyteller, and his medium was light, capturing the nascent dawn of a world reborn.

CHAPTER SEVEN

SEEDS OF DISCORD

The hum of the bio-filters had become a constant, almost soothing, soundtrack to their lives. It was the sound of progress, of a world slowly coaxing itself back from the brink. Mika's ingenuity, combined with Luis's tireless green thumb and Jax's powerful visual storytelling, had undeniably begun to weave a tapestry of recovery. The water, once a source of fear and illness, now flowed from communal taps, clear and life-affirming. Luis's garden, a vibrant anomaly in the ochre landscape, was yielding produce that tasted of sunshine and rain, not the metallic tang of poisoned earth. Yet, as the initial euphoria of these tangible improvements began to settle, a new, more insidious tension began to prickle at the edges of their hard-won peace. It was the quiet, creeping shadow of resource scarcity, a ghost that had haunted humanity for generations, now reasserting its spectral grip.

The problem, in its simplest form, was that *Chloris purificans*, while a miracle, was not an inexhaustible solution. Its ability to purify water was remarkable, but the processing capacity of the existing bio-filters was finite. Each unit, painstakingly assembled from scavenged materials and powered by the gentle efficiency of microbial action, could only handle so much. Similarly, while the *Chloris* could reclaim and enrich soil, the process was not instantaneous. The most fertile plots, like Luis's prized garden, were a testament to months, even years, of dedicated cultivation. The areas that had been most heavily contaminated, the true toxic scars of the old world, required even more time and careful management.

This fundamental limitation meant that access to the most precious commodities – clean water and fertile land – was no longer a given, but a privilege that had to be carefully managed. And management, in a community forged from the ashes of inequality, was a loaded word. Before the

Chloris and Mika's filters, access to these resources had been dictated by a brutal, informal hierarchy. Those who were strong, or cunning, or simply lucky enough to have established themselves in the more viable pockets of land, had controlled what little there was. They had hoarded water, dictated terms for its use, and monopolized the few areas where anything edible could be grown. Now, with the potential for widespread improvement, those established power dynamics were being tested.

The first subtle signs of discord manifested around the communal water taps. While the taps themselves were accessible to all, the flow was not always consistent. Mika, with her pragmatic approach, had divided the settlement into zones, each with a scheduled access period for water collection. This was a necessary measure to ensure equitable distribution and prevent the filters from being overwhelmed. However, the allocated times, while logical from an engineering standpoint, did not always align with the needs or desires of everyone.

The families who had lived on the more elevated, less desirable terrain before, the ones who had always struggled with access to even the most basic necessities, found their scheduled water collection times often fell during the hottest parts of the day, or when their children were meant to be attending educational sessions. Conversely, some of the families who had previously occupied more central, strategically advantageous positions, now found their traditional routines disrupted by these new timetables. They grumbled about the inconvenience, about having to wait, about the perceived unfairness of having their long-established habits dictated by a schedule.

"It's not like it used to be," grumbled old Silas, his voice raspy with disuse, as he watched a group of children from the outer zones fill their containers. Silas's family had always lived near the old administrative building, a location that had offered them a degree of protection and proximity to the dwindling pre-collapse resources. They had been among the first to establish a small, albeit precarious, garden on land that, while not pristine, was less contaminated than most. "Now everyone thinks they're entitled to a constant flow. We used to have to *earn* our water, show we were responsible."

His words, delivered with a self-righteous air, were overheard by Elara, a woman whose home was in one of the newly designated 'outer' zones. Elara had been a young mother when the collapse hit, and had spent years scrabbling for scraps, her children often going hungry. The advent of the *Chloris* and the bio-filters had been a lifeline, offering a hope she hadn't dared to entertain for a decade.

"Earn it, Silas?" Elara's voice was quiet but firm, carrying an edge of weariness that spoke of countless struggles. "We've always earned it. We earned it by enduring the thirst. We earned it by watching our children sicken. This schedule, it's the first time in my memory that the water reaches our homes at all. Before, your 'responsibility' meant we got nothing."

The exchange, though brief, encapsulated the underlying friction. It wasn't just about water anymore; it was about perceived entitlement, about the rebalancing of a deeply ingrained social order. Those who had previously held the reins of resource control felt their influence waning, while those who had been on the fringes tasted a newfound, albeit fragile, sense of equality.

This tension was amplified by the increasing demand for land suitable for cultivation. While the *Chloris* could break down toxins and improve soil structure, it required time and consistent watering. The most productive and easily accessible plots were now highly coveted. Luis, acting as the de facto overseer of agricultural efforts under Mika's broader guidance, found himself at the center of numerous requests, pleas, and sometimes outright demands.

"Luis, my neighbor's plot is struggling. The young shoots are wilting. Could you spare some of the filtered water for them? Just a little, to get them through."

"Luis, I heard you managed to clear that patch near the old market square. It's prime real estate. My family could make good use of it. We've got a good seed stock."

"Luis, the council says we can't expand our plot beyond the marked boundaries, but the

Chloris is spreading towards the south. Surely that land is just going to waste if we don't cultivate it."

Luis, a man whose hands were perpetually calloused and stained with earth, found himself navigating a minefield of social pressures. He understood the desperation driving these requests. He remembered the gnawing hunger, the gnawing fear of scarcity. But he also understood the delicate balance. Over-cultivation could deplete the soil, even with the *Chloris*'s restorative properties. Over-reliance on the filtered water for every single plot could strain the bio-filtration system beyond its capacity.

He found himself having to explain, repeatedly, the limitations. "The *Chloris* needs time to work," he would patiently explain, wiping sweat from his brow. "And the water, it's precious. We must use it wisely. Every drop counts."

He began to implement a tiered system for land allocation and water distribution, based on need and demonstrated effort. Those with existing, productive plots who showed they were actively tending to them, composting, and practicing water conservation, were prioritized. New allocations were given to families who had previously had no access, but only after a period of training and demonstration of commitment. This system, while logical and intended to foster sustainable practices, was not universally popular.

Some saw it as favoritism. They pointed to families who had always been more established, who had managed to secure prime locations early on, and who now continued to reap the benefits, their harvests consistently larger and more reliable. They whispered about backroom deals, about Mika or Luis showing partiality based on old allegiances or perceived social standing.

"It's not fair," muttered a younger man named Kael, his voice laced with resentment, as he watched Luis carefully inspect a row of burgeoning gourds. Kael's family had been allocated a patch of land on the edge of the settlement, a more challenging area where the soil was still compacted and the

Chloris growth was slower. They had received a basic ration of filtered water, but nothing like the quantity that seemed to be directed towards the more established gardens. "Luis always helps the 'old guard.' They get the best land, the most water. We're left with the dregs."

His words were overheard by Anya, a woman who had arrived at the settlement only a few years prior, after a long and perilous journey from a distant, ravaged region. Anya's family had lost everything, and their arrival had been met with suspicion and a grudging acceptance. They had been given a small plot of land, similar to Kael's, and had worked tirelessly, their efforts often yielding meager results.

"Dregs?" Anya's voice was sharper than Kael's, laced with a raw pain that silenced him. "We are grateful for any water, any earth that will sustain us. My children have not known a full meal in years. If Luis is helping those who have proven their dedication, who understand the value of what they have, then I see no injustice. We must earn our place, Kael. We must show we can be trusted with this bounty."

Anya's perspective was a stark reminder of the spectrum of experiences within the community. For some, the new system was a slight inconvenience, a challenge to their established comfort. For others, like Anya, it was the difference between survival and oblivion. Yet, the underlying issue remained: the finite nature of the resources, and the human tendency to view them through the lens of personal gain and perceived fairness.

Jax, with his ever-present camera, documented these burgeoning tensions with a keen, if somber, eye. He captured the furrowed brows of those who felt overlooked, the tight-lipped expressions of those who guarded their water barrels, the subtle shifts in body language that spoke of unspoken resentments. He photographed the queues at the water taps, the anxious glances exchanged between neighbors, the carefully measured portions of produce being shared, or sometimes not shared.

He also saw the counter-narrative. He documented the communal work parties where people, despite their grievances, came together to help clear new plots or repair a faltering filtration unit. He photographed instances of genuine generosity: a family sharing their meager harvest with a neighbor whose crops had failed, an elder teaching younger children how to properly tend the

Chloris tendrils, not for personal gain, but for the collective good. He saw Mika and Luis, often weary and overwhelmed, patiently explaining the science and the logistics, trying to maintain a sense of calm and reason amidst the rising anxieties.

One particular incident highlighted the deep-seated divisions. A small, experimental plot of land on the outskirts of the settlement, one that had been particularly stubborn to reclaim due to lingering chemical contamination, had finally shown signs of significant improvement. A group of families, who had been among the first to embrace the

Chloris and had consistently lobbied for access to more challenging terrain, had been granted permission to work it. They had toiled for weeks, using a combination of filtered water and a painstakingly developed compost mix, and the rewards were beginning to appear – small, hardy root vegetables pushing through the darkened soil.

However, a family who had previously occupied a more central, well-watered plot, and whose own harvests had recently dipped due to a minor pest infestation, saw this burgeoning success as an opportunity. They claimed the newly fertile land was rightfully theirs, citing an obscure, pre-collapse land registry document they had 'discovered' which, they argued, gave them prior claim. Their assertion was met with outrage from the families who had invested their labor and hope into the plot.

The dispute escalated quickly, drawing in others. Some sided with the 'old guard,' citing tradition and established rights. Others, sympathetic to the tireless efforts of the families working the new plot, argued that dedication and contribution should supersede dusty old documents. Mika and Luis were called to mediate, their authority stretched thin. Jax, observing from a distance, his camera capturing the heated exchanges, the angry gestures, the palpable division rippling through the crowd, felt a familiar pang of despair. It was the same old song, the same old human failing – the inability to share, the insatiable hunger for more, the willingness to sow discord over even the smallest of advantages.

Mika, her voice resonating with a weariness that belied her years, eventually brokered a compromise. The families who had cultivated the land would be allowed to harvest its initial yield, a testament to their efforts. However, the land itself would be designated as a communal testing ground, managed by a rotating committee, ensuring that its benefits would be shared more broadly in the future, and its development would be a collaborative effort. It was a fragile peace, a temporary reprieve from the simmering resentments.

The incident left a mark. The subtle whispers of discontent grew louder. Those who felt marginalized now harbored a deeper sense of injustice, while those who had previously held power felt their grip weakening further, prompting them to cling more tightly to what they perceived as their dwindling privileges. The clean water and the burgeoning green spaces, symbols of hope and renewal, were also becoming focal points of contention, breeding grounds for suspicion and envy.

Jax knew that his photographs could not solve these deeply ingrained human issues. He could document the beauty of the *Chloris* and the efficiency of the filters, he could capture the joy of a successful harvest, but he could not force generosity, nor could he legislate fairness. He could only bear witness, and perhaps, through his lens, remind people of the preciousness of what they were fighting over, and the potential for that fight to consume them, just as it had consumed their predecessors. The seeds of discord were being sown, not in the poisoned earth, but in the fertile ground of human nature itself, threatening to choke the very life that they were so desperately trying to cultivate. The struggle for survival had evolved, from battling the external forces of a ruined world, to navigating the internal landscape of a community grappling with the age-old challenges of scarcity and the intoxicating, dangerous lure of power.

The night had a way of amplifying anxieties. In the hushed hours, when the settlement settled into a restless sleep, the rustling of wind through dried leaves sounded like furtive footsteps, and the distant cry of a scavenging nocturne could be mistaken for a human whisper. It was during one such night, a night that had been particularly still, that the first tangible crack appeared in the fragile veneer of their shared hope.

Mika was the first to discover it. She had been performing a late-night diagnostic on Filter Unit Beta, a routine she performed with obsessive regularity. The unit, a complex arrangement of repurposed pipes, microbial cultures, and salvaged membranes, was the lynchpin of their water purification system for the eastern sector of the settlement. As her gloved hands traced the smooth, cool surface of the primary diffusion chamber, her fingers brushed against an anomaly. A hairline fracture, almost invisible in the dim glow of her headlamp, snaked across the reinforced polymer. It was subtle, yet devastating. This was no accidental stress fracture; the mark was too clean, too precise. It spoke of deliberate, targeted force.

Her heart sank, a cold, heavy stone in her chest. She knew the fragility of the materials she worked with, the constant battle against decay and degradation. But this was different. This was malice. She carefully documented the damage, her movements precise, her mind racing. Who would do this? And why? The filter unit was vital to everyone, a shared resource that benefited every single inhabitant of their small community. The thought of someone actively working against their collective survival was a chilling one, a betrayal that cut deeper than any physical wound. She spent the rest of the night painstakingly sealing the breach, working with a desperate urgency, the weight of responsibility pressing down on her. The hum of the bio-filters, usually a source of comfort, now seemed to thrum with an undercurrent of unease.

The next morning, the air in the settlement was thick with a tension that had nothing to do with the usual morning bustle. Mika, despite her efforts, had only managed a temporary fix. The damage was significant enough that the filter's efficiency was compromised, and the water output for the eastern sector would be reduced, even if it didn't stop entirely. She gathered the council, her voice tight with suppressed emotion as she explained what she had found. Whispers, like creeping vines, began to spread through the assembled group. Paranoia, a venomous seed long dormant, began to sprout.

Luis, his hands still bearing the telltale green stains of his work, arrived at the council meeting with his own grim news. He had been tending to his meticulously cultivated plots near the southern perimeter, the ones that were showing the most promise, the most resilience. His prized row of protein-rich tubers, the ones he had been nurturing for months, had been ravaged. Uprooted. Torn from the soil, their tender roots exposed to the harsh, unforgiving air. Some were simply scattered, others were trampled into the mud, their life force extinguished. It was an act of pure vandalism, a senseless destruction of nourishment.

"It was done at night," Luis explained, his voice rough with a mixture of anger and despair. He held up a gnarled tuber, its once-proud form now broken and wilting. "Someone came in, under the cover of darkness, and just... destroyed it. Not for food. Not to steal. Just to ruin it."

The implication hung heavy in the air. This wasn't about desperation; it was about sabotage. It was a direct assault on their progress, on their ability to sustain themselves. The clean water, the fertile land – these were not merely resources; they were the tangible symbols of their collective effort, their hard-won victory over the desolation. To attack them was to attack the very foundation of their renewed community.

Jax, ever the silent observer, had been present at both discoveries. His camera, usually held with a practiced ease, now felt like a weight in his hands. He had captured the stark image of the fractured diffusion chamber, the faint, almost apologetic hairline crack that spoke volumes of deliberate damage. He had also documented the scene in Luis's garden, the chaotic disarray of uprooted plants, the brutal testament to a night of malicious intent. He knew these images, when shown, would fan the flames of suspicion, but he also knew the truth needed to be seen.

"Who would do this?" the question echoed, not just from the council members, but from the faces of the people who had gathered, drawn by the growing tension. The usual camaraderie, the shared sense of purpose that had characterized their interactions, began to fray. Suspicion, once a faint undercurrent, now surged to the surface. Every sidelong glance, every hushed conversation, felt laden with accusation.

Mika, ever the pragmatist, tried to steer the conversation back towards solutions. "We need to understand *why* this is happening," she urged, her voice steady despite the turmoil churning within her. "This isn't random. This is a targeted attack on our progress. We need to consider who stands to lose from our recovery. Who benefits from our fear?"

Luis, his gaze fixed on the ruined tubers, his knuckles white, added, "Some people... they don't like change. They don't like that things are getting better for everyone. They're used to being in control, or they feel left behind. This is their way of lashing out."

The idea that the sabotage was rooted in resentment, in a refusal to accept the new order, resonated with many. There were still those who felt their previous status had been diminished, those who had benefited from the scarcity of the old world and now saw their advantage eroding. They were the ones who grumbled about the water schedules, who complained about land allocation, who whispered about Mika and Luis playing favorites.

"It's the people from the 'old guard' sectors," muttered a woman from the outer zones, her voice laced with bitterness. "They think they own this place. They think they deserve more. They don't want the rest of us to have clean water or food."

"And what about those who arrived recently?" countered another, his gaze flicking towards the newer arrivals who were still finding their footing. "They haven't put in the work. Maybe they're trying to destabilize things, to make us all vulnerable again."

The accusations flew, each one a tiny dart aimed at a perceived enemy. The unity that had been so carefully constructed was beginning to splinter under the weight of suspicion. The fragile trust, painstakingly built through shared hardship and mutual reliance, was being eroded by unseen forces. The very progress they had celebrated was now becoming a source of division, a battleground for those who clung to the past and those who feared the future.

Mika knew that a visible response was needed. Locking down the settlement wasn't an option; their survival depended on cooperation and movement. But they couldn't let these acts of sabotage go unaddressed. She proposed an increase in nighttime patrols, not just by the able-bodied, but by volunteers, ensuring that more eyes were watching, more ears were listening. She also suggested a series of community meetings, focused not on assigning blame, but on understanding the underlying frustrations, on creating a space for people to voice their grievances before they festered into destructive acts.

"We need to remind everyone," Mika stated, her voice carrying a new steeliness, "that the old world died because of division and selfishness. If we fall back into those patterns, we are dooming ourselves. This is not just about damaged filters or uprooted plants. This is about our collective will to survive, and to thrive."

Luis nodded in agreement. "We can replant the tubers. We can repair the filters. But we can't replant trust once it's been poisoned. We have to actively work to rebuild it, to show that we are all in this together, that our progress is for everyone."

Jax, his lens capturing the worried expressions, the averted gazes, the subtle shifts in posture that betrayed unspoken fears, felt the weight of his responsibility acutely. His photographs had always been about documenting reality, about revealing the truth, however harsh. Now, he had to decide how to present this new truth. Would his images of the damaged filter and the ravaged garden serve to unite them, by showing the common enemy, or would they further divide them, by fueling the accusations and suspicions?

That night, as the patrols began their slow, deliberate rounds, a chilling realization settled over Mika. The sabotage wasn't just an act of defiance; it was a calculated move to sow discord. It was designed to make them turn on each other, to consume their energy and their hope in internal conflict, leaving them vulnerable to whatever other threats the ravaged world might still hold. The seeds of discord, sown in the darkness, were beginning to bear bitter fruit, threatening to choke the very life they had so painstakingly cultivated. The struggle for survival had indeed evolved, moving from the external battle against a ruined planet to the insidious, internal war for the soul of their fledgling community. The night, once a time of respite, had become a canvas for fear, and the shadows held more than just the chill of the wind. They held the potential for betrayal, and the unsettling certainty that their most dangerous enemy might not be outside their walls, but within.

The hum of the bio-filters, usually a lullaby of progress, had become a discordant thrum in Mika's ears. Sleep offered little respite; her dreams were a chaotic montage of cracking polymers, wilting roots, and accusing faces. Each rustle of the wind outside her meager dwelling sounded like a clandestine whisper, a harbinger of further destruction. The fragile peace of their settlement had been shattered, not by the elements, but by the insidious work of an unseen hand.

Mika found herself caught in a maelstrom of doubt and defense. The meticulous repair of Filter Unit Beta had been a temporary balm, a necessary act of preservation. But the knowledge that it had been deliberately damaged gnawed at her. It wasn't just about a water purification system; it was about the integrity of their shared purpose. The same night she discovered the fracture, a chilling realization had begun to take root: her innovations, her tireless efforts to engineer their survival, were not universally welcomed. They were, in fact, becoming a target.

Her days were now consumed by an almost frantic vigilance. She spent hours in her workshop, a converted storage shed crammed with salvaged components, circuit boards, and repurposed tools. The air was thick with the metallic tang of solder and the faint scent of microbial cultures. She wasn't just repairing; she was reinforcing. Every pipe fitting was double-checked, every seal scrutinized, every circuit re-routed with an added layer of protection. She worked with a desperate urgency, her brow furrowed in concentration, her hands moving with a practiced, almost desperate, precision. She scavenged for stronger alloys, for more resilient membranes, for anything that could withstand a deliberate blow. It felt like she was building a fortress around a spring, the very source of life under siege.

The sabotage of Luis's tubers was a brutal echo of her own experience. The senseless destruction of the protein-rich plants, the very sustenance of their community, was an act of primal rage. It wasn't about survival; it was about negation. And the common thread that ran through both incidents was a chillingly deliberate intent to undermine their progress, their hard-won fight against the desolation.

"It's the engineers' fault," a voice had hissed in the marketplace, just loud enough for Mika to overhear. "They're building all these fancy contraptions, making things too easy. It's not natural. It's upsetting the balance."

The words struck her like a physical blow. Upsetting the balance? Was her dedication to providing clean water and reliable food a disruption? Was her desire to alleviate suffering a cause for resentment? She had always believed that progress, true progress, was about lifting everyone, about creating a more equitable and sustainable future. But now, she was beginning to see the darker side of human nature, the stubborn refusal to adapt, the fear of losing perceived privilege.

She found herself scrutinizing every face, every interaction. Was it the disgruntled few who had enjoyed a position of power in the old world? Were they the ones who felt their authority slipping away with each functioning water filter and ripening crop? Or was it the newly arrived, those still struggling to integrate, who saw the established settlers' advancements as a barrier to their own inclusion?

The ambiguity was a torment. Every hesitant smile, every averted gaze, felt like a potential accusation.

One evening, while recalibrating the nutrient flow to the algae farms, she overheard a hushed conversation near the perimeter fence. Two figures, their faces obscured by the twilight shadows, spoke in low, urgent tones.

"...can't let them get too comfortable," one said, their voice a gravelly whisper. "If things get too easy, people forget what it's like. They forget who's in charge."

"But the water... the food... it's helping everyone," the other voice replied, a hint of unease in its tone.

"Helping *them*," the first voice spat, the venom in the word sharp and chilling. "Not us. This isn't how it's supposed to be. This is artificial. And artificial things... they break."

Mika froze, her blood turning to ice. They weren't just talking about the filter or the tubers. They were talking about her. About her

work. The phrase "artificial things... they break" echoed in her mind, a direct threat. It wasn't just vandalism; it was a philosophy of resistance, a desperate attempt to cling to a past that was already dust.

The realization that her own creations were now a focal point for this discontent was a heavy burden. Had her focus on technological solutions inadvertently created a new kind of dependency, a disconnect from the natural order that some people craved? Was she, in her attempt to engineer their salvation, becoming an agent of unintended consequences? The thought was deeply unsettling. She had always seen her role as a facilitator, a builder of bridges to a better future. Now, she felt like a lightning rod, attracting the very storms she had hoped to dissipate.

She began to double-check her own work with an almost paranoid intensity. Every component, every connection, was a potential point of failure, not due to natural decay, but due to malicious intent. She developed an elaborate system of coded markings, subtle indicators of tampering that only she would recognize. It was a lonely task, a secret war waged in the quiet hours of the night, armed with ingenuity and a growing sense of dread.

Jax's photographs, which he had discreetly shared with her, were a stark testament to the damage. The almost surgical precision of the fracture on the filter, the brutal disarray of Luis's garden – they painted a grim picture. But they also served a purpose. They were irrefutable evidence, proof that these were not accidents. They were deliberate acts.

"What do we do, Jax?" she had asked him, her voice barely a whisper as they stood in the dim light of her workshop, examining the prints. "How do we fight an enemy we can't see? An enemy that might be our neighbor?"

Jax, ever the quiet observer, had simply handed her another photograph. It was a close-up of a single, uprooted tuber, its tendrils exposed and fragile. "The truth," he said, his voice low. "We show them the truth. And we trust them to see it."

But Mika wasn't so sure. The truth, she was learning, was a complex thing. It could illuminate, but it could also ignite. And the fire spreading through their settlement was fueled by fear and resentment, a potent cocktail that threatened to consume them all. She felt a profound sense of isolation. Her ingenuity, once a source of pride, now felt like a dangerous liability. She was the one who pushed for the new irrigation system, the one who optimized the solar arrays, the one who had devised the microbial filtration process. She was the innovator, the problem-solver. And now, she was the perceived threat.

She started to question her own motives, her own judgment. Had her drive to improve their lives blinded her to the emotional cost of change? Had her focus on efficiency overshadowed the need for community consensus? The lines between her good intentions and the resulting discord blurred, leaving her adrift in a sea of uncertainty.

"Perhaps they have a point," a quiet voice had said during one of the heated community meetings. It was Elara, a woman who had always been reserved, her hands roughened by years of manual labor. "We have so much now. More than many dared to dream of. But it's all... manufactured. It's not the land itself, not directly. It's through machines and processes. What happens if the machines break? Or if the people who understand them... leave?"

Her words, spoken without accusation, carried a heavy weight. They touched upon a primal fear, a vulnerability that Mika had tried to shield them from. Her reliance on technology, on complex systems, was indeed a form of dependency. And those who didn't understand those systems, or felt excluded from them, were understandably apprehensive.

The personal nature of the attacks began to weigh on her. It wasn't just the damage to the systems; it was the implication that *she* was the problem. The whispers about her ambition, her supposed desire for control, stung more than any physical injury. She spent sleepless nights poring over schematics, not just for structural integrity, but for any subtle flaw that could be exploited, any vulnerability that had been born from her own design. It was a maddening cycle of self-doubt and tireless effort.

She initiated a series of smaller, more localized projects, seeking to involve more people in the hands-on aspects of maintenance and cultivation. She taught basic repair skills, encouraged the formation of small work crews, and actively sought out individuals with latent mechanical aptitudes. It was a conscious effort to decentralize knowledge, to diffuse the perception that she held a monopoly on progress. She wanted to empower others, to show that their collective ingenuity was the true engine of their survival, not her singular vision.

One afternoon, while demonstrating how to calibrate a pressure valve on a secondary water line, a young man named Kael, a recent arrival who had been quiet and withdrawn, asked a question. "Mika," he began, his voice hesitant, "all this... it's amazing. But what if... what if it fails? What if the power goes out, or the filters clog beyond repair? We wouldn't know what to do."

His question, devoid of malice, was a direct reflection of the fear that was being deliberately sown. It was a fear she understood, a fear she had worked to mitigate. "That's why we're learning," she replied, her voice gentle. "That's why we're building redundancy. And that's why we're not just relying on one person, or one system. We are all learning, together. We are building a community that can adapt, no matter what." She gestured to the other people gathered, their faces a mixture of curiosity and concern. "This is about shared knowledge, Kael. Not just shared resources."

Yet, even as she tried to foster this sense of shared responsibility, the underlying anxiety persisted. The saboteur, whoever they were, was still out there, their actions a constant reminder of the fragility of their progress. Mika found herself increasingly drawn to the security of her workshop, to the predictable logic of circuits and mechanics. It was a refuge from the unpredictable chaos of human emotions, from the gnawing suspicion that the greatest threat to their future might lie not in the ravaged landscape, but within the very heart of their community. She was acutely aware that her dedication, her very existence as a problem-solver, had inadvertently made her a target, forcing her to confront the disheartening truth that even the most earnest attempts to build a better world could breed envy, fear, and ultimately, destruction. The struggle for survival had become a deeply personal one, a battle not just for resources, but for the very soul of their shared endeavor.

The encroaching twilight painted long, distorted shadows across the settlement, each one a phantom of unease for Luis. His gaze, usually steady and focused on the nascent life within his small plot, now darted with a new, sharp vigilance. The gentle rustle of the wind, once a soothing murmur, now carried the sharp edge of suspicion. It whispered through the hardy stalks of the invasive tubers, each movement a potential prelude to another act of senseless destruction. He clutched the worn wooden handle of his digging hoe, the rough texture a familiar comfort, yet in his hands, it felt less like a tool of cultivation and more like a clumsy weapon. The night was no longer a period of rest, but an extension of his workday, a crucial vigil.

He had never considered himself a guardian. His hands were meant for coaxing life from barren soil, for understanding the subtle needs of a struggling plant. But the sight of those mutilated tubers, ripped from the earth with a brutal, almost gleeful abandon, had ignited something primal within him. It was more than just the loss of food; it was an assault on hope, a deliberate act of extinguishing a future he had so painstakingly nurtured. He felt the weight of every seed he had sown, every watering can he had emptied, every weed he had meticulously uprooted. These weren't just plants; they were the tangible results of his tireless efforts, a testament to his contribution to their precarious existence. To see them ravaged was to see a piece of himself desecrated.

His small garden, a patch of resilience carved out of the scarred earth, had become his sanctuary, and now, his battleground. He had reinforced the flimsy fencing, weaving scavenged wire and tough, pliable branches into a more formidable barrier. He had dug shallow trenches around the perimeter, not deep enough to impede growth, but enough to make stealthy approach a noisy, clumsy affair. Each night, he took up his post, a silent sentinel against the encroaching darkness and the unseen enemies it concealed. He would find a spot near the edge of his plot, shrouded by the sparse foliage, his senses honed to the subtlest sound – the snap of a twig, the scuff of a boot, the hushed exchange of words.

He found himself replaying the events of the past few days, the whispers and accusations that had rippled through the settlement like a poison. He had heard them, of course. The murmurs about Mika's "artificial" creations, the complaints that progress was making them "soft," that they were "upsetting the balance." He hadn't fully understood the depth of the resentment until his own livelihood, his own contribution, had been targeted. Now, the words resonated with a chilling clarity. It wasn't just about Mika's water filters or the solar arrays; it was about anything that challenged the status quo, anything that represented a departure from the harsh, unforgiving simplicity of the past. And he, with his stubborn dedication to cultivating these tenacious, life-giving plants, had become a symbol of that change.

The irony was not lost on him. He, a man of quiet habits and simple needs, was now embroiled in a conflict that felt far larger than himself. He had always found solace in the predictable rhythms of nature, the steady cycle of growth and decay. But this was different. This was the unpredictable, irrational chaos of human emotion – fear, jealousy, resentment – twisted into a destructive force. He couldn't fathom how anyone within their community, people who shared the same struggle, the same hope for survival, could inflict such damage.

He remembered the day he had discovered the devastation. The sun had been climbing, painting the dew-kissed leaves with a soft, golden light, a morning that promised sustenance. He had approached his plot with the familiar anticipation of tending to his plants, only to be met with a scene of brutal disarray. The tubers, usually nestled securely in the earth, were strewn haphazardly, their roots torn, their flesh bruised and exposed. Some were crushed, their precious stores of energy splattered on the ground. The air, usually alive with the earthy scent of soil, was now tainted with the acrid tang of destruction. A cold dread had settled in his stomach, heavy and suffocating. He had felt a surge of anger, hot and blinding, but it had quickly given way to a profound sense of bewilderment. Who? Why?

He had knelt, his calloused fingers gently touching a bruised tuber, trying to assess the extent of the damage. His initial thought had been wildlife, but the nature of the damage was too precise, too deliberate. This wasn't the opportunistic raid of a hungry animal; this was an act of calculated malice. The precise way the plants had been uprooted, the almost surgical severing of some roots, spoke of a human hand. And that realization was far more terrifying than any wild beast.

His nights became a blur of wakefulness, punctuated by the chirping of insects and the distant, mournful cry of scavengers. He forced himself to stay alert, his senses on high alert. He would sip lukewarm water from his canteen, his mouth dry and tasting of dust, and scan the darkness, searching for any anomaly, any movement that seemed out of place. He trained his eyes to distinguish the familiar shapes of the settlement's structures from the fleeting silhouettes of intruders. The security lights, meager as they were, cast a pale, flickering glow that did little to dispel the oppressive darkness, but it was enough to catch the glint of something metallic, or the tell-tale ripple of disturbed earth.

He tried to rationalize it. Perhaps it was an accident, a misunderstanding. But the deliberate nature of the damage to Mika's filter, and now to his garden, argued against such optimism. These were not isolated incidents. They were connected, part of a pattern of sabotage that threatened to unravel the very fabric of their community. He thought of the hushed conversations he'd overheard, the veiled criticisms directed at Mika and her efforts. Were these the same people? Were they so afraid of change, so resistant to progress, that they would resort to such desperate measures?

The thought that the enemy might be someone he knew, someone he shared meals with, someone he had perhaps even exchanged pleasantries with, was a bitter pill to swallow. He had always believed in the inherent goodness of people, in their capacity for cooperation and mutual support, especially in their shared struggle for survival. This was a betrayal of that belief, a stark reminder that even in the face of common adversity, the seeds of discord could still take root.

One night, a sound, distinct from the usual symphony of the nocturnal world, pierced the quiet. It was a faint, rhythmic scraping, coming from the direction of the eastern perimeter, not far from his garden. He froze, his heart pounding against his ribs like a trapped bird. He pressed himself deeper into the shadows, his hoe held ready, its edge glinting dully in the sliver of moonlight. He strained his ears, trying to pinpoint the source of the noise. It was faint, intermittent, as if someone was trying to move stealthily, but failing.

He waited, every muscle tensed, for what felt like an eternity. The scraping stopped. Then, a low murmur, too indistinct to make out words, reached him. He peered through the sparse vegetation, his eyes scanning the area. He saw nothing but the play of light and shadow. But the feeling of unease, of a tangible presence just beyond his sight, was overwhelming. He stayed in his hiding spot, unmoving, until the first hint of dawn began to lighten the eastern sky. The sounds, whatever they were, had ceased.

As the sun finally broke over the horizon, casting a warm, reassuring glow, Luis emerged from his vigil, weary but undeterred. He surveyed his garden, his gaze sweeping over the resilient plants that had, against all odds, survived the night. The reinforced fencing held firm. The shallow trenches were undisturbed. He breathed a sigh of relief, a small victory in the face of mounting tension. But the memory of the sound, the phantom murmur, lingered. It was a constant reminder that his vigilance was necessary, that the threat was real and ever-present.

He began to work, his movements methodical, almost ritualistic. He checked the soil moisture, gently loosened the earth around the base of a few of the more mature tubers, and meticulously removed any stray weeds that had dared to sprout. As he worked, his mind drifted back to the words he had overheard, the insinuations that their progress was "unnatural." He didn't understand that. Was the cultivation of plants unnatural? Was the purification of water unnatural? What was natural, then? The slow, inevitable decay of their world? The hunger that gnawed at their bellies? The thirst that parched their throats?

He saw his garden, and Mika's carefully maintained systems, not as a disruption, but as a defiance. They were acts of rebellion against the desolation, against the forces that sought to push them back into a primitive, desperate existence. They were proof that even in the harshest of environments, life, and progress, could find a way. He felt a surge of quiet pride, a determination to protect what he had helped to build.

He observed the other settlers with a new, critical eye. He saw the faces of those who seemed to resent Mika's innovations, the ones who spoke with longing for a past that was irrevocably lost. He saw the apprehension in the eyes of those who felt left behind, who didn't understand the technology, who feared being excluded. He understood their fear, their uncertainty. But he couldn't condone their destructive response. There had to be another way.

He continued his nightly vigils, the digging hoe always within reach. He became intimately familiar with the sounds of the settlement at night – the creak of the wind turbines, the distant hum of the bio-filters, the scuttling of small creatures in the undergrowth. Any deviation from this familiar soundscape would trigger his immediate attention. He started to notice subtle signs that might have escaped him before – a footprint too deep in the mud near the perimeter, a branch broken in a way that didn't seem natural, a faint scent of something out of place.

He even began to develop a rudimentary system of observation, noting down any anomalies in a small, tattered notebook he kept tucked in his tunic. The time, the location, the nature of the observation, however minor. It was his own small attempt to bring order to the chaos, to find a pattern in the apparent randomness of the sabotage. He knew it was a long shot, that his observations might lead nowhere, but the act of documenting, of actively seeking to understand, gave him a sense of purpose beyond mere defense.

He remembered a conversation he'd had with Mika a few weeks ago, before the sabotage had escalated. She had been explaining the complex interplay of microbial cultures and nutrient cycling in the algae farms, her eyes alight with the passion for her work. He hadn't understood all the technical jargon, but he had understood her conviction, her unwavering belief that these systems were crucial for their survival. He had nodded, offering a simple, "It sounds like you're building a future, Mika." Now, he knew that building a future was a dangerous act in their fractured world, an act that invited not only admiration but also fear and hatred.

The weight of his self-imposed duty was heavy. Sleep became a luxury he could rarely afford, and when he did drift off, his dreams were filled with images of uprooted plants and broken machinery. But with each passing night, his resolve only seemed to harden. He would not let these acts of vandalism go unchallenged. He would stand guard, a silent guardian of the fragile seeds of hope, determined to protect the future he believed in, even if it meant facing the darkness alone. He found a strange sort of peace in his vigilance, a sense of purpose that transcended his weariness. He was no longer just a cultivator; he was a protector, a silent sentinel standing between his community and the encroaching shadows of fear and destruction. His quiet determination was a small beacon of defiance in the encroaching gloom, a testament to the enduring strength of the human spirit, even when faced with the darkest manifestations of its own failings.

Jax moved with a practiced stillness that belied the turmoil brewing beneath the surface of Haven. His optical recorder, a sleek, almost invisible device integrated into a worn leather wristband, hummed with a low, almost imperceptible frequency. It was an extension of his senses, a silent witness to the creeping shadows of discord. He'd spent weeks meticulously documenting the everyday rhythms of the settlement: the synchronized clang of the hydroponics bays, the murmur of the water purifiers, the drone of the solar arrays soaking up the relentless sun. Now, his focus had shifted, honing in on the subtle dissonances, the discordant notes in Haven's otherwise carefully orchestrated harmony.

He found himself drawn to the periphery, to the spaces where conversations died and eyes darted away. It wasn't always about outright confrontation; often, it was the unspoken, the implied, that held the most weight. He saw it in the way certain individuals clustered together, their voices low and urgent, their gazes often sweeping towards the more technologically advanced sectors of Haven, particularly Mika's hub and the nascent agricultural plots. He'd captured a series of images, almost impressionistic in their ambiguity, of a group of elders – men and women who had weathered the initial collapse with a fierce adherence to old ways – gathered near the crumbling remnants of the old world, their faces etched with a mixture of nostalgia and something harder, something that bordered on resentment. Their gestures were sharp, their expressions tight, and the undertone of their hushed dialogue, even through the muffled audio capture of his device, was one of disapproval, of a deeply ingrained skepticism towards the new methods of survival.

One afternoon, while ostensibly calibrating a sensor array near the western perimeter, Jax's attention was snagged by a hushed exchange beneath the skeletal remains of a pre-Collapse overpass. It was Kael, a burly man whose hands were as skilled with a wrench as they were with the crude defenses of Haven, speaking with Elias, a former community leader whose influence had waned with the rise of Mika's technological solutions. Jax remained partially obscured by a rusted girder, his recorder zoomed in. Kael's body language was tense, his usual boisterous energy subdued. Elias, his face a mask of practiced diplomacy, gestured emphatically, his words too soft to be clearly distinguished, but the visual cues were potent: a subtle shake of the head from Kael, followed by Elias placing a hand on Kael's shoulder, a gesture that seemed to convey a mixture of appeasement and urgency. Jax zoomed in on Kael's face as he finally spoke, his voice a low growl captured by the recorder: "They call it progress, Elias. I call it a betrayal of what we are. We're forgetting how to bleed, how to truly survive." The words hung in the air, heavy with unspoken implications. Jax cataloged the interaction, tagging it with keywords: Kael, Elias, resentment, dialogue, perimeter, unease.

Later that week, during the communal meal – a sparse but vital ritual of unity – Jax observed a subtle shift in dynamics. Elara, a fierce advocate for Mika's sustainable farming techniques, was explaining the efficiency of the new nutrient delivery system to a small group. Jax, positioned at a discreet distance, his recorder discreetly scanning the room, noticed that several members of the "traditionalist" faction, led by the elder Silas, deliberately turned away, their conversation becoming more animated amongst themselves, their laughter a little too loud, a little too forced. Silas himself, his gaze fixed on Elara with an expression that was difficult to decipher – a blend of scorn and perhaps a touch of pity – was seen to subtly shake his head, a gesture lost on most, but a clear signal to those who watched him. Jax's recorder caught a fleeting micro-expression on Silas's face, a tightening around the eyes that spoke volumes about his disapproval, his deeply rooted resistance to anything that veered from the harsh pragmatism of their immediate past.

Jax wasn't an investigator by nature. His skills lay in observation, in the silent accumulation of data. He believed in the power of evidence, in the way that small, seemingly insignificant details could coalesce to form a larger, undeniable truth. He began to spend more time in the less-trafficked areas of Haven – the abandoned sectors, the forgotten storage bays, the edges of the settlement where the salvaged technology met the encroaching wilderness. It was in these liminal spaces that the seeds of discord seemed to find the most fertile ground.

He witnessed furtive meetings, brief and shadowed. A quick exchange of what appeared to be a small, metallic object between two individuals near the atmospheric processors, followed by nervous glances in every direction. He captured the image of a woman, known for her quiet but staunch support of Mika's initiatives, pausing abruptly as she noticed someone watching her from a shadowed alcove; her subsequent haste and averted gaze were damning. These weren't direct acts of sabotage, not yet, but they were the subtle tremors preceding an earthquake, the hushed plotting that hinted at a growing divide.

He meticulously documented these moments, cross-referencing them with his growing database of Haven's inhabitants. He noted who met with whom, the times and locations, the general tenor of their interactions. He discovered patterns, not in overt actions, but in the subtlest of behaviors. The way certain individuals, particularly those who felt their traditional roles were being eroded by new technologies, would often find themselves congregating after dusk, their faces illuminated by the dim glow of salvaged lanterns, their expressions a mixture of frustration and quiet defiance.

One evening, Jax positioned himself overlooking a disused observation deck, its rusted railings a testament to a forgotten era. Below, in the deepening twilight, a small group had gathered. He recognized Kael, Elias, and a few others who had been vocal in their skepticism of Mika's more ambitious projects. They weren't arguing; their discussion was almost mournful, punctuated by heavy sighs and the occasional muttered phrase that spoke of lost skills and a perceived abandonment of their hard-won self-sufficiency. Jax's recorder captured Kael gesturing towards the distant, glowing hub of Mika's laboratory, his voice, though low, carrying a distinct edge of bitterness: "They build their towers, Elias, but they forget the foundations. What happens when the lights go out? Who will know how to mend the simple things?" Elias, his face shadowed, offered a quiet, almost resigned reply, "The winds of change are strong, Kael. Sometimes, they can erode even the strongest stone." Jax felt a prickle of unease. It wasn't just about technological advancement anymore; it was about a fundamental philosophical divide, a clash between two visions of survival.

His photographic evidence began to paint a picture, not of direct perpetrators, but of a brewing discontent, a palpable tension that was starting to fray the edges of their community. He captured images of Elias sharing what appeared to be maps with Kael, their heads bent low, their concentration absolute, suggesting a level of planning or strategizing beyond mere conversation. He photographed Silas, the elder, in quiet conversation with a younger man named Finn, a skilled but disillusioned mechanic, whose resentment towards the reliance on Mika's complex systems was well-known. The images showed Silas placing a reassuring hand on Finn's arm, his expression one of encouragement, as if sanctioning Finn's growing discontent.

Jax continued his silent surveillance, his optical recorder a tireless eye in the gathering storm. He observed a moment of accidental, yet revealing, interaction between Elara and a member of Silas's faction, Mara. Elara, her hands still faintly stained with nutrient paste from the hydroponics, had approached Mara to ask about a shared resource. Mara, her face impassive, had curtly dismissed Elara, her body language subtly recoiling, as if contact with Elara's "modern" work was somehow contaminating. The fleeting look of hurt on Elara's face, quickly masked by her characteristic resilience, was a stark illustration of the burgeoning animosity. Jax zoomed in on Mara's downcast eyes as she walked away, a subtle, almost imperceptible smirk playing on her lips, a chilling sign of her satisfaction in her small act of ostracization.

He also noticed a recurring theme: the subtle undermining of Mika's authority and innovations. Whispers of "unnatural" processes, of "playing God" with life, were amplified in hushed tones amongst certain groups. Jax captured a brief, almost surreptitious, meeting between Kael and Finn near the edge of the recycling plant. Kael seemed to be passing Finn something small and dark, which Finn quickly pocketed. The furtive nature of the exchange, the way they both scanned their surroundings before parting ways, suggested something more than a casual handover. Jax couldn't identify the object, but its clandestine transfer was a clear indicator of illicit activity.

The visual evidence was mounting, a mosaic of furtive glances, hushed meetings, and subtle gestures of discontent. Jax understood that he wasn't witnessing the act of sabotage itself, but the fertile ground from which such actions sprang. He was documenting the growing chasm, the slow, deliberate erosion of unity that paved the way for more overt acts of aggression. His recorder continued its silent vigil, capturing the nascent signs of discord, the visual whispers of a community on the brink of fracturing, each photograph a stark testament to the unseen observer's growing awareness of the insidious currents running beneath Haven's fragile surface. He was piecing together a narrative, not with words, but with irrefutable images, a silent chronicle of the seeds of discord being sown.

CHAPTER EIGHT
THE WHISPERING FLAMES

The air, once merely thin and carrying the metallic tang of the processors, now held a gritty weight. It settled on skin, in lungs, and on every surface, a constant, unwelcome reminder of the planet's weary sigh. The sun, a harsh, unfiltered orb in the bruised sky, beat down with an intensity that felt less like warmth and more like a deliberate, suffocating embrace. The prolonged dry spell was no longer a prediction whispered by the climate monitors; it was a palpable, choking reality. Every breath was an effort, each exhalation laced with the fine, grey particulate that coated everything in Haven, from the salvaged metal structures to the carefully tended hydroponic bays.

The whispers of the wind had changed. They were no longer the gentle sighs that sometimes offered a fleeting respite from the perpetual hum of survival machinery. Now, they carried a dry, rasping sound, like the friction of a thousand tiny stones being dragged across bare rock. It was a premonition, a low, insistent murmur that spoke of parched earth and brittle vegetation. Even the hardy, opportunistic flora that had managed to sprout in the cracks of the ruined landscape, those stubborn green veins that Jax had documented with cautious optimism, were succumbing. Their leaves, once a vibrant, defiant green against the grey, were curling inward, turning a sickly yellow, then a brittle brown. The invasive scrub, usually so tenacious, looked defeated, its branches desiccated and skeletal.

Jax felt it most acutely when he was outside the filtered confines of the main hab structures. The fine dust, invisible in the weak light of the settlement's interior, became a visible haze in the open air, swirling in lazy eddies that danced with an unsettling permanence. He would watch it, his optical recorder capturing the way it clung to his worn boots, the way it powdered the surfaces of the external sensors he was tasked with maintaining. He'd seen the water levels in the main reservoir dip, the reclaimed moisture systems working overtime to extract every last drop from the atmosphere, but it was a losing battle. The arid air seemed to drink their efforts with an insatiable thirst.

The communal gatherings, usually marked by a somber but steady rhythm, now carried an undercurrent of anxiety. Conversations, once focused on the day's tasks and the subtle machinations within Haven, inevitably drifted to the increasingly dire environmental conditions. Elara, her brow perpetually furrowed with concern, would present the latest data projections, her voice strained as she described the dwindling moisture reserves and the alarming rise in ambient temperature. Her reports, once met with a thoughtful silence, were now often punctuated by nervous coughs or the shuffling of feet. The visual acuity of Jax's recorder captured the subtle signs: the slight tremor in Elara's hands as she adjusted the holographic display, the way individuals would instinctively run a hand over their dry lips, the quick, almost furtive glances towards the sky, as if hoping to will rain clouds into existence.

Silas, the elder, remained a stoic presence, but even his pronouncements, usually a blend of stoic acceptance and subtle guidance, seemed to carry a new weight of gravity. He spoke of the old ways, of times when the land was more forgiving, but his words now held a less nostalgic, more cautionary tone. He'd recount tales of droughts from his youth, not as historical anecdotes, but as stark warnings. Jax's recorder, trained on Silas's weathered face during these pronouncements, noted the deepening lines around his eyes, the way his gaze seemed to fix on some distant, unseen horizon. He didn't offer solutions, not the kind that involved technological intervention, but his quiet pronouncements served to anchor the community, to remind them of their resilience, even as the ground beneath them turned to dust.

Kael, ever the pragmatist, was vocal about the immediate concerns. He'd often be seen inspecting the perimeter defenses, his large hands running over the reinforced plating, his brow furrowed in thought. He spoke of the increased risk, the heightened vulnerability. "This dry air," he'd grumble to anyone who would listen, his voice a low rumble that carried the grit of the environment, "it's like a tinderbox waiting for a match. One wrong spark, and everything we've built goes up in smoke." His words, once dismissed as the typical anxieties of a security man, now resonated with a chilling accuracy. Jax's recorder captured Kael pointing towards the desiccated scrublands that ringed Haven, his gestures sharp and urgent. He saw Kael discussing with Finn, the young mechanic, the state of the portable water pumps, their faces etched with a shared concern as they examined the stressed, vibrating machinery.

The pervasive dust meant that visibility was often limited. The sun, high overhead, bleached the landscape into a uniform palette of pale browns and greys. The distant, jagged outlines of the pre-Collapse ruins were often blurred, softened by the atmospheric haze. Jax found himself relying more on his audio sensors, the subtle shifts in the wind's pitch, the rustle of desiccated foliage, the distant, almost imperceptible crackle that might be the wind or something more... ominous. His optical recorder's enhanced thermal imaging struggled to differentiate between the ambient heat of the sun-baked earth and any potential nascent fires. The environment itself seemed to conspire to obscure and disorient, mirroring the growing unease within Haven.

The constant dryness had an effect on the very structure of their existence. The recycled water, while essential, had a faint, metallic aftertaste that was becoming more pronounced. Personal hygiene, always a carefully managed aspect of their enclosed lives, required more effort. The dust seemed to cling to everything, requiring constant wiping and cleansing. The hum of the air purifiers, a constant sonic backdrop to life in Haven, seemed to work harder, their whirring intensifying as they battled the encroaching particulate. Jax recorded the subtle visual cues of this strain: the slightly warmer housings of the purification units, the way the intake filters accumulated dust at an accelerated rate, requiring more frequent cleaning and replacement.

During one of his perimeter patrols, Jax noticed a new phenomenon. The wind, as it swept across the barren plains, was picking up more than just dust. It was carrying embers, tiny, incandescent specks that glowed briefly before being extinguished. He'd captured a series of high-resolution images of these fleeting sparks, their erratic flight paths a visual metaphor for the precariousness of their situation. He'd even felt the faint warmth of one on his exposed cheek, a terrifying sensation that sent a shiver down his spine despite the oppressive heat. The dry wind wasn't just a whisper of dust; it was becoming a carrier of nascent destruction.

The community leaders, including Mika, were not unaware of the escalating danger. Emergency preparedness drills, once conducted with a routine efficiency, now had a palpable urgency. Jax's recorder captured the hushed, intense meetings held in Mika's control center, the holographic displays showing alarming projections of fire spread, the simulated scenarios of potential ignitions. He saw Mika, usually so composed and analytical, her face illuminated by the glow of her data streams, her jaw tight with a worry that even her carefully constructed professionalism couldn't entirely conceal. He observed her engaging in extended dialogues with Kael, their discussions animated, their gestures conveying a sense of rapid problem-solving and a shared understanding of the imminent threat.

Elara, in her own domain, was working feverishly to find solutions. She was researching drought-resistant strains of the hardy grains they cultivated, experimenting with more efficient irrigation techniques that minimized water loss. Jax's recorder captured her long hours in the hydroponic bays, the sterile white of the environment contrasting with the wilting plants that were the subject of her urgent attention. He saw her poring over schematics, her face illuminated by the soft glow of a salvaged tablet, her brow furrowed in concentration. He also saw the frustration in her eyes when a particular experiment yielded disappointing results, a fleeting micro-expression that spoke volumes about the immense pressure she was under.

The elders, including Silas, held their own counsel, their discussions taking place in the quieter, more traditional spaces of Haven. Jax, from a discreet distance, observed them gathered around a salvaged, flickering lantern, their faces etched with the wisdom of experience.

They spoke of ancient fire-fighting techniques, of clearing brush, of creating firebreaks using methods that predated the widespread use of advanced technology. While Mika and her team focused on technological countermeasures, the elders offered a parallel approach, a grounding in the fundamental principles of survival that had served humanity for millennia. Jax's recorder captured Silas gesturing with a gnarled finger towards a faded diagram of a historical firebreak, his voice a low, resonant murmur that spoke of accumulated knowledge passed down through generations.

The narrative of the looming threat was reinforced by external signs. The local fauna, those few hardy creatures that had adapted to the harsh environment, were becoming more desperate. Jax had observed a small group of scavengers, their fur matted with dust, venturing closer to Haven than usual, their gaunt forms a visual testament to the scarcity of resources. He'd captured footage of them digging near the settlement's water collection points, their desperation palpable. These sightings, once unusual, were becoming more frequent, a clear indication that the entire ecosystem was under immense strain.

The constant, dry wind carried a sound that was becoming increasingly unnerving. It was a low, persistent hiss, punctuated by sharp cracks and snaps that sounded like dry twigs breaking underfoot. Jax, with his enhanced audio equipment, began to isolate and analyze these sounds. He recognized the natural creaking of stressed metal in the older structures, the rasping of dust against the solar panels, but there were other sounds, subtler ones, that he couldn't immediately categorize. A faint, intermittent popping, a low, guttural rumble that seemed to emanate from the very earth. He began to tag these sounds, compiling an auditory map of the settlement's increasing vulnerability.

His recorder's thermal sensors, usually a reliable tool for detecting heat signatures, were now often confused by the intense ambient heat. Distinguishing a potential fire from the sun-baked surfaces was becoming a complex algorithmic challenge. He spent hours calibrating his sensors, refining their sensitivity, trying to develop a protocol that could differentiate between residual heat and active combustion. The visual data was often ambiguous, requiring careful cross-referencing with audio cues and wind patterns. He captured images of Elara painstakingly monitoring the temperature readings from the perimeter sensors, her face a mask of intense concentration as she tried to filter out the noise of the environment itself.

The psychological toll of the persistent dryness and the threat of fire was also becoming evident. Jax observed a subtle shift in the community's interactions. There was an increased edginess, a shorter fuse. Minor disputes, usually resolved with a degree of patience, were now more likely to escalate. He saw Kael, usually so jovial, snap at Finn over a minor mechanical issue, his voice louder and sharper than usual. He captured the brief, tense exchange, noting the flicker of surprise and then hurt on Finn's face before he quickly regained his composure. These were small incidents, but they were symptomatic of a community under growing stress, a populace pushed to its limits by the relentless environmental pressure.

The elders, while offering wisdom, also provided a grounding in shared tradition. They organized small, informal gatherings where stories were told, not of the present anxieties, but of past triumphs, of times when Haven had faced adversity and emerged stronger. Jax's recorder captured these moments, the dim light illuminating the faces of the community members as they listened, their expressions shifting from worry to a quiet sense of shared heritage. Silas, in his measured voice, would speak of the importance of inner strength, of the resilience that came from understanding one's roots and supporting one another. These moments, while not directly addressing the fire threat, provided a vital emotional bulwark, a reminder of what they were fighting to preserve.

The dry wind continued its ceaseless lament, a constant auditory reminder of the danger. Jax found himself listening to it, analyzing its nuances, trying to decipher its silent language. He would often stand at the perimeter, his optical recorder scanning the horizon, his audio sensors picking up the subtle shifts in the wind's song. He was documenting not just the physical state of their environment, but the growing sense of apprehension, the palpable tension that hung in the air, as dry and suffocating as the dust itself. The warning was clear, carried on every gust, a relentless, parched premonition of what was to come if they failed to heed its somber message. The tinderbox was ready. It was only a matter of time before the spark.

The sun dipped below the jagged, dust-choked horizon, not with the gentle descent of a dying day, but with a harsh, abrupt plunge. The twilight that followed was not a soft unveiling of stars, but a deepening of the perpetual, bruised greyness that had become their sky. Jax stood at the observation deck, his worn boots tracing familiar patterns on the metal grating. The air, thick and gritty, offered little respite, each inhalation a deliberate act. He adjusted the focus on his optical recorder, its lens sweeping across the desolate western expanse, a panorama of scorched earth and skeletal remains of what was once vibrant flora. The wind, a constant, dry rasp against his exposed skin, carried the familiar scent of desiccated earth, but tonight, it seemed to hold something else – a subtle, acrid undertone, like burnt sugar and something far more primal, something that set his teeth on edge.

He'd been tracking the temperature anomalies for hours, subtle fluctuations that Elara had flagged as concerning. They were outliers, anomalies in the predictable ebb and flow of the arid climate. But as the last vestiges of daylight bled from the sky, the anomalies coalesced, coalesced into a visual phenomenon that stole the breath from his already labored lungs. A faint, nascent glow, an almost imperceptible blush against the deepening gloom, began to paint the western horizon. It was too low to be the lingering heat of the sun, too defined to be a trick of the dust. Jax zoomed in, his recorder's magnification pushing the limits of its optical capabilities. The glow intensified, a hesitant ember igniting in the vast darkness.

It began as a fragile flicker, like a distant, dying star. But within minutes, it was a palpable presence, a smudge of molten orange against the bruised canvas of the sky. The wind, as if sensing the change, seemed to pick up speed, its dry whisper transforming into a more insistent murmur, carrying with it the faintest, yet undeniably present, crackle. Jax's audio sensors, finely tuned to the subtlest sonic shifts, registered it first – a distant, erratic popping, like a thousand tiny embers colliding in the wind. Then, a low, resonant hiss, a sound that spoke of fuel consuming itself with an insatiable hunger. It was the sound of combustion, raw and untamed.

His heart hammered against his ribs, a frantic drumbeat against the monotonous hum of Haven's life support. He raised his hand, not in a gesture of alarm, but to steady himself as he adjusted his recorder's spectral analysis. The light was not uniform; it pulsed, it flickered, it ebbed and flowed with an unnerving life of its own. Shades of fiery red and incandescent orange began to bleed into the ash-laden atmosphere, pushing back the oppressive grey, casting long, distorted shadows across the barren landscape. This was no natural celestial event. This was a wildfire, a monstrous, elemental force unleashed upon their fragile existence.

He turned, his gaze sweeping across the faces of the few others who were still on the observation deck, drawn by the subtle shift in the environment. Elara stood by her monitoring station, her usual analytical calm replaced by a stark, dawning horror. Her fingers, usually flying across holographic interfaces, were frozen mid-air, her eyes wide as she stared at the encroaching inferno. Mika, her face grim and etched with the weight of command, stood beside her, her gaze fixed on the same horizon, a silent assessment of the unfolding disaster. Kael, his usual boisterous energy subdued, stood a little apart, his broad shoulders tense, his hand instinctively reaching towards his side where his repurposed plasma cutter usually rested. Even Silas, who had been observing the stars with a detached serenity, had turned, his ancient eyes squinting, his lips moving in a silent prayer or a word of caution.

The crackling grew louder, more distinct. It was no longer a subtle whisper carried on the wind, but a chorus of hungry flames. Jax amplified the audio feed, and the raw sound of burning brush, of dry vegetation surrendering to the heat, filled the small space. It was a visceral sound, primal and terrifying. It confirmed their deepest fears. The prolonged drought, the desiccated scrublands, the tinderbox conditions that Kael had so often warned about – they had all culminated in this. The post-cataclysmic environment, with its fragile ecosystem and weakened defenses, had become the perfect incubator for disaster.

"It's... it's closer than the projections anticipated," Elara stammered, her voice barely a whisper, strained against the rising din. She gestured frantically at her display, the lines of projected fire spread now wildly deviating from their predicted paths. The wind, their constant tormentor, had become their enemy's ally, fanning the flames and accelerating their relentless advance. The dry air, so inimical to life, was now the very medium that allowed the fire to surge forward with such terrifying speed.

Mika's voice, when it came, was clipped and urgent, cutting through the growing dread. "All personnel to their designated stations. Kael, initiate Level Three alert. Finn, secure the auxiliary water reserves. Elara, keep me updated on wind direction and speed, and any potential ignitions closer to the perimeter. Jax, continue visual and audio reconnaissance, but do not compromise your safety." Her words were a cascade of commands, a desperate attempt to impose order on the chaos that was rapidly descending.

Jax nodded, his gaze still fixed on the horizon, his recorder diligently capturing every nuance of the approaching conflagration. The glow was no longer a distant ember; it was a substantial wall of fire, a monstrous entity devouring the landscape. He could discern the fiery tendrils reaching upwards, licking at the darkened sky, painting the underside of the ash clouds with an infernal light. It was a scene of terrible beauty, a testament to the destructive power of nature, a power amplified by the world they now inhabited.

He zoomed out, his recorder sweeping across the immediate vicinity of Haven. The salvaged metal structures, the carefully maintained hydroponic bays, the solar arrays that hummed with their precious energy – all stood starkly illuminated by the unnatural light. They seemed impossibly fragile, specks of defiance against the encroaching inferno. He thought of the community, of the faces he'd seen in the communal hall just hours before, their conversations now a distant memory, replaced by the stark reality of this immediate threat.

He thought of the children, safely ensconced in the deeper, more protected sectors of Haven, unaware of the fiery specter looming on their doorstep.

The fire's crackle was now a distinct roar, a sound that vibrated through the very metal beneath his feet. It was a sound of consumption, of inevitable destruction. He could feel the heat, a subtle but persistent wave rolling across the plain, even at this distance. It was a testament to the immense energy being unleashed, an energy that threatened to consume everything they had painstakingly built, everything they had fought to preserve. This was not just a fire; it was a harbinger of oblivion, a stark reminder of their precarious existence on a wounded planet. The whispers of the wind had become a roar, the dry breath of the land now a raging inferno. The time for observation was over. The time for action, for survival, had begun. The first glow on the horizon was no longer a warning; it was a declaration of war.

He continued to document, his recorder capturing the subtle shifts in the fire's behavior. The wind, ever fickle, seemed to be gusting now, pushing the leading edge of the inferno in sporadic bursts. He saw patches of the fire leap ahead, igniting isolated pockets of dry brush and creating new fire fronts, making the overall shape of the conflagration a chaotic, unpredictable beast. The orange and red hues deepened, becoming more vibrant as the flames encountered more fuel. It was a terrifyingly beautiful spectacle, a maelstrom of heat and light consuming the desolate landscape.

"The wind is shifting," Elara's voice crackled over the comms, laced with urgency. "It's picking up speed from the northwest. It's... it's pushing it directly towards us."

Mika's terse reply followed. "Understood. Kael, report on perimeter status. Have you deployed the atmospheric suppressants?"

"We're deploying them now, Mika," Kael's voice boomed, strained with effort. "But the wind... it's so damn strong. They're not holding as long as we'd hoped. The scrub on the outer perimeter is already igniting in several places."

Jax's recorder picked up the distinct sound of the atmospheric suppressant canisters being fired from the outer defense turrets – a series of sharp, percussive blasts followed by a faint hiss. He zoomed in on the perimeter, his recorder capturing the brief, localized fogs of retardant that billowed out, attempting to form a barrier against the encroaching flames. But the wind was a relentless adversary, snatching the suppressant particles away, diluting their effectiveness before they could fully coalesce. He saw small ignitions occur just beyond the suppressant clouds, small sparks that quickly grew into flickering tongues of flame, only to be swallowed by the larger, more powerful inferno behind them.

He focused on the ground, his recorder's high-resolution optics picking up the frantic scurrying of small, desert-adapted creatures. They were fleeing their desiccated homes, driven by an instinct far older than any of Haven's technological defenses. These were the very creatures Jax had observed and documented, their resilience a source of his cautious optimism. Now, their desperate flight was a stark visual representation of the existential threat they all faced. He saw a family of burrowing rodents darting across the barren earth, their small bodies a blur against the encroaching orange glow, their destination uncertain, their only hope a blind flight from the destructive force behind them.

The roar of the fire was now a constant presence, a deafening symphony of destruction. Jax could feel the vibration of it through the deck plating, a low thrum that resonated deep within his bones. The air, already thin and dry, was becoming noticeably warmer, infused with the radiant heat of the approaching inferno. He could see the dust clouds that were being whipped up by the fire's intense updraft, creating a swirling vortex of ash and smoke that was beginning to obscure the already dim light. The sky, once a bruised grey, was now a chaotic tapestry of fiery oranges, reds, and a sickly, acrid yellow where the smoke began to dominate.

"The eastern flank is holding for now, but the western edge is accelerating," Elara reported, her voice tight with suppressed fear. "The wind is gusting at thirty-five klicks and rising. We're getting reports of ember showers reaching the outer solar arrays."

Jax swiveled his recorder, capturing the terrifying sight of incandescent particles raining down on the arrays. Some sparks pinged harmlessly off the hardened surfaces, but others found purchase in the accumulated dust and debris, igniting small, defiant fires that the automated maintenance drones were frantically attempting to extinguish. It was a desperate battle on multiple fronts, a struggle against an enemy that was both relentless and opportunistic.

Mika's voice was calm, measured, but carried an unmistakable edge of command. "Kael, pull back the perimeter teams if they are in immediate danger. Prioritize personnel safety. Finn, activate the reserve water pumps. We need every drop we can get for the internal fire suppression systems. Jax, maintain your position if it is safe, but do not hesitate to retreat. We need eyes on the fire, but not at the cost of losing you."

Jax understood. His role was to observe, to record, to provide critical data. But he was also a part of this community, a lifeblood within Haven's intricate system. He would not be the first to retreat, but he would not be foolish. He adjusted his recorder's night vision and thermal imaging capabilities, preparing for the increasing darkness and the potential for the fire's heat signature to become the dominant visual element.

The crackling intensified, morphing into a deep, guttural roar that seemed to shake the very foundations of Haven. He could feel the heat now, a tangible wave washing over the observation deck, making the metal under his boots warm to the touch. The smell of burning vegetation was overpowering, acrid and suffocating, a stark reminder of what was being lost. He saw the flames cresting the low hills to the west, a horrifyingly beautiful wall of fire advancing with terrifying speed. It was a primal force, untamed and unforgiving, bearing down on their fragile sanctuary. The fight for survival had truly begun, and the first glow on the horizon had now become an all-consuming inferno.

The immediate threat of the encroaching wildfire had irrevocably shifted Mika's focus. The architect of Haven's nascent agricultural systems, the visionary who had painstakingly coaxed life from the barren earth, now found herself tasked with the grim, yet utterly essential, duty of orchestrating its potential abandonment. The vibrant greens of the hydroponic bays, the promising sprouts in the soil enrichment labs – they represented hope, growth, a future. But that future was now precariously balanced on the razor's edge of survival. The embers weren't just falling on the solar arrays; they were falling on the very foundations of their existence.

Mika's characteristic drive, once channeled into the intricate dance of photosynthesis and nutrient cycling, was now redirected towards the complex, volatile choreography of an evacuation. Her mind, honed by years of problem-solving in the unforgiving environment of their world, began to process the unfolding disaster not as an insurmountable force, but as a colossal logistical challenge. The whispering flames on the horizon, which had sent tremors of fear through the community, were a deafening siren call to action for Mika. She moved with a renewed, almost frenetic, energy, her gaze no longer fixed on the potential for growth, but on the stark, undeniable imperative of preservation.

She established a dedicated command center within the deeper, more shielded levels of Haven. The familiar hum of the life support systems, usually a comforting constant, now served as a percussive backdrop to the urgent dialogues and rapid data streams that filled the air. Her primary concern was the dissemination of clear, actionable evacuation protocols. This wasn't a drill; this was a real-time crisis, and confusion would be as deadly as the flames themselves. She began by breaking down the community into manageable units, assigning responsibility and defining clear chains of command. Every individual, from the seasoned scouts to the youngest children, needed to understand their role, their immediate objective, and their designated safe zone.

Her technical acumen, so adept at designing irrigation systems and optimizing atmospheric processors, was now applied to the creation of intricate communication networks. Redundant channels were established, both within Haven's internal comms and through long-range emergency beacons. She worked tirelessly, her fingers flying across holographic interfaces, inputting data, cross-referencing schematics, and running simulations. The goal was to ensure that no one was left behind, that information flowed seamlessly, and that even in the face of overwhelming chaos, vital instructions could reach their intended recipients. She understood that in a crisis, effective communication was not a luxury; it was a lifeline.

The concept of "safe zones" had always been a theoretical component of Haven's long-term survival plans, a contingency for scenarios like this. Now, these theoretical spaces had to be identified, secured, and prepared with an urgency that bordered on desperation. Mika pored over topographical maps of the surrounding region, cross-referencing them with real-time environmental data. She factored in wind patterns, potential firebreaks, and the availability of any natural resources that could offer temporary refuge. She knew the limitations of these zones; the post-cataclysmic landscape offered few truly secure havens. But they were better than direct exposure to the inferno. Her analysis had to be swift, precise, and account for every variable, from the potential for flash floods from any unexpected rain to the presence of dangerous, mutated fauna driven from their habitats by the fire.

She initiated the process of identifying and prioritizing the most vulnerable members of Haven's population. The very young, the elderly, those with pre-existing respiratory conditions exacerbated by the air quality, and individuals with limited mobility – their needs were paramount. Mika ensured that specific evacuation teams were assigned to assist these individuals, equipped with specialized transport and medical supplies. She meticulously compiled lists, cross-checked against population registries, and ensured that each designated caregiver understood the critical importance of their charge's safety. Her own anxiety, a cold knot in her stomach, stemmed from the sheer scale of this undertaking and the immense responsibility resting on her shoulders. She was no longer just an innovator; she was a guardian, and the weight of that role was immense.

The initial deployment of atmospheric suppressants had been a valiant effort, but Kael's report confirmed their limited efficacy against such a powerful, wind-driven fire. Mika understood that these were temporary measures, buying them precious time, but not a solution. Her focus now shifted to the internal containment protocols and the secondary evacuation routes within Haven itself. She reviewed the blueprints of the habitat, identifying access points to the deeper subterranean levels, the reinforced bunkers originally designed for seismic events, and the sealed atmospheric zones. These would become their immediate refuges should the exterior defenses fail.

She remembered her early days, sketching designs for self-sustaining biodomes, envisioning a future where life flourished against all odds. That same passion for life, for its inherent value, now fueled her efforts to protect it from annihilation. She worked alongside Elara, her scientific mind a perfect complement to Elara's analytical prowess. They analyzed sensor readings, predicted fire behavior, and constantly recalculated the optimal evacuation routes. Elara's data streams, once focused on atmospheric composition and soil nutrient levels, now painted a terrifying picture of thermal fronts, ember trajectories, and wind shear patterns.

"The western quadrant is proving highly volatile, Mika," Elara reported, her voice a low, steady hum over the comms, despite the visible strain on her face. "The wind is pushing the main front with unprecedented speed. Our projections for containment are... optimistic at best. We're seeing secondary ignitions miles ahead of the main body."

Mika absorbed the information, her mind already racing through contingency plans. "Understood. What are the current wind speeds and projected direction in the next six hours?"

"Thirty-eight klicks and rising, primarily from the northwest. The simulation indicates a potential shift towards north-northwest within the next three hours, which would further accelerate the western advance. If the wind pattern holds, it will be directly upon us within eight hours, possibly less."

Eight hours. The words hung in the air, heavy with unspoken dread. Eight hours to evacuate a community, to move hundreds of people and essential resources through potentially compromised pathways, all while a wall of fire advanced with relentless fury. Mika took a deep, steadying breath, the recycled air doing little to calm her racing heart. She had to remain calm, to project an aura of control, even as the inferno roared outside. Panic was a contagion she could not afford to spread.

"Kael," Mika's voice cut through the tense atmosphere, firm and unwavering. "Initiate the 'Deep Shelter' protocol for Sector Gamma and Delta. Prioritize the children and the infirm. Ensure all personnel in those sectors are accounted for and moved to the sub-levels. Deploy auxiliary power to the bunker access points and seal them once cleared."

"On it, Mika," Kael's voice responded, a gruff affirmation of his readiness. He was a warrior, a pragmatist, and in this moment, his unwavering obedience was a bulwark against the encroaching chaos.

"Finn, I need an update on the auxiliary water reserves," Mika continued, her gaze sweeping across a holographic display of Haven's internal infrastructure. "Are the pumps primed and ready for direct feed to the internal suppression systems? We need to be prepared for breaches."

"Pumps are operational, Mika. Reserves are at ninety percent capacity. We're diverting all non-essential power to ensure maximum pressure if needed. The internal teams are prepped and ready with portable extinguishers and fire blankets, but you're right, we need to prepare for the worst." Finn's voice was tinged with a similar urgency, but also with a quiet determination.

Mika's attention then turned to Jax, whose observational posts were now crucial for real-time intelligence. "Jax, your priority is to maintain a secure vantage point for as long as possible. We need continuous updates on the fire's behavior, any significant changes in its intensity, direction, or speed. If your position becomes compromised, retreat to the nearest designated safe point and relay your data. Your eyes on the ground are invaluable."

"Understood, Mika," Jax replied, his voice steady despite the sounds of crackling in the background of his comms feed. "I'm documenting the ember showers and their proximity to the structures. The heat is increasing noticeably even at my current location."

Mika acknowledged his report with a curt nod, though he couldn't see it. The heat. It was a physical manifestation of their threat, a tangible wave of destruction bearing down on them. She glanced at a small, framed photograph on her console – a younger Mika, standing amidst a vibrant, thriving greenhouse, her face alight with the joy of creation. It was a stark contrast to the grim reality she now faced. But it was also a reminder of what they were fighting for.

She initiated the community-wide alert, a series of pulsing red lights and a low, resonant tone that signaled the activation of emergency protocols. The message, broadcast across all internal channels, was clear and concise: "This is Mika. A significant wildfire is approaching Haven. All personnel are to proceed to their designated sector assembly points immediately. Follow instructions from your assigned evacuation teams. Prioritize the safety of the vulnerable. Repeat, this is not a drill. Proceed to your assembly points."

Her own anxiety was a constant undercurrent, a thrumming beneath her outward composure. The responsibility for the lives of hundreds weighed heavily on her. She had designed systems to foster life, to make it thrive. Now, she had to design systems to ensure it endured, to orchestrate its escape from the jaws of oblivion. The intricate web of protocols she was weaving was a testament to her resilience, her unwavering commitment to her community. She was no longer just an architect of growth; she was an architect of survival, and her designs would be tested by the fiercest fire they had ever faced.

The hours that followed were a blur of activity, a symphony of controlled urgency. Mika, at the heart of the command center, remained the steady hand, the clear voice in the storm. She fielded reports, rerouted teams, and made split-second decisions based on the rapidly evolving situation. She saw her meticulously crafted plans put into action, witnessing the community's disciplined response, a testament to the preparedness and training they had undergone. But she also saw the fear in the eyes of those around her, a fear that she had to constantly quell with her own resolve.

She monitored the progress of the evacuation, her gaze flicking between the holographic displays that showed personnel movement within Haven and the external sensors that tracked the fire's relentless advance. The sound of the inferno, a distant roar that had grown steadily louder, now seemed to vibrate through the very metal of the habitat. The air within Haven, once so carefully regulated, began to carry a faint, acrid scent, a chilling premonition of the external atmosphere's contamination.

Elara's voice crackled, laced with a new urgency. "Mika, we're detecting significant heat signatures around the eastern perimeter solar arrays. It looks like they're igniting. The fire's reach is extending further than anticipated."

Mika's jaw tightened. The solar arrays were their primary source of power, their lifeblood. Their loss would cripple their defenses and significantly hamper any chance of sustained survival. "Understood. Kael, assess the damage to the arrays and the integrity of the outer wall in that sector. If there's any risk of breach, prioritize sealing and reinforcing the internal defenses. We cannot afford a direct ingress."

"We're seeing multiple ignitions along the eastern fence line, Mika," Kael reported back, his voice strained. "The suppressants are overwhelmed. It's... it's bad. The metal is glowing in places."

Mika's mind raced. The fire was a hydra, and every time they severed a head, two more seemed to sprout. She had to make a difficult decision, a decision that would sacrifice a vital resource for the immediate safety of the community. "Finn, if the arrays are beyond salvage, initiate the automated shutdown sequence. We need to conserve the internal power reserves. Divert all available energy to the life support systems and internal fire suppression. We'll have to operate on emergency power for an extended period if necessary."

"Acknowledged, Mika," Finn replied, his voice somber. The loss of the solar arrays was a significant blow, a testament to the fire's destructive power. It meant a future plunged into deeper twilight, reliant on finite stored energy.

Mika continued to coordinate, her resolve hardening with each new challenge. She understood that the protocols she had devised were not merely procedures; they were the manifestation of her hope, her belief in their collective will to survive. She was transferring not just people, but the very essence of Haven – its knowledge, its spirit, its potential for a future – to the deeper, more secure levels. Her focus remained on the preservation of life, on ensuring that the whispers of the flames did not become the final eulogy for their community. Her anxiety hadn't vanished, but it had been transmuted into a fierce, unwavering determination. The architect of creation was now the architect of salvation, and she would not falter. She would ensure that Haven, in whatever form it took, would endure.

The roar of the approaching inferno was no longer a distant threat; it was a visceral presence, a physical wave of heat that pressed against the dwindling sanctuary of Haven. Inside the hastily established command center, the air, though still breathable thanks to the life support systems, was thick with a tension that mirrored the smoke seeping through unseen cracks. Mika, her face etched with fatigue but her eyes burning with an unwavering focus, had just finished coordinating the initial phase of the internal evacuation. The primary objective – getting the most vulnerable to the deepest shelters – was underway. But the external threat still loomed, a vast, insatiable maw inching closer.

It was then that Kiley's voice, rough and commanding, cut through the low murmur of anxious chatter. "Mika, we need more than just hiding. We need to fight back, on our terms."

Mika turned, her gaze meeting Kiley's. Kiley, the community's most seasoned survivalist, a woman whose practical skills were as legendary as her stoic demeanor, stood with a grim determination that was both reassuring and alarming. Her hands, calloused and strong, were already clutching a salvaged, heavy-duty axe.

"What do you have in mind, Kiley?" Mika asked, her voice betraying none of the gnawing uncertainty that she felt.

"A firebreak," Kiley stated simply, as if it were the most obvious solution in a world that had seemingly abandoned all logic. "A big one. We can't outrun this thing forever, and our suppressants are being overwhelmed. We need to create a gap. Something the flames can't cross easily."

Mika's mind, accustomed to the intricate dance of agricultural systems and atmospheric processors, grappled with the brutal simplicity of Kiley's proposal. A firebreak. It was a raw, primal strategy, born of necessity in a world that had long forgotten the luxury of untouched forests. It meant mobilizing the remaining able-bodied survivors, pushing them to their physical limits, and exposing them to the very danger they were trying to escape.

"It's... it's a massive undertaking, Kiley," Mika admitted, her brow furrowed. "The terrain is treacherous, and the fire is moving so fast. We don't have the heavy equipment for something like this."

Kiley gave a short, sharp laugh that held no humor. "We have hands, Mika. We have tools, scavenged and sharpened. And we have a will to survive that's stronger than any fire." She gestured to the handful of individuals who had gathered around, their faces a mixture of apprehension and grim resolve. "We've already started gathering what we can. Axes, shovels, makeshift pry bars. Anything that can tear at the earth and strip away the fuel."

Mika looked at the faces around Kiley. They were the builders, the engineers, the few who still possessed the physical strength and the mental fortitude to undertake such a grueling task. Their usual roles – tending to the hydroponics, maintaining the generators, scouting for resources – were temporarily set aside for this desperate gambit.

"The western flank," Kiley continued, her gaze fixed on a holographic map that displayed the encroaching fire front, "that's our best bet. The ground slopes there, and there's a natural clearing that we can expand. If we can clear a fifty-meter swathe, a hundred if we're lucky, we might just give ourselves a fighting chance. It'll be a hell of a lot of work, and it'll be dangerous as hell, but it's a chance."

Mika understood. Hiding in the deep shelters was a temporary reprieve, a postponement of the inevitable if the fire found a way in. A firebreak was an active defense, a physical assertion of their will against the encroaching destruction. It was a gamble, a desperate throw of the dice, but in the face of annihilation, gambles were all they had left.

"Alright, Kiley," Mika said, her voice firm, cutting through the rising tide of fear. "You have my full support. Mobilize everyone you can. Prioritize those with experience in manual labor and any who have demonstrated resilience under pressure. Jax, I need you to provide Kiley with the most accurate, real-time topographical data for the western sector. Mark out the optimal path for the firebreak, factoring in wind direction and potential ember spread."

Jax, who had been monitoring the external sensors, nodded curtly. His usual role was observation, but in this dire moment, his analytical skills were being repurposed to aid Kiley's monumental task. He began inputting data, his fingers flying across the holographic display, highlighting inclines, identifying areas of denser vegetation that would need the most attention, and flagging potential hazards like unstable rock formations.

"Kiley, who will be leading the effort on the ground?" Mika asked.

"I will," Kiley stated without hesitation. "I'll take the first shift. We'll work in rotations, as long as we can. We'll need water, medical supplies, and constant updates on the fire's progress. Finn, I'll need you to coordinate the resupply and medical teams. Make sure they're ready to move in quickly if needed."

Finn, his face grim, nodded. "Water carriers and first-aid kits will be staged at the western access point. We'll have a mobile medical unit ready to respond. My people will be on standby, but... tell them to be careful, Kiley. This isn't a training exercise."

Kiley's eyes, usually filled with a steely calm, held a flicker of something akin to fear, but it was quickly suppressed. "We know the risks, Finn. But standing still is a death sentence. We move, we work, we survive."

As Kiley and her assembled team began to move towards the western sector, a palpable shift occurred within Haven. The quiet desperation of the evacuation was replaced by a surge of determined, if anxious, energy. The sound of tools being gathered, the low rumble of salvaged vehicles being prepped for transport, and the terse, encouraging words exchanged between individuals formed a new soundtrack to their survival.

Stepping out of the command center and into the hastily prepared staging area near the western access point was like stepping into a furnace. The air, even this far from the main inferno, was thick with smoke, stinging the eyes and catching in the throat. The oppressive heat was a tangible force, sapping strength and making every breath a labor. Yet, the determined faces of Kiley's crew, silhouetted against the smudged orange glow of the horizon, were a testament to their unwavering resolve.

Kiley, now fully clad in reinforced, heat-resistant gear that looked more like repurposed industrial safety wear than anything remotely comfortable, surveyed the assembled group. There were about fifty individuals, a mix of men and women, their faces grim, their bodies tense with anticipation. They carried an assortment of tools: heavy-duty axes, their blades gleaming ominously; sturdy shovels, their edges sharpened to a dangerous point; saws, both manual and a few precious, jury-rigged powered ones that would need careful management of their limited energy supply.

"Listen up!" Kiley's voice, amplified by a portable comm unit clipped to her gear, cut through the rising hum of the approaching fire. "The fire's moving fast. The data suggests we have a maximum of six hours before it reaches this perimeter. That's not a lot of time. We need to create a buffer zone, at least fifty meters wide, all the way to the old ravine. It's going to be backbreaking work. The smoke will be thick. The heat will be intense. You will feel like you can't go on. But you

will go on. We are not going to be consumed. We are going to carve out a space for ourselves, a line in the dirt that this fire will not cross."

She gestured towards the landscape ahead, a tangled mess of desiccated scrub, brittle, fire-prone trees, and dry, crackling undergrowth. "Our objective is simple: remove all combustible material. Every leaf, every twig, every dead branch. We dig down to the bare earth if we have to. We clear it all. Jax's data will guide us.

He'll be marking out the precise path, showing us the areas that need the most work. Stay within the marked zones. Do not stray. And watch out for each other."

Kiley paused, her gaze sweeping over each individual, her eyes locking with theirs. "We work in shifts. Two hours on, one hour to rest and rehydrate. Water will be brought to you. Medical teams are on standby. If you feel unwell, if you can't breathe, if you're injured, report it immediately. Don't be a hero. We need everyone to finish this. We need everyone to survive."

The first wave moved out, a determined, grim procession heading towards the designated starting point of the firebreak. Kiley led the way, her axe swinging with a practiced, powerful rhythm, biting deep into the dry wood of a small, stunted tree. The sharp crack of splitting timber echoed against the deeper, more sinister roar of the approaching flames.

The work was brutal, unforgiving. The smoke was a constant torment, blurring vision and making breathing a desperate struggle. The heat was relentless, seeping through their gear, baking them from the outside in. Sweat poured from every pore, stinging their eyes and plastering their clothes to their skin. Each swing of an axe, each heave of a shovel, felt like an act of defiance against an overwhelming force.

Among the crew was Elias, a former engineer who had spent years meticulously calibrating Haven's atmospheric processors. Now, his strong hands, once accustomed to delicate instruments, wielded a heavy-duty saw, its whine a desperate song against the encroaching inferno. He worked alongside Anya, a botanist whose knowledge of plant life was now being used to identify and prioritize the most flammable species.

"This scrub is like tinder," Anya gasped, hacking at a patch of dry, brittle bushes with a sharpened machete. "It'll go up in seconds. We need to get it all cleared."

Elias grunted, his saw chewing through a thick, dead branch. "The earth itself feels baked. One spark and this whole sector could ignite."

Further down the line, a group of younger survivors, teenagers who had grown up within Haven's controlled environment, were tasked with hauling away the cleared debris. Their faces were streaked with dirt and sweat, their young bodies pushed to the absolute limit. They moved with a desperate energy, their youthful exuberance replaced by a grim determination born of shared purpose. They understood, perhaps more than anyone, what was at stake. This was their world, their only home, and they were fighting for its very existence.

Kiley moved through the ranks, her presence a constant source of encouragement. She didn't offer platitudes; she offered practical advice, a steadying hand, a brief word of shared resolve. She helped haul a fallen, burning branch away from the cleared path, her movements efficient and sure. She checked on individuals, offering a canteen of precious water or a quick word of encouragement.

"Keep moving, Rylan! Don't let that heat get to you. Focus on the next swing!" she'd call out to a young man struggling with a particularly stubborn root. To another, she'd say, "Anya, watch your footing. That ground's unstable."

The smoke was their most insidious enemy, not just for its physical discomfort, but for its ability to obscure the true progress and the encroaching danger. Visibility was often reduced to a few meters, forcing them to rely on the marked lines on the ground, the shouted instructions, and the gut feeling that something was terribly wrong. Occasionally, a gust of wind would whip the smoke aside, revealing a terrifying panorama: a wall of orange and red flames, impossibly tall, stretching as far as the eye could see, consuming everything in its path. The sound was deafening, a constant, hungry roar that seemed to vibrate through their very bones.

"It's getting closer!" someone shouted, their voice barely audible over the din.

Kiley's head snapped up. She squinted through the haze, her eyes scanning the horizon. "Jax! Status report!"

Jax's voice crackled over the comms, laced with urgency. "The main front is approximately two kilometers out. Wind speed is still high, pushing it directly towards us. We're seeing increased ember activity ahead of the main line. Sparks are landing further out than predicted."

Kiley's jaw tightened. Two kilometers. And the ember activity meant that sparks were already igniting fuel beyond the main fire line, potentially creating new fronts that would leapfrog their efforts.

"We need to accelerate!" Kiley yelled, her voice raw. "First shift, you've got another hour. Second shift, be ready to move in immediately! We can't afford to stop!"

The urgency rippled through the ranks. Exhausted bodies pushed themselves harder. The rhythm of chopping and digging became more frantic, more desperate. The concept of "rest" faded into the background, replaced by the singular, overwhelming imperative: finish the firebreak.

As the first shift neared the end of their grueling two-hour stint, a wave of intense heat washed over them. The air shimmered, and a shower of glowing embers began to fall around them. A collective gasp went up as a section of dry scrub, just beyond their cleared path, ignited with a terrifying whoosh.

"Fire!" someone screamed.

Kiley reacted instantly. "Water!" she roared, pointing to a nearby cluster of survivors who had been tasked with carrying large water bladders. "Get water on it! Don't let it spread!"

The second shift, already positioned and eager to take over, surged forward, their shovels and makeshift tools now being used not just for clearing, but for beating out small flames. The air filled with the hiss of water on burning embers and the acrid smell of wet ash. It was a brutal reminder of the fire's tenacity, its refusal to be contained.

For a few terrifying minutes, it looked as if their efforts were in vain. The fire, small but fierce, threatened to consume the edge of their painstakingly cleared zone. But the combined efforts of the first and second shifts, their movements desperate and coordinated, managed to contain and extinguish the blaze. The victory was small, hard-won, and came at the cost of further depleting their precious water reserves.

Kiley surveyed the scene, her chest heaving. The firebreak was far from complete, but they had managed to push back the immediate threat. The line they had drawn in the earth, though smudged with ash and scarred by small burns, was holding.

"We did it," she said, her voice hoarse, more to herself than to anyone else. "We held the line."

But the victory was tempered by the grim reality. The main fire front was still a significant distance away, and the ember showers were becoming more frequent, more intense. They had bought themselves time, but not necessarily salvation.

As the second shift settled into the grueling work, Kiley took a moment to lean against a sturdy, cleared tree stump, her muscles screaming in protest. She watched the survivors, their faces etched with exhaustion and fear, but also with a fierce, unyielding determination. They were a testament to the human spirit, a flickering flame of hope against the encroaching darkness.

She thought of Mika, back in the command center, orchestrating the internal evacuation, a different kind of battle being fought there. She thought of all the people they were fighting for, the children huddled in the deep shelters, the elderly, the sick. This firebreak wasn't just about saving their physical structures; it was about saving those precious lives, about giving them a chance to see another dawn.

The work continued, a relentless, backbreaking effort under a sky choked with smoke. Every swing of the axe, every shove of the shovel, was a prayer, a testament to their refusal to surrender. They were carving out their defiance, one meter of cleared earth at a time, a testament to Kiley's pragmatic, unyielding will to fight for every last inch of their survival. The fire raged, a monstrous entity of destruction, but on the western flank of Haven, a desperate, human-made barrier was slowly, painstakingly, rising to meet it.

The inferno was no longer a distant spectacle. It was a palpable entity, its breath hot and suffocating even at the periphery of Haven's hastily constructed defenses. Jax, his face grimy and his eyes narrowed against the stinging smoke, felt the primal urge to retreat, to burrow into the earth like the terrified creatures he'd sometimes glimpsed during his environmental surveys. But his purpose here was different. He wasn't fleeing; he was documenting. His camera, a battered but reliable piece of scavenged tech, was clutched in his gloved hand, its lens a singular, unblinking eye trained on the encroaching terror.

He moved with a calculated caution, his boots crunching on the parched earth. The air thrummed with a low, guttural roar, a symphony of destruction that seemed to vibrate in his very bones. The sky, once a familiar canvas of muted greys and occasional blues, was now a roiling, bruised canvas of ochre and crimson, choked with a dense, acrid smoke that obscured the sun. It wasn't just a visual assault; it was a sensory bombardment. The heat radiating from the fire front was an oppressive blanket, thick and heavy, making each breath a conscious effort, a deliberate act against the suffocating atmosphere.

Jax stopped, raising his camera. Through the viewfinder, the scene was both horrifying and breathtaking. The flames, impossibly tall, writhed and danced, a chaotic ballet of destruction. They leaped from the desiccated scrub, devoured dry trees with a ravenous hunger, and sent plumes of incandescent sparks spiraling into the already choked sky. It was a raw, untamed power, a force of nature unleashed, and for a fleeting moment, Jax felt a humbling sense of his own insignificance. But that feeling was quickly chased away by a surge of grim determination. This was his home, these were his people, and he had a duty to bear witness.

He began to photograph, his fingers instinctively adjusting the settings. He captured the sheer scale of the inferno, the way it consumed the landscape, leaving behind only blackened husks and smoldering earth. He zoomed in on the details: the molten glow of embers, the twisted, skeletal remains of trees, the way the heat warped the air, creating shimmering illusions on the horizon. Each click of the shutter was a small act of defiance, an attempt to freeze a moment of this cataclysm, to preserve it, to understand it, and to show others its terrible reality.

But the fire wasn't the only subject that demanded his attention. He panned his camera towards the firebreak, a stark, raw scar carved into the earth. There, amidst the choking smoke and the searing heat, were the figures of his community. They moved with a desperate, focused energy, their faces set in grim masks of exertion and fear. He recognized some of them: Anya, her normally gentle hands now wielding a sharpened machete with fierce precision, hacking at the dry brush; Elias, his brow furrowed in concentration as he maneuvered a salvaged saw through a thick, dead branch.

Jax moved closer, documenting their struggle. He captured the sweat beading on their brows, the grime caked on their faces, the sheer physical strain etched into their every movement. He photographed the makeshift tools they wielded, the determined set of their jaws, the way they encouraged each other with brief, shouted words lost in the roar of the fire. These were not soldiers, but ordinary people, thrust into an extraordinary, life-or-death struggle. Their courage was not the absence of fear, but the mastery of it, the decision to act in its presence.

He focused his lens on Kiley, the architect of this desperate defense. She was a whirlwind of motion, directing, assisting, her presence a steadying force in the chaos. He saw her pull a burning branch away from the cleared path, her movements economical and sure, a testament to her years of experience. He saw her pause to offer a canteen of water to a struggling survivor, her voice, though strained, carrying a tone of unwavering resolve. Jax captured the grim set of her shoulders, the steely glint in her eyes as she surveyed the ever-approaching threat. She was the embodiment of their resistance, a human bulwark against the encroaching destruction.

The smoke was a constant, suffocating presence, a tangible barrier that amplified the sense of isolation and danger. It swirled and billowed, obscuring vision, making it difficult to gauge the true proximity of the fire. At times, it would thin, revealing a terrifying panorama of flames, a monstrous wall that seemed to stretch to the very edges of the world. At other times, it would thicken into an impenetrable fog, reducing visibility to mere meters, forcing reliance on instinct and the faint, distorted voices carried on the wind. Jax documented this atmospheric assault as well, capturing the eerie, diffused light, the way the smoke painted the landscape in shades of muted orange and sickly yellow. He photographed the small, flickering lights of their work lamps, small beacons of humanity struggling against the overwhelming darkness.

He felt a searing heat on his cheek and instinctively flinched, raising his camera just in time to capture the terrifying spectacle. A shower of incandescent embers, glowing like malevolent stars, rained down around them, igniting patches of dry scrub just beyond their meticulously cleared firebreak. A collective gasp went up from the workers, followed by shouts of alarm.

"Fire!"

The word, a primal scream of warning, cut through the din. Jax didn't hesitate. He zoomed in, documenting the immediate ignition, the terrifying speed with which the flames took hold of the dry vegetation. He photographed the frantic efforts of the second shift, their movements a blur of desperate action as they rushed forward with water and shovels, beating back the encroaching flames. He captured the hiss of water on burning embers, the acrid smell that filled the air, the sheer terror in the eyes of those caught closest to the nascent blaze. It was a visceral, terrifying demonstration of the fire's relentless nature, its insidious ability to exploit any weakness, any lapse in their defenses.

For a few heart-stopping minutes, it seemed as if their hard-won gains were about to be undone. The small, fierce fire threatened to leapfrog their efforts, to consume the very edge of the cleared zone they had fought so hard to create. Jax documented this desperate battle, the raw, unvarnished struggle for survival. He focused on the determined faces, the sweat-soaked clothing, the sheer exhaustion that was etched into every line of their bodies, yet still they fought.

When the immediate threat was finally extinguished, a collective sigh of relief, heavy with exhaustion, rippled through the ranks. Jax captured the aftermath: the smoldering remnants of the scrub, the blackened earth, the weary figures of the survivors, their faces streaked with ash and sweat. They had held the line, but it was a victory that came at a steep cost, evidenced by the dwindling water supplies and the heightened sense of urgency that now permeated the air.

He continued his photographic journey, moving along the firebreak, documenting the painstaking work that was still to be done. He captured the vastness of the landscape that still lay exposed, the seemingly endless expanse of dry, flammable material that remained a potent threat. He photographed the small, but crucial, details: the cleared earth, stripped bare of any potential fuel; the haphazard piles of debris that had been hauled away; the faint, but visible, markings on the ground that guided their relentless efforts.

As the shifts rotated, and the initial wave of exhaustion began to take its toll, Jax continued to document. He photographed the faces of those taking a brief respite, their bodies slumped with fatigue, their eyes distant, yet still holding a spark of resilience. He captured the way they shared meager rations of water, the quiet, almost ritualistic way they tended to minor injuries, their faces a testament to the sheer physical and mental toll of their endeavor.

He even found himself drawn to the periphery, to the very edge of the fire's reach. He wanted to capture the full scope of the threat, the raw, terrifying majesty of the inferno in its full glory. He ventured further, his heart pounding a frantic rhythm against his ribs, his camera held steady. The heat intensified with every step, the roar of the flames growing louder, more all-consuming.

Through his lens, he saw a world consumed by fire. Trees, once majestic, were now skeletal pyres, their branches writhing in the heat. The ground itself seemed to glow, an inferno mirrored beneath his feet. The air was thick with a swirling, incandescent haze, and the sheer force of the heat was almost unbearable, pressing in on him from all sides. He photographed the way the flames consumed everything in their path, the relentless, unstoppable march of destruction. He captured the stark contrast between the vibrant orange and red of the fire and the blackened, desolate landscape it left behind.

He documented the movement of the fire, the way it seemed to breathe and surge, propelled by the wind. He saw entire sections of the forest erupt into a chaotic inferno, the roar reaching a deafening crescendo. It was a terrifying spectacle, a raw display of nature's power that dwarfed human endeavor. But even amidst this overwhelming display of destruction, Jax found himself focusing on the small pockets of resistance, the faint, stubborn signs of life clinging to existence. He saw a lone, unburnt tree standing defiant against the onslaught, a testament to its resilience. He saw a small, dark patch of earth, somehow spared the flames, a promise of future growth. He felt a sudden, sharp blast of heat on his exposed arm, a reminder of the immense danger he was in. He knew he couldn't stay here much longer. His role was to document, not to become another casualty. He retreated, his camera still clicking, capturing the receding, yet still terrifying, spectacle of the inferno.

Back near the firebreak, he found Kiley overseeing the work, her face smudged with soot, her body moving with a weariness that was becoming increasingly evident. He approached her, lowering his camera.

"It's... it's immense, Kiley," Jax said, his voice hoarse. "The scale of it..."

Kiley nodded, her gaze fixed on the approaching fire. "We knew it would be. But we're not fighting it head-on. We're creating a space. A gap. Something it has to overcome, and in doing so, we slow it down, we give ourselves more time." She turned to him, her eyes, though tired, held a fierce resolve. "Did you get what you needed, Jax?"

"I think so," he replied, holding up his camera. "I captured the fire itself, the scale. And... I captured them. The ones working here. Their fight." He paused, then added, "It's... it's important that people see this. Understand what's happening."

"They will," Kiley said, her voice firm. "They will see it, and they will know what we endured. They will know what we fought for."

Jax continued to move amongst the survivors, his camera a silent observer. He documented the moments of quiet camaraderie, the shared glances of understanding, the small gestures of support. He saw a young woman offer her own water ration to an older man whose hands were trembling. He saw a group huddled together, sharing whispered words of encouragement. These were the moments that truly defined their struggle, the small acts of humanity that shone brightest against the backdrop of destruction. He photographed the weary faces of those taking their rest, the lines of exhaustion etched deep, but also the unwavering determination in their eyes. He captured the way they leaned against each other for support, the silent acknowledgment of their shared burden. Even in their exhaustion, there was a refusal to surrender, a quiet strength that pulsed through the entire group.

As the day wore on, and the inferno continued its relentless advance, Jax's camera became an extension of his will. Each photograph was a testament to their courage, a silent scream against the encroaching darkness. He documented the smoke-choked sky, the desperate efforts of the firebreakers, the sheer, terrifying majesty of the flames. His images were not just records; they were a narrative, a story of resilience, of a community fighting for its very existence, one cleared meter of earth at a time, against the terrifying, insatiable hunger of the whispering flames. He knew, with a certainty that chilled him to the bone, that his documentation was not just about preserving the past, but about ensuring a future, a future that was being forged in the heat and smoke of this desperate, brutal stand.

CHAPTER NINE

THE FIREBREAK BATTLE

The acrid bite of smoke had become a constant companion, a stinging reminder of the relentless maw of the wildfire. Yet, something remarkable was happening within Haven. The all-consuming terror, the primal fear that had threatened to splinter their fragile society, was instead acting as a potent, unifying force. The air, thick with the stench of burning pine and dry earth, also carried the hum of a shared purpose, a collective breath drawn in unison against the encroaching inferno. Jax, his camera still slung around his neck, now found himself observing not just the fire, but the intricate tapestry of human interaction it was weaving.

He'd witnessed it from the moment the alarm had been raised with more urgency than usual. Old Man Hemlock, his face a roadmap of stubborn lines, who had always grumbled about the 'newcomers' trampling the old ways, was now shoulder-to-shoulder with Lena, a refugee whose arrival had been met with quiet suspicion just weeks prior. Hemlock, his gnarled hands surprisingly steady, was using his years of experience felling timber to guide a crude, hand-cranked saw, clearing thicker underbrush that others struggled with. Lena, her movements precise and efficient, was working beside him, her focus absolute as she hacked away at tenacious, dry brambles with a scavenged sickle. There was no preamble, no awkward exchange; just the silent, urgent rhythm of shared labor. The fire had no time for old grievances.

Further along the hastily widened firebreak, a group usually found bickering over water rations or territory disputes were now engaged in a different kind of contest: who could clear the most ground. Young Finn, known for his reckless bravado and frequent run-ins with the council, was now the unlikely leader of a small brigade of older children and adolescents. Their energy, usually channeled into petty mischief, was now a whirlwind of determined activity. They hauled away debris, dragged fallen branches, and used their small frames to wriggle into tight spaces, clearing away every scrap of potential fuel. Their laughter, usually a raucous sound that grated on older ears, was now tinged with a shared exertion, a boyish competition to outdo each other in their contribution to the defense. Even Mrs. Gable, who usually confined herself to her small garden, meticulously tending her precious herbs, was there. Her usual sharp tongue was silenced, replaced by a quiet efficiency as she helped shuttle water and offered small, comforting words to those most visibly distressed by the heat and exertion.

Jax raised his camera, not to capture the flames for a moment, but to focus on these human interactions. He zoomed in on Hemlock and Lena, their faces etched with fatigue, but their eyes meeting with a flicker of respect, a silent acknowledgment of each other's worth. He captured the determined set of Finn's jaw as he barked instructions to his young crew, his youthful energy a beacon of hope amidst the grim reality. He saw Mrs. Gable offer a damp cloth to a panting survivor, her movements gentle, a stark contrast to the harshness of their surroundings. These were the details that mattered, the threads of connection being spun in the crucible of crisis.

Kiley, her face a mask of grim determination, was everywhere at once, her voice a constant, steadying presence. She moved between groups, offering practical advice, encouragement, and a firm hand where needed. She understood that this defense wasn't just about clearing land; it was about reinforcing the bonds that held their community together. She'd seen the cracks, the resentments, the quiet divisions that had festered in Haven. She knew that if they were to survive not just the fire, but the aftermath, they needed to find a way to bridge those divides.

"We need more hands on this section!" Kiley's voice, though strained, cut through the growing roar of the fire. "This is where the wind is pushing hardest. Elias, can you get that larger branch shifted? Margo, see if you can find more water for the southern line. Anyone who can carry anything, now is the time!"

Her calls were answered not with hesitation, but with a surge of renewed effort. The refugees, their faces often etched with a weariness that spoke of past traumas, were working with an intensity that belied their struggles. They had lost homes before; the fear was a familiar ghost, but this time, there was a different kind of hope. They were fighting *for* something, not just running *from* it. They saw the faces of the Haven residents, people who had initially viewed them with suspicion, now working alongside them, united by the same threat. It was a powerful, unspoken acknowledgment, a foundation for a future built on shared survival.

Jax felt a surge of emotion as he documented their efforts. He saw a young refugee woman, her hands blistered and raw, carefully tending to an older Haven resident who had stumbled, offering him a swig from her own nearly empty water skin. There was no language barrier in that simple, humane gesture. He saw a former council member, known for his rigid adherence to rules, now following the directions of a young woman who had arrived with nothing but the clothes on her back, her knowledge of the terrain proving invaluable. The old order was dissolving, replaced by a meritocracy of courage and necessity.

The firebreak itself was a testament to their collective will. It was a raw, uneven scar across the landscape, a messy but effective barrier. Where once there had been dense scrub and dry, whispering grasses, there was now a wide swathe of bare earth, punctuated by hastily piled debris. Every shovel-full of earth, every branch dragged away, was a victory, a small act of defiance against the overwhelming power of the inferno. Jax captured the sheer physical exertion, the strained muscles, the sweat-soaked clothes, but he also captured the determined expressions, the shared glances of encouragement, the quiet nods of acknowledgment that passed between strangers who were rapidly becoming allies.

Even the animals seemed to sense the shift. The normally skittish birds had fled, their panicked cries fading into the smoke, but the domestic animals, the few dogs and cats that remained, seemed to move with a subdued awareness, staying close to their human companions. Jax saw a scruffy mutt, usually a lone wanderer, now trotting faithfully beside Lena, its tail tucked low but its eyes fixed on her.

As the day wore on, and the sun became a hazy, distant disc through the smoke-choked sky, a profound weariness began to settle over Haven. Yet, with the weariness came a quiet sense of accomplishment. They had created their defense. They had pushed back the immediate threat, and in doing so, they had forged something more precious than a firebreak. They had forged a community. The old walls of distrust and division had crumbled, not under the force of any grand decree, but under the relentless, unifying pressure of the flames. Jax continued to photograph, his lens now focused on the quiet moments of shared relief, the slumped shoulders that spoke of exhaustion but not defeat, the hands clasped in silent solidarity. He saw the raw, undeniable truth: that in the face of utter destruction, humanity's greatest strength lay not in its individual might, but in its collective heart. The fire was a brutal teacher, but its lesson was one of unity, a stark, burning reminder that survival was a shared endeavor, a fight waged not alone, but together.

The cacophony of the wildfire was a symphony of destruction, yet beneath its roar, a new melody was emerging within Haven – the hum of coordinated effort. Kiley, a whirlwind of focused energy, was the conductor of this desperate orchestra. Her voice, raspy from smoke and exertion, was a constant thread weaving through the chaotic symphony. "More water on the western flank! It's starting to creep near the old storage shed!" she'd shout, her eyes scanning the horizon, perpetually searching for the next ember, the next surge of flame. She wasn't just barking orders; she was strategizing, adapting, her mind a rapid-fire calculation of risk and resource. The firebreak, a raw testament to their collective will, was not static; it was a living, breathing defense, constantly needing reinforcement, constantly threatened by the fire's insatiable hunger.

Under her implicit direction, the community had fractured into an intricate, yet surprisingly effective, network of specialized teams. There were the ground crews, their faces smudged with ash and sweat, wielding shovels and crude axes with a ferocity born of desperation. Their primary task was the relentless clearing of any flammable material. They moved with a grim, synchronized rhythm, a human chain passing debris further back from the fire's edge.

Each fallen branch, each tuft of dry grass, was a potential sacrifice, removed to deny the fire its sustenance. Among them, the familiar faces of Haven residents worked alongside the newcomers, their shared struggle erasing the lines that had once divided them. Old Man Hemlock, his back bent but his spirit unyielding, demonstrated the most efficient way to dig a shallow trench, his instructions punctuated by gruff coughs. Beside him, a young woman named Anya, whose hesitant arrival had been met with wary glances, now worked with a practiced hand, her movements sure and strong as she cleared a stubborn patch of gorse. The fire, in its indiscriminate fury, had become the ultimate equalizer, forcing collaboration where it had been reluctant to bloom.

Another critical contingent was tasked with the precious task of dousing. Their resources were meager – a collection of salvaged buckets, leaky barrels, and a few precious, hand-cranked pumps salvaged from defunct irrigation systems. This was the most dangerous work, requiring them to venture dangerously close to the encroaching flames, their faces shielded by damp cloths, their lungs burning with every breath. Water, once a mundane commodity, was now more valuable than gold. Every drop was accounted for, rationed with agonizing care. Lena, her movements economical and precise, had taken charge of a small team near the eastern edge, where the fire was licking at the edge of the dried-out marsh. She orchestrated the careful distribution of water, ensuring that the most critical areas received immediate attention, her calm demeanor a stark contrast to the inferno they faced. She'd seen such desperation before, the primal fear of thirst, and she understood the weight of every single drop.

Beyond the immediate firebreak, a third crucial group acted as the eyes and ears of Haven. These were the scouts, a mix of seasoned woodsmen and agile youths, tasked with venturing beyond the established perimeter to detect new outbreaks. Their job was perilous, requiring them to navigate the smoky, treacherous terrain, their senses heightened for the faintest scent of smoke, the smallest tell-tale glow. Luis, his face etched with a deep understanding of the land, was a natural leader for this group. He knew the hidden gullies, the wind patterns, the pockets of dry fuel that the fire would inevitably seek. He'd been a reluctant participant in many of Haven's council meetings, preferring the quiet solitude of the forest, but now, his knowledge was invaluable. He'd point with a dirt-stained finger, his voice barely a whisper above the crackling flames, "The wind is shifting. It'll push towards the old oak grove next, likely ignite the deadwood there." His insights allowed Kiley to redeploy resources, to anticipate the fire's next move, buying them precious time.

Mika, usually found tinkering with salvaged electronics in the quiet corners of Haven, had found her calling in the heart of the chaos. She had managed to cobble together a rudimentary communication network using a collection of old radio transceivers, their static-filled voices a lifeline connecting the disparate teams. Stationed at a makeshift command post – a cleared area near the communal hall, shielded by a hastily erected screen of tarps – she became the central nervous system of their coordinated effort. Her face was illuminated by the flickering screens of the radios, her fingers flying across the dusty dials, relaying crucial updates. "Ground crew on the western flank, Kiley reports increased activity near the shed. Repeat, increased activity near the shed. Need immediate water support." Her voice, amplified by a small speaker, cut through the din, a steady beacon of information. She was the conduit, ensuring that no team operated in isolation, that the right people knew what was happening where, and when.

The challenge was immense. The fire was a vast, unpredictable beast, and their resources were finite. But the beauty of their coordinated efforts lay not just in the efficiency of their actions, but in the transformation of their relationships. The old hierarchies, the petty grievances, the lingering suspicions – all were being consumed by the all-encompassing urgency of survival. Jax, his camera now a silent observer, captured it all. He saw the way a refugee, barely able to communicate in Haven's dialect, would nod in understanding when Kiley pointed to a section of the firebreak that needed clearing, then immediately set to work with a borrowed shovel. He saw the pride in the eyes of a young girl, no older than ten, as she proudly displayed a bucket of water she had hauled, her small contribution acknowledged with a warm smile from a hardened farmer.

Luis, with his intimate knowledge of the terrain, was not just identifying vulnerable spots; he was actively guiding the efforts to fortify them. He'd lead small teams into the denser patches of woodland that bordered the firebreak, teaching them how to quickly create "fuel breaks" by clearing underbrush and strategically felling smaller trees, creating gaps that would slow the fire's advance and give the main firebreak a better chance of holding. He'd explain, his voice low and steady, "The wind here funnels through this ravine. If we can clear this ridge, it'll create a natural backdraft, pushing the flames away from the main line." His instructions were not academic; they were born of years of walking these woods, of understanding their subtle language. He would point out the tell-tale signs of dry rot in tree trunks, the types of undergrowth that burned with the most ferocity, the hidden streams that, while perhaps dry on the surface, might still hold water a few feet down if a desperate digging was required.

Mika's radio transmissions were more than just factual reports; they were the threads that bound them all together. "Mika to Luis. Report from the northern scouts – possible flare-up near the old logging trail. Repeat, possible flare-up near the old logging trail. Advise caution." Her voice was calm, measured, even as she relayed potentially dire news. This calm projection was crucial; panic was as dangerous as the fire itself. She understood that her role was to maintain a semblance of order, to ensure that information flowed accurately and without delay, allowing Kiley and the team leaders to make informed decisions. She was the silent anchor in the storm, the one who kept them all connected, even when the smoke threatened to swallow them whole.

The collaborative efforts extended beyond the immediate task of fire containment. Kiley, ever practical, had also organized teams to secure the community's most vital resources. A group was dedicated to safeguarding the dwindling water supply, ensuring it wasn't wasted on non-essential tasks. Another was tasked with moving essential supplies – food, medical kits, blankets – to a more secure location, a small, rocky outcropping on the far side of the community that the fire was less likely to reach. This foresight, this planning for contingencies, was a testament to Kiley's leadership and the growing maturity of Haven's collective consciousness. They were not just fighting the fire; they were fighting for their future.

Jax watched as a group of younger children, their faces streaked with dirt and worry, were guided by Anya and Lena to form a bucket brigade, their small hands working with surprising speed. They weren't fighting the fire directly, but their contribution was vital, ferrying water from the creek to the dousing teams. It was a small act, but it was part of the larger tapestry of their coordinated defense. Anya, who had once been so shy, now spoke with confidence, her gestures clear and encouraging to the children. Lena, her eyes weary but kind, would offer a word of praise for each full bucket. The fire had given them a common enemy, but in fighting it, they were building something new: a shared sense of responsibility, a mutual reliance.

Luis's understanding of the land also extended to recognizing areas that, while appearing safe, held hidden dangers. He warned Kiley about a section of the firebreak that ran near a dense cluster of pine trees, their needles incredibly dry and flammable. "The heat is radiating off them," he explained, pointing. "Even if this line holds, the embers will jump and ignite them. We need to clear a wider buffer zone there, Kiley. Now." His warning was immediate, and Kiley, trusting his judgment, redirected a portion of the ground crew to that critical area. It was this constant communication, this interplay of Kiley's strategic oversight and the specialized knowledge of individuals like Luis, Mika, Lena, and Hemlock, that formed the backbone of their coordinated defense.

The synchronized efforts were not always perfect. There were moments of miscommunication, of fatigue-induced errors, of sheer terror that threatened to break the fragile order. But each time, the collective will of Haven reasserted itself. A dropped bucket was immediately retrieved by another. A hesitant step back from the heat was met with a steadying hand and a quiet word of encouragement. The fire, in its relentless advance, was inadvertently forging a community stronger and more resilient than any of them had ever imagined. They were no longer isolated individuals; they were a single, determined entity, each part playing its role in the grand, desperate battle for survival. The rhythm of their work, the shared breaths, the silent nods of understanding – this was the symphony of their resilience, a defiant melody against the roaring inferno. Jax continued to document, capturing the raw, unflinching spirit of a community finding its strength not in isolation, but in each other.

Mika's usual domain was one of quiet circuits and salvaged processors, of coaxing life back into dead tech. But the wildfire had a way of reordering priorities, of thrusting the unlikely into the heart of the inferno. Stationed at her makeshift communication hub, the crackle of static and urgent voices had become her new soundtrack, but her mind, ever analytical, had begun to dissect the threat not just in terms of communication, but in terms of physical defense. She couldn't wield a shovel or douse flames directly, but she could engineer, improvise, and defend. The firebreak was a crucial barrier, but embers, like desperate scouts, would inevitably leap over it, seeking new tinder. It was this insidious threat, the embers that threatened to reignite everything behind their painstakingly cleared line, that Mika began to focus on.

Her gaze, often fixed on flickering screens, now swept over the structures bordering the firebreak – the communal workshop, the granary, the storage shed that Kiley had worried about. These were the most vulnerable, their wooden frames and dry contents prime fuel for any stray spark. The existing defense was the firebreak itself, a scar of cleared earth. But what about the aerial assault? Mika's fingers, accustomed to delicate soldering, began to sketch out designs on a scrap of salvaged paper, her brow furrowed in concentration. She remembered the old, hand-cranked water pumps, relics of a time when Haven had a more robust water system before the wells had begun to falter. Most were rusted and seized, but in the communal workshop, amidst a chaotic jumble of tools and discarded machinery, she'd seen a few that might be salvageable.

"Jax, can you bring me those old pump mechanisms from the west shed?" she called out, her voice a little strained from the smoky air. Jax, his camera slung around his neck, nodded, his usual observant demeanor tinged with a new respect for Mika's quiet intensity. He understood that her current project was as vital as any shovel-wielding crew. Within minutes, he returned, dragging two heavy, grimy contraptions. Mika examined them, her fingers probing for weak points, for signs of life. One was in worse shape than the other, its crank handle snapped clean off. But the second... the second had potential.

She worked with a focused frenzy, her usual meticulousness amplified by the urgency of the situation. She cleaned away the rust with abrasive pads, oiled the moving parts, and, with a stroke of sheer inspiration, began to adapt a section of a defunct agricultural sprinkler system she'd salvaged weeks ago. She attached a length of cracked, but still serviceable, rubber hose to the pump's output, then to the sprinkler head. It was crude, makeshift, but it was a start. "If we can position these strategically," she murmured to herself, "and keep them supplied with water, we can create a localized deluge to catch those embers."

Her attention then turned to the hoses. The salvaged ones were a patchwork of repairs, brittle and prone to bursting. But she remembered a stash of reinforced fire hose, remarkably intact, that had been part of the old community emergency supplies, tucked away in the deepest, driest part of the town hall's sub-basement. Lena, whose meticulous nature ensured such things weren't entirely forgotten, had a rough idea of their location.

"Lena, I need your help locating those old fire hoses," Mika called over the comms, her voice sharp and clear. "The ones with the brass couplings. And I need a couple of the old pressure tanks from the defunct irrigation system. The ones meant for chemical spraying." Lena's voice, calm even in the chaos, responded, "On my way, Mika. I know where they are. Be careful, it's dusty down there."

The task of collecting these items, and then transporting them to Mika's improvised defense zone, was a significant undertaking. The smoke was thicker now, a choking, acrid curtain that made visibility a challenge. But the community, sensing the importance of Mika's endeavor, rallied. A small group of able-bodied individuals, guided by Lena and Mika's increasingly precise instructions, began to haul the heavy, coiled hoses and the bulky, metal tanks towards the western flank, near the storage shed.

Mika had already identified the most critical points. The shed, filled with stored dry goods and salvaged materials, was a prime target. The communal workshop, with its flammable oils and volatile chemicals, was another. And then there was the cluster of dwellings closest to the fire's edge, the homes of those who had arrived most recently, who had fewer established defenses of their own.

She began connecting the hoses to the salvaged pumps, her hands working with practiced speed. The pressure tanks, when finally in place, were filled by a dedicated team with buckets of water, a precious and laborious task. Mika then devised a system of quick-release valves, using salvaged plumbing fixtures. The idea was that if an ember was spotted nearing a structure, the nearest team could activate the pump, drawing water from the tanks and sending it through the hoses to either the hand-cranked pumps or, in a more targeted fashion, directly onto the threatened building's roof and eaves.

"This needs to be a rapid response," Mika explained to the small team assembled around her, her voice firm. "As soon as a flare-up is spotted near a structure, you activate the nearest pump. Don't wait for confirmation. The fire doesn't wait. If it's a false alarm, you just shut it down and refill the tank. Better to waste a little water than lose a building." She demonstrated the quick-release valve, a simple lever that, when pulled, would engage the pump and send a stream of water arcing through the air.

She also developed a system for containing embers that might fly *over* the firebreak. She had noticed the way small, dry bushes and heaps of leaves, even small branches, tended to accumulate on the leeward side of the firebreak, waiting to be cleared. These were perfect tinderboxes for errant sparks. Her solution was crude but ingenious: "ember traps." Using lengths of salvaged metal sheeting, she fashioned them into shallow, angled barriers, designed to catch falling embers and direct them *back* towards the cleared firebreak, or at least into areas where they would be less likely to ignite a larger blaze. These were then supplemented with damp burlap sacks, strategically placed near vulnerable points, ready to be thrown over any small ignition.

"The goal isn't to stop every single ember," she explained, her eyes scanning the smoky horizon with a fierce intensity. "It's to significantly reduce the chances of a secondary ignition, to buy us time, to protect what we can." She had also managed to jury-rig a series of small, battery-powered alarms, using salvaged motion sensors and sirens. These were placed strategically along the perimeter, wired to Mika's central hub. If a significant movement was detected near a structure – indicating a possible ember landing – the alarm would sound, a shrill, urgent cry cutting through the roar of the fire, alerting the nearest defense team.

The sheer ingenuity born of desperation was palpable. Mika, the quiet technician, had become a frontline defender, her tools not shovels and axes, but wires, pumps, and a relentless, analytical mind. She was the architect of a defense-in-depth, an improvised network designed to catch the fire's insidious tendrils before they could find purchase. She understood that the firebreak was the primary shield, but her system was the secondary line, the crucial safeguard against the unpredictable nature of the inferno.

The first real test came with a sudden surge in the wind. The flames, which had been advancing with a more measured intensity, seemed to gain a renewed ferocity. Kiley's voice, strained over the comms, confirmed it. "Wind's picking up, western flank! It's pushing embers towards the shed!" Mika's fingers flew across the dials of her radio. "Team Gamma, activate pumps at the shed! Ember traps engaged! All personnel, be alert for secondary ignitions!"

Across the chaotic landscape, the response was immediate. The hand-cranked pumps groaned to life, sending arcs of water onto the dry timbers of the shed. The makeshift sprinkler heads sputtered, then began to spray a fine mist, wetting down the roof and eaves. Jax, positioned nearby with his camera, documented the scene. He saw a small ember, glowing like a malevolent star, descend from the smoky sky, landing on the edge of the shed's roof. Before it could even begin to smolder, a quick-thinking resident, alerted by the growing hum of the pumps and the visual of the water spray, grabbed a damp burlap sack and expertly smothered it. Another ember landed near a pile of dry straw just behind the firebreak, but it fell into the shallow, angled metal barrier Mika had constructed, sliding harmlessly back onto the cleared earth.

Mika, watching the readouts from her proximity alarms and listening to the reports filtering through her comms, felt a surge of grim satisfaction. It wasn't a perfect system, but it was working. The water was being delivered, the ember traps were doing their job, and the alarms were providing the crucial seconds of warning. She saw, in the determined faces of the teams manning the pumps, in the swift actions of those dousing small ignitions, a reflection of her own struggle – to push back, to innovate, to deny the fire its easy victories. Her defenses weren't about brute force; they were about precision, about disrupting the fire's destructive flow, about protecting the vulnerable heart of Haven from the embers that threatened to consume it from within. She knew the battle was far from over, but for the first time, she felt a sense of agency, of being able to directly fight back against the encroaching darkness with more than just words and radio waves. She was building a shield, one salvaged pump and repurposed hose at a time. The ingenuity was a testament to their collective will, a silent testament to the fact that even in the face of overwhelming destruction, the human spirit could find ways to build, to protect, and to persevere. The embers were a constant threat, a reminder of the fire's unyielding nature, but Mika's improvised defenses were a defiant whisper back, a promise that Haven would not go down without a fight, one spark at a time. She continued to monitor her screens, to refine her placements, her mind already racing ahead to the next potential weakness, the next ember, the next improvised solution.

From her vantage point on the low rise overlooking the firebreak, Kiley was a statue carved from resolve. The wind, a capricious adversary, whipped strands of hair across her face, but her gaze remained fixed, sharp and unblinking, on the roiling inferno to the west. Smoke, thick and acrid, billowed upwards, a grim testament to the fire's insatiable appetite. Below her, the firebreak – a raw, ragged scar carved into the earth – represented their thin, desperate line of defense. It was a stark contrast to the verdant life it was meant to preserve, and Kiley's mind, a finely tuned instrument honed by countless simulations and a deep understanding of Haven's vulnerabilities, worked at a fever pitch.

"Status report, north sector!" Her voice, amplified by a portable comm unit, cut through the low roar of the flames and the rising chorus of worried murmurs from the surrounding populace. It was a voice of authority, not born of arrogance, but of an absolute necessity. She was the conductor of this desperate symphony of survival, and every note, every pause, mattered.

A harried voice crackled back, "Kiley, north sector holding. Embers are crossing, but the water crews are on it. They're holding the line, but it's tight. Real tight."

Kiley's jaw tightened. "Understood. Conserve water where possible. Prioritize structures. Jax, are your teams in position at the eastern flank?"

"Affirmative, Kiley," Jax's steady reply came through. "We've got the western flank of the shed secured. The wind is pushing towards us, but the men are ready. The... those ember traps you designed, Mika's creations, they're catching a lot of the smaller ones."

"Good. Keep me updated on any direct impacts. We need eyes on everything. This isn't just about the firebreak anymore; it's about preventing secondary ignitions. Mika's systems are our early warning and first response for those." Kiley scanned the horizon, her eyes tracing the unpredictable dance of the flames. The wind was their enemy, a relentless bellows fanning the conflagration, but it was also their informant. It dictated where the greatest danger lay, where the embers would be flung with the most destructive force.

She mentally mapped the vulnerabilities. The communal workshop, a treasure trove of salvaged materials and volatile chemicals, sat perilously close to the fire's path. The granary, its dry timbers a beacon for any errant spark, was another critical point. And then there were the newer dwellings on the western edge, homes built by those who had arrived more recently, their defenses still nascent, their understanding of Haven's fragility less ingrained. These were the places that Kiley focused her strategic gaze upon, the lives and livelihoods she was determined to shield.

"Lena, I need an assessment on the water reserves. How much are we holding in the auxiliary tanks?" Kiley's questions were rapid, precise, each one aimed at gathering a crucial piece of the puzzle.

"We're down to about forty percent, Kiley," Lena's voice, though strained, was laced with a steely determination. "We've been running the pumps almost non-stop for the last hour. The teams are working to refill them from the deepest well, but it's slow going."

Forty percent. That was a grim number. Kiley's mind raced, calculating usage rates, projecting potential consumption. "Understood. We need to be judicious. If the wind shifts, and it looks like it might, we'll have to make some tough choices about where to allocate the remaining water. Jax, Kiley again. On the eastern flank, if the shed is threatened directly, I want you to pull your teams back to the granary. The shed is replaceable. The granary's contents are not."

"Copy that, Kiley. We'll maintain position until then, but we're ready to disengage and reposition on your command." Jax's response was immediate, a testament to the trust they all placed in Kiley's judgment. She was the steady hand in the storm, the one who could see the broader picture when others were overwhelmed by the immediate terror.

Kiley's strategic mind was not simply about reacting; it was about anticipating. She understood the fire's momentum, its tendency to exploit any weakness, any lapse in vigilance. She'd studied historical accounts of fire behavior, pouring over salvaged meteorological data. The wind was picking up, a dangerous omen. It was creating updrafts, carrying burning debris further and faster than usual. This meant the firebreak, while still vital, was not an impregnable fortress. It was a buffer, and the real battle would be fought in the moments after embers leaped over it, seeking new fuel.

"To all teams," Kiley's voice boomed, carrying a new urgency. "The wind is increasing. Expect increased ember activity. Mika, are your proximity alarms functioning optimally?"

"All systems green, Kiley," Mika replied, her voice calm and clear, a surprising counterpoint to the growing inferno. "I'm tracking several potential ember landings near the workshop. My automated systems are alerting the closest response teams, but visual confirmation is still crucial. We can't afford any false alarms, but we also can't afford to miss a single real threat."

Kiley nodded, though Mika couldn't see her. "Understood. Vigilance is paramount. We are shifting to a defense-in-depth strategy. The firebreak is our first line. Mika's ember traps and water spray systems are our second. Direct fire suppression by our ground crews is our third. Every layer must be robust. If one fails, the next must hold."

She gestured towards a cluster of dwellings on the western edge, their roofs a patchwork of salvaged metal and tarpaulin. "Those homes on the fringe – they are our highest priority for secondary ignition. Jax, once you've secured the granary, if the threat to it subsides, I want you to redeploy some of your men to reinforce that sector. Focus on wetting down the roofs and surrounding vegetation. Douse anything that looks like it could catch."

The weight of her decisions pressed down on her, a tangible burden. She had to balance the immediate need to fight the flames with the long-term need to preserve Haven's resources. Every decision involved trade-offs, a calculated risk assessment under the most extreme of pressures. To commit too many resources to one area was to leave another vulnerable. To hold back too much was to invite disaster.

"Kiley, we have a flare-up near the south end of the workshop," Jax reported, his voice tight with concern. "It looks like a larger ember landed right on the roof. Mika's alarms went off, and the team there is moving in with the pump."

Kiley's attention snapped to that sector. She could see the faint orange glow through the swirling smoke. "Report damage, Jax. And Kiley to Lena: divert one of the auxiliary tanks to the workshop sector, if possible. Prioritize that structure; its contents are too volatile to risk."

"Working on it, Kiley," Lena responded. "It'll take a few minutes to reroute the hose, but it's done."

Kiley watched, her heart in her throat, as a stream of water arced towards the workshop roof. She saw figures moving, silhouetted against the fire's infernal light, dousing the burgeoning flames. It was a close-run thing, a testament to the speed of Mika's system and the bravery of the crews.

"Workshop roof is contained," Jax announced, relief evident in his voice. "Minor scorching, but no structural damage. Mika's system worked. The team got there in under a minute from the alarm."

A small, almost imperceptible nod of acknowledgment from Kiley. "Excellent work, Jax. And well done, Mika. Keep those systems operational and maintained. We need them ready for the next onslaught."

She knew the battle was far from over. The fire's fury was not abating; it was merely shifting, testing their defenses, probing for weaknesses. But in that moment, watching the skilled coordination of her people, the effective deployment of improvised technology, Kiley felt a surge of fierce pride. They were not merely reacting to the fire; they were fighting it, strategically, intelligently, with every ounce of their ingenuity and collective will. Her leadership was the pivot point, the central node through which all information flowed and all decisions were disseminated. She was the anchor in the tempest, ensuring that Haven's desperate struggle remained focused, coordinated, and, above all, hopeful. She continued to scan the horizon, her mind already formulating contingency plans, preparing for the inevitable next challenge, her resolve as unyielding as the firebreak itself. The wind gusted again, carrying a fresh wave of embers, and Kiley met its challenge with unwavering determination.

Jax lowered his camera, the familiar weight of it a grounding sensation amidst the chaos. The acrid scent of smoke, once a symbol of destruction, now carried a strange, potent perfume of defiance. He had spent the better part of the last hour moving through the makeshift lines of defense, his lens focused not on the terrifying expanse of the inferno, but on the faces of the people fighting it. Each click of the shutter was a small act of preservation, an attempt to bottle the essence of this desperate moment.

He'd seen fear, undoubtedly. It was etched in the sweat-slicked brows of the young men hauling water in repurposed barrels, their muscles straining under the load. It flickered in the eyes of an older woman shielding a child with her body as embers rained down, her lips moving in silent prayer. But what had struck Jax, what he had worked to capture, was the courage that burned brighter than any flame. It was in the grim set of their jaws, the way they leaned into the wind, their bodies angled against the heat, as if their sheer presence could somehow push back the encroaching danger.

He'd trained his lens on Mika, her face smudged with soot, her brow furrowed in intense concentration as she monitored the readouts from her intricate sensor network. Sparks, tiny, incandescent messengers of destruction, were being tracked, their trajectories calculated. Her hands moved with a surgeon's precision over the controls of the repurposed drone, guiding it to drop water precisely where it was needed most, a testament to her brilliant, often unconventional, mind. It wasn't the typical image of heroism, this quiet, cerebral battle, but Jax knew it was as vital as any physical act of defiance. He'd captured a shot of her, her face illuminated by the glow of the screens, a single tear tracking a clean path through the grime on her cheek – a silent acknowledgment of the immense pressure, the fear she undoubtedly felt, but also her unwavering commitment.

Then there was Lena, her voice hoarse from shouting instructions, her normally neat braid unraveling as she directed the flow of precious water from the auxiliary tanks. Jax had caught her in a moment of pure exhaustion, slumped against a water pump, her chest heaving, but her eyes still scanned the horizon, her mind clearly on the next task, the next potential threat. He'd framed her against a backdrop of smoke and flickering light, her silhouette a powerful symbol of perseverance. It was a portrait of endurance, a testament to the sheer grit it took to keep going when every fiber of your being screamed for rest.

He moved closer to the eastern flank, where Jax's own teams were positioned, their primary objective now the granary. The wind howled, a relentless force that seemed intent on ripping the very air from their lungs. He saw men, their faces caked in dirt and sweat, their clothes singed at the edges, working in a grim ballet of fire suppression. They were armed with shovels, with buckets, with an unshakeable resolve. He captured a close-up of a pair of hands, rough and calloused, gripping a shovel so tightly that their knuckles were white. The image spoke volumes of the desperate fight to hold the line, to protect not just themselves, but the very sustenance of their community.

He saw a younger recruit, barely more than a boy, falter, his breathing ragged, his eyes wide with terror as a large ember landed precariously close to a pile of dry straw. Before anyone could react, an older, grizzled man, his face a roadmap of hardship, lunged forward. He didn't shout or admonish. He simply placed a steadying hand on the boy's shoulder, his gaze conveying a silent, powerful message of reassurance, before swiftly smothering the ember with his boot. Jax caught that moment, the connection between the two men, the unspoken transfer of strength and experience. It was a powerful depiction of community resilience, of how the older generation was anchoring the younger, imbuing them with the courage they needed to face the inferno.

He continued to document the acts of mutual aid, the small gestures that meant everything in the face of overwhelming destruction. He saw someone offering a swig of water to another, their throats parched and burning. He saw individuals working together to reinforce a section of the firebreak that threatened to crumble. He saw the quiet dedication of those tending to minor burns, their faces etched with concern but their movements efficient and steady. These weren't grand pronouncements; they were the quiet, vital threads that wove the fabric of their survival.

His photographs were becoming more than just images; they were a chronicle. A chronicle of the raw, unvarnished courage that emerged when people were pushed to their limits. He saw the resilience not just in the grand strategies Kiley was orchestrating, but in the individual acts of bravery, in the shared glances of determination, in the simple refusal to surrender.

He paused to capture a wider shot, the firebreak a fragile line against the monstrous, advancing fire. The smoke churned, obscuring the horizon, but through the haze, he could see the determined figures of his community, silhouetted against the inferno, a testament to their indomitable spirit. Their faces, streaked with soot and sweat, were turned towards the flames, their bodies taut with effort, their eyes fixed on the task at hand. These were not the faces of despair, but of defiance. These were the faces of people who understood the stakes, who knew what they were fighting for – their homes, their future, their very existence.

Jax adjusted his lens, zooming in on a group working near the communal workshop, their movements urgent as they reinforced the perimeter. He saw the fear in their eyes, yes, but it was tempered by a fierce protectiveness. The workshop held not just tools and salvaged materials, but the promise of rebuilding, of creating anew. It was a symbol of their ingenuity, and they were not about to let it fall. He captured the intensity of their focus, the way they communicated with urgent gestures and brief, clipped words, their shared purpose a palpable force.

He moved towards the western edge, where the newer dwellings stood, more vulnerable than the established core of Haven. Here, the wind seemed to whip the embers with even greater ferocity. He saw families huddled together, their faces pale, but the men and women among them were already out, working with makeshift tools to clear brush, to wet down roofs. He focused on a young couple, their faces etched with worry, but their hands working in tandem to douse their roof with water from a bucket. The wife's eyes met his for a fleeting moment, and in them, he saw not just fear, but a fierce resolve, a mother's determination to protect her child, who was visible peeking from behind her. He felt a pang of empathy, a surge of admiration for their courage in the face of such overwhelming odds.

Jax knew that these images, once the immediate crisis had passed, would serve a purpose far beyond mere documentation. They would be a reminder. A reminder of what they had faced, and a reminder of how they had faced it. They would serve as a testament to the strength that lay within them, the collective will that had allowed them to stand against the inferno. He saw it in the way his fellow survivors were pushing themselves beyond their limits, their actions fueled by a deep-seated instinct for self-preservation, yes, but also by a profound sense of community. This was not just a fight for individual survival; it was a fight for Haven, for the fragile society they had built from the ashes of the old world.

He continued his silent work, his camera a conduit for the raw emotions of the moment. He captured the sheer physical exertion, the sweat pouring down, the muscles burning, the lungs aching for clean air. But more importantly, he captured the spirit that transcended the physical. He saw it in the shared nods of encouragement, in the quick, reassuring handclaps, in the determined glint in every eye. This was courage in its purest form: not the absence of fear, but the triumph over it, a conscious decision to act in the face of overwhelming danger.

He saw an elderly man, his back bent with age, diligently clearing debris from a path, his movements slow but steady. Jax zoomed in, capturing the lines on his face, the determination in his weathered eyes. This man might not be on the front lines of fire suppression, but his contribution was no less vital. He was maintaining the arteries of their defense, ensuring that the flow of resources and personnel remained unobstructed. It was a quiet heroism, easily overlooked in the heat of the battle, but Jax was determined to give it its due.

He moved back towards Kiley's vantage point, needing to capture the broader perspective of the command center, the nexus of their coordinated efforts. He saw Kiley, her stance still unwavering, her gaze fixed on the ever-shifting panorama of smoke and flame. Her face, though strained, was a mask of unwavering resolve. He captured a shot of her, the fire's reflection dancing in her determined eyes, her silhouette sharp against the smoky sky. It was a portrait of leadership under duress, of the immense responsibility she carried.

He knew that his photographs would become part of Haven's story, visual echoes of this pivotal moment. They would remind future generations of the sacrifices made, of the resilience demonstrated, of the unbreakable bonds forged in the crucible of the fire. He had witnessed firsthand that courage was not a singular act, but a persistent spirit, a collective will that manifested in countless small, vital ways. And he, Jax, with his lens, was here to ensure that this spirit, this enduring flame of humanity, would never be extinguished. He raised his camera again, the familiar weight a comfort, and continued to document the unwavering courage of his people.

CHAPTER TEN
ASHES AND AFTERMATH

The last tendrils of smoke curled and dissipated into the bruised twilight sky, surrendering their dominion over Haven. The inferno, a ravenous beast that had threatened to consume everything, was finally subdued. Not vanquished, for the scars it etched upon the land were too deep, too raw, to ever truly heal, but contained. A fragile, hard-won peace settled over the community, a stark contrast to the roaring fury that had raged for what felt like an eternity.

An unnerving silence descended, a palpable void where the roar of the fire had been. It was a silence pregnant with exhaustion, with the ghosts of what might have been. The only sounds were the faint, dying whispers of the blaze – the occasional, mournful crackle of an ember surrendering to the inevitable, the soft hiss of water meeting superheated earth. The air, once thick with the suffocating stench of burning wood and thatch, now carried a more complex perfume: the sharp, metallic tang of scorched soil, the bitter aroma of ash, and beneath it all, a faint, sweetish undertone of ozone, a lingering exhalation of the fire's immense power. It was the smell of devastation, yes, but also the scent of survival.

Jax lowered his camera, its familiar weight a grounding anchor in the surreal calm. He had spent the preceding hours in a state of heightened awareness, his senses honed to a razor's edge, capturing the raw, unflinching courage of his people. Now, as the adrenaline ebbed, a profound weariness settled into his bones. He looked out over the landscape, his gaze sweeping across the perimeter of Haven. The firebreak, a hastily constructed scar across the earth, had held. Barely. It was a testament to the desperate, unyielding efforts of those who had stood on its edge, their sweat and determination forming a more formidable barrier than mere earth and stone.

The immediate outskirts of Haven bore the most grievous wounds. Homes that had stood for generations were now skeletal remains, charred timbers jutting out like broken bones against the darkening sky. Fields that had promised a bountiful harvest were reduced to blackened, smoking expanses, the earth itself seemingly weeping ash. The familiar contours of the landscape were brutally altered, reshaped by the fire's brutal artistry. Yet, amidst this desolation, Haven itself stood. Bruised, battered, undeniably marked, but intact. The communal buildings, the heart of their rebuilt society, had been largely spared, a testament to the strategic brilliance of Kiley and the tireless efforts of every man, woman, and child who had fought tooth and nail to protect them.

A wave of profound relief washed over Jax, so potent it made his knees tremble. It was a relief that was almost painful in its intensity, a stark counterpoint to the gnawing dread that had gripped him for so long. They had faced the abyss, and they had, by some miracle, pulled back from the brink. He saw figures moving in the dimming light, weary silhouettes against the smoldering backdrop. They were moving with a heavy, deliberate slowness, their bodies speaking of a depletion of strength that went beyond mere physical fatigue. It was a deep, soul-wearying exhaustion that came from staring into the face of annihilation and refusing to blink.

Mika, her face streaked with soot and what Jax suspected were tears, was coordinating the final patrols, her voice, though hoarse, still carrying an undercurrent of authority. Her innovative sensor network, a marvel of salvaged technology and ingenious adaptation, had proven invaluable, not only in predicting the fire's path but also in identifying its most dangerous tendrils. He saw her give a weary nod to Lena, who was overseeing the distribution of what little water remained, her usual efficient bustle replaced by a quiet, almost somber diligence. Lena, too, looked utterly spent, her shoulders slumped with the weight of the night's demands, but her eyes still held that familiar spark of resilience, a quiet promise that she would continue, no matter the cost.

Jax felt a surge of gratitude for these people, for their unwavering spirit. He had documented their fear, yes, but what he had truly captured, what would forever be etched in his memory, was their courage. It wasn't the absence of fear, but the quiet, determined decision to act in its presence. It was the small gestures of solidarity, the shared glances of resolve, the sheer, stubborn refusal to surrender. He had seen the old man, his back bent with age, still diligently clearing debris from a vital pathway, his slow, steady movements a silent defiance of the chaos. He had seen the young recruit, trembling but resolute, working alongside a seasoned veteran, the transfer of courage passing between them like a tangible current.

He walked towards the granary, a vital structure that had been a focal point of the defense. The smell of smoke was strongest here, the air thick with the memory of heat. But the granary stood, its thick stone walls having offered a formidable shield. The immediate area around it was a patchwork of scorched earth and hastily dug trenches, but the vital stores of grain, the very sustenance of Haven, were safe. He saw a small group of Kiley's teams, their faces illuminated by the flickering light of hand-held lanterns, beginning the painstaking process of assessing the damage, of ensuring that the precious cargo within was secure. Their movements were slow, methodical, each action a deliberate step towards reclaiming their future.

The wind, which had been such a relentless antagonist, had finally begun to abate, its fury spent. But its passage had left behind a landscape of eerie beauty and profound sadness. The sky, no longer a canvas for the fire's destructive dance, was now a muted palette of grays and purples, the remnants of the smoke clinging to the horizon like a shroud. The setting sun, a molten orb, cast long, distorted shadows across the devastated terrain, imbuing the scene with a spectral quality. It was a landscape that whispered of loss, but also of a stubborn, unyielding hope.

Jax stopped, his gaze fixed on the skeletal remains of a dwelling that had stood near the eastern edge. He remembered the family who had lived there, a young couple with a bright-eyed child. He had seen them, moments before the fire had reached their door, working frantically to douse their roof, their faces a mask of terror and determination. He scanned the area, a knot of anxiety tightening in his chest. He saw a small cluster of figures gathering near what remained of a garden, and his heart leaped. It was them. They were alive. He saw the young woman being held tightly by her husband, their child clinging to her leg, their faces smudged with soot but their eyes holding a flicker of dazed relief. A silent cheer rose in Jax's throat. They had survived.

The immediate threat had receded, leaving behind a profound quietude that was almost as overwhelming as the preceding pandemonium. It was the silence of the aftermath, a period of reckoning and gentle, hesitant reawakening. The crackle of dying embers was a constant reminder of the fire's power, a lingering echo of the fury that had been unleashed. But it was a fading sound, a signal that the immediate crisis had passed. The air, heavy with the scent of destruction, also carried an unmistakable undercurrent of relief. A collective sigh seemed to ripple through the weary survivors. Haven was saved. The surrounding lands, however, bore the unmistakable, brutal signature of the inferno's passage. It was a stark, visual testament to the battle that had been waged, a landscape forever altered by the fiery maw of destruction.

Jax turned his camera towards the community gathering at the edge of the firebreak. They weren't celebrating, not yet. There was no room for jubilation in the face of such loss. Instead, there was a quiet solidarity, a shared understanding that transcended words. People were checking on one another, offering silent embraces, sharing meager rations of water. The shared ordeal had forged a bond, a deep, unwavering connection that was more potent than any fear. He saw Kiley, her face etched with exhaustion but her eyes still sharp, moving through the crowds, offering words of comfort and assurance. Her leadership had been instrumental in navigating the crisis, but it was the collective will of the people that had truly turned the tide.

He focused his lens on a group of children, huddled together, their faces pale and wide-eyed, still processing the enormity of what they had witnessed. An older woman, her own home miraculously spared, was speaking to them softly, her voice a soothing balm. She was telling them a story, Jax realized, a story of resilience, of courage, of how even in the darkest of times, the human spirit could find a way to endure. It was a vital act of preservation, an attempt to shield these young minds from the full horror of the night, to plant seeds of hope in the fertile ground of their fear.

The smell of smoke, though less intense, was still pervasive. It clung to their clothes, to their hair, to their very skin. It was a constant reminder of the near-catastrophe, a sensory imprint of the battle they had just fought. But for the first time in what felt like days, it no longer carried the chilling premonition of doom. Instead, it was a reminder of their collective strength, of the unwavering determination that had allowed them to stand against the inferno. It was the smell of survival, and in its wake, a fragile but undeniable sense of relief began to settle over the community. The immediate threat had receded, leaving behind a landscape scarred but not broken, a testament to the indomitable spirit of Haven. The silence that followed the roar of the fire was not an empty void, but a pregnant pause, a moment to breathe, to assess, and to begin the long, arduous journey of rebuilding. The air, thick with the scent of ash and destruction, was also tinged with the faint, sweet aroma of hope, a promise of the dawn that would inevitably follow this long, fiery night.

The first hesitant rays of dawn, pale and watery, began to bleed across the horizon, illuminating a landscape irrevocably altered. The embers, which had glowed like malevolent eyes in the darkness, had now faded to dull, ashy mounds, their fiery fury extinguished. A profound stillness had descended, a quiet so deep it felt heavy, oppressive. It was the stillness of a world holding its breath, waiting for the verdict of what remained.

Emerging from the communal shelters, where they had huddled through the longest night of their lives, the people of Haven moved with a newfound caution, their eyes wide, their movements tentative. They were like newborns, blinking in the harsh light of a world they no longer fully recognized. The air, though cooler now, still carried the acrid perfume of ash, a constant, gnawing reminder of the inferno's passage. It was a scent that clung to their clothes, their hair, their very souls, a tangible imprint of the night's terror.

Jax, his camera still slung around his neck, felt a familiar pang of professional instinct, but it was muted by a deeper, more personal apprehension. He scanned the faces around him, searching for the familiar contours of resilience, for the glint of determination that had seen them through the immediate crisis. He found it, to be sure, but it was tempered by a dawning realization of the immense scale of their loss.

The heart of Haven, their cluster of sturdy, communal structures, had indeed been spared the worst. The granary stood firm, its stone walls a testament to the foresight of their ancestors. The workshops, the medical bay, the central meeting hall – all remained, scarred but functional. This was their anchor, the core from which they would begin to rebuild. A wave of gratitude, potent and humbling, washed over Jax as he looked at these steadfast buildings, a silent acknowledgment of the collective will that had protected them. Kiley's strategic planning, Lena's organization of the water brigades, Mika's early warning systems – all had played their part in preserving this vital nucleus.

But the victory was a hollow one, a gilded cage when the surrounding wilderness, their lifeblood, had been consumed. As the survivors ventured beyond the immediate perimeter of their homes, the true devastation began to unfold. The forests, once a verdant tapestry of life, were now a monochrome nightmare of charcoal and ash. Towering pines, which had stood for centuries, were reduced to skeletal husks, their once proud branches blackened and brittle, reaching out like skeletal fingers towards a sky that offered no solace.

The air here was even thicker with the smell of smoke, a suffocating blanket that made each breath a conscious effort.

Jax walked with Mika, her usual brisk pace subdued, her eyes scanning the desolate expanse with a mixture of scientific assessment and raw grief. "The timber," she murmured, her voice raspy, gesturing to the ravaged trees. "Most of it is compromised. Burned too deeply to be of much use for construction, not without extensive treatment. And even then, the structural integrity..." She trailed off, shaking her head. The loss of timber meant a delay in repairs, in expansion, in the very ability to rebuild what had been lost outside their core. It meant relying on salvaged materials for far longer than anticipated, a finite resource in a world of infinite needs.

He remembered the vibrant ecosystem that had thrived just beyond their walls. The rustling of leaves, the chirping of unseen birds, the occasional glimpse of a deer or a rabbit darting through the undergrowth – these were sounds and sights that were now relegated to memory. The fields that had promised a late harvest, the carefully cultivated plots that had been their buffer against leaner times, were now barren wastelands. They were expanses of blackened earth, still smoldering in places, the delicate roots of their crops vaporized. The rich topsoil, the very foundation of their agricultural endeavors, had been stripped away by the inferno, leaving behind a sterile, cracked surface.

"Hunting grounds," Jax said, his voice barely a whisper, echoing Mika's unspoken fears. "Our primary source of protein, beyond the granary stores. Gone. For how long, Mika?"

Mika kicked at a loose clump of ash. "Generations, Jax. It will take generations for the forest to truly recover its biodiversity. The smaller game... the insects... the soil itself... all of it is decimated. The seeds are burned. The habitats are destroyed. We've lost more than just trees. We've lost an entire biome." Her scientific detachment warred with the raw emotion in her voice. She had always been the pragmatist, the one who saw the intricate web of life, and now she was witnessing its brutal unraveling.

They encountered small groups of people already venturing out, their faces grim. Kiley was directing a team near the edge of the forest, their movements purposeful as they marked trees that might be salvageable, a futile effort in the face of such widespread destruction. Lena, her usual energetic stride replaced by a slow, measured gait, was with a group assessing the damage to the water catchment systems, their efficiency likely compromised by the ash and debris. Even the usually stoic individuals of Haven seemed subdued, the sheer scale of the loss pressing down on them.

Jax raised his camera, but the act felt almost sacrilegious. How could he capture this desolation without trivializing the struggle they had just endured? How could he frame this devastation in a way that wasn't just a testament to ruin, but a prologue to rebuilding? He focused on small details: a single, blackened wildflower stubbornly pushing its way through the ash, a testament to nature's indomitable will to survive. He captured the weary but determined faces of his people, their eyes fixed on the horizon, not in despair, but in quiet contemplation of the task ahead.

The immediate concern was food. The granary, while intact, held the fruits of previous harvests. The fire had obliterated any chance of a new one for months to come. The hunting grounds were barren. The foraging opportunities – berries, roots, edible fungi – that had supplemented their diet throughout the year were now ashes. Lena,

Jax knew, would be running simulations, calculating their reserves, rationing every grain, every dried fruit. The thought sent a shiver down his spine, a chill that had nothing to do with the morning air.

"We underestimated the wind," Mika said, her voice soft, almost accusatory. "We thought the firebreak would hold, that we could contain it. But the embers... they carried so far."

Jax nodded. He had seen it himself – glowing cinders sailing through the air, igniting distant patches of dry grass, creating new fronts of the inferno faster than they could be fought. The wind, their enemy during the fire, was now a silent accomplice in the devastation.

He walked past a small, charred clearing where a grove of fruit trees had once stood. He remembered the sweet scent of ripe apples in late summer, the crisp crunch of a freshly picked pear. Now, only the gnarled, blackened trunks remained, a somber monument to their lost bounty. This wasn't just about sustenance; it was about the sweetness of life, the simple pleasures that had made Haven more than just a place of survival.

The ecological impact was a chilling prospect. The intricate balance of the surrounding environment had been shattered. What would happen to the insect populations that pollinated their remaining crops? What about the soil's ability to regenerate without the microbial life that had been incinerated? Mika had spoken of generations, and Jax understood why. This wasn't a quick fix, a matter of planting new seeds and waiting. This was a deep wound, a scar that would take far longer to heal than any they had suffered.

He saw a group of children, their faces smudged with ash, looking out at the blackened forest with a mixture of fear and awe. One of them, a young girl named Elara, pointed towards the distant, smoking hills. "Will it come back?" she asked, her voice a thin thread of anxiety.

An older woman, Mara, who had lost her small cottage on the outskirts, knelt beside her. "No, child," Mara said, her voice firm, though her eyes held the sorrow of her own loss. "The fire is gone. But look," she gestured to the new dawn, "the sun is still shining. And we are here. We will learn to grow again, even in the ashes."

Jax felt a surge of pride for Mara, for her unwavering strength. It was this spirit, this refusal to be defined by their losses, that would see them through. But he also saw the fear in Elara's eyes, a fear born from witnessing something truly terrifying. The long-term psychological impact, especially on the children, was another layer of damage to contend with.

He continued his slow circuit, documenting the stark reality. The river, their life-giving artery, flowed on, but its banks were blackened, choked with debris. The water itself looked murkier, laden with ash. Mika had already dispatched a team to test its purity, to ensure it was safe for consumption, but the visual evidence was concerning. The fire had not respected natural boundaries, and its reach had extended to the very water they depended upon.

The scale of the damage was overwhelming. It was easy to be consumed by the sheer magnitude of it all, to feel a crushing despair at the sight of the ruined landscape. But Jax forced himself to focus on what remained: the unyielding spirit of his people, the sturdy buildings of Haven, the life-sustaining river, the promise of the rising sun, however pale.

He saw an old man, Silas, meticulously gathering shards of blackened pottery from the ruins of his home. He wasn't salvaging anything of practical value, not really. He was gathering fragments of memory, of a life that had been. Jax paused, observing him. Silas looked up, his weathered face etched with a profound sadness, but his eyes met Jax's with a flicker of something else – a quiet resolve. He held up a partially intact shard, its once vibrant glaze now dulled by soot. "This," he said, his voice rough, "was from my wife's favorite bowl. It still holds a story, even like this."

Jax understood. They were not just rebuilding structures; they were rebuilding their lives, their histories, their very sense of self, from the remnants of what had been. The damage was profound, deeply etched into the land and the lives of its inhabitants. But as the sun climbed higher, casting its hesitant light on the scarred earth, a new determination began to stir within the weary hearts of Haven. The assessment of the damage was a somber, necessary task, a brutal reckoning with their new reality. But it was also the first step, a crucial foundation upon which the long, arduous journey of rebuilding would begin. The ashes were a stark reminder of their vulnerability, but the rising sun was a silent, undeniable promise of renewal.

Mika moved with a purpose, a stark contrast to the stunned inertia that seemed to grip many of Haven's inhabitants. The acrid bite of smoke still lingered in the air, a constant, unwelcome reminder of the night's fury, but it was the hum of potential failure beneath the surface that occupied her mind. Her gaze, usually sharp and analytical, now swept over the skeletal remains of what had once been their vital lifelines – the communication towers, the conduits that carried power, the very arteries of their connected existence. The fire, a voracious entity, had not been selective in its consumption. It had devoured infrastructure with the same indiscriminate hunger it had shown for the ancient trees and the fertile soil.

Her first objective, after the immediate safety checks, was the communication array. It was more than just a luxury; it was their only link to any potential outposts or, however unlikely, to the scattered remnants of the outside world. Even if no one else answered, maintaining internal communication was paramount for coordinating the monumental task of rebuilding. She approached the main relay tower, or what remained of it. The metal was twisted and warped, blackened like charcoal, a grotesque sculpture against the bruised sky. Sparks, minuscule and pathetic, still flickered from frayed wires, like the dying breaths of a once-powerful beast.

"Anything?" Jax asked, his voice a low rumble beside her, his camera a silent observer. He understood the significance of her work, the technical underpinnings of their survival.

Mika ran a gloved hand over a fused junction box, the heat a lingering echo of the inferno. "Compromised. Severely. The primary antenna is slag. The secondary... it's twisted beyond recognition. The transmission relays are melted. We're looking at a complete rebuild of the main mast, at minimum." She gestured to a tangle of wires, now fused into a single, useless mass. "And the power supply. The solar arrays were integrated into the tower's structure. They're gone. Completely obliterated."

Her focus shifted, her mind already cataloging the damage, mentally sketching out schematics for repair, for improvisation. She moved to the auxiliary power conduits, buried for protection, but the heat had been so intense that even the earth had offered little sanctuary. "The buried lines... some might be salvageable if the insulation held, but the ground temperature must have been astronomical. I need to test the integrity of each segment. We might have a few working channels, enough for local communication within Haven, perhaps even to the outer agricultural zones if they're still operational, but long-range is out of the question. For now."

The implications were immediate and stark. Without reliable communication, coordinating efforts would be significantly hampered. Information would travel at the speed of a runner, or the unreliable crackle of a short-range radio, if she could even get one functioning. This wasn't just an inconvenience; it was a potential bottleneck for rescue, for resource allocation, for the very act of organized survival. She pulled out a multi-tool, its metallic gleam a comforting contrast to the surrounding desolation. Her fingers, nimble and sure, began to meticulously inspect the exposed wires, probing for continuity, for signs of life.

"The generators," Jax prompted, knowing her next thought.

"The diesel generators," Mika confirmed, her voice tight with a familiar tension that always accompanied the assessment of their fuel reserves. "They were housed in the reinforced bunker. The bunker held. But the fuel lines leading to the main grid... I need to check those. And the fuel itself. Contamination from the ash? Heat damage? We need to run diagnostics. If those are down, even our local grid is in serious jeopardy."

She moved towards the bunker entrance, the heavy steel door a symbol of their foresight. Inside, the air was cooler, less choked with smoke, but a fine layer of ash had permeated even this sanctuary. The generators themselves stood silent, imposing metal titans waiting for a spark. Mika began her methodical process, checking fuel lines, inspecting filters, her brow furrowed in concentration. She connected diagnostic tools, the small screens flickering to life, displaying streams of data that only she could truly decipher.

"Engine block temperature stable," she murmured, reading a gauge. "Fuel pump pressure... nominal. The issue might be ignition. The electrical surge from the fire could have fried the ignition coils. Or... the fuel itself is compromised." She pulled a sample of the diesel into a small vial, observing its clarity, its viscosity. "It looks clean, but that doesn't mean much. We'll have to run a burn test."

While waiting for preliminary readings from the generators, Mika's attention was drawn to the environmental monitors she had deployed weeks ago, before the fire had become an uncontrollable inferno. These were her eyes and ears into the health of their ecosystem. The readings from the nearest stations were alarming. The air quality index was off the charts, registering levels of particulate matter that were frankly dangerous.

"The ash isn't just a visual problem," she explained to Jax, pointing to a handheld sensor that beeped insistently. "It's loaded with fine particulates, carcinogens. Even with our filtration systems working at full capacity, breathing this air long-term is going to have significant health impacts. We need to reinforce our air filters, especially in the shelters and the living quarters. And everyone needs to be wearing masks when they're outside, even if it's just for short periods."

She continued to monitor the readings, her scientific mind racing through the cascading consequences. The ash would settle on everything, coating the leaves of any surviving plants, a suffocating blanket that would inhibit photosynthesis. It would leach into the soil, altering its pH, potentially introducing toxic elements. And then there was the water.

"The water filtration systems," she said, her voice taking on a more urgent tone. "They're our biggest immediate concern after power and communication. The primary filtration beds are designed to handle sediment, organic matter. But this much ash... it's a different beast entirely. It's finer, more pervasive. It will clog the filters faster, potentially bypass them if not managed carefully. And if the ash is leaching heavy metals..." She shuddered, the thought of contaminated water a more terrifying prospect than the flames themselves.

She pulled up the schematics for their multi-stage filtration system, a complex network of pumps, sedimentation tanks, and microfiltration units. She needed to assess the capacity of each stage, to determine if they could handle the increased load of ash. "We'll need to increase the frequency of backwashing and cleaning the primary filters. We might even need to implement an additional pre-filtration stage, something to capture the bulk of the ash before it reaches the main system. I need to reconfigure the intake valves, possibly reroute some of the flow to bypass certain stages temporarily while others are being cleaned. It's going to be a constant battle to keep the water pure."

She walked towards the main water processing plant, a robust structure designed to withstand the elements, but even its exterior was coated in a thick layer of grey ash. The hum of the pumps, usually a reassuring sound of constant activity, was now tinged with a note of strain. She opened an access panel, revealing a tangle of pipes and machinery. Her hands, stained with ash, expertly traced the flow, her mind a whirlwind of calculations and potential adjustments.

"The intake from the river," she mused, "it's drawing in a lot more ash than usual. The riverbanks are devastated, the soil loose. Any rain, even a light shower, is going to wash a significant amount of ash into the waterway. We're not just filtering water anymore; we're trying to purify a slurry." She opened a valve, checking the flow rate, the pressure. "The sediment tanks are already filling up faster than anticipated. We'll need to find a safe place to dump the collected ash, away from any water sources, and we'll need to do it frequently."

Her technical expertise, honed by years of studying environmental systems and engineering, was now their most critical asset. She was not just a scientist; she was a lifeline, piecing together the shattered remains of their infrastructure. The immediate repairs were complex, but the long-term implications were even more daunting. The fire had not just destroyed; it had fundamentally altered their environment, creating new challenges that required constant vigilance and adaptation.

"If we can't get the power back online consistently," Mika continued, her voice a low hum of concern, "the pumps for the water filtration will falter. That's the real bottleneck. No power, no clean water. And if the generators aren't reliable, we're in trouble. I need to get those diagnostics finished. We need to know if we can rely on them, even for essential services."

She returned to the bunker, her pace quickening. The generator readings were finally coalescing. She scanned the data, her eyes darting across the numbers. "Ignition coils are fried," she stated, a grim finality in her tone. "And one of the fuel injectors is seized. But... the primary engine is structurally sound. We can replace the coils. We can clean or replace the injector. It's repairable." A flicker of relief, infinitesimally small, crossed her face. "We can get at least one of them running. It won't power everything, not at full capacity, but it will be enough for the water filtration, for essential lighting in the shelters, and for the local communication relays. It's a start."

She turned to Jax, a spark of her usual resolve returning to her eyes. "So, we have power, albeit limited. We have a path forward for communication, again, limited. And the water filtration... it's going to be a constant battle, but it's manageable, for now. The immediate technical crises are identified. Now comes the constant, grinding work of repair and adaptation."

Her thoughts, however, were already drifting to the broader environmental picture. The air quality, the potential for long-term soil contamination, the impact on the remaining flora and fauna – these were not problems with quick fixes. They were generational challenges. The fire had not just burned; it had reset their world, forcing them to re-evaluate their relationship with the environment, to understand its fragility and their own vulnerability.

"The ash is a temporary problem," Mika said, her gaze sweeping over the desolate landscape visible through the bunker's reinforced doorway. "It will eventually wash away, settle, be incorporated into the soil. But the damage to the ecosystem... that's the long game. The loss of biodiversity, the disruption of natural cycles... it's profound. We'll have to reintroduce species, manage new pest outbreaks, monitor the soil composition for years, maybe decades, to come. We've lost so much that we took for granted."

She tapped a finger on her tablet, displaying a complex diagram of nutrient cycles. "The microbial life in the soil, essential for plant growth, has been incinerated. Rebuilding that will take time, perhaps even inoculation with specific strains. And the larger animals... their habitats are gone. They'll either migrate, if they can, or perish. This will impact our hunting grounds for generations, just as Jax predicted."

Her scientific mind, while capable of immense detail and logical progression, also grasped the interconnectedness of it all. The power, the communication, the water – these were the immediate needs, the tangible building blocks of their survival. But the environmental degradation was the insidious, long-term threat, a silent enemy that would continue to challenge them long after the last ember had died.

"We need to start planning for reforestation," Mika stated, her voice gaining a determined edge. "Not just planting saplings, but actively managing the land to encourage the return of native species. We need to study the soil, identify what's missing, what needs to be replenished. And we need to consider drought resistance, fire-resistant species, if we want to avoid this kind of devastation again."

She looked at Jax, her expression a mixture of weariness and steely resolve. "This fire was a wake-up call. We were complacent, perhaps. We took the stability of our environment for granted. Now, we have to work with what's left, and we have to learn from it. The technical challenges are significant, but the ecological ones... they require a fundamental shift in our approach to living here." She paused, taking a deep breath, the filtered air still carrying the faint scent of ash. "But we will adapt. We always do."

Luis's calloused fingers, usually stained with the rich loam of his garden, were now coated in a fine, grey powder. The scent of smoke, though beginning to recede from the air Mika had been meticulously cleaning, still clung stubbornly to everything, a morbid perfume of destruction. He'd spent the initial hours after the fire subsided helping with the immediate rescue efforts, his strength and steady hands proving invaluable in clearing debris and assisting the injured. But his heart, and his mind, remained tethered to the small patch of earth he had so painstakingly cultivated, the living testament to his belief in nature's ability to heal.

He approached his garden cautiously, a knot of dread tightening in his chest. The perimeter of Haven, particularly the areas bordering the wilder fringes, had borne the brunt of the inferno. He had seen the monstrous flames lick at the ancient trees, their roars echoing the primal fear that had gripped the community. His own small haven, his carefully nurtured ecosystem, felt impossibly vulnerable. He braced himself for devastation, for the sight of blackened stumps and scorched earth where vibrant life had once thrived.

What he found, however, was a starkly different tableau. The outer edges of his cultivated land, the zones he had designated for the experimental growth of bio-filtration plants, had indeed been scorched. The dry, papery leaves of some of the more delicate species were brittle and blackened, crumbling at the slightest touch. A palpable sense of loss washed over him. He had poured so much of himself into this project, believing it to be a crucial component of Haven's long-term sustainability, a living shield against the encroaching toxins and imbalances of their altered world.

Yet, as he moved deeper into the garden, a surprising sight began to unfold. The plants closest to the network of shallow bio-filtration channels, the very systems designed to purify water and air, seemed to have weathered the storm with an astonishing degree of resilience. The broad, waxy leaves of the 'cleansing green,' as the community had affectionately nicknamed the hardy, fast-growing species he'd introduced, were remarkably intact. While some bore tell-tale scorch marks along their edges, the core of the plants remained a vibrant, if ash-dusted, green. The water channels themselves, designed to mimic natural marshland filtration, had held moisture, and this vital element had seemingly acted as a crucial buffer against the heat.

Luis knelt by one of the channels, the damp earth cool beneath his fingers. He carefully brushed away the layer of ash, revealing the rich, dark soil beneath. The water, though now cloudy with ash particles, was still flowing, a testament to the underlying integrity of the system. He observed the roots of a particularly robust specimen of

Arundo donax, its dense root system clinging tenaciously to the muddy bank. This species, known for its aggressive growth and exceptional ability to absorb contaminants, had been a gamble, introduced into an environment still struggling to find its balance. Now, it appeared to be a gamble that had paid off spectacularly.

He ran his hand along the thick stalks of the *donax*, feeling a faint warmth that spoke of recent struggle, but also of life. These plants, so often viewed with a mixture of curiosity and mild skepticism by some of the less scientifically inclined members of Haven, had effectively created a living, breathing firebreak. Their sheer density, combined with the inherent moisture retained by the bio-filtration system, had absorbed and dissipated the heat, preventing the flames from breaching deeper into the garden and, by extension, closer to the residential sectors.

A wave of profound relief, mingled with a surge of almost forgotten optimism, washed over Luis. He had always believed in the power of nature to endure, to adapt, to find a way. He had seen it in the resilience of weeds pushing through cracked pavement, in the tenacious growth of trees reclaiming abandoned structures, in the quiet persistence of life in even the harshest environments. But to witness it firsthand, in the face of such a devastating event, was profoundly moving.

He moved further into the garden, his gaze scanning the various plots. The areas where he had experimented with different species for soil remediation seemed to have fared less well. The fine, powdery ash had settled more deeply, and the lack of dedicated water channels in these sections meant that the heat had been more direct and destructive. Some of the younger saplings he had planted to help regenerate the soil's depleted nutrients were little more than blackened sticks. His disappointment was a dull ache, but it was tempered by the undeniable success of the bio-filtration zones.

He recalled the initial skepticism when he had proposed the extensive cultivation of these 'cleansing greens.' Some had questioned the practicality, the allocation of precious water and resources to something that wasn't directly edible. They had argued for more immediate solutions, for crops that could sustain them in the short term. But Luis had argued, with the quiet conviction of a man who understood the intricate web of life, that true sustainability lay in nurturing the very systems that supported them. He had spoken of the delicate balance of the ecosystem, of the need to heal the land itself, not just to extract from it.

He remembered a particularly heated discussion with old Silas, a man whose pragmatism was as weathered as his face. Silas had scoffed, "What good are these weeds, Luis, if they can't fill our bellies or mend our broken tools? The fire might take our food, but it won't take our hunger." Luis had replied, "Silas, these 'weeds' are the lungs and the kidneys of our land. If we poison them, we poison ourselves. If we let them burn, we burn our future. They are not just plants; they are our shield, our medicine." It was a difficult argument to make, especially when faced with immediate needs, but Luis had persevered, driven by an instinctual understanding of ecological principles.

Now, looking at the thriving bio-filtration plants, he felt a vindication that was both personal and communal. They were not just plants; they were a living testament to foresight, to an understanding of natural processes that transcended immediate utility. They were a tangible symbol of hope, a promise of a quicker, more robust recovery for Haven. The fire had been a brutal lesson, a stark reminder of their vulnerability, but it had also illuminated the vital role of these carefully cultivated allies.

He continued his survey, his movements slow and deliberate. He examined the symbiotic relationships he had tried to foster within his garden – the nitrogen-fixing legumes interspersed with nutrient-absorbing grasses, the insect-repelling herbs planted strategically to protect the more sensitive species. Even in the damaged areas, he could see the underlying structure of his design, the intended ecological architecture. It was like looking at a damaged blueprint, where the foundation remained, suggesting the possibility of rebuilding.

He carefully collected samples from the soil near the bio-filtration channels. The ash was present, of course, but under it, the soil felt moist and alive. He knew that further analysis would be needed, a detailed assessment of nutrient levels, pH, and the presence of any lingering toxins. But the initial visual and tactile evidence was overwhelmingly positive. The plants' ability to absorb water and their dense root structures had likely prevented the ash from binding too tightly to the soil particles, and perhaps even facilitated its partial removal through the filtration channels.

Luis envisioned the immediate next steps. He would need to work with Mika, to understand the exact composition of the ash and its potential impact on the soil and water. He would need to devise a plan for clearing the remaining ash from the plants and the filtration channels, a process that would require careful choreography to avoid further damaging the delicate root systems or overwhelming the filtration capacity. He would also need to begin the arduous task of replanting the areas that had been completely destroyed, selecting species that were not only beneficial but also highly fire-resistant.

He thought about the concept of ecological resilience, a term he had often discussed with Mika. It wasn't just about bouncing back from a disturbance; it was about the capacity of an ecosystem to absorb such disturbances and reorganize while undergoing change so as to still retain essentially the same function, structure, identity, and feedbacks. His bio-filtration system, he realized, was a deliberate attempt to *engineer* resilience into their environment. The fire had tested that engineered resilience, and in a crucial sector, it had not only held but thrived.

He stood up, stretching his aching back. The sun, a pale disc in the hazy sky, cast long shadows across the scorched and surviving landscape. The air, though still carrying the smoky scent, also held a faint, earthy aroma from the damp soil. It was the smell of life, a subtle but persistent counterpoint to the devastation.

He looked out beyond his garden, towards the surrounding areas that had been consumed by the flames. The devastation there was absolute, a stark contrast to the partial survival he had witnessed within his own cultivated patch. He knew that the rebuilding effort would be immense, a monumental undertaking that would require the collective will and effort of everyone in Haven. But in the heart of his garden, amidst the ash and the remnants of the fire, he had found a tangible source of hope. The 'cleansing green' had proven its worth, not just as a theoretical solution, but as a practical, living defense.

He knew his work was far from over. In fact, it had just entered a new, more challenging phase. The fire had underscored the fragility of their existence, but it had also revealed the strength inherent in their connection to the natural world, a connection he had dedicated his life to understanding and nurturing. The resilience of his roots, the roots he had planted and tended, offered a beacon in the aftermath, a promise that even from ashes, new life could emerge. He would need to communicate this discovery, to explain its significance to those who might have overlooked the importance of his unconventional methods. He would need to harness this newfound knowledge, to expand upon it, to integrate it more deeply into the fabric of Haven's survival strategy. The fire had taken much, but it had also taught them a vital lesson, a lesson etched in the very resilience of the green shoots pushing through the grey dust. The journey ahead would be arduous, but Luis felt a renewed sense of purpose, a quiet confidence that stemmed from the undeniable, tenacious life that had survived the inferno. He would use this, he vowed, to help Haven not just rebuild, but to emerge stronger, greener, and more resilient than before. He would advocate for the expansion of these bio-filtration zones, for a deeper integration of ecological restoration into their rebuilding efforts. The fire had been a setback, a brutal test, but it had also been a revelation, highlighting the profound power of nature's enduring spirit. He saw not just a garden that had survived, but a living blueprint for Haven's future, a testament to the power of cultivated resilience in the face of utter destruction.

The acrid bite of smoke still clung to Jax's nostrils, a phantom sensation that lingered long after the roaring inferno had been tamed. He walked through what remained of Oakhaven, his camera a familiar weight against his chest, a silent witness to the devastation. Each click of the shutter was a small act of defiance against the all-consuming grey that threatened to swallow their world. The air, thick with the scent of burnt timber and despair, felt heavy on his lungs, a tangible manifestation of the collective grief that had settled over the survivors.

His lens swept across the landscape, a mosaic of destruction and nascent hope. Charred skeletons of buildings stood sentinel against the bruised sky, their once proud facades now gaping wounds. The streets, usually bustling with the quiet rhythms of community life, were choked with debris – splintered wood, twisted metal, and the heartbreaking remnants of lives interrupted. Yet, amidst the desolation, he saw them: the people of Oakhaven.

They moved with a grim determination, their faces smudged with ash and exhaustion, but their eyes held a spark that the flames had failed to extinguish. He saw Elias, his usually jovial face etched with worry, organizing a chain of people passing buckets of water to douse lingering embers. He saw Mara, her hands bandaged from minor burns, meticulously sifting through the rubble of her small bookshop, her brow furrowed in concentration as if expecting to find a miraculously intact first edition. He saw children, their innocence a fragile counterpoint to the grim reality, helping to clear smaller debris, their small hands mimicking the tireless efforts of the adults.

Jax focused his lens on a group of them, their backs bowed in unison as they heaved a fallen beam from the remains of the town hall. Sweat trickled down their temples, mixing with the omnipresent ash, but their movements were synchronized, a testament to an unspoken understanding, a shared burden. It was in these moments of raw, unvarnished effort that the true spirit of Oakhaven began to reveal itself, not in grand pronouncements, but in the quiet, dogged persistence of ordinary people.

He captured the stark contrast between the char and the intact. A sturdy brick building, miraculously spared the full brunt of the fire, stood as a beacon of resilience, its windows reflecting the hazy sky like stoic eyes. Beside it, a once vibrant market stall was reduced to a charred husk, its canvas awning a tattered flag of surrender. These juxtapositions told a story of chance, of the fire's capricious path, but also, Jax suspected, of the desperate efforts of those who had fought to defend their homes and livelihoods. He saw the scorched earth, a canvas of despair, but he also saw the first tentative shoots of green pushing through the ash in Luis's experimental garden, a stubborn refusal to yield.

He spent hours documenting the cleanup, his camera capturing the grit and the grace of the survivors. He photographed the weary smiles exchanged between those who found a salvaged heirloom, the quiet comfort offered to those who had lost everything. He zoomed in on the details: the determined set of a jaw, the gentle touch of a hand on a neighbor's shoulder, the shared glance that conveyed volumes of unspoken empathy. These were the images that mattered, the ones that spoke of a community not broken, but reshaped.

As the sun began its descent, painting the smoke-filled sky in hues of orange and purple, Jax found himself on the edge of town, overlooking the valley. The scale of the destruction was breathtaking, a vast expanse of black and grey stretching as far as the eye could see. It was easy to succumb to despair when faced with such overwhelming loss. But then, his gaze fell upon a cluster of lights flickering to life in the distance. Small, determined pinpricks of illumination against the encroaching darkness. They were the survivors, huddled together, rekindling their hearths, and in doing so, rekindling their hope.

He raised his camera, the familiar weight grounding him. He wouldn't let this be a story of defeat. He would tell the story of Oakhaven's resilience, of the unyielding spirit of a people who, even in the face of utter devastation, chose to rebuild. He would capture the ash, yes, but he would also capture the afterglow, the enduring light of their collective will. He knew that the road ahead would be long and arduous, a path strewn with the remnants of their former lives. But he also knew that the people of Oakhaven, forged in the crucible of this disaster, were capable of more than just survival; they were capable of rising from the ashes, stronger and more united than ever before. He continued to shoot, his finger finding its rhythm on the shutter release, each click a promise to remember, to bear witness, and to tell their story. He had to frame this narrative not just with images of loss, but with the quiet, persistent, and ultimately powerful narrative of human endurance. The sheer will to continue, to find a way forward when all seemed lost, was a story that deserved to be told, and Jax intended to tell it with every frame he captured. He saw the community's efforts extending beyond mere cleanup; he saw the beginnings of a new infrastructure of support, a network of shared resources and tasks that were being forged in the immediate aftermath. People were sharing tools, food, and shelter, their usual individualistic tendencies giving way to a collective necessity. This wasn't just about rebuilding structures; it was about rebuilding the very fabric of their society.

He documented individuals who, despite suffering immense personal loss, were stepping up to help others. There was Anya, whose own home was leveled, yet she was seen tirelessly tending to the injured at the makeshift infirmary set up in the town's still-standing community hall. Her medical knowledge, once a quiet asset, was now proving invaluable to the entire community. Then there was young Finn, barely sixteen, who had lost his parents, but was now using his surprising agility to navigate the dangerous debris fields, scouting for trapped individuals and delivering vital supplies. His youthful energy, once channeled into games and studies, was now a beacon of selfless service.

Jax's lens also captured the silent communication that passed between people. A shared nod of understanding from two individuals who had both lost their homes, a quiet embrace between a rescuer and a survivor pulled from the wreckage, a look of gratitude from someone receiving a salvaged item. These were the micro-narratives of resilience, the small, intimate moments that spoke volumes about the human capacity for empathy and connection, especially in times of crisis. He meticulously framed these fleeting interactions, understanding that the true story of Oakhaven's survival lay not just in the grand gestures of rebuilding, but in the countless acts of kindness and mutual support that sustained them day by day.

He observed the pragmatic solutions that were already emerging. People were pooling their remaining resources, sharing scarce water supplies, and organizing foraging parties into the less affected outlying areas. There was an ingenuity at play, a rapid adaptation to new realities. He saw makeshift shelters being erected from salvaged materials, clever systems for collecting rainwater, and communal kitchens being established to ensure that everyone had access to at least one warm meal a day. These were not just acts of desperation; they were demonstrations of resourcefulness and an innate drive to create order from chaos.

Jax's attention was drawn to the children again. They were adapting with an almost unnerving speed. Their games had changed, incorporating elements of the fire and the rescue efforts, but there was also a palpable sense of community among them. They were helping each other, sharing what little they had, and their laughter, though sometimes subdued, was a precious sound that cut through the somber atmosphere. He captured a group of them playing with a salvaged toy, their faces lit by the flickering glow of a salvaged lantern, a poignant image of childhood resilience.

He understood that his photographs would serve a dual purpose. They would be a historical record, a testament to the catastrophe that had befallen Oakhaven. But more importantly, they would be a source of inspiration, a visual narrative that would remind the people of what they had overcome, and what they were capable of achieving together. He had to convey not just the sorrow of the loss, but the indomitable spirit that refused to be extinguished. He saw the resilience not just in the people, but in the very landscape itself, in the stubborn green shoots that Luis was tending to, a visual metaphor for the hope that was beginning to take root in the hearts of the survivors.

As he continued to document, he realized that his role as a photographer was evolving. It was no longer just about capturing images; it was about bearing witness, about amplifying the voices of the survivors, and about preserving the memory of their struggle and their triumph. He felt a profound sense of responsibility, a need to do justice to the courage and determination he was witnessing. He would ensure that these images would not just document the aftermath, but would serve as a powerful reminder of the strength of the human spirit in the face of adversity. The quiet dignity of the survivors, the unwavering commitment to each other, the sheer grit that was propelling them forward – these were the elements he would weave into his visual chronicle. He would capture the raw emotion, the vulnerability, but also the unwavering resolve. His camera became an extension of his own will to see Oakhaven not just as a victim of disaster, but as a testament to the enduring power of community and the unyielding flame of hope. He knew that future generations would look at these photographs, and they would see not just a town that had burned, but a people who had refused to be consumed. He was meticulously choosing his shots, not just for their aesthetic appeal, but for their narrative power. He wanted each image to tell a story, to evoke an emotion, to convey a message of resilience. He saw a woman carefully tending to a small, potted plant that she had managed to salvage from her home, her face a mixture of sorrow and fierce protectiveness. This tiny green sprout, amidst the grey ashes, became a symbol for him, a microcosm of Oakhaven's own struggle and its burgeoning hope. He continued to work, his spirit invigorated by the very resilience he was documenting, understanding that his photographs would become the visual legacy of a community that had faced the abyss and chosen to climb back into the light.

CHAPTER ELEVEN

THE DAWN OF FUTURE-FIRST

The acrid tang of smoke, though fading, served as a constant, visceral reminder. It was a scent woven into the very fabric of their new reality, a pervasive aroma that spoke of loss and the terrifying power of nature unleashed. Yet, for the people of Oakhaven, that same scent was also becoming a symbol of a hard-won lesson. The fire, in its indiscriminate fury, had stripped away their illusions of security, leaving them exposed and vulnerable. But in that raw, exposed state, they had also discovered a depth of resilience and an unshakeable interconnectedness they hadn't fully appreciated before.

The immediate aftermath was a blur of soot-stained faces and weary movements, a community united in the monumental task of salvaging what they could and burying what they couldn't. But as the smoke thinned and the embers cooled, a different kind of work began to take hold. It was the work of reflection, a collective introspection born out of necessity and a gnawing awareness that the disaster had been a brutal, albeit unintentional, teacher. Gathered in the relative safety of the still-standing community hall, their voices, hoarse from smoke and exhaustion, began to articulate the lessons learned.

Elias, his usual jovial demeanor replaced by a thoughtful gravity, was among the first to voice the palpable shift in their collective consciousness. "We always thought we were prepared," he began, his gaze sweeping across the faces illuminated by the flickering lanterns. "We had our emergency kits, our evacuation plans. But the fire... it showed us how fragile those plans were when faced with something so overwhelming. It wasn't just about having supplies; it was about having each other." He spoke of the moments when a neighbor, with no thought for their own dwindling resources, had shared water or offered a place to sleep. He recalled the sheer power of collective action, how the coordinated efforts to contain the flames, even when they felt futile, had forged a bond stronger than any timber.

Mara, her hands still bandaged, echoed his sentiment, her voice quiet but firm. "My shop... it's gone. Everything I built. But in the days before, when the fire was closing in, the younger folk, the ones I'd only ever seen passing by, they came. They helped me move what they could, helped board up the windows. They didn't have to. They just did. That's the lesson, isn't it? We're not just individuals living near each other; we're a single entity, and when one part is hurt, the whole body feels it." She spoke of the vulnerability of their isolated existence, how the fire had highlighted the fact that a localized disaster could have far-reaching consequences for everyone.

The conversation flowed, a communal unburdening and a shared charting of new territory. They analyzed the vulnerabilities: the lack of easily accessible water reserves beyond the town's aging reservoir, the insufficient firebreaks around the perimeter of their homes, the reliance on a single, aging power grid that had sputtered and died under the strain. Each of these identified weaknesses wasn't a source of shame, but a call to action. The fire had been a diagnostic tool, revealing the unseen ailments within their community's infrastructure and their social fabric.

Luis, his experimental garden a testament to his belief in nature's enduring capacity, spoke with a quiet passion about the need for foresight. "We always built for the present," he said, gesturing towards the charred remains of what had been a row of picturesque cottages. "We built what was needed now, without truly considering what

might be needed tomorrow. The fire taught us that 'tomorrow' can arrive with terrifying speed and unforgiving intensity. We need to build with resilience in mind, not just convenience. We need to think about sustainability not as a choice, but as a survival imperative." He shared his observations of how the areas with more natural vegetation, the established windbreaks, had offered some resistance, while the densely packed, dry-brush-laden areas had been the most susceptible. This led to discussions about responsible land management, about reintroducing native, fire-resistant flora, and about creating decentralized water systems that could withstand such widespread destruction.

The children, too, had learned their lessons, though their understanding was expressed in hushed tones and newfound seriousness. They had witnessed fear, loss, and the courage of their elders. They had helped carry water, cleared debris, and held the hands of those who cried. Their games, once filled with playful abandon, now sometimes involved elaborate reenactments of the fire drills, their small faces earnest as they simulated rescue scenarios. Jax, his camera capturing these moments of innocent solemnity, saw in their eyes a dawning awareness of the world's precariousness, but also a nascent understanding of their own agency, their ability to contribute even in the smallest ways.

The concept of 'Future-First' began to take root in these conversations. It wasn't merely a catchy slogan; it was a philosophy born from the ashes. It meant prioritizing long-term survival and well-being over immediate gratification or convenience. It meant investing in infrastructure that could withstand future shocks, whether from fire, drought, or whatever else the changing climate might throw at them. It meant fostering a culture of preparedness, not out of fear, but out of a profound respect for the delicate balance of their existence.

The shared experience of fighting the fire had, paradoxically, brought them closer. The usual social barriers seemed to have dissolved in the shared danger and the common struggle. People who had previously only exchanged polite nods now knew each other's strengths and weaknesses, their fears and their courage. This newfound camaraderie was not a fleeting emotion; it was a solid foundation upon which they could begin to rebuild. The very act of survival had become a collective act of community building. They had faced their greatest fear together, and in doing so, had discovered their greatest strength: their unity.

The lessons weren't always easy to digest. There were moments of profound grief, of acknowledging the lives lost and the livelihoods destroyed. There were arguments, too, as differing opinions on how to proceed clashed. But underlying it all was a shared commitment to learning and to moving forward. The fire had been a devastating force, but it had also been a catalyst, an unwelcome harbinger of change that forced them to confront their realities and to reimagine their future. They understood that the path ahead would be long and arduous, but they also knew, with a certainty forged in the heat of the inferno, that they would walk it together, their eyes firmly fixed on a future that was not just about survival, but about thriving. This collective awakening, this shared understanding of their interconnectedness and their responsibility to one another, was the most valuable lesson the fire had bestowed. It was a lesson etched not in textbooks or speeches, but in the very soot and ash that still clung to their homes and their hearts, a permanent reminder of what they had endured and what they now understood. The vulnerability they had felt during the fire had transformed into a deep-seated understanding of their interdependence, and this understanding was the bedrock upon which their 'Future-First' approach would be built. They recognized that individual resilience was important, but it was collective resilience, born from genuine connection and mutual reliance, that would truly see them through whatever challenges lay ahead. This realization was a profound shift, moving them from a community of individuals living in proximity to a truly cohesive, interdependent society. The shared trauma had, in a very real sense, rewired their social DNA.

The discussions that followed the initial reflection sessions were not simply about rebuilding what was lost, but about reimagining what could be. Elias, with his pragmatic leadership, initiated the formation of several working groups, each tasked with addressing a specific vulnerability exposed by the fire. One group focused on water security, exploring options for rainwater harvesting on a larger scale, the creation of more robust catchment systems, and even the feasibility of underground reservoirs. Another group took on the critical task of fire mitigation, devising plans for expanded firebreaks, implementing a community-wide program for responsible brush clearing, and investigating the potential for early warning systems that utilized technology beyond simple human observation. Mara's group focused on community resilience, looking at ways to diversify local economies, ensuring that no single livelihood was as vulnerable as it had been, and establishing a more comprehensive system for mutual aid and resource sharing in times of crisis. Luis, naturally, led the charge on ecological restoration, focusing on replanting with native, fire-resistant species, and advocating for land-use practices that worked in harmony with, rather than against, the natural cycles of the region.

These were not quick fixes. They were long-term strategies, requiring significant investment of time, resources, and collective effort. But the 'Future-First' mindset permeated every discussion. Decisions were no longer made based on what was easiest or cheapest in the short term, but on what would provide the greatest long-term security and sustainability. This meant embracing new technologies, sometimes unfamiliar and expensive, but with a clear understanding of their potential to safeguard their future. It meant a commitment to ongoing education and training, ensuring that everyone in the community had the knowledge and skills to contribute to these new initiatives.

Jax's camera continued to document this transition. He captured the earnest discussions in the working groups, the focused intensity of people learning new skills, the collaborative spirit as they cleared land for new firebreaks or constructed new water collection systems. He saw a different kind of effort now, not the frantic, desperate struggle against an immediate threat, but the steady, determined work of building a more secure tomorrow. He photographed the seedlings being carefully planted in Luis's restored areas, a tangible representation of the hope and foresight that now guided them. He captured the shared meals in the community hall, no longer just a place of solace but a hub of planning and collaboration, where ideas were exchanged and commitments were solidified.

The fire had been a brutal interruption, a moment of profound crisis. But in its wake, it had cleared the ground, not just of burning trees and homes, but of complacency and short-sightedness. It had forced them to look beyond the immediate horizon, to confront the potential for future disasters, and to proactively build a community that could withstand them. The lessons learned were etched not only in their memories but in the very landscape they were now meticulously and intentionally reshaping. The fire had been a devastating teacher, but its lessons, however painful, were proving to be the most vital Oakhaven had ever received. They understood that the future was not a passive destination to be reached, but an active creation, built day by day through conscious choices and a deep-seated commitment to each other's well-being. The embers of the fire had long since faded, but the embers of their renewed purpose glowed brighter than ever.

The inferno had scoured Oakhaven, not just of its physical structures, but of its deeply ingrained assumptions about the future. The raw, visceral experience of loss had stripped away layers of complacency, revealing a profound truth: survival wasn't merely about enduring the present, but about actively safeguarding what was to come. This revelation, forged in the crucible of smoke and fear, began to coalesce into something more tangible than shared memory. It became a guiding principle, a conscious decision to recalibrate their entire societal compass. The term 'Future-First' itself, initially a tentative whisper, gained momentum, evolving from a reactive coping mechanism into a proactive, deliberate philosophy. It was no longer just a reaction to the fire, but a fundamental shift in their collective consciousness, a commitment to building a society that actively anticipated and mitigated future challenges.

This adoption of a 'future-first' ethos was not a sudden, overnight transformation. It was a gradual but persistent evolution, nurtured in the quiet aftermath of disaster. Elias, ever the pragmatist, recognized the need to formalize this nascent sentiment. He convened a series of community gatherings, not in the salvaged community hall, which was still undergoing repairs, but in the open air, under the vast, smoke-hazed sky. These meetings became the crucible where abstract ideals were hammered into concrete policy. The initial discussions, born from the emotional urgency of the fire, began to mature into strategic planning. The raw lessons learned – the fragility of their infrastructure, the critical importance of interconnectedness, the devastating impact of ignoring ecological balance – were meticulously dissected and translated into actionable directives.

The 'Future-First' philosophy, as it took shape, was multi-faceted. At its core lay an unwavering commitment to long-term sustainability. This meant a radical departure from the short-sighted practices that had, in part, contributed to their vulnerability. Decisions about resource allocation, land use, and community development would henceforth be measured against their impact on future generations. Every new construction project, every agricultural initiative, every community policy would be subjected to a rigorous "future impact assessment." This wasn't about stifling progress, but about redefining it. Progress was no longer measured by immediate returns or convenience, but by the lasting resilience and health of Oakhaven and its surrounding environment.

Resource management became a paramount concern. The fire had exposed the precariousness of their reliance on external, and often unreliable, systems. The dwindling water reserves, the single point of failure in their aging power grid, the limited local food production – these were not just inconveniences, they were existential threats. The 'Future-First' mandate therefore prioritized the development of decentralized, robust, and sustainable resource systems. This involved a significant investment in infrastructure that could weather future crises. For water, this meant scaling up rainwater harvesting systems, not just for individual households, but for community-wide reservoirs, drawing inspiration from ancient, forgotten techniques of water conservation and augmenting them with modern engineering. The exploration of greywater recycling and the implementation of strict water usage policies became commonplace. For energy, the focus shifted towards renewable sources, with ambitious plans for solar arrays and wind turbines strategically placed to maximize efficiency and minimize environmental impact. The idea of a single, vulnerable power source was deemed an unacceptable risk for the future.

The concept of collective well-being was elevated to an almost sacred principle. The fire had demonstrated, in the starkest possible terms, that individual prosperity was inextricably linked to community health. The days of "every man for himself" were over. The 'Future-First' ethos enshrined a commitment to equity and mutual support. This translated into tangible policies designed to protect the most vulnerable members of their society and to ensure that everyone had a stake in the community's future. A comprehensive mutual aid network was established, formalizing the ad-hoc support that had emerged during the fire. This network not only provided immediate assistance in times of crisis but also facilitated skill-sharing and resource pooling on an ongoing basis. For instance, those with carpentry skills could offer their services to those who needed repairs, while those with knowledge of medicinal herbs could contribute to a community-wide health initiative.

Mara, whose entrepreneurial spirit had been tested by the fire, played a pivotal role in shaping this aspect of the 'Future-First' philosophy. Her own experience of losing her shop, but gaining a deeper understanding of community support, fueled her efforts. She championed the idea of a diversified local economy, advocating for initiatives that would reduce Oakhaven's reliance on any single industry or trade. This included promoting small-scale artisanal production, supporting local agriculture with a focus on diverse and resilient crops, and developing new skill-training programs to equip residents for emerging sustainable industries. Her vision was a community where economic security wasn't dependent on the whims of external markets or the fragile state of a single enterprise, but on the collective strength and adaptability of its members.

Luis's work in ecological restoration and land management became a cornerstone of the 'Future-First' approach to environmental stewardship. The fire had been a brutal lesson in the consequences of neglecting the delicate balance of nature. His vision was not simply about replanting trees, but about fostering a symbiotic relationship with the land. This involved an intensive program of reintroducing native, fire-resistant flora, creating robust windbreaks, and developing land-use practices that mimicked natural ecosystems. The 'Future-First' philosophy demanded that they think like the land itself, understanding its cycles, its vulnerabilities, and its inherent capacity for regeneration. This meant embracing a slower, more deliberate approach to development, one that respected the ecological footprint of every action. Decisions about where and how to build, where to cultivate, and where to conserve were now guided by ecological principles, ensuring that their expansion did not come at the cost of future environmental health.

The children, the inheritors of this new Oakhaven, were at the heart of the 'Future-First' vision. Their education was reoriented to reflect the community's new values. Schools incorporated curriculum that emphasized environmental stewardship, resourcefulness, critical thinking about long-term consequences, and the importance of civic engagement. They learned about the principles of sustainability not as abstract concepts, but as practical skills necessary for their future survival and prosperity. Jax's photographs, which had captured the initial shock and then the dawning realization after the fire, now documented this generational shift. He photographed children participating in community planting days, meticulously tending to seedlings that would grow into the windbreaks of tomorrow. He captured them in classrooms, engaged in debates about responsible water usage or the ethical implications of different energy sources. He saw in their earnest faces a reflection of the community's renewed purpose, a generation being raised with a deep understanding of their responsibility to the planet and to each other.

The formal adoption of the 'Future-First' philosophy was marked by a symbolic act. The community council, now comprised of representatives chosen for their commitment to these new ideals, drafted and ratified the Oakhaven Charter for Sustainable Futures. This document, written on durable recycled paper and displayed prominently in the rebuilt community hall, wasn't just a collection of rules; it was a declaration of intent, a solemn promise to future generations. It outlined the core principles of sustainability, equity, and resilience, and established frameworks for ongoing community dialogue and adaptation. It was a living document, designed to be reviewed and revised as Oakhaven learned and grew.

This shift in values was not without its challenges. There were those who clung to the old ways, who felt that the focus on long-term planning was an unnecessary burden on the present. Debates were frequent, sometimes heated, as the community grappled with the implications of these new ideals. Reallocating resources towards expensive, long-term projects meant foregoing immediate comforts. Implementing strict conservation measures required significant behavioral changes. But the shared experience of the fire had created a powerful impetus for change. The memory of the inferno served as a constant, sobering reminder of the costs of inaction and the fragility of their existence.

The 'Future-First' philosophy thus became more than just a set of policies; it permeated the very culture of Oakhaven. It influenced their art, their music, their storytelling. Tales of resilience, of innovation, and of collective action became the new legends, replacing older narratives that might have focused on individual heroism or past glories. The scent of smoke, once a symbol of destruction, began to transform in their collective imagination. It became a reminder of the lessons learned, a catalyst for their renewed commitment to building a future that was not just secure, but also vibrant and sustainable. The spirit of 'Future-First' was about embracing a proactive, hopeful vision of tomorrow, built on the hard-won wisdom of today, and etched into the very fabric of their revitalized community. It was a conscious, collective decision to move beyond mere survival, and to actively cultivate a thriving future, ensuring that the sacrifices made, and the lessons learned, would not be in vain. This profound commitment to intergenerational responsibility was the bedrock upon which Oakhaven's new dawn was built.

Mika's workshop, once a cluttered space filled with discarded electronics and experimental contraptions born from a desire for efficiency and sometimes, sheer curiosity, had undergone a subtle yet profound transformation. The air, still carrying a faint hum of salvaged machinery, now also smelled of treated wood, beeswax, and the earthy aroma of cultivated fungi. Gone were the impatient sprints towards quick fixes. Instead, her movements were deliberate, infused with the quiet intensity of someone meticulously weaving the future. The 'Future-First' mandate, resonating through every facet of Oakhaven's rebuilding efforts, had found its most tangible expression in Mika's inventive mind. Her work was no longer about simply making things work; it was about making them work *for* the long haul, for generations yet to come, and for the recovering planet.

Her primary focus had shifted to energy generation, not through the brute force of old-world fossil fuels, but through the elegant, understated power of natural systems. Mika was no longer chasing the elusive promise of perpetual motion machines; she was studying the subtle dance of the wind and the relentless persistence of the sun. One of her most promising innovations was the 'Whisperwind Turbine' – a series of low-profile, multi-directional turbines designed to capture even the faintest breezes that rustled through the reforested edges of Oakhaven. Unlike the towering, anachronistic structures of the past that had been vulnerable to extreme weather and visually intrusive, these turbines were almost camouflaged, their blades crafted from a reinforced, bio-composite material derived from fast-growing bamboo and a binding agent extracted from processed kelp. The turbines were small enough to be integrated into the architecture of new buildings, their quiet operation ensuring they wouldn't disturb the burgeoning wildlife. They were also modular, allowing for easy replacement and upgrade, a testament to the 'Future-First' principle of adaptability. Mika had spent weeks in the high plains surrounding Oakhaven, meticulously mapping wind patterns with sensitive anemometers and acoustic sensors, not just for the strongest gusts, but for the consistent, almost imperceptible currents that wind experts had previously dismissed. Her research revealed that the cumulative energy generated by these smaller, strategically placed turbines, when networked together, could rival the output of a single, large, and far more precarious unit.

Complementing the Whisperwind Turbines were Mika's advancements in solar energy. She had moved beyond the brittle, inefficient silicon panels that had been standard before the fire. Her new designs utilized advanced perovskite solar cells, which were not only more efficient at capturing a broader spectrum of light, including diffuse light on cloudy days, but were also flexible and could be integrated into a wider range of materials. She had developed a method for embedding these cells into roofing tiles, turning every dwelling into a micro-power station. Furthermore, she was experimenting with translucent solar films that could be applied to windows, allowing buildings to generate electricity without compromising natural light. This was a radical departure from the past, where solar installations were often bulky afterthoughts, an addition to a structure rather than an integral part of it. Mika envisioned entire neighborhoods powered by a decentralized grid of these integrated solar and wind systems, a network resilient to the failures of any single component, and harmoniously blended into the landscape. The excess energy generated during peak production times was stored not in clunky, chemical-heavy batteries, but in a series of innovative thermal energy storage units that utilized molten salt and phase-change materials, a system designed for longevity and minimal environmental impact at the end of its lifecycle.

Waste reduction was another area where Mika's ingenuity shone, embodying the circular economy principles that were now central to Oakhaven's ethos. She had developed a bio-digester system for organic waste that was far more efficient and contained than previous iterations. This wasn't just about composting; it was about extracting valuable resources. The digester produced biogas, which could be used for cooking and heating, and a nutrient-rich slurry that was perfect for fertilizing the community's expanded agricultural plots. But Mika's vision extended beyond mere waste conversion. She was pioneering methods for reclaiming and repurposing materials from the salvaged remnants of the old world. Her workshop was a testament to this: shelves lined with meticulously sorted plastics, metals, and glass, each destined for a new life. She had developed a low-energy process for shredding and re-forming certain plastics into durable building materials, and had perfected a method for purifying and reusing metals with minimal energy expenditure.

One of her most ambitious projects was the creation of a community-wide 'resource reclamation hub'. This wasn't just a recycling center; it was a vibrant ecosystem where discarded items were not seen as waste, but as raw materials. Mika designed and built automated sorting systems using salvaged sensors and AI algorithms to identify and categorize materials with remarkable precision. She then developed specialized processing units for each material type. For instance, glass was crushed and melted into decorative tiles and countertops, or finely ground into aggregate for new construction. Metals were sorted by alloy and melted down for casting into tools, bicycle parts, and even intricate sculptures that began to adorn Oakhaven's public spaces. Even the salvaged wood, scarred and weathered, was given new life. Mika developed a technique of impregnating it with a natural sealant derived from tree sap, making it resistant to rot and insects, and then used it for furniture, decorative paneling, and structural elements in new builds. Her workshop became a demonstration of this principle – her workbench was a beautifully finished slab of reclaimed oak, her chair a marvel of bent plywood and recycled metal, all crafted from materials that would have once been destined for a landfill or incinerator.

Mika's commitment to environmental remediation was deeply intertwined with her design work. The scars of the fire were still visible in the surrounding landscape, and she saw her inventions as tools for healing. She had developed a series of 'phytoremediation modules' – self-contained units that utilized specially selected plants and microorganisms to break down residual toxins in the soil and water. These modules, often integrated into drainage systems and permeable paving, were designed to work passively, requiring minimal maintenance once established. She was also experimenting with bio-engineered fungi that could consume specific pollutants, and had developed portable bioreactors that could be deployed to clean contaminated water sources. Her designs were not just functional; they were aesthetically considered, often incorporating living elements that added to the beauty of Oakhaven's revitalized spaces. She saw the integration of nature into technology as a fundamental principle of 'Future-First' design, a way of moving beyond the anthropocentric view that had led to so much environmental degradation.

The design process itself was a departure from the old. Mika spent less time hunched over screens, and more time in the field, observing, listening, and understanding the natural world. She walked the regenerating forests, studied the behavior of local fauna, and consulted with Luis on the best ecological strategies for integrating her technologies. Her blueprints were not just schematics; they were detailed ecological assessments, mapping out the potential impact of her designs on the surrounding environment, ensuring that every innovation contributed to the overall health and resilience of the ecosystem. She adopted a philosophy of 'minimal intervention, maximum harmony'. Her machines were designed to be quiet, unobtrusive, and to work *with* natural forces, rather than against them.

One of Mika's most intriguing projects involved the development of a bio-luminescent lighting system. Inspired by the glowing fungi and deep-sea creatures she had studied, she had engineered a stable, long-lasting bio-luminescent bacteria that could be cultivated in sealed, transparent conduits. These conduits could be integrated into pathways, building exteriors, and even interior lighting fixtures, providing a soft, ambient glow at night with virtually no energy consumption. The bacteria were fed a nutrient solution derived from the very organic waste that her bio-digesters processed, creating a closed-loop system that was both beautiful and entirely sustainable. This wasn't just about illumination; it was about reintroducing a sense of natural wonder into their lives, a stark contrast to the harsh, energy-guzzling artificial lights of the past. The gentle, ethereal glow emanating from these systems transformed Oakhaven's nights, creating an atmosphere of peace and quietude that had been lost in the pre-fire era.

The adoption of Mika's designs wasn't instantaneous. There were still lingering doubts, the ingrained habits of a society that had once prioritized immediate gratification and convenience above all else. Some residents were wary of the 'unfamiliar' technologies, the reliance on biological processes, or the absence of the familiar, noisy hum of combustion engines. However, Mika, with her characteristic blend of patience and conviction, was a masterful educator. She didn't just present her designs; she demonstrated them, showcasing their efficacy, their low impact, and their long-term benefits. She held workshops, inviting residents to her transformed workshop, to see the bio-digester in action, to touch the recycled materials, and to witness the Whisperwind Turbines quietly spinning. She explained the science behind the bio-luminescent lights, demystifying the process and highlighting the natural beauty it brought.

Her approach was always collaborative. She worked closely with Elias on the community-wide infrastructure planning, ensuring that her decentralized energy systems were seamlessly integrated into Oakhaven's overall rebuilding strategy. She partnered with Luis to identify optimal locations for her phytoremediation modules, ensuring they would have the greatest ecological impact. And she collaborated with Mara to explore how her reclaimed materials could be used in new artisanal products, fostering small-scale, sustainable enterprises that aligned with the 'Future-First' economic vision. Mika understood that true sustainability wasn't just about creating innovative technologies; it was about fostering a collective understanding and acceptance of these new ways of living.

Her inventions were more than just functional objects; they were physical manifestations of Oakhaven's renewed purpose. Each Whisperwind Turbine humming softly in the breeze, each solar-tiled roof quietly converting sunlight into energy, each lamp glowing with natural bio-luminescence, was a quiet declaration of their commitment to a future that was not just survivable, but thriving. Mika's workshop had become a beacon of this new era, a place where the ashes of the past were being transformed into the building blocks of a more resilient, harmonious, and beautiful tomorrow. The ingenuity that had once been focused on personal gain or mere technological advancement was now channeled into a profound service to the community and the planet, a testament to the transformative power of a shared, future-focused vision. Her work was a constant, tangible reminder that innovation, when guided by wisdom and a deep respect for the natural world, could indeed lead to a brighter dawn. The hum of her machinery was no longer just the sound of progress, but the quiet, persistent song of regeneration.

Luis's journey towards a comprehensive agro-ecological vision began not with grand pronouncements, but with the quiet observation of what the land itself was offering, even in its wounded state. He had always been drawn to the resilience of nature, the persistent green shoots pushing through ash, the tenacious roots anchoring themselves in compromised soil. Before the fire, his focus had been primarily on ensuring immediate sustenance, on coaxing enough food from the earth to feed himself and those closest to him. But the scale of destruction, the sheer devastation that had swept through their land, had forced a re-evaluation. It was no longer enough to simply survive; they had to learn to thrive, to rebuild not just their structures, but their relationship with the earth. This required a shift from individual survival to collective regeneration, a transition that felt both daunting and exhilarating.

He spent countless hours walking the periphery of Oakhaven, meticulously documenting the plant life that had emerged from the ruins. He observed how certain species, often those previously considered undesirable or even invasive, were now acting as ecological pioneers, their robust root systems stabilizing the soil, their rapid growth providing shade and moisture retention for more delicate native flora struggling to re-establish. The tenacious spread of a particular variety of bindweed, for instance, its deep taproots reaching far into the earth, was preventing further erosion on the slopes. Certain tough, scrubby bushes, previously seen as mere undergrowth, were now acting as nurse plants, creating microclimates that allowed seedlings of oak and pine to take root. Luis began to see these plants not as weeds to be eradicated, but as allies, as crucial components in a complex, emergent ecosystem.

His research into permaculture principles, once a theoretical pursuit, now became a practical necessity. He devoured the texts he had salvaged, re-reading them with a new urgency, translating the abstract concepts of closed-loop systems, polycultures, and ecological succession into tangible strategies for Oakhaven. He realized that their own resourcefulness, coupled with an understanding of these natural processes, could forge a path towards true self-sufficiency, a resilience that was not imposed from without, but grown from within.

The 'Future-First' mandate, resonating through every aspect of Oakhaven's rebuilding, found a profound expression in Luis's evolving philosophy. It wasn't just about building structures that lasted, or energy systems that were sustainable; it was about cultivating a food system that was deeply integrated with the land, a system that actively contributed to the health and vitality of the ecosystem. He envisioned a network of interconnected food forests, carefully designed permaculture gardens, and integrated animal husbandry, all working in concert to provide for the community while simultaneously healing the scars of the past.

One of his initial breakthroughs came from studying the invasive kudzu vines that had aggressively carpeted vast swathes of the surrounding wilderness. Before the fire, these vines had been a symbol of nature's unchecked power, a tangled menace that choked out native vegetation. But Luis observed their extraordinary growth rate, their ability to fix nitrogen in the soil, and their surprisingly palatable young shoots. He began to experiment with incorporating them into the diet, not as a staple, but as a valuable supplement. He developed methods for harvesting the tender leaves and young vines, processing them through blanching and light pickling to mitigate their slightly bitter taste, and found they were a rich source of vitamins and minerals, particularly during the lean early months. More importantly, by actively harvesting and utilizing the kudzu, they could manage its spread, preventing it from overwhelming the slower-growing, native species that were crucial for long-term ecological recovery.

He worked with Mika, sharing his observations of how the Whisperwind Turbines, when strategically placed in open areas, could also help aerate the soil and create micro-patterns of wind that influenced seed dispersal and the growth of certain plants. He saw their innovations not as separate entities, but as interlocking pieces of a larger, regenerative puzzle. Mika's phytoremediation modules, designed to cleanse contaminated soil and water, became an integral part of his agricultural planning. He worked to identify the most effective plant and microbial combinations for different types of contamination, strategically placing these modules within the planned garden areas, turning remediation into a fertile ground for future food production.

Luis's vision extended to the creation of a comprehensive seed bank, not just for the crops they intended to grow, but for the wild and resilient flora that were proving vital to the ecosystem's recovery. He understood that preserving genetic diversity was paramount for long-term survival, especially in a world prone to unpredictable environmental shifts. He began meticulously collecting, drying, and storing seeds from the hardy pioneer species, from the nitrogen-fixing legumes that enriched the soil, and from the drought-resistant grains that could withstand challenging conditions. This seed bank became a symbol of their commitment to a future that was deeply rooted in the past, yet prepared for the uncertainties ahead.

He meticulously mapped out Oakhaven's agricultural potential, identifying areas best suited for different types of cultivation based on soil composition, water availability, and sunlight exposure. His plans included not only the cultivation of familiar crops but also the integration of a wide array of underutilized or wild edibles. He recognized the nutritional and ecological value of plants like wild sorrel, dandelion greens, and various species of edible fungi that were beginning to re-emerge. He developed simple, effective methods for propagating these plants, ensuring their availability without depleting wild populations.

The concept of guilds became central to his garden design. He would group plants that mutually benefited each other – for example, planting nitrogen-fixing clover around fruit trees to enrich the soil, or companion planting aromatic herbs like rosemary and lavender to deter pests from vegetable patches. He experimented with 'chop and drop' techniques, where he would harvest biomass from fast-growing cover crops, chop it into smaller pieces, and leave it on the surface of the soil to decompose, acting as a natural mulch and fertilizer. This not only reduced the need for external inputs but also helped to build soil structure and retain moisture.

Luis's understanding of animal integration was also evolving. He saw small-scale, pastured livestock – chickens for pest control and egg production, goats for managing brush and providing dairy, and rabbits for meat – not as separate entities, but as active participants in the agro-ecosystem. Their manure, when properly composted, would feed the soil. Their grazing, when managed rotationally, could help to stimulate plant growth and prevent the re-establishment of aggressive, invasive species in controlled areas. He was particularly interested in creating symbiotic relationships between the animals and the flora. For instance, he envisioned allowing chickens to forage in the orchards during certain seasons, their scratching helping to break up the soil and their droppings fertilizing the trees, while they themselves would consume insects and weeds.

The implementation of his vision was a gradual process, a constant cycle of observation, experimentation, and adaptation. He began by transforming a small, relatively untouched plot of land on the outskirts of Oakhaven into a demonstration garden, a living laboratory where he could showcase the principles of permaculture and agro-ecology. This garden became a focal point for the community, a place where residents could come to learn, to ask questions, and to witness firsthand the potential of working *with* nature rather than against it.

He hosted workshops, not with the air of an expert imparting wisdom, but as a fellow learner sharing discoveries. He showed people how to identify edible wild plants, how to build simple compost bins, how to create natural pest deterrents using household ingredients, and how to plant a diverse range of crops that would provide a continuous harvest throughout the growing season. He emphasized the importance of observation, encouraging everyone to become attuned to the subtle cues of the land – the way the soil felt, the patterns of rainfall, the behavior of the local insects and birds.

His collaboration with Mika was a testament to the interconnectedness of their efforts. He provided her with data on soil conditions and microclimates to help her refine the placement and effectiveness of her bio-luminescent lighting systems, which he envisioned not only illuminating pathways but also attracting beneficial nocturnal insects. He also worked with her to integrate his waste-management strategies, ensuring that the nutrient-rich slurry from her bio-digesters was perfectly balanced for his crops. He saw her energy innovations as crucial enablers for his agricultural ambitions, providing the power needed for irrigation pumps, processing equipment, and even the gentle warmth required for seed starting in cooler months.

The concept of resilience was at the core of Luis's agro-ecological designs. He understood that the old ways of monoculture farming, reliant on single crops and external inputs, were inherently fragile. By diversifying crops, by integrating perennial plants, by building healthy soil, and by fostering a network of beneficial organisms, he was creating a food system that could withstand disease, pest outbreaks, and the vagaries of weather. He was actively working to create a system that was not only productive but also self-repairing, a system that could bounce back from setbacks with a minimum of external intervention.

He began to document the progress of his demonstration garden meticulously. He recorded yields, noted pest pressures, and observed the increasing diversity of insect and bird life. He created visual aids, diagrams, and charts that explained the complex interactions within the garden, making the principles of agro-ecology accessible to everyone. He also began to train a new generation of community gardeners, passing on his knowledge and fostering a sense of shared responsibility for Oakhaven's food security.

The initial skepticism that greeted some of his more unconventional ideas, such as utilizing certain invasive plants, gradually gave way to a grudging respect as people witnessed the tangible benefits. The young shoots of kudzu, once feared, were now seen as a welcome addition to the spring harvest. The deep roots of the bindweed, once a nuisance, were now recognized for their soil-stabilizing properties. Luis's approach was always rooted in practicality and demonstrable results, and as Oakhaven moved further into its 'Future-First' era, his work became increasingly central to the community's newfound self-sufficiency and its commitment to ecological restoration. He was not just growing food; he was growing a future, one that was deeply intertwined with the health and vitality of the land. His vision was a testament to the idea that even from the ashes of devastation, life could re-emerge, stronger, more diverse, and more resilient than before, nurtured by a profound understanding and respect for the natural world. He was, in essence, teaching Oakhaven to speak the language of the earth once more, to listen to its whispers and respond with wisdom and care. His understanding of the land was not just scientific; it was becoming spiritual, a recognition of their place within a larger, interconnected web of life. The success of his initiatives began to ripple outwards, inspiring a deeper appreciation for the natural world, fostering a sense of stewardship, and laying the groundwork for a truly sustainable and harmonious existence for Oakhaven. He was planting seeds, not just in the soil, but in the hearts and minds of his community.

Jax felt the familiar weight of his camera, a comfortable, grounding presence against his shoulder. The silence of early morning in Oakhaven was a canvas, and he was ready to paint it with light and shadow, with the nascent beauty of their rebuilt world. The 'Future-First' philosophy, a guiding star in their collective consciousness, felt less like an abstract concept and more like a tangible force of nature, one he felt compelled to capture and share. His photographic manifesto, as he'd started to think of it, wasn't just about documenting their progress; it was about weaving a narrative, a visual testament to their shared journey towards a sustainable and regenerative existence.

He started with the periphery, where the raw power of nature was most evident, now coaxed into a collaborative dance with human ingenuity. His lens focused on the whispering Whisperwind Turbines, their sleek, elegant forms not as sterile machines imposing themselves on the landscape, but as partners. He positioned himself to frame them against the rising sun, the first rays catching the spinning blades, turning them into ethereal dancers against a sky painted in hues of rose and gold. He captured the way their subtle hum seemed to harmonize with the gentle rustling of new growth pushing through the scorched earth. One image, still nascent in his mind's eye, would show the turbines silhouetted against a sky filled with the returning migratory birds, a symbol of restored ecological balance. He wanted to show that technology, when designed with respect for the natural world, could be an extension of it, not an adversary.

He moved into the newly established permaculture gardens, his camera finding stories in the meticulous design. Luis's vision was everywhere, a vibrant tapestry of life reclaiming what was lost. Jax framed shots of the diverse polycultures, capturing the intricate interplay of plants that Luis had so carefully orchestrated. He focused on the lush, nitrogen-fixing clover carpeting the ground around young fruit saplings, its presence a subtle visual cue of the soil's enrichment. He got close, his macro lens revealing the dew-kissed leaves of a resilient bean variety climbing a bamboo trellis, its tendrils reaching out with a quiet determination. He photographed the 'chop and drop' material, a vibrant mulch of green, creating a rich, fertile bed for new life. The image he envisioned here was one of abundance, of a system where every element served a purpose, where decay was not an end but a vital beginning. He saw the interconnectedness, the elegant efficiency that mirrored the complex systems of the natural world.

His gaze then turned to the community itself, the heart and soul of Oakhaven's resilience. He found his subjects in the hands of builders, weathered and strong, carefully fitting reclaimed timber into new structures, each piece a testament to their resourcefulness. He captured the collaborative spirit in a shot of children, their faces alight with curiosity, helping Mika's team tend to the phytoremediation modules, their small hands carefully planting hardy reeds that would cleanse the earth. He photographed the shared meals, the laughter echoing in the communal dining hall, the plates laden with food grown from their own revitalized soil, a visual representation of their collective effort and shared sustenance. He sought to convey the warmth, the camaraderie, the unspoken understanding that bound them together. One particular scene he longed to capture was a group of elders sharing stories with the younger generation, their faces etched with the wisdom of the past, their eyes reflecting the hopeful future they were building together. This was not about individual heroism, but about the strength of their collective will.

Jax ventured further, seeking out the subtle signs of the land's recovery, the beauty that was emerging from the ashes. He found it in the delicate unfurling of a fern frond amidst the charcoal-stained earth, its vibrant green a defiant splash of life. He discovered it in the shimmering iridescence of a beetle's wing, a tiny marvel of evolution thriving in the newly fertile ground. He captured the resilience of the old oak, a solitary sentinel that had survived the inferno, its gnarled branches now adorned with new, tender leaves, a symbol of enduring strength. He was drawn to the way the water, channeled by Mika's innovative systems, meandered through the landscape, reflecting the clear, blue sky, a mirror to their renewed clarity of purpose. He wanted his images to showcase that recovery wasn't just about rebuilding what was lost, but about discovering a new, perhaps even more profound, beauty in the process of regeneration.

He dedicated a whole section of his photographic series to the integration of Mika's technological advancements with the natural world. He photographed the bio-luminescent pathways, not just as functional illumination, but as ethereal trails of light weaving through the twilight landscape, attracting beneficial insects with their gentle glow. He captured the Whisperwind Turbines not just as sources of power, but as sculptures in motion, their forms harmonizing with the movement of clouds and the bending of trees. He sought to illustrate how technology, when thoughtfully designed and implemented, could enhance, rather than detract from, the natural environment. He envisioned a striking image of a phytoremediation module, its purpose of cleansing the earth, being embraced by flowering plants, its utilitarian design softened by the beauty of organic life.

Jax felt a surge of excitement as he reviewed the early shots on his camera's display. He saw the potential for his project to become more than just a collection of photographs; it could be a living document, a visual manifesto that would inspire and guide. He imagined these images displayed throughout Oakhaven, a constant reminder of their shared aspirations, their hard-won progress, and the beauty of the future they were actively creating. His aim was to create a visual language that spoke to the core of their 'Future-First' philosophy, a language of hope, resilience, and profound connection to the earth.

He spent days meticulously scouting locations, waiting for the perfect light, the ideal moment to capture the essence of Oakhaven's transformation. He framed a shot of a flock of chickens foraging in a young orchard, their busy scratching and pecking a visible demonstration of Luis's integrated animal husbandry, their droppings a promise of future fertility. He captured the subtle glow of Mika's energy-efficient lighting in the community kitchen, where residents were preparing meals from their abundant harvests, the light reflecting the warmth of their shared endeavor. He sought out the quiet moments, the contemplative spaces, where the profound connection between humanity and nature was most palpable.

His process was a form of meditation, a deep immersion into the spirit of Oakhaven. He would spend hours observing the intricate patterns of insect life in the newly planted wildflower meadows, the patient work of bees pollinating the burgeoning fruit blossoms, the steady progress of native grasses reclaiming the scarred slopes. He saw these as visual metaphors for their own journey, the slow, persistent, and ultimately triumphant return of life. He was particularly drawn to the contrast between the remnants of the fire – the stark beauty of blackened trees standing sentinel – and the vibrant green shoots pushing through the ash at their base. This juxtaposition, he felt, perfectly encapsulated the essence of their rebuilding efforts.

One of his most ambitious ideas was to create a series of panoramic shots that would capture the breathtaking sweep of Oakhaven's transformation. He envisioned a triptych: one panel showing the raw, scarred landscape before the conscious rebuilding effort, another capturing the nascent stages of development with the

Whisperwind Turbines and initial gardens, and a third depicting the integrated ecosystem that was slowly, steadily emerging. This would serve as a powerful visual timeline, a testament to their journey and a beacon of hope for what was yet to come.

He also focused on the smaller details, the intimate moments that spoke volumes about their progress. He photographed the careful labeling of seeds in Luis's expanding seed bank, each packet a promise of future harvests, a repository of resilience. He captured the gleam of satisfaction in the eyes of a community member as they harvested their first basket of plump tomatoes, a tangible reward for their collective labor. He sought out the expressions of joy and wonder on the faces of children as they discovered a ladybug or watched a butterfly alight on a newly bloomed flower, their connection to the natural world being nurtured from its earliest stages.

Jax understood that his role was not just to document, but to interpret, to translate the complex principles of their rebuilding into a universally understandable visual language. He sought to evoke emotion, to inspire awe, and to foster a sense of profound appreciation for the delicate balance they were striving to achieve. He wanted his images to be a conversation starter, a catalyst for further innovation and a constant reaffirmation of their commitment to a 'Future-First' approach. He believed that by showcasing the tangible beauty and inherent logic of their regenerative practices, he could inspire a deeper level of engagement and commitment from every member of the community.

He considered the power of repetition and pattern in his work. He would photograph the same turbine from different angles and at different times of day, capturing its constant, silent work. He would revisit the gardens throughout the seasons, documenting the cyclical rhythm of growth, bloom, and harvest. He saw a parallel in the community's own cyclical efforts – periods of intense labor followed by seasons of nurturing and fruition. This rhythmic approach, he believed, would underscore the sustainable and enduring nature of their 'Future-First' philosophy.

The collaborative aspect of their rebuilding was also a crucial theme he aimed to capture. He took portraits of individuals working alongside each other, their shared effort evident in their posture, their expressions, their interwoven tasks. He photographed the passing of knowledge, the patient guidance of an experienced builder helping a younger apprentice, the shared laughter and mutual respect that characterized their interactions. He wanted to convey that their success was not built on individual brilliance, but on a foundation of shared purpose and mutual support.

He found himself returning to the metaphor of the emergent ecosystem. He saw the Whisperwind Turbines as the emergent canopy, providing a vital function while allowing light to filter down. He viewed Luis's gardens as the understory, a diverse and complex layer of life supporting the larger system. Mika's technologies, he felt, were the vital microbial communities and nutrient cycles, working unseen but essential to the overall health of the biome. His photographs aimed to illustrate this intricate web, this delicate and powerful interdependence. He saw his photographic manifesto as a key to unlocking a deeper understanding of this intricate design, making it accessible and inspiring for all. He knew that a single image, if framed correctly, could convey more than a thousand words, and he was dedicated to finding those powerful visual narratives.

CHAPTER TWELVE

THE RESOURCE LIBRARY

The concept of a 'Resource Library' began as a quiet murmur, a necessity born from the stark realities of their existence. It wasn't a grand pronouncement, but a pragmatic response to the scattered nature of their efforts, the occasional duplication of resources, and the constant need for access to specialized tools that a single individual might not possess. The 'Future-First' philosophy, which Jax had so eloquently captured with his lens, demanded a system that reinforced their collective survival and ensured that no one was left behind, struggling in isolation. Thus, the Resource Library was conceived, not as a dusty archive of the past, but as a dynamic, breathing hub for the present and a vital cornerstone for their future.

Its physical manifestation was as thoughtful and considered as any of Mika's energy systems or Luis's permaculture designs. Located in what had once been the town's community center, a building that had miraculously survived the eruption with minimal damage, it was a space reimagined. The cavernous main hall, previously used for town meetings and celebrations, was now divided into distinct zones. The air, once thick with the scent of recycled food and the low hum of communal chatter, now carried a more utilitarian aroma: the faint metallic tang of well-maintained tools, the earthy fragrance of preserved seeds, and the subtle, pleasing scent of treated lumber and salvaged textiles.

The design of the library was a testament to their collaborative spirit. Mika, ever the pragmatist, ensured that the building was fully integrated with their sustainable energy grid. Solar panels, discreetly integrated into the roofline, powered the energy-efficient LED lighting that illuminated the space with a steady, consistent glow. The heating and cooling systems were managed by Mika's proprietary geothermal pumps, ensuring a stable, comfortable environment for both the stored resources and the people who utilized them, regardless of the external weather. Luis, with his keen understanding of flow and function, designed the internal layout. He envisioned not just storage, but an ecosystem of resources. Sections were clearly demarcated, not with rigid walls, but with thoughtful arrangements of shelving units, repurposed industrial racks, and cleverly constructed partitions made from salvaged materials. Pathways were wide enough to accommodate the larger equipment, and strategically placed workbenches allowed for immediate use of borrowed items.

The core of the library was its diverse inventory. At its heart, of course, were the tools. Not just any tools, but a curated collection of the best, the most robust, and the most versatile that Oakhaven possessed or had managed to salvage. There were hand tools for every conceivable task: saws of all sizes, hammers, axes, chisels, planes, wrenches, screwdrivers, and an array of specialized implements for plumbing, electrical work, and carpentry. These were meticulously organized, cleaned, and sharpened by a rotating roster of community members who had proven their aptitude for maintenance. Each tool was tagged, not just with its name and inventory number, but with a small QR code. This code, when scanned with a common device, would bring up a brief instructional video or a set of written guidelines on its proper use and maintenance, a direct manifestation of the knowledge-sharing ethos.

Beyond hand tools, the library housed a collection of larger, more specialized equipment. There were electric drills and saws, powered by rechargeable battery packs that were themselves maintained and charged by Mika's energy system. There were welding kits, a borrowed but invaluable set of agricultural machinery for tilling and harvesting larger plots, and even a meticulously maintained 3D printer, a marvel of salvaged technology that could fabricate replacement parts for almost anything, given the correct digital schematics. Access to these larger items was managed through a simple sign-out system, ensuring that heavy-duty equipment was available to those who genuinely needed it for community projects and that it was returned in good working order. The library's custodians, a dedicated team of volunteers, were trained in the basic operation of all the equipment, serving as an initial point of contact and guidance for users.

The seed bank was another vital component, overseen by Luis himself. Housed in a climate-controlled section of the library, it was a testament to Oakhaven's commitment to food security and biodiversity. Varieties of grains, legumes, vegetables, and herbs, all adapted to the local climate and soil conditions, were carefully cataloged and stored in airtight containers. These weren't just generic seeds; they were seeds that had been grown, harvested, and saved by the community, selected for their resilience and yield. Each seed packet bore not only the name of the plant but also information on its optimal planting conditions, expected germination time, and any specific pest or disease resistance it possessed. This was more than just a pantry; it was a living archive of Oakhaven's agricultural heritage, a promise of future harvests. There were also sections dedicated to medicinal herbs and other useful plants, ensuring that traditional knowledge of natural remedies remained accessible.

Salvaged materials formed another significant part of the library's collection. The eruption had left behind a landscape littered with the debris of the old world, and Oakhaven had become adept at repurposing and recycling. The library served as a central hub for these salvaged treasures. Sorted by material and potential use, there were piles of reclaimed lumber, stacks of metal sheeting, bundles of electrical wire, rolls of fabric, and an assortment of plumbing fixtures, all cleaned, processed, and made ready for reuse. This ensured that valuable resources weren't sitting idle in individual homes but were available for any community project, preventing unnecessary new production and further minimizing their environmental footprint. A dedicated section was even established for electronic components and circuitry, allowing for the repair and revitalization of salvaged devices.

But the Resource Library was far more than just a repository of physical objects. Its true value lay in its function as a hub for shared knowledge, a living, breathing embodiment of the 'Future-First' philosophy. This aspect was meticulously curated and fostered by a dedicated team, often led by individuals with a knack for organization and communication. They understood that knowledge was as crucial a resource as any tool or seed. To this end, dedicated bays within the library were set aside for the dissemination of practical information.

One area was dedicated to what they called the "Technological Blueprints." Here, digital copies of schematics for Mika's various inventions were stored, accessible via networked terminals. Anyone with a project that could benefit from solar power integration, water purification, or efficient lighting could access the plans, learn how the systems worked, and even download designs for component fabrication if they had access to the 3D printer. This wasn't just about providing access to blueprints; it was about fostering understanding. Accompanying the schematics were detailed explanatory notes, often recorded by Mika herself or her apprentices, breaking down complex engineering principles into digestible segments. There were also case studies of successful integrations and common troubleshooting guides.

Another crucial section was devoted to "Regenerative Practices." Luis was the primary curator here, ensuring that the knowledge gathered from their successes and failures in permaculture, soil regeneration, and integrated pest management was readily available. This included detailed guides on companion planting, natural fertilization techniques, water harvesting strategies, and the cultivation of specific resilient crops. These guides weren't just dry text; they were often supplemented with visual aids. Jax's photographs, far from being confined to his personal archive, found a prominent place here, illustrating the practical application of these techniques. There were also video recordings of Luis demonstrating specific gardening methods, explaining the symbiotic relationships between different plants, or showcasing the benefits of no-till farming. Oral histories were also collected, with recordings of elders sharing traditional agricultural knowledge that had proven surprisingly relevant in their new world.

The "Salvage and Repair" section was a treasure trove of practical ingenuity. This area focused on the art of making do and making better. It contained guides on identifying useful materials from salvaged wreckage, techniques for cleaning and treating various substances, and instructions for repairing common household items and tools. This was where the community's collective ingenuity truly shone. Many residents contributed their own expertise, creating instructional videos on how to mend a broken appliance, how to repurpose old clothing into durable fabric, or how to re-wire a salvaged electrical component. These contributions were vetted for safety and effectiveness by a small committee, ensuring that the knowledge shared was reliable and practical.

Beyond these structured sections, the library served as a nexus for informal knowledge exchange. The workbenches, equipped with basic tools and lighting, were often buzzing with activity. Community members would gather there to work on personal projects, to collaborate on repairs, or simply to discuss challenges and share solutions. The librarians, a group of individuals with diverse skills and a passion for community building, acted as facilitators. They were adept at connecting people with the knowledge they needed, whether it was pointing someone to the correct blueprint, introducing them to an elder with expertise in a particular craft, or simply helping them navigate the library's extensive catalog.

The sign-out system for tools and equipment was designed with fairness and transparency in mind. A digital log, accessible via the networked terminals, tracked who had borrowed what, and for how long. This wasn't for punitive measures, but for accountability and to ensure that valuable resources were not being hoarded or neglected. If an item was overdue, a friendly reminder would be sent, or a librarian would follow up. The system also allowed for requests to be placed on popular items, ensuring that those who needed them for critical projects were prioritized. This equitable distribution was a cornerstone of their 'Future-First' approach, ensuring that progress was a shared endeavor, not a race for individual acquisition.

The library also played a crucial role in the ongoing education of Oakhaven's younger generation. Workshops were regularly held within its walls, introducing children to basic tool usage, gardening techniques, and the principles of sustainable technology. These weren't just theoretical lessons; they were hands-on experiences. Children would help maintain the seed bank, assist in the repair of simple tools, or learn to identify useful plants in the library's small demonstration garden. This practical education instilled in them a deep respect for resources and a sense of responsibility for their community's future.

The impact of the Resource Library on Oakhaven's collective spirit was profound. It fostered a sense of interdependence, a tangible reminder that their strength lay in their unity. When someone needed a specialized tool for a unique repair, they didn't have to search endlessly or go without; they knew the library had it, and someone there could help them find it and use it. When a new gardening challenge arose, they knew the collective knowledge of their community, curated within the library, held the solutions. This shared access to resources and knowledge reduced individual burdens, fostered innovation, and built a stronger, more resilient society.

The library also served as a beacon of hope. It represented Oakhaven's proactive approach to rebuilding, their commitment to learning from the past and building a better future. It was a physical manifestation of their "Future-First" philosophy, a place where ideas were nurtured, skills were honed, and community bonds were strengthened. It was a testament to the belief that by sharing what they had, both tangible and intangible, they could not only survive but thrive, creating a legacy of resourcefulness and collaboration that would endure for generations to come. The shelves, filled with tools, seeds, salvaged materials, and the wisdom of their collective experience, were more than just storage; they were a promise of continuity, a testament to the enduring power of shared purpose. Jax's photographs, now prominently displayed in designated areas of the library, served as visual reminders of the journey, the challenges overcome, and the beauty of the future they were diligently constructing, one shared resource, one learned skill, at a time.

Kiley's approach to the Resource Library was not one of grand pronouncements or abstract theory, but of meticulous, ground-level functionality. Where others saw a collection of salvaged goods and borrowed knowledge, Kiley saw a complex ecosystem that demanded rigorous order to truly flourish. Her background, though not rooted in formal academia, had honed an almost instinctive understanding of logistics. She'd spent years coordinating the complex dance of supply and demand in the pre-eruption era, a skill that translated with uncanny precision to the post-cataclysmic needs of Oakhaven. For Kiley, the library wasn't just a place to store things; it was the operational heart of their nascent society, and it needed to beat with unwavering efficiency.

Her initial survey of the space, which had initially been a chaotic jumble of donated items and hastily erected shelves, was swift and decisive. She moved through the aisles with a focused intensity, her eyes scanning, categorizing, and mentally rearranging. The previous efforts, while well-intentioned, lacked a cohesive strategy. Tools were grouped by type but not by project applicability; salvaged materials were piled loosely, their potential uses obscured by dust and disarray; the seed bank, while secure, lacked an intuitive browsing system.

Kiley recognized that true accessibility wasn't just about having the item; it was about making it findable, understandable, and ultimately, usable by every single member of the community.

Her first major undertaking was the establishment of a robust cataloging system. This wasn't to be a dusty ledger, but a dynamic, searchable database. She worked with Mika to integrate a simplified, low-power terminal system throughout the library. Each item, from the smallest screw to the largest piece of salvaged machinery, was assigned a unique identifier. This identifier was then linked to a digital profile containing a wealth of information. For tools, this included its exact location within the library, its maintenance history, any specialized skills required for its operation, and even a link to relevant instructional videos or schematics within the library's knowledge base. Salvaged materials were tagged with their composition, dimensions, and potential applications, drawing from a growing community-contributed list of ideas. The seed bank was meticulously cross-referenced, detailing not only the plant variety but also its ideal growing conditions, historical yield data from Oakhaven's trials, and even cross-pollination compatibility.

Kiley understood that a comprehensive catalog was only half the battle. The other half was ensuring that the physical layout facilitated easy retrieval and return. She envisioned a system of clear, color-coded zones, each dedicated to a specific category of resource. The tool section was further subdivided into categories like "Construction," "Repair," "Gardening," and "Specialty." Within these, hand tools were grouped by function, and power tools were stored in designated charging stations, their slots clearly marked. The salvaged materials section was organized by material type – metals, woods, textiles, plastics, electronics – and then further by size and potential use. Shelving was reinforced, aisles were widened, and clear, universally understandable signage, often incorporating pictograms designed by Jax's team, was erected. She even designed a system of mobile shelving units for bulkier items, allowing for flexible rearrangement of the space as needs evolved.

Crucially, Kiley's organizational genius extended beyond the purely physical. She was deeply invested in ensuring that the library served

everyone. This meant considering accessibility for individuals with varying physical abilities and skill sets. She advocated for the inclusion of assistive tools – modified grips for wrenches, rolling work platforms, and magnifying lamps – and ensured these were clearly identified and readily available. She also recognized that many in Oakhaven had skills that were not traditionally valued in the old world, and that these skills held immense practical value now. The cataloging system included fields for "User Expertise," allowing individuals to voluntarily list skills they possessed related to specific tools or materials, and for "Learning Opportunities," where someone could indicate a desire to learn about a particular resource, effectively creating informal mentorship pairings facilitated by the library's interface.

To further democratize access, Kiley implemented a tiered sign-out system, designed to balance immediate need with long-term planning. Emergency requests for critical repairs or essential planting could be fast-tracked. Community projects, requiring multiple tools or significant quantities of materials, had a clear proposal and approval process that prioritized communal benefit. For personal projects, a simple, time-based sign-out system was in place, with gentle reminders and a community-driven accountability system to ensure timely returns. She also instituted a "Resource Wishlist" function, where community members could anonymously request items that were not currently in stock. This data was invaluable for guiding future salvage operations and prioritizing acquisitions.

Kiley's relentless pursuit of efficiency was not about imposing rigid rules, but about freeing up collective potential. She saw that by removing the friction of searching, by clarifying availability, and by making resources intuitively accessible, she was not just organizing objects, but empowering people. She understood that in a society built on shared responsibility and collective progress, the infrastructure that supported that effort had to be as robust and accessible as the ideals themselves. Her meticulous system was a quiet but powerful testament to the belief that true progress stemmed from a foundation of order, fairness, and universal access, ensuring that every member of Oakhaven had the tools, the knowledge, and the opportunity to contribute their unique talents to building their shared future.

The initial rollout of Kiley's system was met with a mixture of awe and trepidation. The sheer scale of her organization was, for some, overwhelming. The pre-eruption world had been a place of information overload and often, opaque systems that benefited the few. Oakhaven, by contrast, had thrived on a more organic, word-of-mouth exchange. Kiley's methodical approach felt, to some, like a return to a more structured, perhaps even bureaucratic, way of doing things.

However, Kiley was a master of demonstration and gradual integration. She didn't just present the system; she lived it. She could be found daily, not behind a desk, but on the floor of the library, guiding individuals through the cataloging process, helping them tag new acquisitions, or demonstrating the efficient use of the sign-out terminals. She patiently explained the rationale behind each step, emphasizing how her system was designed to *enhance* their collaborative spirit, not stifle it.

"Think of it like Luis's irrigation system," she'd explain to a curious gardener, her voice calm and steady. "It's not just pipes and water. It's about precise delivery, ensuring every plant gets what it needs, when it needs it, without waste. This catalog, these zones – they're our irrigation system for resources and knowledge. It ensures nothing dries up, nothing gets lost, and everyone benefits."

Her focus on inclusivity was particularly evident in her design of the user interface for the cataloging terminals. Recognizing that not everyone was tech-savvy, she worked with Jax's team to develop a visually intuitive interface. Icons were large and clear, text was concise and easy to read, and the search functions were designed to be flexible, allowing users to search by keyword, category, or even by a descriptive phrase like "thingy to hammer nails with." For those who struggled even with this, she implemented a "Librarian Assistance" button that would alert a human helper, a role she often filled herself in the early days.

Kiley also recognized the value of the intangible. She understood that the "Resource Library" was more than just tools and seeds; it was also a repository of skill and experience. To that end, she initiated the "Skill Share" program, an extension of the library's knowledge dissemination. This program encouraged individuals to volunteer to teach short workshops on topics they excelled in. A retired carpenter might offer a session on joinery techniques, a former seamstress could teach visible mending, or a seasoned forager might share their knowledge of local edible plants. These workshops were scheduled and advertised through the library's system, and attendance was logged, creating a record of who had shared what knowledge and who had learned.

The success of the Skill Share program was a direct testament to Kiley's foresight. It not only reinforced the knowledge base within the community but also fostered deeper social connections. People who might have previously only interacted in passing now found common ground through shared learning experiences. Kiley ensured that these workshops were open to all, with special consideration for scheduling around existing community duties and for providing necessary materials through the library itself. She saw these skill-sharing sessions as vital threads in the fabric of Oakhaven, weaving together the practical needs of survival with the human desire for connection and personal growth.

Moreover, Kiley's organizational prowess extended to the very concept of waste reduction within the library itself. She implemented a rigorous "Return and Refurbish" protocol. Any returned tool was immediately inspected. Minor issues were addressed on the spot by designated "Tool Tenders" – individuals trained in basic maintenance. Items requiring more extensive repair were routed to the appropriate specialists, with their progress tracked in the catalog. This not only ensured that tools were always in optimal working condition but also created a consistent demand for repair skills, providing valuable work and training opportunities.

For salvaged materials, Kiley introduced a "Repurposing Idea Board" in a prominent location. Community members were encouraged to post their ideas for how discarded items could be transformed into something useful. This fostered a collective problem-solving approach, turning potential waste into a source of creative inspiration. If an idea gained traction, Kiley could then easily facilitate the retrieval of the necessary materials from the library's inventory. She saw this as a way to tap into the latent ingenuity of the entire community, making everyone a co-creator in Oakhaven's resourcefulness.

The sheer volume of salvaged goods meant that storage and accessibility were constant challenges. Kiley's solution was a dynamic inventory management system. Periodically, she would organize "Inventory Audits," where designated teams would systematically review sections of the library, re-categorize items that had been mislabeled, and identify materials that had been sitting idle for extended periods. These audits were also opportunities to assess the condition of stored goods and to brainstorm new uses for slow-moving inventory. Kiley believed that an active, engaged approach to inventory was essential to prevent the library from becoming a stagnant repository of forgotten potential.

Her dedication also extended to the physical well-being of those who worked within and utilized the library. She ensured adequate lighting, good ventilation, and ergonomic considerations for the workstations. She was a staunch advocate for regular breaks and fostered a culture where seeking help was seen not as a weakness, but as a smart utilization of communal resources. Her calm, organized presence became a reassuring constant for the community, a living embodiment of the stability and foresight that Oakhaven was striving for.

Kiley's genius lay in her ability to see the interconnectedness of all things within Oakhaven. She understood that the efficiency of the Resource Library directly impacted the success of Mika's energy projects, Luis's agricultural endeavors, and Jax's documentation efforts. By creating a system that was transparent, accessible, and highly functional, she was not just managing inventory; she was actively nurturing the resilience, ingenuity, and collaborative spirit that defined their new way of life. She had transformed a collection of disparate items into a vital, living organ of their community, ensuring that the future they were building was not only sustainable but also grounded in the principle of equitable access to the means of creation and survival. The Resource Library, under Kiley's meticulous stewardship, was becoming far more than a building filled with things; it was becoming a testament to their collective potential, a tangible manifestation of their shared commitment to a future where everyone had the opportunity to contribute and to thrive.

Mika's arrival at the Resource Library, following Kiley's foundational organizational overhaul, felt less like an addition and more like a vital infusion of intellectual and practical energy. While Kiley had masterfully organized the physical and digital infrastructure, Mika brought a wealth of specialized knowledge and a unique approach to its utilization. Her contributions weren't merely about adding more inventory; they were about deepening the library's capacity to foster self-reliance and innovation, particularly in the realm of essential infrastructure.

Her initial offerings were a revelation. She personally delivered a carefully curated collection of salvaged technical equipment. These weren't random assortments of wires and components; they were meticulously selected items that represented critical nodes in the functioning of their community's life support systems. Among the haul were several high-capacity water pumps, their casings scarred but their internal mechanisms surprisingly intact. Beside them lay spools of specialized, high-tensile wiring, crucial for extending power grids or reinforcing critical conduits. There were also advanced filtration components, salvaged from industrial purification plants, each piece bearing the subtle, almost artistic, sheen of precision engineering. These weren't items one could easily stumble upon during routine salvage runs; they were the product of Mika's keen eye for identifying the truly indispensable, the components that, if understood and maintained, could make the difference between a sputtering existence and a thriving community.

Accompanying this hardware was an equally significant trove of knowledge, encoded not just in data chips but in meticulously drafted schematics and comprehensive instructional guides. Mika had always possessed a knack for translating complex technical jargon into understandable diagrams and step-by-step procedures. Her filtration systems, which had become a lifeline for Oakhaven, were a prime example. She presented Kiley with a complete set of schematics for her multi-stage filtration units, detailing everything from the initial sediment removal stages to the UV sterilization and final polishing filters. But Mika didn't stop at mere blueprints. She had painstakingly documented the maintenance requirements for each component, the diagnostic steps for identifying common malfunctions, and, most importantly, the procedures for DIY repairs and even for fabricating replacement parts using readily available salvaged materials.

These weren't just theoretical manuals; they were practical, hands-on guides designed for the community member with a wrench in their hand and a problem to solve. For instance, one set of instructions, accompanied by clear, hand-drawn diagrams, walked users through the process of replacing a worn pump impeller using a salvaged bicycle chain and a carefully shaped piece of durable polymer. Another detailed how to recalibrate flow sensors using simple magnetic field adjustments, a technique that bypassed the need for specialized, irreplaceable electronic components. Mika's understanding of the post-eruption reality was profound; she knew that reliance on original equipment manufacturer parts was a luxury they could no longer afford. Her schematics and guides were a testament to her ability to innovate within constraints, to find elegant solutions using the detritus of the old world.

Beyond the physical items and documentation, Mika's most impactful contribution was the establishment of a dedicated workshop space within the Resource Library. Recognizing that access to schematics and tools was only one part of the equation, she understood that true empowerment came from shared learning and hands-on experience. She identified a section of the library, previously underutilized and somewhat dusty, and began to transform it. With Kiley's logistical support, she cleared the space, erected sturdy workbenches from salvaged metal framing and repurposed countertops, and installed overhead lighting powered by a dedicated, low-draw generator she'd brought with her.

This workshop was not intended to be a private domain for Mika's expertise, but a communal learning hub. Her vision was to democratize knowledge, to equip individuals with the skills and confidence to tackle their own technical challenges. She began by offering a series of introductory workshops, open to anyone interested. Her first sessions focused on the fundamental principles of her filtration systems. She'd gather a small group, perhaps six or eight individuals, around a disassembled filtration unit, her hands moving with practiced grace as she explained the function of each component. She'd demonstrate how to properly seal a pipe joint using reclaimed rubber and a heat-fusion technique, how to identify and replace a clogged filter cartridge, and how to conduct basic flow rate tests.

The response from the community was immediate and enthusiastic. People who had previously only known the "black box" of their water systems now felt a sense of agency. A young woman, who had been responsible for maintaining the filtration unit in her sector, found herself not just reporting malfunctions but actively troubleshooting and resolving them. An older gentleman, whose days of intricate mechanical work were thought to be behind him, discovered a renewed sense of purpose as he patiently guided younger members through the intricacies of pump assembly. Mika fostered an environment where questions were encouraged, where mistakes were seen as learning opportunities, and where collaborative problem-solving was the norm. She would often say, with a warm smile, "The goal isn't for everyone to become an expert engineer. The goal is for everyone to understand enough to keep the water flowing, to keep the lights on, and to feel empowered to fix what's broken in their own corner of Oakhaven."

Her approach to teaching was iterative. She understood that the "Resource Library" was a living entity, constantly receiving new acquisitions and experiencing new challenges. She encouraged workshop attendees to bring their own tools and materials, to experiment and to share their own findings. If someone discovered a more efficient way to repair a particular component, Mika would encourage them to document it, perhaps with Jax's help, and add it to the library's growing knowledge base. This created a virtuous cycle of learning and improvement, where the community's collective experience continuously refined the available resources and knowledge.

One of Mika's most innovative ideas was the creation of a "Troubleshooting Log" within the workshop space. This was a physical whiteboard, prominently displayed, where individuals could post specific technical problems they were encountering. They would describe the issue, list the equipment involved, and note any troubleshooting steps they had already taken. Other community members, whether they were attending a workshop or simply passing through, were encouraged to contribute their own suggestions, insights, or even offer hands-on assistance. This turned the workshop into a dynamic hub for real-time problem-solving, often leading to unexpected but highly effective solutions. A persistent issue with a flickering light in the agricultural sector, for instance, was eventually resolved by a suggestion posted on the board by a former electrician who had noticed a subtle resonance frequency in the power cables, a problem that wouldn't have been apparent through traditional diagnostics alone.

Mika also recognized the importance of documenting the "why" behind her designs. She didn't just provide instructions; she shared the underlying principles. In her workshops, she would often delve into the physics of fluid dynamics for the filtration systems, or the principles of electrical conductivity for the wiring. This was not to intimidate, but to foster a deeper understanding. She believed that by grasping the fundamental science, individuals would be better equipped to adapt her designs to new situations or to invent entirely novel solutions. This intellectual foundation was, in her eyes, just as critical as the physical tools and schematics. It was about cultivating a mindset of inquiry and innovation that would serve Oakhaven far beyond the immediate needs of repair.

The integration of Mika's contributions into the Resource Library's existing framework was seamless, largely due to her collaborative spirit and Kiley's foresight. The schematics and guides she provided were digitized and linked within the library's cataloging system, cross-referenced with the specific tools and components required for their implementation. The salvaged equipment was cataloged, its condition and any known maintenance history meticulously recorded. The workshop space itself became a designated area within the library's layout, clearly marked and equipped with the necessary resources, including a selection of common tools that Mika had supplemented from her own salvaged stashes.

Furthermore, Mika worked with Kiley to establish a system for tracking the success of the workshop and the dissemination of her knowledge. Attendance records for workshops, the frequency of certain troubleshooting requests on the log, and even informal feedback from community members were all collected. This data allowed Mika and Kiley to identify areas where further training or resources might be needed, ensuring that the library's educational offerings remained relevant and responsive to the community's evolving needs. They began to see patterns emerge: a surge in requests related to basic electrical repairs after a particularly harsh storm, or an increased interest in hydroponic system maintenance following a successful harvest cycle. This feedback loop was invaluable, allowing them to proactively address potential bottlenecks and to foster specialized skill sets where demand was highest.

Mika's presence transformed the Resource Library from a mere repository of physical goods and information into a dynamic center for applied knowledge and practical skill development. Her technical expertise, combined with her passion for teaching and her unwavering belief in the capacity of others, was a powerful catalyst for Oakhaven's continued resilience. She didn't just provide the means to fix things; she cultivated the understanding, the confidence, and the collaborative spirit necessary for the community to truly thrive, proving that the most valuable resource of all was not the salvaged scrap, but the empowered mind. She had, in essence, helped to forge the tools of self-sufficiency and then generously handed them to everyone in Oakhaven, along with the knowledge of how to use them, ensuring that their future would be built not on chance, but on competence and shared ingenuity. Her workshop became a testament to the idea that knowledge, when shared and practiced, is a force multiplier, capable of transforming scarcity into abundance and dependency into autonomy. This philosophy, embodied in her hands-on approach and her dedication to empowering others, became an integral part of the Resource Library's evolving mission, a mission that was increasingly defined by its capacity to equip every member of Oakhaven with the skills to build and sustain their shared future.

Luis's contribution to the Resource Library was a quiet counterpoint to Mika's buzzing workshop and Kiley's meticulous cataloging. Where others focused on the immediate needs of repair and infrastructure, Luis looked towards the horizon, towards the very foundation of Oakhaven's future: its food. His was a mission rooted in the earth, in the patient waiting of a seed, and in the profound understanding that true resilience began with the ability to grow.

He arrived at the library not with salvaged machinery or complex schematics, but with an assortment of worn canvas bags, intricately woven baskets, and small, meticulously labeled glass vials. The scent of dried herbs, rich soil, and something vaguely floral clung to him, a testament to his hours spent in the untamed fringes of their settlement and the carefully tended plots behind the bio-domes. He wasn't a mechanic or an engineer, but a botanist by inclination, a farmer by necessity, and a guardian of Oakhaven's agricultural future by design.

Luis's initiative was born from a deep concern for the fragility of their food supply. While rationing and salvaged canned goods had seen them through the initial years, he recognized that long-term survival depended on cultivating their own sustenance. He had spent countless hours observing the post-eruption landscape, not just for salvageable materials, but for the plants that stubbornly persisted. These were the true heroes of the new world – the native species that had adapted to the altered climate, the hardy grasses, the resilient root vegetables that pushed through cracked earth, and even the tenacious invasive species that, while often problematic, possessed an undeniable vitality.

He began by systematically collecting seeds. This was not a haphazard endeavor. Luis approached each plant with a botanist's precision, understanding the optimal time for seed collection, the methods for drying and storing them to ensure viability, and the specific needs of each species. He worked tirelessly to document his findings, filling notebooks with observations on germination rates, ideal growing conditions, and even potential medicinal properties. His collection was a testament to the diverse flora that had managed to endure. There were the tiny, dust-colored seeds of a native prairie grass, known for its drought resistance and ability to stabilize soil. Beside them, nestled in a small, airtight vial, were the plump, dark seeds of a fast-growing, nutrient-rich legume, an invasive species that Oakhaven had struggled to control, but which Luis saw as a valuable protein source. He painstakingly gathered seeds from cultivated crops that had managed to survive in the protected bio-domes – hardy strains of potatoes, resilient varieties of corn, and compact, fast-maturing beans, carefully selected for their ability to thrive in the challenging local conditions.

But Luis's vision extended far beyond mere collection. He understood that seeds were only one part of the equation. The earth itself needed to be nurtured, its depleted nutrients replenished, its delicate balance restored. He began to incorporate soil health into his offerings at the Resource Library. He presented Kiley with a series of pamphlets he had painstakingly compiled, filled with hand-drawn illustrations and clear, concise instructions on composting techniques. These weren't generic guides; they detailed how to create effective compost using Oakhaven's specific waste streams – organic refuse from the communal kitchens, shredded bio-dome plant matter, and even carefully processed ash from controlled burns. He explained the science behind decomposition, the role of microorganisms, and how a well-managed compost heap could transform waste into a rich, life-giving soil amendment.

His guidance didn't stop at composting. Luis was a vocal advocate for crop rotation and companion planting, principles he had learned through years of trial and error and a deep reverence for traditional agricultural knowledge. He prepared detailed charts illustrating which crops benefited from being planted near others, explaining the symbiotic relationships – how nitrogen-fixing legumes could enrich the soil for subsequent leafy greens, or how certain aromatic herbs could deter common pests. He even demonstrated techniques for natural pest control, eschewing any reliance on the chemical agents of the old world. He showed how to cultivate beneficial insect populations, how to create simple barriers from salvaged netting, and how to prepare natural deterrent sprays from common plants like garlic and chili peppers.

The Resource Library began to house not just seeds, but the knowledge to cultivate them successfully. Luis established a dedicated section, carefully climate-controlled to preserve the delicate viability of his collection. Shelves lined with small, labeled containers held the promise of future harvests. Beside them, he organized a small but growing collection of gardening tools – trowels, hand cultivators, pruners, and seed-starting trays, all salvaged and meticulously maintained. More importantly, he developed a comprehensive catalog system, cross-referencing each seed variety with its cultivation requirements, germination rates, ideal growing season, and any notes on its resilience or specific challenges. This catalog was accessible both digitally and in print, ensuring that anyone with a desire to grow could find the information they needed.

Luis also recognized the need for practical, hands-on learning. He began offering workshops, mirroring Mika's approach in the technical sphere but focused on the earth beneath their feet. His first sessions were held outdoors, in a small, sheltered plot adjacent to the library, where he could demonstrate his techniques in real-time. He would gather a group of interested individuals, their hands already stained with earth from previous gardening attempts, and guide them through the process of preparing a seedbed. He'd show them how to test soil pH using simple, improvised kits, how to amend the soil with compost, and how to create the ideal environment for germination.

He meticulously demonstrated how to sow seeds, emphasizing the importance of depth and spacing. For the tiny grass seeds, he showed how to mix them with sand to ensure even distribution. For larger seeds like beans or corn, he demonstrated the correct planting depth, explaining how it influenced root development and access to moisture. He would then guide them through the careful process of watering, explaining how to avoid disturbing the delicate seedlings and how to maintain consistent moisture levels.

These workshops were far from solitary lectures. Luis encouraged questions, fostered a spirit of shared discovery, and celebrated every small success. He would often point out the emerging shoots of a previously sown batch of seeds, his voice filled with quiet pride, as he explained what the visible growth indicated about the health of the soil and the viability of the seed. He fostered a sense of camaraderie among the participants, creating a network of nascent gardeners who could share their experiences and learn from each other. A young woman who had struggled to keep her small tomato plants alive discovered the benefits of Luis's companion planting advice, finding that a few strategically placed marigolds significantly reduced aphid infestations. An older man, who had only ever known the harsh, industrial farming methods of his youth, found a new appreciation for the gentler, more sustainable practices Luis advocated, particularly the meticulous care for soil health.

One of Luis's most significant contributions was his initiative to preserve not only the cultivated crops but also the wild, native plants that had demonstrated such resilience. He recognized that these plants held vital genetic diversity, crucial for future adaptation. He began to identify and collect seeds from these hardy species, often venturing further afield than most were willing to go. He would return with small packets of seeds from drought-tolerant wildflowers, nutrient-rich foraging plants, and even species that showed a natural resistance to common blights. He cataloged these with even greater care, understanding that their value might not be immediately apparent in terms of bulk food production, but was essential for the long-term ecological health and genetic resilience of Oakhaven.

He also championed the idea of a community seed exchange. Inspired by the collaborative spirit of the library, Luis proposed a system where individuals could deposit surplus seeds from their successful harvests and, in turn, take seeds from others. This fostered a sense of mutual reliance and ensured that a wider variety of crops could be grown throughout the community. He helped to establish guidelines for the exchange, ensuring that only healthy, viable seeds were contributed and that proper labeling was maintained, preventing accidental hybridization or the spread of diseases. This exchange became a vibrant hub, a testament to the community's growing self-sufficiency and their shared commitment to agricultural diversity.

Luis's work was characterized by patience and foresight. He understood that growing food was not a quick fix, but a continuous process of learning, adapting, and nurturing. His workshops weren't just about planting seeds; they were about cultivating a deep understanding of the cycles of nature, the interconnectedness of life, and the profound importance of respecting the earth that sustained them. He instilled in people a sense of stewardship, encouraging them to see themselves not as exploiters of the land, but as caretakers.

His commitment extended to educating people on seed saving, a vital skill for any community aiming for long-term food security. He would demonstrate how to identify mature seed pods, how to harvest them at the right time, and how to dry and store them properly to maintain viability for future seasons. He emphasized the importance of selecting seeds from the healthiest and most productive plants, a practice that would gradually improve the genetic stock of their cultivated crops. This knowledge, shared freely, empowered individuals to become self-sufficient in their seed needs, breaking the cycle of dependency on salvaged stores or the vagaries of chance.

The seed bank itself became a symbol of hope. Within the climate-controlled environment of the Resource Library, rows upon rows of meticulously labeled containers represented not just future meals, but the promise of a sustainable future. It was a tangible embodiment of Oakhaven's ability to not just survive, but to thrive, to regenerate, and to build a lasting legacy from the fragments of the past. Luis, with his quiet dedication and his profound connection to the earth, had sown the seeds of Oakhaven's agricultural independence, ensuring that the community's ability to feed itself would endure for generations to come. His initiative underscored the fundamental truth that while salvaged technology could mend the present, a well-tended garden, nurtured by knowledge and a deep respect for life, was the only true guarantee for the future. His quiet dedication was a powerful reminder that even in a world transformed by cataclysm, life, in its most fundamental form, possessed an extraordinary capacity to endure and to flourish. The simple act of preserving a seed, of nurturing a seedling, was an act of defiance against despair, a testament to the enduring power of nature and the unwavering human spirit to cultivate life, no matter the odds.

Jax's contribution to the Resource Library was a vibrant splash of color and clarity in a space that could easily have become dense with text and schematics. Where Luis meticulously documented the life-giving potential of seeds and Mika conjured intricate blueprints for salvaged machinery, Jax translated that knowledge into a universal language: images. He believed that understanding shouldn't be a privilege, a skill reserved for those who could decipher dense manuals or grasp abstract scientific principles. In Oakhaven, with its diverse population of survivors, many carrying the scars of a world that valued specialized knowledge over holistic understanding, visual aids were not just helpful; they were essential.

He moved through the library with a quiet purpose, his canvas satchel filled not with tools or specimens, but with an array of salvaged cameras, rolls of film he painstakingly developed himself, and a stack of thick, blank paper. His workspace, a corner cleared near the larger communal tables, was soon adorned with his work. Initially, he focused on the practicalities of daily life, the everyday tasks that had become more complex in the post-eruption landscape. His first series of guides tackled the operation and maintenance of essential salvaged equipment. There were step-by-step visual sequences demonstrating how to properly start and maintain the communal water purification system, complete with close-up shots of the critical filters and diagrams illustrating the flow of water. Another set of images clearly depicted the safe operation of the thermoelectric generators, highlighting the crucial safety checks and the correct way to monitor fuel levels, each action accompanied by a simple, bold icon indicating "Safe" or "Caution."

Jax's photography was characterized by its accessibility. He didn't use professional models; he enlisted anyone who was willing, often finding them in the midst of performing the very task he was documenting. His images showed real hands, weathered and capable, performing the actions. For a guide on basic tool maintenance, he captured Mika patiently showing a younger scavenger how to properly hone a salvaged axe blade, the sharp glint of steel on whetstone frozen in time. Another featured Lena, her brow furrowed in concentration as she demonstrated how to re-thread a stripped bolt using a specialized die set, the worn metal of the tools stark against the clean white background Jax had managed to arrange. His accompanying text was minimal, often just a single, descriptive word or a short, declarative sentence, allowing the images to carry the bulk of the informational load.

Beyond mechanical repairs, Jax turned his lens to the crucial task of food cultivation, working closely with Luis to translate his botanical expertise into easily digestible visual formats. He recognized that Luis's detailed notes, while invaluable, could be intimidating for those new to farming. Jax's approach was to show, not just tell. He created a series of "Planting Guides," each dedicated to a specific crop. For Oakhaven's hardy strain of blight-resistant potatoes, he produced a multi-panel poster. The first panel showed a plump seed potato, marked with distinct "eyes." The subsequent panels illustrated the correct way to cut it, ensuring each piece had at least one eye. Then came the visual progression of planting: the preparation of the soil, the digging of the hole to the precise depth Luis had recommended, the placement of the potato piece, and its covering. Each image was accompanied by a small infographic showing the ideal planting season and spacing.

He extended this visual narrative to other crops. For the fast-growing, nutrient-rich legumes Luis had identified as a vital protein source, Jax documented the entire lifecycle. He captured the appearance of the young seedlings, their delicate leaves unfurling. He photographed the vibrant purple flowers that preceded the pods, and then, the satisfying image of mature pods, plump with beans, ready for harvest. His guides often included "troubleshooting" sections, presented as simple visual comparisons. For instance, a guide on growing resilient corn might feature a panel showing a healthy, green stalk next to a panel depicting a yellowing stalk, with a small, red "X" over an image of over-watered soil. This allowed individuals to quickly diagnose common problems without needing to sift through lengthy explanations.

Jax's commitment to accessibility also meant adapting his methods to different literacy levels within the community. He created a set of

"Tool Identification Cards," each featuring a clear, high-resolution photograph of a tool on one side and simple, universally recognized pictograms on the other, indicating its primary function and safety warnings. A wrench, for example, might be depicted alongside icons of turning bolts and nuts, with a clear "do not overtighten" symbol. For those who struggled with numbers, he developed visual measurement guides for common tasks, such as a diagram showing how much compost to add to a planting hole, represented by a shaded area on a scaled drawing.

He also documented Oakhaven's salvage and repair efforts, creating a visual logbook of their progress. This was not just for practical instruction; it served as a powerful morale booster. He captured the triumphant moment when Mika and her team managed to coax life back into a derelict power conduit, the images showing the intricate wiring and the final, satisfying spark of re-energized light. He documented the ongoing efforts to fortify the outer perimeter, showing the stacking of salvaged materials, the reinforcement of structural points, and the careful placement of warning signs, all rendered in clear, actionable visual sequences. These guides became living documents, updated as new techniques were learned or new salvage discoveries were made.

One of Jax's most innovative contributions was the creation of "Troubleshooting Trees." These were not literal trees, but branching visual diagrams displayed prominently in the library. Starting with a common problem – for example, a sputtering generator – the tree would branch out to potential causes, each illustrated with a representative image or icon. Following a specific branch would lead to a visual solution, often a direct link to one of Jax's more detailed guides or a diagram showing the exact repair needed. This allowed individuals to self-diagnose and often self-correct issues with minimal assistance, freeing up the more experienced members of the community for more complex challenges.

His approach was inherently collaborative. He would spend time observing Luis in the bio-domes, photographing the nuances of grafting techniques. He documented Kiley's meticulous cataloging process, capturing the satisfying order of the organized shelves and the precise way she labeled each item. He even worked with the younger members of Oakhaven, teaching them basic photography skills and inviting them to contribute their own visual observations of the surrounding environment, fostering a new generation of citizen-documentarians.

Jax's visual guides transformed the Resource Library from a passive repository of information into an active, dynamic learning center. His images demystified complex processes, making knowledge accessible to everyone, regardless of their background or prior experience. He understood that in a world rebuilding from scratch, clear communication was as vital as clean water or fertile soil. His visual storytelling bridged gaps, empowered individuals, and solidified the library's role as the beating heart of Oakhaven's collective effort to not just survive, but to thrive, one clear, compelling image at a time. The quiet click of his camera became a soundtrack to their recovery, each captured moment a testament to their ingenuity and their shared determination to rebuild a future where knowledge was a tool for everyone.

The impact of Jax's visual approach rippled through Oakhaven's rebuilding efforts. His guides were not confined to the library walls.aminated copies were posted in communal areas, in workshops, and even near the bio-dome entrances. A young scavenger, tasked with maintaining a perimeter sensor, could simply glance at the laminated card tacked near the device, its clear diagrams showing how to recalibrate the sensitivity after a dust storm, eliminating the need to trek back to the library for clarification. The communal kitchens benefited immensely from Jax's illustrated guides on food preservation techniques, showcasing the correct methods for drying herbs, pickling salvaged vegetables, and smoking meats, presented in a way that was easily understood by everyone who shared the responsibility of feeding the community.

He even tackled the often-overlooked aspect of waste management with his visual clarity. Jax created a series of posters detailing the sorting of refuse for recycling and composting. Using distinct color-coding and simple icons, he illustrated which materials belonged in the compost bins, which could be repurposed for repairs, and which needed to be safely stored as hazardous waste. This seemingly minor initiative significantly reduced contamination in their composting efforts, leading to a richer, more effective soil amendment, directly benefiting Luis's agricultural projects.

His dedication extended to creating visual narratives of Oakhaven's history and its ongoing challenges. He compiled "Day in the Life" sequences, capturing the rhythm of their community – the early morning patrols, the bustling activity in Mika's workshop, the quiet contemplation in Luis's growing plots, the shared meals in the communal hall. These visual stories, displayed in a dedicated section of the library, served as a constant reminder of their collective journey and their shared purpose. They were a powerful antidote to despair, a visual testament to the resilience and tenacity of the human spirit.

Jax's influence was also felt in the subtle ways it fostered a culture of shared learning. When someone encountered a problem, their first instinct became to consult Jax's visual guides. This not only solved immediate issues but also empowered individuals to tackle new tasks with confidence. A former office worker, now vital to the community's textile production, found herself able to repair salvaged sewing machines thanks to Jax's clear photographic instructions, a skill she never would have imagined acquiring in her previous life. Similarly, a young orphan, with limited formal education, became proficient in basic electrical maintenance by diligently following Jax's visual diagrams for simple circuit repairs.

The effectiveness of Jax's work lay in its inherent simplicity and universality. He had a knack for distilling complex information into its most essential visual components, stripping away jargon and technicalities. This made knowledge accessible to the elderly, the very young, and those who had never had the luxury of formal education in the old world. The Resource Library, under his visual guidance, became a true hub of democratized knowledge, where learning was an active, engaging, and inclusive process. Jax's camera was not just a tool for documentation; it was a conduit for empowerment, a brush painting a clearer, more hopeful future for Oakhaven, one frame at a time. He proved that sometimes, the most profound communication didn't require words, but rather a well-composed image that spoke directly to the practical needs and the innate intelligence of every member of their recovering community. His visual guides were more than just instructions; they were windows of understanding, illuminating the path forward.

CHAPTER THIRTEEN

ECHOES IN THE WETLANDS

The air in the wetlands hung thick and heavy, a damp shroud that clung to skin and filtered the already weak sunlight into anemic shafts. It was a place whispered about in Oakhaven, a place few dared to venture into, and fewer returned from with their wits entirely intact. The very ground seemed to breathe, a slow, Gurgling exhalation of methane and decay. Jax, ever the observer, found himself drawn to the unsettling beauty of the place, his camera a familiar weight against his side. He trailed behind Elara and Rhys, their faces set with a grim determination that mirrored the oppressive atmosphere. They were here for salvage, for resources that might lie hidden beneath the stagnant surface, but even Elara, usually so pragmatic, cast wary glances into the murky expanse.

Rhys, his weathered face etched with years of hard-won experience, pointed a gloved finger towards a cluster of skeletal trees, their branches gnarled like arthritic fingers reaching for a sky they could no longer touch. "That's where the readings were strongest last time," he rasped, his voice a low rumble against the symphony of unseen insects and the distant, mournful cry of some unseen bird. "Scavengers used to talk about strange lights out here, but most dismissed it as swamp gas or delirium."

Elara, ever the pragmatist, adjusted the strap of her pack, her eyes scanning the horizon. "Swamp gas doesn't pulse, Rhys. And delirium doesn't leave behind a faint scent of ozone, no matter how diluted." She had a keen nose for the unusual, a sensitivity that had often saved them from unseen dangers. Today, that sensitivity was on high alert, a prickling sensation that ran beneath her skin.

They moved with a practiced caution, their boots sinking into the soft, yielding earth, the waterlogged soil sucking at their soles with every step. The silence here was not an absence of sound, but a presence of something else, a quietude that felt pregnant with unspoken secrets. Jax, usually so attuned to the visual, found himself straining to hear, to discern the subtle shifts in the wetland's murmur that might betray its hidden nature. He adjusted his camera, the lens cap a familiar barrier between him and the unknown, a tool that allowed him to observe without fully immersing himself.

It was when they neared the edge of a particularly large, still pool, its surface reflecting the bruised sky like a shattered mirror, that it began. A faint, almost imperceptible glow, like embers smoldering beneath ash. At first, Jax dismissed it as a trick of the light, a reflection of the dying sun on some unseen mineral deposit. But the glow intensified, not with the brightness of reflected light, but with an inner luminescence, a soft, verdant pulse that seemed to emanate from the very heart of the murky water.

"Did you see that?" Elara whispered, her voice barely audible. Her hand instinctively went to the sidearm holstered at her hip. Rhys, who had been examining a patch of strange, almost iridescent moss clinging to a fallen log, straightened up, his eyes wide with a dawning comprehension.

"The lights," he breathed, his earlier skepticism dissolving into a profound awe. "The old stories. They weren't just stories."

Jax raised his camera, his fingers fumbling slightly with the focus. He'd photographed countless things in his time – derelict machinery, resilient flora, the determined faces of Oakhaven's survivors. But this... this was something entirely new. The light wasn't the harsh, artificial glow of salvaged lamps, nor the organic warmth of bioluminescent fungi he'd encountered on the fringes of the old forests. This was ethereal, a soft, cool light that seemed to breathe with a life of its own, pulsing with a gentle rhythm. It was a soft, emerald green, a color that felt alien and yet strangely inviting against the muted browns and grays of the wetlands.

He pressed the shutter. The click of the camera, usually a reassuring sound, felt strangely intrusive in the hushed stillness. He took another shot, then another, trying to capture the subtle shifts in intensity, the way the light seemed to ebb and flow like a slow heartbeat. The luminescence wasn't constant; it would fade for a moment, then bloom again, a silent testament to an unknown force at work beneath the surface.

"What is it?" Elara asked, her voice a tight knot of curiosity and apprehension. She edged closer to the pool, her gaze fixed on the pulsing light. The water itself seemed undisturbed, no visible ripples betraying any movement beneath. Yet, the glow was undeniable, a beacon in the suffocating gloom.

"I don't know," Rhys admitted, running a hand through his salt-and-pepper hair. "Never seen anything like it. Not even in the old texts. They spoke of rare phosphorescent algae, but this... this is different. This has a... a deliberate quality to it."

Deliberate. The word hung in the air, heavy with implication. Life, thriving in an environment that should have choked it, creating its own light, its own energy. Jax zoomed in with his camera, trying to discern any pattern, any structure within the glow. It seemed to originate from multiple points within the murky depths, scattered like fallen stars. He adjusted his aperture, trying to capture the subtle diffusion of the light, the way it softly illuminated the water around it, hinting at unseen forms just beyond the reach of his lens.

He began to meticulously document his findings. He captured images of the surrounding flora, the strange, gelatinous growths clinging to the submerged roots of the skeletal trees, the unusually large, pale insects that flitted near the water's surface, their wings almost translucent. He took readings with his handheld scanner, though the device struggled to make sense of the ambient energies. It registered faint spikes, anomalies that defied easy categorization. He focused his lens on the water's edge, noting the subtle sheen that seemed to coat the mud, a faint, almost oily iridescence that mirrored the glow below.

"It's not just algae," Jax murmured, reviewing the images on his camera's small screen. "The patterns are too complex. And look at this." He showed Elara and Rhys a magnified shot. Within the soft glow, faint, filament-like structures were visible, weaving and branching like an intricate, living tapestry. They pulsed with the same light, seemingly the source of the luminescence.

"They look almost like... neural pathways," Elara mused, leaning closer. "Or perhaps vascular systems. But for what?"

The questions hung heavy, unanswered. This was more than just a salvage mission now. This was an encounter with the profoundly unknown. The wetlands, already a place of peril, had revealed a secret, a hidden life that defied their understanding of biology, of chemistry, of what was possible. Jax felt a familiar thrill, the scientist in him battling with the artist. How could he possibly convey the sheer, unearthly beauty of this phenomenon? How could he capture the silent symphony of light and life that pulsed beneath the stagnant surface?

He continued to shoot, experimenting with different exposures, different angles. He tried to capture the way the light seemed to shift and coalesce, forming brief, fleeting shapes before dissolving back into the general glow. He wondered if these were individual organisms, or a collective consciousness, communicating through light. The thought sent a shiver down his spine.

Rhys, meanwhile, had cautiously dipped a long, salvaged pole into the water, gently probing the area where the light was most concentrated. "It feels... dense," he reported, his brow furrowed in concentration. "Not like just water. There's a resistance, but it's not solid. It's yielding, like pushing through thick syrup, but also... alive." He carefully withdrew the pole, examining the tip. It was coated in a fine, almost luminous slime, the same iridescent sheen they had observed at the water's edge.

"The scanner is picking up trace amounts of unusual compounds," Elara said, her eyes glued to the device's display. "Organic, but nothing I recognize. And there's a faint electromagnetic signature, very low frequency, but persistent. It seems to be tied to the light's pulses."

Jax, his mind racing, began to set up a makeshift tripod, his camera now locked onto the pulsing center of the pool. He intended to take a long exposure, to try and capture the full extent of the luminescence, to create a visual record that would speak volumes. He adjusted his settings, the sounds of the wetlands fading into a distant hum as he focused on the task. This was what he lived for, the moments of discovery, the chance to document the extraordinary.

As the shutter opened, bathing the scene in the soft glow of the camera's timer light, he saw it. Not just the light, but something *within* the light. A subtle, swirling motion, a pattern forming and reforming. It was like watching a nebula coalesce, but on a microscopic scale, a dance of light and shadow played out in the murky depths. He held his breath, the seconds stretching into an eternity.

When the shutter finally closed, he eagerly reviewed the image. It was astonishing. The long exposure had captured a ethereal bloom of green light, revealing the intricate, branching structures in their full glory. They were indeed like veins, or roots, of pure light, interconnected and pulsing in unison. And at the very center, a slightly brighter, more defined core of luminescence seemed to be the nexus of the entire phenomenon.

"It's beautiful," Jax whispered, the word inadequate to describe the spectacle. "And terrifying."

Rhys nodded slowly. "Beautiful, yes. But 'terrifying' is probably the more accurate assessment. We don't know what this is, what it does, or if it's even safe."

Elara, however, seemed more intrigued than fearful. "This could be... anything. A new form of life, adapted to this toxic environment.

Or perhaps something else entirely. An energy source we haven't dreamed of." She picked up a small, smooth stone from the edge of the pool and tossed it gently into the glowing area. As the stone sank, the light seemed to momentarily gather around it, an almost inquisitive embrace, before returning to its rhythmic pulsing. There was no splash, no disturbance, as if the water itself had absorbed the stone without resistance.

Jax continued to photograph, documenting every subtle change, every shift in the light's intensity. He captured the way the surrounding reeds, even those submerged, seemed to faintly absorb some of the glow, their tips taking on a ghostly luminescence. He noticed that the air here felt cleaner, paradoxically, despite the decay. There was a strange, almost electric crispness to it, a faint scent of something akin to petrichor, but sharper, cleaner.

He wondered about the implications. If life could not only survive but *thrive* in such a toxic mire, creating its own light and energy, what did that mean for Oakhaven? For their own struggles to reclaim a world ravaged by pollution and decay? This was a testament to resilience, to adaptation, on a scale they hadn't yet comprehended.

The pulsing continued, a silent, mesmerizing spectacle. Jax felt a profound sense of privilege, of being privy to a secret the world had kept hidden for so long. He knew that these images, these observations, would become a vital part of the Resource Library, a testament to the fact that even in the most desolate places, life, in its myriad and wondrous forms, could find a way. The wetlands, once a symbol of all that was broken, had become a beacon of unexpected hope, its mysterious bio-luminescence a silent promise of the undiscovered wonders that still lay hidden in the scarred remnants of their world. He continued to shoot, his fingers working with a renewed purpose, driven by the urge to capture and understand this luminous enigma, this pulse of life in the heart of decay. He documented the gradual fading of the light as the sun dipped lower, the glow becoming more pronounced against the encroaching twilight. He captured the subtle interplay of the bioluminescence with the emerging stars, a celestial mirroring in the terrestrial depths. He knew this was just the beginning of their understanding, a tantalizing glimpse into a hidden ecosystem. The wetlands had given them more than salvage; they had given them a mystery, a question that would echo in the minds of Oakhaven long after they left its treacherous embrace.

The journey back to Oakhaven was a quiet one, punctuated only by the soft crunch of their boots on the damp earth and the persistent hum of the wetlands' unseen inhabitants. The images Jax had captured, flickering on his camera's small screen, were a constant, mesmerizing presence, a tangible reminder of the profound mystery they had unearthed. The emerald glow, so vibrant in the murky depths, seemed to cast its own subtle luminescence on their thoughts, imbuing the familiar trek with an undercurrent of wonder and disquiet. Elara, usually so focused on practicalities, found her gaze drifting towards the shadowed fringes of the marsh, as if half-expecting to see the ethereal light bloom again. Rhys, ever the stoic, kept his silence, but the thoughtful lines on his brow deepened with each passing mile, betraying the wheels turning within his experienced mind.

As they re-entered the familiar, albeit weathered, structures of Oakhaven, the palpable shift in atmosphere was immediate. The subdued bustle of the community, the weary resilience etched onto every face, felt like a sanctuary after the unnerving openness of the wetlands. Yet, the secret they carried, the visual evidence of the pulsing, luminous phenomenon, cast a long shadow. They knew that the whispers would begin as soon as their discovery was even hinted at, the fertile ground of Oakhaven's collective anxieties ready to sprout a thousand theories. The wetlands, already a place steeped in local folklore and tinged with the dread of the unknown, had now provided fodder for a new generation of apprehension.

Jax, meticulously cataloging his photographic evidence back in his cramped, makeshift darkroom – a space where salvaged bulbs cast a stark, utilitarian light – felt the weight of their findings. He knew that these images, stark and compelling against the backdrop of Oakhaven's grim reality, would spark more than just curiosity. They would ignite speculation, fear, and perhaps, a desperate hope. The glow, so alien and yet so undeniably alive, was a disruption to the established order of their understanding, a question mark etched in light onto the very fabric of their world.

"It's unlike anything I've ever documented," Jax murmured, poring over a particularly striking shot of the intricate, light-emitting filaments. "The complexity... it's almost architectural. Like something designed, not grown. But by whom? Or what?" He turned to Elara, who was examining his scanner's readings, her brow furrowed in concentration. "The energy signatures are so... unique. Not quite biological, not quite chemical. It's like a third category altogether."

Elara tapped a section of the readout. "These trace compounds are still baffling. They're organic, yes, but their molecular structure... it doesn't align with any known terrestrial life. And the electromagnetic pulses, they're so regular, so patterned. It suggests a form of communication, or perhaps regulation of its own metabolic processes. If it *is* a process, that is." She looked up, her gaze meeting

Jax's. "Some of the older folks will say it's just the swamp reclaiming its own, a more potent form of methane seep or some mutated fungi. They'll tell you it's best left undisturbed, a warning from the old earth."

Rhys, who had been observing from the doorway, his hands clasped behind his back, finally spoke, his voice a low, resonant rumble that always commanded attention. "The old stories. They always spoke of the wetlands as a place where the veil between worlds was thin. Some said spirits resided there, others spoke of gateways to forgotten realms. They called it the 'Whispering Mire' for a reason." He paused, a flicker of something akin to wonder in his usually stern eyes. "Perhaps those stories weren't entirely allegorical. Perhaps they were attempts to describe something that defied their understanding, something like what you found, Jax."

The initial dissemination of Jax's photographs within Oakhaven was met with a predictable spectrum of reactions. In the communal mess hall, where the aroma of simmering algae stew usually dominated, hushed conversations erupted around the few printouts Jax had made. Old Man Hemlock, his face a roadmap of a life lived under the harsh sun, peered at the glowing images through thick, cracked spectacles. "See!" he declared, his voice raspy with age and a hint of triumph. "I told you. I told the council, years ago, that the wetlands weren't just dead ground. There's life there. Different life. Life that remembers the old ways, before the Collapse. It's a sign, I tell you. A sign that nature is fighting back, finding new ways to thrive where we failed." He pointed a gnarled finger at the images. "Look at that light! It's the earth's own magic, waking up."

Others, like Mara, the pragmatic head of the Oakhaven scavenging teams, viewed the discovery with a more cautious, analytical eye.

"It's certainly intriguing, Jax," she admitted, her arms crossed as she studied the prints. "And if those energy readings are consistent, it could represent a new, untapped resource. Think of it – self-sustaining light, perhaps even a power source. But we have to be realistic. We don't know what this is. Is it toxic? Is it aggressive? Is it even truly alive in a way we can understand?" She gestured towards the shadowy edges of the wetlands, visible even from their vantage point. "That place has always swallowed people. This light might just be a lure, a beautiful trap. It's one thing to document it, another to try and harness it."

Then there were those who saw the phenomenon through a lens of fear, their imaginations already conjuring darker possibilities. Young Silas, who had lost his parents to a fever that swept through the settlement years ago, clutched a printout as if it were a cursed artifact. "It's an omen," he whispered, his eyes wide and darting. "The wetlands are a scar on the land. This... this unholy light... it's a manifestation of that scar. It's a new kind of sickness, a sickness of the light. The old stories say things come out of the mire when it's disturbed. Things that aren't meant to see the sun." His voice trembled. "It's not life, it's... corruption. A warning that the rot is spreading, and it's found a way to illuminate itself."

The discussions filtered through Oakhaven like ripples across a still pond, each conversation adding a new layer of interpretation, a fresh wave of trepidation. The scientific curiosity that Jax and his companions felt was overshadowed, for many, by the primal fear of the unknown. The wetlands, a place already synonymous with danger and decay, had now become the source of something wondrous, yet profoundly unsettling. This wasn't the familiar struggle against mutated pests or dwindling resources; this was an encounter with something that hinted at a fundamental shift in the understanding of life itself, a biological anomaly that defied easy categorization.

"It's the 'deliberate quality' Rhys mentioned," Elara mused, replaying Jax's description in her mind as she sat with a small group of Oakhaven elders, trying to contextualize the visual evidence. "That's what unsettles people. If it were merely a strange reaction to pollution, or an unusual adaptation, they might accept it as another aspect of our harsh reality. But the patterns, the pulsing, the way it seems almost... aware. That taps into something deeper, something superstitious." She gestured to the crude drawings on the table, depicting various swamp-dwelling creatures and shadowy figures from Oakhaven's folklore. "They've always attributed sentience to the unknown, to the things they couldn't explain. This light, in its strangeness and beauty, presents itself as the ultimate enigma."

One of the elders, a woman named Anya who had lived on the fringes of Oakhaven her entire life, her face weathered like ancient parchment, traced a symbol on the table with her finger. "The old ones spoke of lights in the bogs," she said, her voice a low murmur. "Not just marsh gas, but lights that would dance. They said it was the souls of those lost to the mire, trapped between worlds. They said if you followed them, you'd never return." She looked at Jax's photographs with a mixture of awe and apprehension. "This... this is different. This is too organized for lost souls. This feels... primal. Like the earth itself is dreaming, and this is its dream made manifest."

Another elder, Kael, a former engineer before the Collapse, scoffed. "Dreams don't leave electromagnetic signatures, Anya. This is a biological or geological anomaly. A highly complex one, granted. Perhaps some symbiotic relationship between extremophile bacteria and a newly discovered mineral deposit. The energy output could be a byproduct of its metabolic process. The 'deliberate' aspect might be a complex chemical reaction, mimicking intelligent design. We've seen stranger adaptations in the irradiated zones." He tapped his finger on a section of the printout depicting the filaments. "If this is a living organism, or a colony of organisms, it's evolved to survive in an environment that would kill most known life forms. That alone is remarkable. But it doesn't mean it's supernatural."

Yet, Kael's rational explanation did little to assuage the underlying unease. The very fact that it was so unlike anything known amplified the fear. It was the alienness of it, the suggestion that life, or some force mimicking life, could exist and even flourish in the toxic crucible of the wetlands, that truly stirred the pot of anxieties. It challenged their carefully constructed understanding of survival, of what it meant to adapt. Their world had been defined by decay and struggle, by the slow, arduous process of clinging to existence. This discovery offered a glimpse of a radically different kind of existence, one that generated its own light and energy from the very substances that poisoned their own world.

Jax, in his quiet study, felt a kinship with both the scientists and the mystics. He understood Kael's desire for a logical explanation, for a framework to contain this anomaly. But he also felt the tug of Anya's interpretation, the primal resonance of something ancient and profound. The patterns in the light, the almost rhythmic beating he had felt through the water, spoke of a force that transcended simple chemistry. It was a testament to the sheer, unyielding persistence of life, but also a potent reminder of how little they truly understood about the world they inhabited.

The trepidation wasn't just about potential danger, though that was a significant factor. It was about the implications for Oakhaven's future. If such a robust, self-sustaining phenomenon could exist in the poisoned heart of the wetlands, what did that say about their own efforts to reclaim and rebuild? Was their struggle a futile one against an environment that had evolved beyond their comprehension? Or was this a sign of hope, a demonstration that even in the most corrupted places, life could find a way to manifest its brilliance?

"We have to consider all possibilities," Elara stated firmly, her voice cutting through a particularly heated debate in the council hall. "Theories range from a hyper-adaptive extremophile colony to... well, to whatever the more imaginative among us are conjuring. But until we have more data, dismissing anything is premature. The fear is understandable. The wetlands have always been a place of mystery and danger. This discovery only amplifies that. But fear shouldn't blind us to potential understanding, or potential solutions." She held up a detailed diagram Jax had created based on his photographs. "This isn't just pretty lights. This is an ecosystem, or a process, that has found a way to thrive in extreme toxicity. That, in itself, is a scientific marvel. We need to approach this with caution, yes, but also with an open mind. It's a testament to life's boundless adaptability, and perhaps, a lesson for our own survival."

Jax continued to work, refining his photographic techniques, attempting to capture the subtle nuances of the light's pulsation and intensity. He spent hours comparing his images, searching for patterns, for any clue that might unlock the mystery. He felt a sense of responsibility, not just to document, but to try and bridge the gap between the fear and the wonder. The echoes from the wetlands, he knew, were not just in the images on his camera, but in the hearts and minds of every inhabitant of Oakhaven, resonating with a mixture of awe, apprehension, and a dawning, fragile hope for what might still be possible in their broken world. The pulsing green light, he suspected, was merely the opening note in a much larger, and as yet unheard, symphony of the unknown.

Mika's fingers, stained with nutrient paste and smudged with fine dust from salvaged components, moved with practiced efficiency. The salvaged sensor array, a Heath Robinson contraption of repurposed comms equipment and repurposed atmospheric samplers, lay spread across her workbench in the Oakhaven's repurposed research nook. It hummed with a low, expectant thrum, a testament to her uncanny ability to coax life from dead technology. While Jax had captured the visual spectacle of the emerald glow, and Elara wrestled with its potential biological implications, Mika's focus was on the invisible architecture of the phenomenon: the air, the ground, the very essence of the wetlands that nurtured this anomaly.

She had spent the better part of the last cycle meticulously calibrating the array. The core of the device was a modified spectral analyzer, salvaged from a pre-Collapse weather drone, capable of detecting not just chemical compositions but also subtle shifts in electromagnetic frequencies. Surrounding it were an array of humidity sensors, particulate counters, and a surprisingly robust Geiger counter, all jury-rigged to transmit their readings wirelessly to a salvaged tablet. The wireless range was a gamble, a hopeful stab in the dark given the interference that often plagued the wetlands. She'd chosen a spot on the periphery of the illuminated area, a precarious balance between proximity and safety. The fear in Oakhaven was palpable, a thick fog that settled over every conversation, but Mika's scientific curiosity was a more potent force, an unquenchable thirst for understanding. She believed, with a conviction that bordered on defiance, that knowledge was the most potent weapon against the encroaching darkness, both literal and metaphorical.

"Alright, old girl," she murmured, patting the sensor array affectionately. "Let's see what secrets you can whisper to us." With a final twist of a connector, she activated the transmission sequence. The tablet flickered to life, displaying a cascade of raw data – numbers, graphs, and fluctuating bar charts that represented the unseen symphony of the wetlands. Her brow furrowed in concentration as she initiated the first set of comparative readings, capturing baseline data from a relatively untouched patch of land a few kilometers away from the anomaly. This was crucial. Without a control, any readings from the wetlands themselves would be suspect, potentially misinterpreting normal post-Collapse environmental degradation as evidence of the anomaly.

The initial readings from the control site were as expected, a familiar tapestry of degraded atmospheric conditions. Elevated levels of residual radiation, a persistent, low-level particulate haze from forgotten industrial sites, and a complex, often chaotic, mixture of volatile organic compounds, the lingering ghosts of widespread ecological collapse. The air itself felt heavy, laced with the bitter tang of decay and the faint, metallic scent of irradiated dust. Even the Geiger counter, usually a comforting companion in its steady clicking, registered a slightly elevated background hum, a constant reminder of the planet's wounded state. Mika meticulously logged these figures, her internal database cross-referencing them against known pre-Collapse environmental data, a futile exercise, perhaps, but one that grounded her in the scientific method.

Then, she directed the array towards the heart of the phenomenon. The trek to the deployment site was fraught with a different kind of tension than Jax and Elara had experienced. While they had navigated the physical dangers of the wetlands, Mika's concern was with the invisible forces at play. She moved with deliberate steps, her eyes scanning the terrain, her senses attuned to any subtle change. The air grew noticeably warmer as she approached the zone of luminescence, a disconcerting sensation in the otherwise cool, damp environment. The humidity, already high, seemed to cling to her skin like a second layer, thick and cloying.

The moment the sensors were positioned, the tablet's display erupted. The change was immediate and dramatic. The Geiger counter's steady hum escalated into a frantic clicking, not at a level that indicated immediate danger, but a significant, anomalous increase. "Whoa," she breathed, her voice barely a whisper. "That's... unexpected." She ran the calibration checks again, her heart hammering against her ribs. The readings held. The anomaly was not only emitting light, but also a measurable, though not acutely harmful, level of ionizing radiation. This immediately complicated Elara's biological theories. While some extremophiles could tolerate radiation, such a pronounced localized increase suggested a more direct source or a powerful interaction with the environment.

The spectral analyzer was even more revealing. While the control site showed a predictable mix of common atmospheric gases and industrial pollutants, the wetlands' readings were a confounding enigma. There were trace amounts of known organic compounds, but their ratios were skewed, and interwoven with them were signatures that Mika had never encountered. One particular spectrum appeared as a series of sharp, distinct peaks, almost crystalline in their definition, clustered around an unusually narrow band. It didn't match any known naturally occurring gas or industrial byproduct in her extensive databanks. It was as if a new element, or a novel molecular compound, had decided to make its presence known.

"This is not methane, not phosphine, not any of the usual suspects," she muttered, zooming in on the peculiar peaks. "The energy requirements to create these specific bond formations... they're significant. Where is it coming from?" She ran a deep-scan analysis, pushing the salvaged equipment to its limits. The results were frustratingly incomplete. The signal was strong, undeniably present, but its origin remained elusive. It seemed to emanate from everywhere and nowhere at once, a pervasive presence that defied pinpointing. The tablet struggled to resolve the source, the triangulation algorithms faltering in the face of such diffuse energy.

Her focus then shifted to the electromagnetic frequencies. While the visual glow was a constant, Mika's sensors detected subtle, rhythmic fluctuations in the ambient EM field, synchronized with the visual pulse of the light. These weren't random bursts of energy; they were structured, almost like a heartbeat. The frequency was low, in the extremely low frequency (ELF) range, a band often associated with geological phenomena or, in more advanced societies, sophisticated communication systems. But the patterns were too complex for simple geological interference, too precise for natural chaotic emissions. It suggested a deliberate modulation, a form of output that was more than just a byproduct.

"It's like it's... breathing," she mused, watching the oscillating waveforms on the screen. "Breathing out light and... something else. Something that's altering the very air around it." She began to correlate the EM pulses with the spectral anomalies. There seemed to be a direct relationship; the spikes in the ELF frequencies coincided with the emission of those strange, crystalline spectral signatures. It was as if the EM pulse was the trigger, or the conduit, for the release of these unknown compounds.

The geological sensors, the least sophisticated part of her setup, offered only fragmented clues. The soil composition in the immediate vicinity of the light showed a higher than usual concentration of certain metallic elements, particularly iron and a cluster of rare earth metals. But this was not entirely surprising; the wetlands were known to be rich in mineral deposits, remnants of ancient geological processes. What was peculiar was the isotopic signature of these metals. They showed a slight deviation from the expected ratios, a subtle enrichment that Mika couldn't immediately explain through conventional geological models. It hinted at an energy source or process that could be actively influencing the surrounding mineral matrix.

"Could it be a chemoautotrophic organism on a scale we've never imagined?" she pondered aloud, scribbling notes furiously on a digital notepad. "One that utilizes exotic minerals and emits radiation and structured EM signals as part of its metabolic cycle? Or is it something entirely inorganic, a geological process triggered by some unknown external influence?" The data, while rich with anomalies, refused to coalesce into a definitive answer. It was a tantalizing puzzle, each piece suggesting a revolutionary scientific concept, but none fitting neatly into place.

She spent hours meticulously logging every reading, cross-referencing every variable. The tablet's battery life was a constant concern, forcing her to run diagnostics and analyses in short, intense bursts. The glow, a constant beacon in the gathering twilight, seemed to mock her efforts, its ethereal beauty intertwined with a profound scientific mystery. She was a scientist, trained to seek rational explanations, but the data she was collecting defied easy categorization. It was like trying to understand a symphony by only listening to a single, distorted note.

As the light intensified with the deepening of night, Mika realized the limitations of her current setup. The wireless transmission was unstable, prone to dropouts, and the range was insufficient to get readings from the absolute center of the most intense luminescence without risking direct exposure. She needed to get closer, to deploy more sensitive, localized sensors. But that would require careful planning, the kind of cautious approach that Oakhaven's general populace, steeped in fear, would never endorse.

She packed up her equipment with a sense of reluctant satisfaction. She hadn't solved the mystery, not by a long shot. But she had gathered invaluable data, data that hinted at a phenomenon far more complex and potent than anyone had initially suspected. The radiation, the novel spectral signatures, the structured EM pulses – these were not the signs of a simple biological mutation or a localized environmental hazard. They pointed towards something... fundamental. Something that was actively shaping its environment, interacting with it on a level that defied current scientific understanding.

Back in her makeshift lab, the tablet's data downloaded onto her primary terminal, Mika began the arduous process of comparative analysis. She ran simulations, tested hypotheses, and cross-referenced her findings with every obscure pre-Collapse scientific paper she could access from the fragmented archives. The more she delved, the more the enigma deepened. The data suggested an energy efficiency that was astounding, a process that seemed to draw power from the very toxic compounds that rendered the wetlands so deadly to most life. It was a testament to nature's unfathomable adaptability, but also a stark reminder of how little they truly understood about the planet they inhabited. The glowing wetlands were not just a strange spectacle; they were a scientific frontier, a challenge to everything

Mika, and indeed all of Oakhaven, thought they knew about life, energy, and the resilience of the natural world. The enigma was only just beginning to unfold.

The insistent hum of Mika's atmospheric sensor array, a sound that had become the background music to his thoughts, did little to distract Luis from the unsettling allure of the wetlands. He found himself drawn to the edge of the settlement, his gaze invariably drifting towards the pulsating, emerald heart of the anomaly. It wasn't just the visual spectacle that captivated him, though the shifting hues and the ethereal light were undeniably mesmerizing. It was a deeper, more primal resonance, a whisper of recognition that prickled at the edges of his consciousness.

He remembered, with a clarity that surprised him, fragmented lessons from his childhood. His grandfather, a man whose hands were as calloused from tending salvaged hydroponics as they were from holding the reins of a long-gone era's tools, would speak of the planet's inherent resilience. He'd described ancient forests that breathed life into the air, vast oceans teeming with a diversity of organisms that now existed only in corrupted data fragments. These weren't just stories; they were blueprints of a world that had once been, a testament to nature's inexhaustible capacity for adaptation and renewal. And now, in the heart of this scarred and fractured landscape, Luis felt a nascent echo of that profound vitality.

While others saw only danger, a testament to the Collapse and its lingering toxins, Luis began to perceive something else: the possibility of evolution. Mika's meticulous data, though riddled with anomalies that defied current scientific understanding, hinted at processes far more complex than mere corruption. The unusual spectral signatures, the structured electromagnetic pulses – these weren't necessarily the death throes of a dying planet, but perhaps the birth pangs of a new one. He envisioned an ecosystem, not succumbing to the harsh realities of their post-Collapse world, but actively, ingeniously, *adapting* to them.

His mind, naturally inclined towards observation and interpretation, began to construct its own hypotheses, weaving together the scientific tidbits Mika reluctantly shared with the ingrained intuition of someone who had grown up understanding the subtle cues of their damaged environment. He'd spent countless hours in the few patches of semi-tamed wilderness surrounding Oakhaven, learning to read the language of the mutated flora, the resilient fauna that had somehow found a way to thrive. He understood the delicate balance of nutrient cycles, the complex interplay of organisms in even the most degraded environments. And the wetlands, with their peculiar glow, felt like the ultimate expression of this intricate, often unseen, dance of life.

He imagined the light not as a beacon of doom, but as a symptom of an extraordinarily efficient metabolic process. Could it be that some organisms, driven by the scarcity of sunlight and the omnipresent radiation, had found a way to harness energy in entirely new ways? Perhaps they were utilizing the very toxins that made the wetlands so perilous, transforming them into something beneficial, something that allowed them to flourish. He pictured vast colonies of extremophiles, not just surviving, but thriving, their biochemical processes so alien that they produced outputs that bewildered even Mika's advanced salvaged technology.

"It's like a living furnace," he mused to himself, sketching in a worn notebook, its pages filled with crude diagrams of interconnected root systems and imagined cellular structures. He drew swirling patterns of energy, depicting hypothetical chemical reactions that might produce both light and the strange spectral emissions Mika had detected. He envisioned a symbiosis on an unprecedented scale, where different species, perhaps even different kingdoms of life, were collaborating in a grand, planetary-scale biochemical project.

The elevated radiation, which had so alarmed Elara, was, in Luis's speculative mind, a potential power source. What if certain organisms had developed mechanisms to not only tolerate radiation but to actively *utilize* it? It was a radical thought, a departure from everything known about biology, but the post-Collapse world was a testament to radical departures. He drew parallels to deep-sea hydrothermal vents, where life thrived in the absence of sunlight, powered by chemical energy. The wetlands, he theorized, could be an aerial or terrestrial equivalent, a testament to life's boundless ingenuity.

His curiosity was a tangible thing, a persistent itch beneath his skin. It wasn't the reckless curiosity of youth, eager to plunge headfirst into danger. It was tempered by a deep respect for the risks. He knew the legends of the wetlands: the lingering chemical pockets, the unstable terrain, the creatures that had adapted in ways that made them terrifyingly formidable. He'd heard the hushed tales of those who had ventured too deep and never returned, or returned irrevocably changed. Yet, the pull remained.

He started by venturing closer to the periphery, his movements slow and deliberate. He paid close attention to the flora, observing how it adapted to the unusual conditions. The reeds, taller and more vibrant than anywhere else, seemed to absorb moisture with an aggressive efficiency, their stalks thicker, their leaves a deeper, almost metallic green. He noticed that some of the mosses and fungi, usually muted in color, pulsed with a faint, bioluminescent glow of their own, a subtle imitation of the larger phenomenon. He collected samples, carefully storing them in sterile containers, his mind already formulating questions about their genetic makeup, their metabolic pathways.

He observed the insect life, or what passed for it in this era. The familiar scavengers were absent, replaced by iridescent beetles with exoskeletons that shimmered with an almost crystalline sheen, and moths with wingspans that seemed impossibly large, their patterns intricate and alien. He watched them interact with the glowing flora, noting how they seemed to navigate the luminescent areas with an innate understanding, their antennae twitching, their movements purposeful. Were they feeding on the plants? Or were they, too, part of the energy cycle, perhaps acting as conduits or pollinators for this new, radiant ecosystem?

His explorations weren't just about observation; they were about listening. He learned to distinguish the subtle sounds of the wetlands: the gentle lapping of water against the mutated reeds, the rustling of their thick stalks in the breeze, the almost imperceptible hum that seemed to emanate from the very earth itself. He tried to correlate these sounds with the visual phenomena, with the fluctuating readings Mika had shared from her sensor array. He began to associate certain low-frequency thrums with periods of heightened luminescence, certain crackling sounds with brief bursts of intense light.

He even began to document the changes in the air itself. While Mika focused on the chemical composition, Luis paid attention to the more visceral sensations. The air, even at the fringes, felt different. It was often heavy, humid, carrying a faint, ozone-like tang that was both invigorating and slightly unnerving. He noticed subtle shifts in temperature, pockets of warmth that seemed to emanate from the ground, as if the earth itself was breathing. He hypothesized that these thermal gradients could be indicators of active biochemical processes, of energy being released or consumed.

He started a new section in his notebook, dedicated to "Ecological Speculations." Under this heading, he began to meticulously document his observations, cross-referencing them with what little ecological knowledge had survived the Collapse. He sketched diagrams of food webs that defied conventional understanding, proposing cycles where waste products became the primary energy source, where radiation was not a threat but a nutrient. He drew hypothetical diagrams of microbial communities working in concert, each species contributing to a larger, overarching biochemical engine.

He wondered about the water. The wetlands were, by definition, waterlogged. But what was in that water? Mika's readings had indicated unusual mineral compositions and trace elements. Luis theorized that these dissolved minerals, perhaps catalyzed by the unique energy emissions, could be playing a crucial role in the metabolic processes of the organisms. He imagined a complex soup of dissolved metals and organic compounds, a primordial broth from which this new, radiant life was emerging.

His curiosity, however, was not purely academic. He felt a profound sense of connection to this emerging ecosystem. It represented a triumph of life, a defiant assertion of existence in the face of overwhelming adversity. It was a vision of the future, not of humanity's dominion over nature, but of nature's enduring power to reinvent itself, to find new ways to thrive. It spoke to a fundamental optimism, a belief that even in the most desolate of circumstances, life would find a way.

He understood that his exploration was fraught with peril. He wasn't a scientist like Mika, with her sophisticated equipment and her cautious, methodical approach. He was a layman, armed with a notebook, a keen eye, and an insatiable curiosity. But he believed that understanding this phenomenon, not just its chemical composition or its energy output, but its *ecological* essence, was crucial. It held clues, not just about the wetlands, but about the potential for life to persist and even flourish in the drastically altered world they now inhabited.

He began to plan more deliberate excursions, venturing further into the fringe areas of the wetlands. He devised simple traps to observe insect behavior, collected soil and water samples with basic tools, and always, always, he watched, he listened, and he recorded. He knew that his observations, while perhaps rudimentary compared to Mika's data, offered a different perspective – a view from the ground up, from the perspective of the flora and fauna that were the living components of this extraordinary, glowing ecosystem. The wetlands were no longer just a dangerous anomaly; they were a nascent world, and Luis felt an undeniable urge to understand its intricate, radiating heart.

The allure of the wetlands, a place whispered about in hushed tones within the confines of Oakhaven, had begun to exert a powerful pull on Jax. While Luis, with his scientific mind and ecological intuition, sought to understand the pulsating heart of the anomaly through observation and deduction, Jax felt its draw on a more visceral, artistic level. He saw not just a scientific puzzle, but a hauntingly beautiful canvas of the post-Collapse world, a place where life, in its most unexpected and resilient forms, was painting itself in hues of ethereal light. His medium was not petri dishes and sensor readings, but lenses and light-sensitive film, salvaged from forgotten eras and painstakingly nurtured back to functionality.

Jax was a creature of the shadows, more comfortable in the quiet solitude of his makeshift darkroom than in the boisterous communal spaces of Oakhaven. His hands, usually steady and precise when adjusting aperture settings or developing prints, trembled slightly as he prepared his equipment. The wetlands were a forbidden zone, a place where the very air seemed to hum with unseen dangers, where the ground itself could swallow the unwary. Yet, the faint, almost imperceptible glow that bled from its depths on the darkest nights was a siren song he could no longer resist. He knew the risks, the tales of those who had ventured too close and never returned, or returned with minds fractured and bodies withered. But the artist in him, the one who craved to capture the essence of their broken world, felt an obligation to bear witness.

His first forays were cautious, conducted under the cloak of the deepest night. Armed with a bulky, salvaged camera and a tripod that felt impossibly flimsy against the encroaching darkness, he'd creep to the very edge of the settlement's perimeter, the familiar, comforting lights of Oakhaven receding behind him like a fading dream. The air grew heavy, thick with the scent of damp earth and something else, something metallic and strangely sweet, a perfume of decay and rebirth. The silence here was different from the quiet of the settlement; it was a listening silence, pregnant with unspoken secrets. The usual chirps of nocturnal insects were muted, replaced by the slow, deliberate drip of water and the almost imperceptible sigh of the wind through the mutated reeds.

He would set up his tripod, each click of the adjustment knobs echoing unnaturally loud in the stillness. His goal was not to capture the spectacular, overwhelming luminescence that Luis described, but the subtle, the fleeting, the *suggestion* of light. He aimed for photographs that spoke of what was *almost* seen, of what lingered at the edges of perception. He was interested in the contrast: the stark, skeletal silhouettes of the dead trees that clawed at the sky against the faint, pulsing heart of the wetlands; the oily sheen of the stagnant water reflecting a ghostly luminescence; the twisted, gnarled forms of the mutated flora, their leaves often dark and leathery, yet occasionally catching and amplifying the faintest of glows.

The photographs that began to emerge from his darkroom were unlike anything Oakhaven had seen. They were not sharp, clear images of a world reborn, but rather evocative, impressionistic renditions of a world in transition. In one, a cluster of reeds, unnaturally tall and slender, seemed to absorb the faint light, their forms appearing almost as dark specters against a backdrop that bled from deep indigo to an unsettling emerald. The water at their base was a mirror of this eerie palette, reflecting not stars, but faint, internal fires. There was no overt depiction of danger, but the absence of clear detail, the play of light and shadow, instilled a profound sense of unease. It was beautiful, undeniably so, but a beauty tinged with sorrow and mystery.

Another photograph captured a patch of what appeared to be stunted, moss-like growth clinging to a decaying log. In the dim light, the moss seemed to shimmer, not with a vibrant, active glow, but with a subtle, almost weary phosphorescence. It was as if the very earth was sighing out its last embers of life. The surrounding landscape was desolation personified – cracked earth, barren scrub, the skeletal remains of structures long since reclaimed by time and neglect. The contrast was stark, a testament to life's tenacious grip even in the face of overwhelming entropy. The image evoked a quiet desperation, a silent plea for recognition.

Jax became particularly fascinated by the reflections. The still, dark waters of the wetlands acted as imperfect mirrors, distorting and amplifying the faint light sources. He would spend hours, sometimes entire nights, waiting for the perfect moment, for the interplay of light and water to create a scene that spoke volumes without shouting. In one striking image, the reflection of an unseen luminescent source beneath the water's surface rippled and distorted, creating a fragmented, almost hallucinatory pattern of greens and blues that seemed to pulse with a life of its own. The surface of the water, a dark, viscous expanse, seemed to hold the secrets of the world beneath, offering only fleeting glimpses of its radiant depths.

He experimented with long exposures, allowing the faint light to imprint itself onto the film over extended periods. This technique often yielded astonishing results, revealing subtle patterns and gradients of luminescence that were invisible to the naked eye. In these longer exposures, the wetlands transformed. The faint glow became more pronounced, revealing a network of interconnected light, a subterranean aurora hinting at processes far beyond human understanding. He saw what looked like veins of light running through the murky water, pathways of energy that pulsed with an organic rhythm. The stillness of the night was broken by a silent, visual symphony of light.

His photographs weren't just about capturing light; they were about capturing atmosphere. He meticulously worked on his prints in the darkroom, using different developers and toners to enhance the mood. He favored sepia tones for images that emphasized decay and nostalgia, and deep blues and greens for those that highlighted the eerie luminescence. He learned to control the grain of the film, sometimes exaggerating it to give his images a dreamlike, almost feverish quality, other times smoothing it out to emphasize the stark reality of the landscape.

The reactions within Oakhaven were varied. Some dismissed his work as morbid, an unhealthy obsession with the desolate beauty of their ruined world. They saw only the decay, the lingering toxins, the reminders of what had been lost. Elara, ever practical and cautious, expressed concern for his safety, her brow furrowed with worry whenever he spoke of his nocturnal excursions. "Why chase ghosts, Jax?" she'd asked him once, her voice laced with a mixture of exasperation and affection. "There's enough light to be found in the here and now, in building something real."

But others, a quieter, more introspective segment of the community, were captivated. They saw in Jax's photographs a reflection of their own internal landscape, a visual metaphor for the persistent, often hidden, sparks of hope that flickered within them. Luis, in particular, found a deep resonance in Jax's work. He saw not just art, but confirmation. The subtle nuances of light and shadow, the atmospheric qualities that Jax so masterfully captured, aligned with his own observations of the wetlands' subtle energies. He would spend hours poring over Jax's prints, his fingers tracing the ghostly luminescence, his mind piecing together a more complete picture of the evolving ecosystem.

"You see it too, don't you?" Jax had said to Luis one evening, as they stood in the flickering lamplight of Jax's workshop, examining a particularly striking print. The photograph depicted a lone, mutated amphibian, its skin shimmering with an internal, faint light, perched on the edge of a glowing pool. "It's not just decay. It's... something else. Something alive. Something that's found a way."

Luis nodded, his gaze fixed on the amphibian. "It's a language, Jax. A language we're only just beginning to decipher. Your photographs... they're like translations. They capture the poetry of it, the raw emotion that the data alone can't convey."

Jax's photographs served as a bridge between the purely scientific and the deeply intuitive. They humanized the anomaly, transforming it from a collection of alarming data points into something both alien and strangely familiar. They evoked a sense of wonder, but also a profound unease, a feeling that they were witnessing something ancient and powerful stirring from a long slumber. The stark beauty of the desolation, juxtaposed with the faint, otherworldly glow, created images that lingered long after they were seen, prompting questions that had no easy answers. What was this light? What strange biological processes were at play? And what did it mean for the future of Oakhaven, and indeed, for life itself in this radically altered world? Jax, with his camera and his darkroom, was not just documenting the present; he was, in his own unique way, capturing the whispered echoes of what was to come. His eerie photographs were a testament to the enduring mystery of life, a hauntingly beautiful reminder that even in the deepest darkness, there could be light, and in the most desolate landscapes, beauty could still bloom, albeit in forms that defied comprehension. He was a chronicler of the strange, an artist unafraid to peer into the abyss and find within it an unexpected, radiant glow. His work was a testament to the resilience of the creative spirit, a spark of human ingenuity in a world that often felt devoid of it. The wetlands, in his captured images, became less a place of dread and more a testament to the indomitable force of nature, a force that continued to shape and reshape itself, even in the ruins of what once was. His images were visual poems, sung in the language of light and shadow, a lament for what was lost, and a whispered promise of what might yet be. The viewers of his photographs often found themselves caught between a sense of awe and a prickle of fear, a recognition of the unknown that lay just beyond their grasp, a profound mystery etched in shades of emerald and indigo.

CHAPTER FOURTEEN

FACING THE UNKNOWN

The faint, almost imperceptible glow that Jax captured on his film was not merely an aesthetic curiosity, a ghostly luminescence emanating from the stagnant pools and mutated reeds of the wetlands. It was, as Luis's meticulous data began to suggest, a symptom of something far more pervasive, a subtle manifestation of an unseen force that was weaving its tendrils through the very fabric of their post-Collapse world. The interconnectedness of it all was becoming chillingly apparent, a complex web of cause and effect that defied their understanding of natural phenomena.

Luis, hunched over his salvaged equipment in the communal science lab, his brow furrowed in concentration, pointed a trembling finger at a series of readings. "Look at this, Jax. The atmospheric pressure anomalies. They're not random. They're... synchronized. They peak precisely when the bioluminescent intensity in the wetlands is at its highest." He gestured towards a graph that plotted fluctuating barometric pressure against spectral analysis of the wetland's glow. The correlation, though subtle, was undeniable. They weren't merely observing a localized phenomenon; they were witnessing the outward ripples of a much larger, more enigmatic event.

Jax, his hands still bearing the faint, tell-tale stains of developing chemicals, nodded slowly, his artist's intuition confirming Luis's scientific deductions. He had noticed it too, in his own way. The nights when the wetlands pulsed with a more vibrant, insistent light were often the nights when the wind, usually a predictable, gentle sigh through the skeletal remains of Oakhaven, would whip into a sudden, almost violent frenzy. It was a localized tempest, a miniature vortex of wind that seemed to emanate from the direction of the glowing marshes, only to dissipate as mysteriously as it arrived. He had initially dismissed it as a quirk of the altered topography, a consequence of the volcanic debris that had reshaped their valley. But now, seeing Luis's data, he recognized it for what it was: a part of a larger pattern, a more active expression of that unseen force.

The synchronized fluctuations weren't confined to the air. The behavior of the local fauna, a hardy and often desperate collection of mutated creatures that eked out an existence in the shadow of Oakhaven, had also become increasingly erratic. Small, rodent-like scavengers, normally skittish and nocturnal, were now observed congregating in unnervingly large numbers near the wetlands' edge during daylight hours, their beady eyes wide and seemingly mesmerized by the faint, ethereal light. More alarmingly, the few larger predators that still roamed the surrounding wastes – the gaunt, wolf-like creatures with their unnatural speed – seemed to be actively avoiding the wetlands, their predatory instincts overridden by an apparent, instinctual dread. Luis had recorded instances of these normally fearless hunters veering sharply off course, their howls of frustration echoing through the desolate landscape, all to avoid even the periphery of the glowing marshlands.

"It's not just that the animals are reacting to the light," Luis mused, his voice low and contemplative, as he reviewed his notes on animal migration patterns. "It's as if the light itself is influencing them. Guiding them, or perhaps, warning them. Some of the smaller, ground-dwelling creatures, the ones that seem to feed on the mutated fungi and mosses near the wetlands, they appear to be more active, almost invigorated, when the glow is strongest. Their reproductive cycles seem to be accelerating, too. We're seeing a surge in their populations. It's... an ecosystem undergoing a rapid, almost directed evolution."

Jax traced the outline of a particularly striking photograph he had developed the previous night. It depicted a cluster of the unusually tall, slender reeds, their dark, leathery surfaces almost entirely obscured by a shimmering, iridescent film. Beneath the surface of the stagnant water, a faint, pulsing green light seemed to emanate, casting an eerie glow upon the submerged roots. He remembered the palpable stillness of the air that night, the oppressive quiet that seemed to absorb all sound, and the strange, almost electric sensation that had prickled his skin as he adjusted his tripod. It was more than just photogenic decay; it was a scene saturated with an invisible energy.

"It feels like the land itself is waking up," Jax said, his voice barely above a whisper. "Like it's breathing again, but with a different kind of breath. Not the air we breathe, but something... else. Something older. Luis, have you noticed how the plants closer to the wetlands are changing? They're not just mutated; they're... adapting. The ones that can withstand the radiation, the ones that seem to absorb the ambient energy, they're growing faster, stronger. Their colors are shifting too, taking on these strange, almost phosphorescent hues."

Luis's eyes lit up with a shared intensity. "Precisely! The flora analysis is showing a significant increase in certain bio-luminescent proteins within the cellular structures of the plants nearest the anomaly. It's not just passive absorption; it's an active integration of this new energy. It's as if the wetlands are a... a nucleus, a catalyst for a new form of life. And the effects are radiating outwards. We're seeing subtle shifts in soil composition, changes in the mineral content of the water table miles away. It's a systemic transformation, Jax, not an isolated event."

The implications of this interconnectedness were profound and deeply unsettling. The volcanic eruption, the catastrophic event that had so drastically reshaped their world, had not merely rendered the land uninhabitable, poisoning the air and choking the skies. It had, it seemed, inadvertently awakened something else, something primal and profoundly alien. The glowing wetlands were not just a testament to the lingering toxins; they were a visible manifestation of a powerful, emergent force that was actively re-writing the rules of their existence.

"We thought we were just surviving the aftermath," Elara said one evening, her voice laced with a growing unease as she listened to Luis and Jax discuss their findings. She had been tending to a patch of hardy, genetically modified vegetables in the communal hydroponic garden, her usual practical demeanor tinged with apprehension. "We thought it was all about finding clean water, rationing supplies, rebuilding what we could. We never imagined... this. This force that seems to be actively shaping the world around us, not just passively existing within it."

Her words hung in the air, a stark acknowledgment of their misperceptions. They had been so focused on the immediate threats, the tangible dangers of radiation, scarcity, and the ever-present fear of the unknown. They had viewed their struggle as one of enduring a static catastrophe. But the evidence accumulating around them – the synchronized atmospheric pressure, the peculiar animal behavior, the rapid adaptation of the flora, and of course, the haunting bioluminescence – painted a far more dynamic and disquieting picture.

"It's like a new evolutionary engine has been ignited," Luis explained, his voice hushed with a mixture of awe and trepidation. "The energy source... whatever it is that's causing the luminescence, it's providing a constant, powerful input. And life, in its most fundamental drive to survive and adapt, is responding. It's not just surviving the post-Collapse world; it's evolving *within* it. And this force, this unseen energy, is the architect of that evolution."

Jax, looking at his photographs of the subtly glowing moss clinging to decaying wood, no longer saw just decay. He saw a dormant seed of adaptation, a testament to life's unyielding will. He saw the tiny amphibian, its skin radiating a faint, internal light, not as a curiosity, but as a harbinger of a new biological paradigm. His artistic lens, which had initially focused on the melancholic beauty of their ruined world, was now capturing glimpses of something far more active, a vibrant, albeit alien, re-creation unfolding before their very eyes.

The community of Oakhaven, once united by the shared experience of disaster and the singular goal of survival, now found themselves confronting a new, far more complex challenge. They were not merely survivors of a geological cataclysm; they were inhabitants of a world undergoing a profound, possibly sentient, transformation. The glowing wetlands were no longer just a forbidden zone, a place of whispered legends and lingering dread. They were the epicenter of a developing mystery, a beacon of an unknown future that pulsed with an eerie, captivating light, beckoning them to confront not just the ghosts of their past, but the vibrant, unsettling specter of a world reborn. The unseen force was no longer merely an abstract concept; it was a palpable presence, its influence seeping into every aspect of their lives, from the very air they breathed to the dreams they dared to dream. They were no longer simply living

in the ruins; they were living *with* a new genesis, a genesis of light and mystery, emanating from the heart of the glowing wetlands. This realization settled upon Oakhaven not with a sudden crash, but with the slow, inexorable pressure of a rising tide, a tide of luminous, unknown potential. The subtle shifts in the environment were no longer random; they were deliberate strokes on a cosmic canvas, guided by an artist whose palette was light and whose medium was life itself. And Oakhaven, a fragile settlement clinging to the edge of this burgeoning wilderness, was now irrevocably a part of its unfolding masterpiece. The scientific measurements, the artistic interpretations, the anecdotal observations – they all converged into a single, undeniable truth: they were no longer just contending with the aftermath of the past; they were now participants in a potent, emergent future, a future inextricably linked to the ethereal glow of the wetlands and the unseen force that animated it. This awakening force was not just altering the environment; it was beginning to subtly alter their perceptions, their fears, and their hopes, weaving a new narrative for humanity's place in a world that was no longer merely broken, but actively, profoundly, and mysteriously transforming. The very air seemed to thrum with this nascent energy, a silent symphony of change that resonated in the rustling of the mutated reeds and the shimmering of the phosphorescent moss. It was a grand, terrifying, and undeniably beautiful unfolding, a testament to life's relentless drive to exist, to adapt, and to illuminate the darkest of corners with its own, peculiar, and ever-evolving radiance.

The luminous anomaly in the wetlands, once a shared enigma that had momentarily united Oakhaven under the banner of scientific curiosity and artistic fascination, was rapidly becoming a wedge. The initial thrill of discovery, the shared wonder at Luis's data and Jax's evocative imagery, had begun to fray at the edges, revealing the familiar fault lines that had always existed beneath the surface of their fragile community. The shared struggle for survival had, for a time, plastered over these cracks, but the emergence of something so fundamentally *new*, so profoundly outside their established understanding of the post-Collapse world, was proving to be a catalyst for their resurfacing.

A palpable tension had begun to weave itself through the communal mess hall, the hydroponic gardens, and even the hushed corners of the repurposed library where they gathered for their infrequent council meetings. The 'future-first' adherents, those who had always championed progress, adaptation, and a proactive approach to rebuilding, found themselves increasingly at odds with a significant portion of the population who, having endured so much, now clung to the hard-won stability of the present with a fierce, almost desperate grip.

"We *must* understand it," insisted Lena, her voice ringing with the conviction of someone who saw opportunity where others saw only peril. Lena, a former bio-engineer whose sharp intellect and relentless drive had been instrumental in developing Oakhaven's self-sustaining agricultural systems, had quickly become one of the most vocal proponents of a thorough, systematic investigation of the glowing wetlands. She saw the luminescence not as a curse, but as a potential key. "Think of the possibilities, Luis! If this energy, this bioluminescent phenomenon, can accelerate plant growth, can it be harnessed? Can it lead to new food sources, more resilient crops? What if it's a source of clean energy, a power that doesn't rely on the fossil fuels that nearly destroyed us?" She gestured animatedly with her hands, her eyes alight with the fire of discovery. "We can't afford to ignore this. To turn our backs on it would be... it would be a dereliction of our duty to build a better future."

Her arguments, logical and compelling, resonated with many of the younger members of Oakhaven, those who had known little else but the struggle and the scarcity, and who yearned for a tangible sign of progress, a glimmer of hope that extended beyond mere subsistence. They were the ones who had internalized the 'future-first' ethos, seeing it not as a radical ideology, but as the only rational path forward in a world that offered no room for complacency. To them, Lena's words were not just persuasive; they were a call to action, a promise of a future where they might not just survive, but thrive.

However, for others, Lena's fervent optimism sounded more like a siren's call, luring them towards an unknown danger. Among them was old Silas, his face a roadmap of hardship etched by years of scavenging in the irradiated ruins. Silas had been one of the original architects of Oakhaven, a pragmatist who had always tempered ambition with caution. He had witnessed firsthand the devastating consequences of unchecked technological advancement and the hubris that often accompanied it.

"Understand it?" Silas's voice was a low rumble, laced with skepticism and a deep-seated weariness. He sat hunched over his plate of reconstituted protein, his gaze fixed on a point beyond Lena's impassioned pronouncements. "We tried to 'understand' the atom, didn't we? We thought we were masters of it, and look where that got us. Look what it unleashed. This... glow... it's unknown. It's *unnatural*. The last time we embraced the unknown with open arms, it nearly wiped us out. My generation, we've paid the price for that curiosity. We've seen what happens when you poke a sleeping dragon."

His words, delivered with the quiet authority of lived experience, struck a chord with a significant segment of the community. These were the individuals who had lost loved ones in the initial Collapse, who bore physical and emotional scars from the ensuing years of environmental catastrophe and societal breakdown. The very idea of venturing into the wetlands, of actively seeking to engage with this strange, luminous phenomenon, filled them with a primal dread. The wetlands, with their eerie glow and mutated inhabitants, had become a symbol of everything they feared: the unpredictable, the destructive, the embodiment of a world that had irrevocably turned against them.

"Silas is right," echoed Anya, a woman whose quiet demeanor belied a steely resolve. Anya ran the infirmary, her days filled with tending to the ailments that still plagued Oakhaven, a constant reminder of the lingering effects of the Collapse. Her hands, often gentle as she bound wounds or administered medicine, were now clasped tightly in her lap, a sign of her inner turmoil. "We've seen too much death, too much suffering, born from trying to control things we don't understand. The wetlands are a place of decay, a place where the old world's poisons still fester. Why would we want to go there? Why invite more danger?"

She looked around the hall, her gaze meeting the worried eyes of many others. "We have what we need here in Oakhaven. We have our farms, our water purifiers, our defenses. We are safe. Why risk that safety for... for a glow in the swamp? It's a risk we cannot afford. We should seal it off, pretend it's not there, and focus on what we *know*."

This division was not merely an intellectual debate; it was a deeply emotional chasm. The 'future-first' faction, led by Lena and buoyed by the energy of the younger generation, saw the wetlands as a frontier, a challenge to be met with ingenuity and courage. They envisioned a future where humanity, having learned from its mistakes, could harness even the most alien of forces for its own betterment. They were driven by a potent blend of scientific optimism and a desperate need to believe that their struggle had a purpose beyond mere survival.

Conversely, the 'cautionary' faction, championed by Silas and Anya, viewed the wetlands with a profound sense of trepidation. Their experiences had taught them that the unknown was rarely benevolent, and that the pursuit of progress often came at a terrible cost. They were the inheritors of a legacy of destruction, and their primary instinct was to protect what little they had managed to salvage. For them, the wetlands were a place best left undisturbed, a reminder of the perils of overreaching and a warning to be heeded.

The 'future-first' ideals were being tested in the crucible of fear and uncertainty. Oakhaven, which had prided itself on its unity in the face of adversity, was now grappling with the very human tendency to fracture when faced with an unprecedented and deeply unsettling enigma. The glowing wetlands, with their silent, pulsing light, were not just an environmental anomaly; they were a mirror reflecting the deepest anxieties and the most divergent hopes of its inhabitants.

Jax, though an artist rather than a scientist or a politician, found himself caught in the middle of this burgeoning conflict. His own fascination with the wetlands was not driven by a desire for power or a fear of the unknown, but by a profound aesthetic and emotional pull. He saw beauty in the luminescence, a melancholic poetry in the adaptation of life, a testament to nature's indomitable spirit. He felt a kinship with the land, a connection that transcended logic or fear.

"It's not about conquering it," Jax explained to Luis one evening, as they watched the distant, faint glow from the safety of Oakhaven's perimeter wall. Jax's voice was soft, contemplative. "It's about understanding our place within it. The wetlands aren't attacking us. They're... changing. And we're part of that change, whether we like it or not. To ignore it is to deny a part of ourselves, a part of the world we live in."

Luis nodded, his gaze distant. "I understand Lena's ambition. The data... it's intoxicating. It suggests possibilities we never dreamed of. But Silas and Anya have a point too. We're not equipped for this. We're survivors, not explorers of the truly alien. Every step we take could lead us into a trap we can't even comprehend." He ran a hand through his already disheveled hair. "The synchronization of atmospheric pressure, the accelerated evolution... it suggests a power that's far beyond our current understanding, far beyond our ability to control. What if Lena's 'harnessing' is just another form of the same reckless ambition that led to the Collapse?"

The council meetings, once forums for collaborative problem-solving, were becoming increasingly acrimonious. Lena would present new data, outlining potential research avenues, suggesting carefully monitored excursions. Silas would counter with grim historical parallels, vivid accounts of past disasters, and impassioned pleas for caution. Anya would speak of the medical implications, the potential for unknown pathogens or environmental toxins, her voice a constant reminder of the fragility of life.

"We're not talking about sending people into the heart of the anomaly," Lena would argue, her patience wearing thin. "We're talking about careful, controlled observation. Small drones, remote sensors. Minimal risk for maximum knowledge."

"Minimal risk is still risk, Lena," Silas would retort, his voice hardening. "And knowledge that we can't act upon, or worse, knowledge that tempts us to act rashly, can be more dangerous than ignorance."

The 'future-first' camp saw the resistance as fear-mongering, a stubborn adherence to the past that would stifle progress and condemn Oakhaven to a perpetual state of scarcity. They accused Silas and his allies of being dinosaurs, clinging to outdated notions of safety in a world that demanded adaptation.

"You want us to live like monks forever, surviving on rations and fear?" a young woman named Clara, a fierce supporter of Lena, challenged Silas during one heated exchange. "The world is changing, Silas. It's offering us something new. Are we going to hide in our bunkers, or are we going to step out and see what it is? Our ancestors took risks. That's how we got here. That's how we survived the Collapse in the first place – by adapting, by finding new ways."

Silas's eyes narrowed. "Your ancestors also built cities that fell into ruin, Clara. They wielded power they couldn't comprehend. Adaptation is one thing; recklessness is another. We survived the Collapse because some people were *smart* enough to *not* rush into the fire, but to huddle around the embers and build something small and safe first. And now, the fire is glowing again, and you want to run towards it. That's not progress, child. That's folly."

The rift was deepening, threatening to split the community down the middle. The 'future-first' idealists, brimming with a nascent belief in humanity's capacity for reinvention, found themselves pitted against the 'cautionary' pragmatists, whose experiences had instilled in them a profound respect for the limits of human knowledge and the destructive potential of the unknown. The glowing wetlands, once a source of shared wonder, had become the focal point of their deepest fears and their most divergent hopes, a stark reminder that even in the face of extraordinary circumstances, the human heart remained a complex tapestry of ambition and anxiety, forever striving for a future while haunted by the specters of its past. Oakhaven's unity, a hard-won achievement, was now being tested by the very mystery that had promised to reveal new possibilities, exposing the inherent divisions within their small, resilient society. The unseen force, pulsing in the distant marshes, was not only transforming the environment; it was also, irrevocably, transforming the social and emotional landscape of Oakhaven itself, forcing them to confront not just the external unknown, but the deeply ingrained uncertainties within their own community. The debate was no longer confined to the scientific implications or the artistic interpretations; it had morphed into a fundamental question of identity and purpose: what kind of future did they truly want, and how much were they willing to risk to achieve it?

Mika sat hunched over her workbench, the dim glow of the communal lighting barely illuminating the scattered notes and sketches before her. The air in her small corner of the repurposed library, usually thick with the scent of old paper and disinfectant, now carried a subtle undercurrent of anxiety. It was a palpable tension, a collective breath held by Oakhaven as it grappled with the luminous enigma of the wetlands. While others debated, argued, and feared, Mika felt a different kind of pressure – the quiet, insistent demand of the unknown to be understood. Her mind, accustomed to the precise language of scientific inquiry, was a storm of possibilities, a restless engine trying to find a framework, a hypothesis, to anchor the swirling uncertainty.

She traced a finger over a diagram of the wetland's micro-ecosystem, a sketch born from Luis's preliminary data and Jax's atmospheric readings. The luminescence, that ethereal, pulsating light, was the undeniable focal point, but what *was* it? The easy answers, the ones that involved simple chemical reactions or known biological processes, felt woefully inadequate. This felt... different. It felt like a fundamental shift, not just a localized anomaly.

Her first tentative hypotheses began to coalesce, not as declarations, but as carefully worded questions. Could this be an unprecedented form of microbial life, an extremophile flourishing in conditions previously thought impossible? Perhaps a symbiotic relationship between known organisms and an entirely novel energy source, a biological process that had evolved in isolation from the rest of the post-Collapse world. She considered the possibility of undiscovered microbial colonies, vast, interconnected networks that fed on residual radiation or geothermal activity, their metabolic byproducts manifesting as this soft, pervasive light. She even entertained the outlandish, the idea of entirely new life forms, silicon-based or something beyond their current biological understanding, adapted to an environment that had long been considered toxic and sterile. She jotted down notes, her handwriting tight and precise: "Hypothesis 1: Novel microbial consortium, extremophilic, bioluminescent. Potential energy pathway?"

But the scale of the phenomenon, the way it seemed to synchronize with atmospheric pressure shifts and affect plant growth in the immediate vicinity, pushed her beyond purely biological explanations. Could it be geological? Had the recent seismic activity, a tremor that had rattled Oakhaven just weeks before the glow appeared, somehow awakened something deep within the earth? Perhaps a hitherto unknown mineral deposit, reacting with groundwater and the unique chemical composition of the wetlands, was undergoing a process that released energy in the form of light. She sketched cross-sections of the earth, imagining subterranean caverns, mineral veins, and the slow, relentless flow of water. "Hypothesis 2: Geochemical reaction, deep-earth mineral activation, catalyzed by seismic event. Energy release via luminescence."

The mention of accelerated plant growth, even if anecdotal at this stage, gnawed at her. If it was biological, was it a pathogen, a parasite that was somehow *enhancing* its host to better serve its own needs? Or was it a beneficial symbiosis, a mutualistic relationship that Oakhaven, with its perpetual struggle for sustenance, could learn from? The idea of harnessing such a force, Lena's fervent dream, was compelling, but the potential for unintended consequences was equally terrifying. The Collapse had been a stark, brutal lesson in the dangers of tampering with forces one did not fully comprehend.

She remembered the early days of Oakhaven, the desperate scramble for resources, the constant threat of famine. The hydroponic systems, their current lifeline, were a testament to human ingenuity, but they were fragile. If this new energy source could truly supercharge their crops, it would be a revolution. But what if it also caused unpredictable mutations? What if it was toxic in ways they couldn't yet detect? The questions multiplied, each one branching into a dozen more, creating a labyrinth of uncertainty.

Mika realized that any attempt to understand this phenomenon had to be grounded in a rigorous, phased approach, prioritizing safety above all else. The passionate debates in the mess hall, while understandable, were too volatile, too driven by fear and ambition. What Oakhaven needed was not more impassioned speeches, but a plan. A scientific plan.

She began to outline a multi-stage investigation. The first phase, she wrote, must be purely observational, non-intrusive. This meant deploying remote sensing equipment, drones equipped with spectral analyzers and atmospheric samplers, operating at a safe distance. They needed to map the extent of the luminescence, measure its intensity, and collect baseline data on the chemical composition of the air and water in and around the glowing areas. "Phase 1: Remote Sensing and Data Acquisition. Objective: Characterize the phenomenon without direct interaction. Safety focus: Maintain significant distance, utilize automated systems."

Only after accumulating a substantial body of data from this initial phase, data that could be analyzed and cross-referenced, should they even consider moving to a second stage. This would involve the deployment of probes, carefully designed to withstand unknown environmental conditions, capable of collecting physical samples – water, soil, plant matter – from the periphery of the glowing zones. These samples would then be brought back to Oakhaven for rigorous analysis in their limited but functional laboratory. Strict quarantine protocols would be paramount, of course, with any retrieved samples handled in the most secure containment possible. Anya's concerns about unknown pathogens were not to be dismissed lightly. "Phase 2: Remote Sampling and Laboratory Analysis. Objective: Gather physical samples for controlled study. Safety focus: Advanced containment, rigorous decontamination procedures, isolation of analyzed samples."

Mika envisioned a third phase, one that would only be initiated if the first two phases yielded results that were deemed sufficiently understood and manageable. This would involve cautious, highly controlled manned excursions, but only to the very edges of the phenomenon, and only after extensive risk assessments and the development of specialized protective gear. The goal would not be to penetrate the heart of the anomaly, but to conduct targeted observations and collect specific samples under direct supervision. "Phase 3: Limited Manned Observation (Conditional). Objective: In-situ observation and targeted sample collection. Safety focus: Specialized suits, designated safe zones, immediate extraction protocols, robust medical support on standby."

She emphasized the conditional nature of each phase. No advancement to the next stage would occur without the full community's understanding and agreement, based on clear, verifiable data. This was not about appeasing Silas's fear or Lena's ambition, but about establishing a framework for rational decision-making in the face of the profoundly unknown. Her goal was to inject logic into the rising tide of emotion, to build a bridge of understanding between the two factions by providing a concrete, scientific methodology.

She began to detail the specific equipment they might need. Drones were readily available, scavenged from pre-Collapse research outposts. Luis had salvaged several atmospheric sensors and a compact mass spectrometer that, with some recalibration, could potentially analyze air samples. For the probes, they might need to adapt existing robotic arms used for hazardous waste management, outfitting them with sampling tools and sealed collection containers. The challenges were immense, but not insurmountable. They had a history of innovation born from necessity.

Mika's own background, a blend of environmental science and a deep understanding of Oakhaven's salvaged technological infrastructure, gave her a unique perspective. She understood the delicate balance of their ecosystem, the reliance on carefully managed resources, and the lingering threats of radiation and mutation that still haunted the world outside their walls. This phenomenon in the wetlands was a radical disruption to that balance, and it had to be approached with the utmost respect for the inherent dangers.

She began to draft a formal proposal, a document that would be presented to the Oakhaven council. It wouldn't be filled with wild speculation or emotional appeals. Instead, it would be a sober, detailed outline of a scientific investigation, a roadmap for de-escalating the fear and channeling the community's energy into productive inquiry. She knew it wouldn't be universally welcomed. Lena would likely find it too cautious, too slow. Silas might see it as an invitation to danger, regardless of the safety protocols. But Mika believed it was the only responsible way forward.

She wrote of the importance of documenting everything, of establishing a baseline of normal environmental conditions in the wetlands before the glow, if such data even existed. She speculated about the possibility of an accelerated evolutionary process, a concept that both thrilled and terrified her. If the wetlands were a crucible of rapid adaptation, what other changes might be occurring just beyond their immediate perception? Were there new pathogens evolving? New toxic flora? Or, conversely, were there new resources, new sources of sustenance, waiting to be discovered?

Her hypothesis about microbial life grew more complex. She considered quorum sensing, inter-species communication, and the possibility of collective intelligence within these hypothetical colonies. Could the luminescence be a form of communication, a signal within the microbial network, or perhaps a byproduct of a vast, interconnected biological system operating on principles they had yet to discover? She even mused on the potential for these microbes to metabolize lingering radiation, offering a natural form of remediation for the scarred landscapes. This was, of course, pure speculation, but it was speculation grounded in scientific principles, a starting point for inquiry.

Regarding the geological hypothesis, she considered the possibility of piezoelectric effects, or some form of chemiluminescence triggered by specific mineral compositions and the presence of water. The recent tremors, however minor, could have fractured underground rock formations, releasing gases or fluids that interacted with known or unknown minerals. She thought of ancient, dormant geothermal vents, their activity perhaps stirred by the seismic shifts. The heat from these vents could provide the energy for life, even in the cold, damp environment of the wetlands.

Mika also began to consider a hybrid hypothesis, one that combined biological and geological elements. Perhaps a geological event had released dormant, resilient microbial life, which then thrived in the new conditions, developing its luminescent properties as a means of survival or energy production. This felt like a more plausible scenario, one that could account for both the physical and biological aspects of the phenomenon. She sketched a layered diagram, showing subterranean rock strata, then a layer of microbial colonies, and finally the luminescent output visible at the surface. "Hypothesis 3: Biogeochemical symbiosis, triggered by seismic event. Geological activity provides energy/nutrients for novel microbial ecosystem, resulting in luminescence and accelerated biological processes."

She knew that each hypothesis, however intriguing, would require extensive testing. Her proposed phased approach was designed to systematically test each possibility, to eliminate variables, and to build a coherent picture of what was happening in the wetlands. She wouldn't be satisfied with simply knowing *that* it was glowing; she needed to understand *why* and *how*.

The document she was crafting was more than just a scientific proposal; it was an attempt to bring order to chaos, to provide a reasoned framework in a time of burgeoning fear and division. It was a testament to her belief that even in the face of the most profound mysteries, human reason and scientific inquiry could provide a path forward. She believed that Oakhaven's survival, and its future, depended on its ability to confront the unknown not with blind panic or reckless ambition, but with careful observation, rigorous analysis, and an unwavering commitment to safety. The light in the wetlands was a challenge, a profound and potentially dangerous one, but Mika was determined to meet it with the tools of her discipline, to illuminate the darkness with the steady, rational glow of scientific understanding.

She meticulously documented the materials they would need for each phase: specialized drone attachments, reinforced sampling probes, portable atmospheric analyzers, and, crucially, upgraded biosafety protocols for the laboratory. She even began to think about the ethical considerations, the potential impact of their investigations on the wetland ecosystem itself, a concern that often got lost in the urgency of survival. If they were to discover a new form of life, what were their responsibilities towards it? This was a question that transcended immediate utility and touched upon the very core of their humanity.

Mika paused, looking out at the faint, almost imperceptible glow that sometimes shimmered on the horizon of the wetlands even from their vantage point within Oakhaven. It was beautiful, in a strange, unsettling way. It held a promise, and a threat. Her hypothesis development was not just an intellectual exercise; it was an act of faith, a belief that understanding was the first step towards navigating the unknown, and that in understanding, they might find a way not just to survive, but to truly thrive, to build a future that was not merely safe, but also informed and purposeful. The path forward would be fraught with difficulty, and the debates would undoubtedly continue, but Mika had laid down a foundation, a scientific blueprint for confronting the mystery, one carefully measured step at a time.

Luis's perspective, often characterized by a quiet pragmatism and an almost poetic appreciation for the resilience of nature, began to weave itself into the growing discourse surrounding the wetland's luminescence. While Mika meticulously charted hypotheses rooted in established scientific paradigms – microbial colonies, geological anomalies, biogeochemical interactions – Luis's mind drifted towards a more intricate, interconnected view. He saw not just isolated phenomena, but a burgeoning symphony of adaptation, a testament to life's persistent drive to find equilibrium, even in the most scarred and unforgiving of landscapes.

He sat with Jax by the edge of the hydroponics bay, the rhythmic hum of the pumps a familiar counterpoint to the hushed urgency that permeated Oakhaven. Jax, ever the pragmatist, was reviewing atmospheric scrubbers, his brow furrowed with the usual concerns of air quality and resource management. Luis, however, was looking beyond the immediate confines of their controlled environment, his gaze fixed on the distant, softly glowing expanse of the wetlands.

"It's not just a light, Jax," Luis murmured, his voice barely above a whisper, as if not to disturb some delicate balance in the air. "It's a conversation. Life trying to talk to itself."

Jax grunted, not looking up from his schematics. "A conversation that's making people nervous, Luis. Mika's got her theories, complex ones, I'll give her that. But this... this glow. It's unprecedented. And unprecedented usually means dangerous."

"Or it means a new kind of opportunity," Luis countered, his eyes alight with a thought that had been germinating for days. "Think about it. The wetlands were poisoned. Toxic. Full of residual radiation, chemicals that would kill most things we know. And yet, life found a way. It always does. But this... this is more than just survival. This is... thriving."

He gestured towards the distant wetlands. "We've been battling those invasive reeds, haven't we? The ones that choke out everything else, the ones we've had to cultivate carefully in the hydroponics because they're so aggressive. They thrive on toxins, on harsh conditions. And now, look. The luminescence is strongest where those reeds are thickest. Coincidence?"

Jax finally turned, his expression skeptical. "Reeds are plants, Luis. They don't glow. Whatever is making that light is something else. Something... in the water, maybe? In the soil?"

"Exactly! But what if those 'somethings' – and I'm imagining them as microscopic, perhaps a complex consortium of microbes, or even a novel fungal network – are not just *living* in the reeds, but *working* with them?" Luis leaned forward, his quiet intensity drawing Jax's attention. "My theory, Jax, is that this luminescence is a byproduct of a massive, emergent symbiotic relationship. The glowing organisms are acting as a colossal detoxification system for the wetlands. They're metabolizing the poisons, the radiation, the very things that made it uninhabitable for so long. And in doing so, they're creating an environment that the invasive plants, with their unique tolerance for harsh conditions, can exploit even further. It's a feedback loop, a mutually beneficial arrangement that's healing the land, or at least, reshaping it into something new."

He paused, letting the idea settle. "Imagine it: these microbes, these little bio-factories, are breaking down the complex, harmful compounds into simpler, inert substances. And perhaps some of those simpler substances are actually nutrients for the reeds. The reeds, in turn, provide a habitat, a substrate, for the microbes. It's a natural adaptation, a wild solution to a catastrophic problem."

Jax rubbed his chin, a flicker of consideration crossing his face. "So, you're saying the glow isn't a sign of danger, but a sign of... environmental repair? Life fighting back, literally, by cleaning up the mess?"

"Precisely," Luis confirmed, a rare, broad smile gracing his lips. "Think of it as nature's immune system kicking into overdrive.

The Collapse left Oakhaven and the surrounding lands riddled with sickness. The wetlands, perhaps due to their unique mineral composition or their isolation, became a crucible for a new kind of biology. Life, under immense pressure, finds a way to evolve, to create novel solutions. This luminescence, this visible manifestation of intense metabolic activity, could be the most profound indicator of that healing process. It's not an invasion; it's an integration. A re-establishment of balance, albeit a very alien one."

He elaborated on his theory, sketching in the air with his hands. "We've been so focused on what we *lost*, on what the Collapse *destroyed*. We see remnants of the old world as dangerous or scarce. But what if Oakhaven's greatest opportunity lies not in rebuilding what was, but in understanding and integrating with what is emerging? This wetland phenomenon... it might be the key. If these organisms are indeed detoxifying the environment, then understanding their processes could unlock revolutionary applications for us. Not just for food production, but for reclamation. Imagine if we could cultivate these symbiotic relationships, harness them to purify our water sources, or even to make previously uninhabitable areas safe again."

Luis's mind raced, connecting this nascent theory to Oakhaven's ongoing struggles. Their carefully cultivated crops, while vital, were a constant drain on resources, requiring precise nutrient mixes and controlled environments. The invasive reeds, by contrast, were self-sufficient, even thriving in conditions that would kill their precious hydroponic produce. If the luminescence was linked to a process that rendered even these hardy, toxin-tolerant plants more productive or, paradoxically, made them a source of benefit, it would be a paradigm shift.

"And what about the invasive plants themselves?" Luis continued, his thoughts flowing with increasing conviction. "We see them as a problem, a nuisance that we've had to learn to manage. But what if their invasiveness is a sign of their own form of adaptation? They are opportunistic, yes, but what if their 'opportunism' is driven by the very detoxification process we're observing? What if they've co-evolved with these luminescent organisms, forming a partnership that allows them to flourish where nothing else can? The glow might not just be a byproduct for the microbes; it could be a signal, a nutrient exchange, a pathway for the plants to access energy or compounds they wouldn't otherwise be able to utilize."

He knew this sounded outlandish to many. The prevailing Oakhaven narrative was one of survival against a hostile world, a world defined by its ruin and its dangers. The idea of 'harmony' or 'symbiosis' with the post-Collapse environment felt almost heretical. Yet, Luis had always found a quiet beauty in the tenacity of life, in the intricate ways it adapted and endured. He saw this luminescence not as a spectral anomaly, but as a vibrant, pulsating indicator of nature's indomitable will to create, to connect, to persist.

"Consider this," he urged Jax, his voice deepening with earnestness. "Our hydroponics require constant energy input. Fertilizers, water purification, light cycles – it's a closed system, inherently fragile. But what if, through understanding this wetland symbiosis, we could tap into a self-sustaining energy source? What if the microbes, by breaking down complex toxins, release usable energy? And what if the plants are somehow acting as conduits, amplifying or directing that energy? It's a speculative leap, I know, but it's a leap based on observing Oakhaven's most pressing needs and the most compelling natural phenomenon we've encountered since the Collapse."

He envisioned a future where Oakhaven wasn't just surviving in isolation, but actively engaging with and learning from the revitalized ecosystems around them. A future where their understanding of biology and environmental science allowed them to foster natural processes, rather than just battling them. This wasn't about reckless exposure or blind faith; it was about intelligent, careful observation and the pursuit of a deeper understanding that could lead to genuine, sustainable prosperity.

"Mika's focus on containment and analysis is crucial, don't get me wrong," Luis conceded, acknowledging the scientific rigor of Mika's approach. "We absolutely need to know what we're dealing with, what the risks are. But while she's mapping the boundaries and cataloging the unknowns, we also need to be thinking about the

potential. What this could *mean* for us. This isn't just about identifying a new organism; it's about recognizing a new *process*. A process that Oakhaven, with its constant struggle for resources, might be able to learn from, perhaps even to emulate. Imagine if we could cultivate a strain of these detoxifying microbes, or understand the specific triggers that lead to this luminescence and accelerated growth, and then apply it to our own systems. It could be a way to naturally enrich our soil, to purify our water, to make our crops more resilient, all by working *with* nature, not just against it."

He looked at Jax, his gaze steady and full of a quiet hope. "This luminescence... it's a beacon, Jax. A sign that life is not only surviving, but evolving. And if we are to truly rebuild, to create something more than just a fortified bunker against the past, we need to be open to what the future is showing us. This is Oakhaven's chance to become more than just a survivor. It's a chance to become a steward, a partner with the resurgent life of this damaged world."

Luis then began to articulate specific areas of inquiry that aligned with his theoretical framework, suggesting observational points that might corroborate his symbiotic hypothesis. He proposed looking for correlations between the density and vibrancy of the luminescent areas and the specific types and health of the surrounding flora, particularly the invasive reeds. Were there specific nutrient gradients in the soil or water that coincided with areas of intense luminescence? Could they observe any physical interactions, however subtle, between the visible organisms and the glowing zones? He also suggested examining the internal structure of the invasive reeds themselves, looking for any unusual biological markers or compounds that might indicate a novel partnership with microbial life. His inquiries were less about immediate danger and more about uncovering the intricate, beautiful tapestry of natural adaptation that he believed was unfolding before their eyes. He was not dismissive of the risks, but he firmly believed that fear should not blind them to the profound possibilities that might lie hidden within the glowing depths of the wetlands. His perspective offered a counterbalance to the prevailing anxieties, a reminder that even in the post-Collapse world, nature possessed an astonishing capacity for renewal and a complex, interwoven beauty that was waiting to be understood.

Jax, the pragmatic engineer, found a different kind of solace in his meticulous documentation. While Luis saw a vibrant symphony in the wetland's glow, and Mika sought to dissect it with cold, hard data, Jax's method was rooted in tangible evidence. He saw the world through the lens of his camera, his journal a repository of observations that grounded the ephemeral in the concrete. He was the chronicler of the uncanny, the visual archivist of Oakhaven's unfolding strangeness. His focus was not on the why, not yet, but on the what. What was changing? How was it changing? And how could he possibly present this cascade of anomalies in a way that made sense, or at least, in a way that preserved the facts for a future that might possess clearer understanding?

He spent hours out in the reclaimed zones, the air thick with the scent of damp earth and the metallic tang of the filtration systems. His camera bag was his most trusted companion, its worn leather smelling of dust and purpose. He'd venture out at dawn, when the mist still clung to the marshy ground, turning the luminescent reeds into ethereal torches. The soft, pulsing light, which Luis described as a conversation, Jax saw as a data point. He'd capture it from every angle, noting the intensity, the color variations – from a pale, ghostly green to an almost electric cerulean. He'd zoom in on the reeds themselves, his macro lens revealing intricate patterns in their chlorophyll-deficient leaves, the way the light seemed to emanate from within, not just reflect off the surface. He'd photograph the unique structures of the re-emerging fungi, some resembling delicate, bioluminescent lace clinging to decaying wood, others squat, phosphorescent mounds that seemed to absorb and re-emit the ambient glow.

His journal entries were terse, factual, interspersed with sketches and photographic captions. "Day 287 post-Reboot. Wetland Sector Gamma. Luminescence intensity estimated at 7.3 lux, fluctuating. Reed density increased by 15% in observed quadrant. No observed precipitation. Atmospheric particulate count within acceptable parameters." These were the baseline facts, the unvarnished reality of what he was witnessing. But beneath the sterile language, a deeper narrative was forming, one that he began to recognize as a cohesive, if bewildering, phenomenon.

It wasn't just the reeds, or the glow. His excursions took him further, to the edges of the zones where the environmental scrubbers worked tirelessly, their hum a constant reminder of Oakhaven's delicate balance. He started noticing anomalies in the insect life. The familiar, hardy species that had managed to survive the Collapse were still present, their chitinous exoskeletons dulled by the harsh environment. But interspersed amongst them were new forms, or perhaps, old forms irrevocably altered. He photographed beetles with iridescent wing casings that shimmered with the same otherworldly hues as the wetland light. He captured images of moths, their wings patterned with intricate, bioluminescent markings that pulsed faintly in the twilight. He even documented a species of dragonfly, its wings impossibly large and translucent, its body a vibrant, almost glowing, emerald green. He labeled these with careful annotations: "Unidentified insect species, potential symbiotic adaptation to luminescent flora."

The plant life outside the immediate wetland periphery also began to show signs of alteration. He noticed how certain lichens, clinging to the weathered concrete of abandoned structures, were developing a faint, internal luminescence, particularly in areas close to the wetland's influence. Some of the hardy, drought-resistant mosses that Oakhaven cultivated for soil stabilization were exhibiting an unusual resilience, growing with a vigor that seemed almost unnatural, their fronds occasionally catching the ambient light and appearing to glow from within. He'd photograph these, often juxtaposing them with images of the struggling hydroponic crops back within Oakhaven's walls, the contrast stark and unsettling.

He meticulously documented atmospheric phenomena, too. While Mika focused on the air quality readings, Jax captured the visual evidence. He'd photograph the shimmering heat hazes that seemed to hang over the wetlands, even on cooler days, distortions in the air that hinted at unseen energies. He noticed subtle shifts in cloud formations, the way certain wisps of vapor seemed to catch and amplify the light, creating ephemeral, glowing patterns against the twilight sky. He recorded instances of strange atmospheric refractions, creating mirages that played tricks on the eye, making the distant landscape appear to warp and shimmer. He even captured peculiar, almost crystalline, dew formations on the fringes of the wetlands, intricate structures that seemed to capture and refract the faintest light, sparkling like a million tiny diamonds.

His workspace, a corner of the engineering bay, became a collage of this strange new world. Photographs were pinned to every available surface: close-ups of glowing fungi, wide shots of the luminous reeds stretching into the mist, images of mutated insects and plants. Beside them, he'd tack hand-drawn diagrams, overlaying soil composition analyses with luminescence intensity maps, plotting the correlation between atmospheric moisture levels and insect activity. He wasn't an artist, but his visual narrative was undeniably powerful. It spoke of a world not merely recovering, but actively transforming, weaving itself into something new, something alien.

The interconnectedness was what struck him most profoundly. It wasn't a series of isolated incidents. The glowing insects seemed to be attracted to the glowing plants. The altered atmospheric conditions often coincided with increased luminescent activity. The unusual plant growth appeared to be concentrated in areas with specific soil compositions that also showed high levels of microbial activity, and by extension, luminescence. He began to see patterns emerge, a complex web of cause and effect that stretched from the microscopic organisms in the soil to the atmospheric haze above.

He started creating composite images, layering different elements to highlight these connections. A photograph of a luminescent beetle would be overlaid with a diagram of the reed's internal structure. An image of a glowing lichen would be juxtaposed with a soil sample analysis, the color spectrum of the lichen mirroring the nutrient density of the soil. These were not scientific papers, but visual arguments, presented with the stark clarity of an engineer's blueprint. He was building a case, not for any particular theory, but for the undeniable reality of radical environmental change.

Luis would often pause by his desk, a quiet observer in the midst of Jax's organized chaos. He'd point to a photograph of a mutated dragonfly, its wingspans unusually broad, its body radiating a soft green light. "See, Jax? It's not just surviving. It's *optimizing*. It's found a way to integrate the energy, to use it. It's a testament to the adaptability you're documenting so beautifully."

Jax would nod, his gaze steady, his fingers tracing the lines of a diagram. "Adaptation, or mutation. The distinction is... becoming blurry. What concerns me, Luis, is the rate. It feels accelerated. As if the environment is not just healing, but undergoing a forced evolution. And we're on the outside, looking in, trying to catch up."

Mika, in her own way, also recognized the value of Jax's work. She'd request specific images, detailed close-ups of fungal structures or insect anatomy, data points that her own sophisticated sensors couldn't always capture with such visceral clarity. "Your photographs, Jax," she'd admit, her voice tinged with grudging respect, "they provide a visual context that my spectral analysis alone cannot. When I see this... this strange bioluminescence on the carapace of that beetle, it prompts a different line of inquiry than a simple chemical signature."

Jax's efforts weren't about grand pronouncements or sweeping theories. They were about observation, about collecting the raw material of understanding. He was the one ensuring that the extraordinary details of Oakhaven's transformation wouldn't be lost, that the subtle shifts, the mutations, the atmospheric anomalies, and the undeniable glow of the wetlands would be preserved. He was building a visual history, a testament to a world remaking itself, one glowing reed, one iridescent beetle, one shimmering haze at a time. His commitment to this visual record was a quiet act of defiance against the encroaching unknown, a steady hand documenting the storm, in hopes that one day, someone might understand the shape of its clouds. He saw his role as that of a cartographer, charting an uncharted territory, not with lines on a map, but with light and shadow, form and texture, creating a visual atlas of a world reborn in a spectrum of alien hues. Each photograph was a fragment of a puzzle, and Jax was diligently collecting every piece, arranging them with an engineer's precision, waiting for the larger picture to emerge from the collective detail. He understood that the story of Oakhaven's survival, and its potential future, was being written not just in their controlled environments or their scientific theories, but in the wild, untamed, and increasingly luminous landscapes that surrounded them. His camera was his tool, his journal his archive, and the visual evidence he painstakingly gathered was becoming an irrefutable chronicle of life's relentless, and in this case, glowing, persistence.

CHAPTER FIFTEEN

HORIZON'S PROMISE

The air within Oakhaven, once a constant reminder of the external decay, now hummed with a different kind of energy. It wasn't the low thrum of life-support systems or the sterile whir of air purifiers, though those were still present. This was a deeper, more resonant vibration, born from shared struggle and emergent resilience. The events of the past cycles – the suffocating ashfall that had threatened to bury them, the corrosive kiss of acid rain that had etched scars onto their structures, the ravenous wildfires that had painted the horizon with a terrifying, vibrant orange – these were not mere historical footnotes. They were the crucibles in which the community of Oakhaven had been reforged. Each averted disaster, each problem solved through collective ingenuity and sacrifice, had tightened the threads of their social fabric, weaving them into a tapestry far stronger than any single strand.

The philosophy of 'future-first' had transcended its initial definition as a mere operational directive. It had become an ingrained ethos, a guiding principle that permeated every decision, every project, every interaction. It was evident in the careful rationing of resources, the meticulous planning for contingencies, and the unwavering dedication to sustainable practices. But more than that, it was visible in the faces of the people. Gone was the pervasive despair that had clung to the early days. In its place was a quiet determination, a steely resolve that spoke of an understanding that their present actions were laying the foundation for generations to come. They were not simply surviving; they were actively building a legacy, brick by painstaking brick, seed by precious seed.

This profound shift was inextricably linked to the burgeoning success of the Resource Library. What began as a humble collection of salvaged manuals and operational schematics had blossomed into the vibrant heart of Oakhaven's collaborative spirit. It was more than just a repository of knowledge; it was a nexus of innovation, a testament to the power of shared learning. Every salvaged component meticulously cataloged, every rediscovered technique thoroughly documented, every successful repair or modification shared openly – these were the building blocks of their collective advancement. The Library wasn't a static archive; it was a living, breathing organism, constantly evolving as the community poured its collective experience and nascent discoveries back into its digital veins.

The architects of this burgeoning community were not monolithic in their approach. Luis, with his artist's eye and a scientist's curiosity, saw the luminescence of the wetlands as a grand, unfolding narrative of adaptation. He spoke of it not just in terms of chemical reactions or energy transfer, but as a testament to life's relentless drive to find new expressions, to embrace and integrate the extraordinary. His explanations often wove poetic imagery with scientific observation, making the seemingly alien phenomenon of the glowing flora and fauna accessible and even inspiring to those who had previously only viewed it with apprehension. He would spend hours by the perimeter of the luminous zones, his sketchbook filled with vibrant depictions of the pulsing reeds and the iridescent insects, his mind buzzing with theories about how this newfound energy might be harnessed for Oakhaven's benefit. He saw not just light, but possibility, a vibrant palette of potential applications waiting to be discovered.

"It's as if the very essence of life here is re-writing itself," he'd explain to anyone who would listen, his voice filled with a reverent wonder. "These organisms aren't just surviving the changes; they're actively *participating* in them. They're weaving this luminescence into their very being, creating a symbiosis with the environment that's unlike anything we've cataloged before. Think of the potential, not just for illumination, but for energy, for new forms of biomaterials, for understanding the very processes that sustain life in extreme conditions."

Jax, the pragmatic engineer, viewed the same phenomena through a different lens, one grounded in meticulous documentation and empirical evidence. While Luis painted with words and broad strokes of scientific inquiry, Jax meticulously captured the details, ensuring that no anomaly went unrecorded. His camera was his primary tool, his journal a testament to his dedication to the observable facts. He sought to quantify the luminescence, to map its fluctuations, to trace its correlation with environmental factors. His work was the bedrock upon which more speculative theories could be built.

"The intensity of the glow in Sector Gamma has increased by an average of 12% over the last reporting cycle," he would state, his voice calm and measured, as he pointed to a series of charts and graphs displayed on his tablet. "This correlates with a 7% increase in atmospheric moisture and a 3% rise in ambient temperature. The spectral analysis of the reed's outer membrane shows a significant increase in a novel protein compound, one we haven't encountered before, which appears to be directly responsible for the bioluminescent reaction. It's not magic, Luis. It's chemistry, and biology, operating at an accelerated pace."

Mika, ever the scientist, approached the transformation with a rigorous analytical framework. While she appreciated the artistic and observational contributions of Luis and Jax, her focus remained on data, on quantifiable outcomes, and on the potential for practical application. Her instruments, humming with advanced sensor technology, were constantly deployed, gathering atmospheric readings, soil composition analyses, and subtle energy signature detections. She saw the luminescence not as a wonder, but as a complex energetic phenomenon, a puzzle to be solved through systematic investigation.

"The energy signature emitted by the wetland flora is anomalous," she'd report during a community council meeting, her tone precise and objective. "It doesn't align with known biological luminescence. We're detecting trace amounts of exotic particle decay, coupled with a unique electromagnetic field oscillation. My hypothesis is that the altered atmospheric composition, particularly the residual radiation from the Collapse, has triggered a novel metabolic pathway within these organisms. My current research is focused on isolating the specific enzymatic processes involved and determining if this energy can be safely and efficiently captured."

Despite their differing methodologies, their individual contributions converged, creating a powerful synergy. Luis's expansive vision inspired new avenues of inquiry, Jax's detailed documentation provided the empirical foundation, and Mika's rigorous analysis offered a path toward practical understanding and application. This collaborative spirit, nurtured by the Resource Library, was the bedrock of Oakhaven's strengthened community.

The library was more than just a place to borrow tools or consult schematics; it was a physical manifestation of their shared commitment. Designated alcoves were set aside for individuals or small groups to present their findings. Regular "Knowledge Exchange" sessions, hosted by the library's dedicated curators – a rotating roster of skilled individuals from various disciplines – became highly anticipated events. These weren't formal lectures, but informal dialogues, where ideas were shared freely, questions were encouraged, and nascent theories were debated with respect and enthusiasm.

One such session, recently held, focused on Jax's ongoing photographic documentation of the altered insect populations. He presented a series of stark, high-resolution images: a beetle with wing casings that shimmered with an ethereal, multi-hued iridescence, a moth whose wings displayed intricate, pulsing bioluminescent patterns, and a dragonfly with wings of an impossible, translucent grandeur, its body a vivid emerald green that seemed to emanate light.

"These are not isolated mutations," Jax explained, his voice resonating with a quiet intensity. "We're seeing a pattern. The insects that interact with the luminescent flora, particularly the reeds in Sector Gamma, exhibit similar chromatic and energetic properties. My hypothesis, based on soil analysis from these areas, is that they are ingesting or absorbing compounds that are not only coloring them but also influencing their metabolism, making them bioluminescent themselves. This is particularly evident in the larval stages of several insect species, where we're seeing an increased concentration of luminescent compounds before they even emerge as adults."

Luis, captivated, leaned forward. "So, it's not just the plants that are adapting, Jax. It's the entire ecosystem! The insects are becoming vectors, carrying this luminescence throughout the environment. Imagine the possibilities! If we can understand how they integrate these compounds, perhaps we can replicate it. Imagine our filtration systems, or even our living quarters, being illuminated by the natural glow of adapted insects, reducing our reliance on energy-intensive lighting."

Mika, ever the pragmatist, countered with a measured caution. "While the aesthetic and potential energy benefits are intriguing, we must also consider the ecological implications. Are these altered insects displacing native species? What are their predatory habits? Are they bioaccumulating these luminescent compounds in a way that could be toxic to other organisms, including ourselves, if they enter the food chain? My current research is focusing on the bio-magnification potential of these novel compounds within the local insect population. We need to ensure that our pursuit of innovation doesn't inadvertently create new environmental hazards."

The ensuing discussion was lively, a testament to the community's intellectual engagement. Ideas bounced back and forth, building upon each other, refining hypotheses, and identifying new avenues of research. Someone suggested testing the luminescence of insect larvae found in areas *without* direct contact with the glowing reeds, to establish a baseline. Another proposed a controlled experiment, introducing a small, isolated population of luminescent insects into a sealed biome within Oakhaven, to observe their behavior and impact in a controlled environment. Jax diligently logged every suggestion, every unanswered question, into the Resource Library's database, cross-referencing them with existing research and flagging them for future investigation.

The spirit of collaboration extended beyond scientific and engineering endeavors. The communal gardens, once a necessity born of food scarcity, had become vibrant social hubs. Neighbors worked side-by-side, sharing gardening tips, exchanging harvested produce, and finding solace in the simple, rhythmic act of tending the earth. The shared experience of coaxing life from the soil, especially after the ravages of ashfall and contaminated rain, had fostered a profound sense of connection. The bright splashes of color from the hardy, genetically resilient vegetables and fruits, now interspersed with experimental crops designed to thrive in slightly altered conditions, were a visual testament to their collective effort.

Children, too, were active participants. Their education was no longer confined to sterile classrooms. They were taken on supervised excursions to the edges of the reclaimed zones, their curiosity nurtured by skilled educators who balanced the inherent risks with the invaluable lessons of direct observation. They learned about the unique properties of the luminescent flora, identified different species of the newly adapted insects, and participated in soil sample collection, their small hands carefully scooping earth under the watchful eyes of experienced scientists. The Resource Library often hosted "Junior Innovator" workshops, where children, guided by adults, could experiment with simple circuits powered by bioluminescent algae cultures or design their own protective gear for exploring the outer zones. Their uninhibited questions often sparked new lines of thought for the adults, reminding them of the fundamental wonder that drove their own pursuits.

The community's resilience was not just about facing external threats; it was about the internal strength they had cultivated. The challenges had stripped away superficialities, forcing them to rely on each other's unique skills and strengths. The engineers worked alongside the botanists, the former soldiers coordinated with the medical staff, the teachers facilitated intergenerational knowledge transfer, and the artists and storytellers preserved their collective memory and inspired hope. This interdependence had created a social safety net so strong that the fear of isolation, a prevalent anxiety in the early days, had largely dissipated.

Even the older generation, initially hesitant to embrace the rapid changes, found their place. Their wisdom, honed by years of experience before the Collapse, provided a valuable historical perspective. They remembered the world as it was, offering context and often caution against reckless innovation. Their stories, shared during communal gatherings, served as potent reminders of what had been lost, but also of the enduring spirit of humanity. These narratives, meticulously recorded and archived in the Resource Library, became a vital part of Oakhaven's collective identity, a bridge between their past and their unfolding future.

The very act of living in Oakhaven had become a form of proactive engagement with the unknown. The constant hum of innovation, the shared commitment to 'future-first' principles, and the unwavering support network forged in the fires of adversity had transformed Oakhaven from a mere sanctuary into a thriving, dynamic society. The challenges were far from over; the mysteries of the glowing wetlands and the broader environmental shifts remained significant. But the community was no longer defined by its fears or its vulnerabilities. It was defined by its unity, its ingenuity, and its unwavering belief in the promise of the horizon, a promise they were actively, collaboratively, and luminously building for themselves, and for all who would come after. The Resource Library, in its role as the central nervous system of this interconnected community, buzzed with the shared energy of discovery, a testament to the fact that even in the face of overwhelming uncertainty, a strengthened community, united by purpose and fueled by hope, could forge a brighter future. The glow from the wetlands, once a source of apprehension, was slowly, surely, being reinterpreted as a beacon of Oakhaven's own burgeoning strength and resilience.

The wetlands, a shimmering tapestry of emerald and sapphire, pulsed with a life that defied easy categorization. The faint, ethereal glow that had once been a source of unease had, over the cycles, woven itself into the very fabric of Oakhaven's perception. It was no longer an anomaly to be feared, but a constant, living presence, a testament to the planet's stubborn, vibrant refusal to yield. Luis, often found sketching at the water's edge, no longer approached it with the detached curiosity of a scientist cataloging the unknown, but with the contemplative gaze of an artist studying a masterpiece, one that was perpetually in motion. He saw in the gentle undulations of the glowing reeds, the fleeting trails of luminescent microorganisms, and the slow, deliberate drift of iridescent aquatic life, a profound beauty that transcended mere scientific explanation.

"It's like the planet is breathing light," he'd murmur to himself, his charcoal dancing across the page, capturing the subtle shifts in intensity, the way the bioluminescence seemed to ebb and flow with an unseen tide. He had begun to think of it not as a chemical reaction to be dissected, but as a symphony, an orchestra of biological processes playing a melody in frequencies beyond human auditory range, but perceivable through the visual spectrum. The very air above the wetlands seemed to hum with this silent song, a gentle vibrance that seeped into the souls of those who lived near it, a constant reminder that their world, though scarred, was far from barren.

Jax, ever the pragmatist, continued his meticulous documentation, but even he had begun to imbue his reports with a subtle sense of wonder. His data points, precise and unyielding, were now accompanied by observational notes that spoke of a growing respect for the phenomenon's inherent mystery. He mapped the luminescence with increasing detail, noting its patterns of diffusion, its responsiveness to atmospheric pressure changes, and its seemingly symbiotic relationship with the local fauna. Yet, he could not, with all his instruments and analytical prowess, pinpoint the ultimate source, the singular catalyst that set this intricate biological light show in motion. It was a puzzle that continued to elude definitive resolution, and in that elusory nature, Jax found a new dimension to his scientific pursuit. He documented the glowing dragonflies that flitted through the twilight, their wings leaving trails of phosphorescent dust, and the water beetles whose carapaces mimicked the starry sky, a reflection of the luminescence within. He noted how the smallest of organisms, the plankton that formed the base of the wetland's food web, pulsed with an internal light, creating a diffused glow that turned the water into liquid starlight.

"The spectral analysis remains consistent," he'd report, his voice devoid of its usual slight edge of impatience, "indicating a high concentration of novel luciferin compounds in the flora. However, the energy output fluctuates by as much as fifteen percent in response to factors we haven't yet identified. There are intermittent, localized energy spikes that don't align with known biological processes. It's... persistent. And its persistence suggests an adaptability that goes beyond our current understanding of cellular biology." He would often pause, his gaze drifting towards the shimmering expanse, a thoughtful furrow in his brow. "We can measure it, catalog it, even predict its general behavior, but truly *understanding* it feels like trying to grasp mist."

Mika, while still driven by the pursuit of definitive answers, had also begun to acknowledge the limitations of absolute certainty. Her laboratory, a sterile haven of gleaming equipment, was now a place where hypotheses evolved into theories, and theories, while striving for proof, were also being re-evaluated in light of the wetland's persistent enigmatic character. She had, in fact, designated a specific section of her research to "Inconclusive Phenomena," a category that, to her initial frustration, was growing at an alarming rate. The luminescence, with its unyielding complexity, was the prime exhibit. She had isolated numerous enzymes and compounds responsible for the light production, tracing intricate biochemical pathways. Yet, the fundamental trigger, the original spark that set these complex reactions in motion, remained elusive. It was as if the very act of being exposed to the altered atmosphere and residual radiation had fundamentally rewired the genetic code of these organisms, a self-activating process that once initiated, perpetuated itself indefinitely.

"We have mapped the cascading enzymatic reactions with 98.7% accuracy," Mika stated during one of the more informal Knowledge Exchange sessions, her fingers gliding over a holographic display of molecular structures. "We understand *how* the light is produced, down to the quantum level of electron excitation and photon emission. What we are still struggling with is the *initiation* event. The energy signature suggests an external trigger, but every controlled experiment designed to replicate pre-Collapse environmental conditions has failed to induce the same level of sustained luminescence. It's as if the wetlands have developed their own internal clock, a rhythm dictated by factors that are no longer present in our controlled environments, or perhaps, factors we simply cannot detect." She sighed, a rare admission of intellectual impasse. "We've come to a point where the system appears to be self-sustaining, exhibiting emergent properties that defy our current understanding of cellular automata. It's... humbling."

The community, in turn, had absorbed this evolving understanding. The initial apprehension that had accompanied the first sightings of the glowing flora had long since receded, replaced by a comfortable coexistence. The wetlands were no longer viewed as a source of potential danger, but as a place of quiet wonder, a natural sanctuary that offered a unique aesthetic and a subtle, ambient energy that seemed to soothe the underlying anxieties of their post-Collapse existence. Children would often bring their parents to the edge of the marshlands, not with tales of fear, but with wide-eyed reports of the most vibrant glowing patches, or the strange, luminous patterns they had observed in the water. The glow became a part of their stories, a mythical element woven into the fabric of their daily lives.

"Look, Papa!" a young girl named Elara, her face smudged with dirt from the communal gardens, would exclaim, pointing a small, grubby finger towards the distant shimmer. "The sky-water is blinking at us today!" Her father, a former mechanic who now curated the Resource Library's tools section, would smile and nod, his gaze following her finger. He understood that Elara wasn't just seeing light; she was seeing a vibrant, living testament to the world's capacity for adaptation, a silent, luminous promise that life, in its most fundamental form, would always find a way. He had even begun to incorporate the wetland's unique properties into his work, designing a series of low-power, ambient lighting systems for the library's reading alcoves using carefully cultivated bioluminescent algae, a direct inspiration from the wetlands' persistent glow.

The philosophy of 'future-first' had, in many ways, found a profound resonance in the wetlands. It was a living, breathing embodiment of adaptation, a testament to the planet's ability to reinvent itself in the face of catastrophic change. The luminescence, inexplicable as it was, represented a vast, untapped potential, a frontier of biological and energetic possibilities that Oakhaven was slowly, cautiously, beginning to explore. Luis's sketches, once purely artistic studies, were now being annotated with speculative notes on bio-integration. Could the luminescent properties of certain plants be transferred to Oakhaven's agricultural crops, reducing the need for artificial lighting in the greenhouses? Could the energy signature, however faint, be harnessed to supplement their power grid? These were questions born not of desperation, but of inspired curiosity, fueled by the ever-present, silent song of the wetlands.

The community council often convened near the perimeter of the wetlands, the soft, ambient glow providing a natural, soothing illumination that facilitated their discussions. It was during one such meeting, as they deliberated on the allocation of precious water resources, that Luis shared his latest artistic interpretations. He had compiled a series of his sketches and digital renderings into a presentation, not of scientific data, but of emotive imagery. He showed the council swirling patterns of light, depicting the interconnectedness of the wetland ecosystem, and the way the luminescence seemed to communicate, a silent dialogue between flora and fauna.

"We often focus on what we can extract, what we can control," Luis began, his voice soft but compelling, gesturing towards an image of a particularly vibrant patch of glowing moss. "But perhaps, the greatest lesson the wetlands offer is not in what we can *take* from it, but in what we can *learn* from its existence. It thrives not by brute force, but by a profound integration, a willingness to embody its environment. It doesn't fight the changes; it becomes them. This luminescence isn't just a chemical reaction; it's a declaration of life's persistence, its ability to find beauty and function in the most unexpected circumstances. We, too, are in a constant state of adaptation. Perhaps our path forward lies not only in engineering solutions, but in embracing this inherent adaptability, in finding our own inner luminescence."

His words resonated deeply within the assembled community. While Jax continued to measure and Mika to analyze, there was a growing acceptance that some aspects of their new world might remain, for a time, shrouded in mystery. The fear that had once been attached to the unknown had transmuted into a profound sense of awe, a humbling recognition of the planet's vast, intricate, and often inexplicable processes. The wetlands, with their silent song of light, had become a powerful symbol of this evolving perspective. They were a constant reminder that even in a world reshaped by devastation, life found a way to flourish, to adapt, and to create beauty in the most unexpected forms.

The luminescent organisms were not merely surviving; they were thriving, weaving this extraordinary light into their very beings. This was not just a biological quirk; it was a paradigm shift in how Oakhaven viewed life itself. The relentless drive for progress, for control, was tempered by an emerging appreciation for the subtle, the inexplicable, the inherently wild beauty of their transformed planet. The wetlands, in their silent, glowing persistence, taught them that understanding did not always equate to mastery, and that sometimes, the most profound lessons were learned through quiet observation and a willingness to simply be present with the mystery. The world was no longer just a canvas for humanity's ambitions, but a living, breathing entity with its own language, its own rhythms, and its own radiant secrets, waiting to be perceived, not just understood.

The constant hum of activity within Oakhaven was now subtly underscored by the gentle luminescence of the wetlands, a visual lullaby that soothed and inspired. It was a reminder that even after the harshest of winters, a new spring could bloom, albeit in forms they had never imagined. The light, once a harbinger of the unknown, had become a symbol of their own nascent resilience, a quiet promise reflected in the shimmering waters, that even in the deepest darkness, life's enduring light could always find a way to shine through. It was a promise they were, day by day, learning to live by, to embrace, and to carry forward into the unfolding dawn. The wetlands' silent song was becoming Oakhaven's own, a melody of adaptation, of hope, and of the enduring, luminous spirit of life itself. This acceptance, this integration of the inexplicable, was perhaps the most significant adaptation Oakhaven had undergone, a testament to their growing maturity as a species facing a truly alien future. They were no longer just surviving the changed world; they were learning to live within its breathtaking, luminous mystery. The glow was not just in the water, but in their hearts.

Mika's laboratory, once a sanctuary of sterile precision, had become a vibrant crucible of applied innovation. The initial frustrations born from the unyielding enigma of the luminescent wetlands had transmuted into a powerful impetus for further exploration. She hadn't just cataloged the biochemical reactions; she had begun to synthesize them, to coax them into controllable, beneficial applications. Her work was no longer solely about understanding the 'how' of the glow, but the 'why' and, crucially, the 'what next.' The inherent adaptability of Oakhaven's flora and fauna, so starkly exemplified by the glowing organisms, had become Mika's guiding principle. If the planet could reinvent itself with such tenacity, so too could its inhabitants, not by conquering nature, but by harmonizing with its evolved forms.

Her current obsession was the integration of bioluminescent algae into Oakhaven's communal greenhouses. The previous season's experimental crops, cultivated under carefully regulated artificial lights, had yielded moderate success, but the energy expenditure had been a significant drain on their nascent power grid. The wetlands, however, offered a far more elegant and sustainable solution. Mika had meticulously cultivated strains of algae that exhibited consistent, controllable luminescence, drawing inspiration from the gentle, perpetual glow of the marsh reeds. These were not the wild, untamed organisms of the wetlands, but carefully selected and bred descendants, their light-producing capabilities amplified and stabilized through controlled environmental conditioning and minor genetic adjustments – always within ethical boundaries, always prioritizing long-term ecological integration.

"The key," Mika explained to a small group of community members who had volunteered to assist in the pilot program, her voice laced with quiet enthusiasm, "is not to replicate the wetlands' intensity, but to mimic their efficiency. These algae utilize minimal energy, primarily drawing sustenance from their nutrient substrate and the ambient light spectrum. Their glow is a byproduct, a beautiful, functional one." She gestured towards a large, transparent tank where a vibrant green culture pulsed with a soft, inviting light. "Imagine an entire crop cycle, from seedling to harvest, bathed in this natural, energy-neutral luminescence. No more strain on the hydro-generators, no more reliance on dwindling power reserves. Just pure, sustained growth, powered by life itself."

The process involved designing specialized bioreactors, sleek, modular units that could be seamlessly integrated into the greenhouse structures. These reactors housed the cultivated algae, their growth medium carefully balanced with recycled nutrients from Oakhaven's composting systems. Tubes carrying filtered water from the central reservoir would circulate through the reactors, picking up the faintly luminous microorganisms and distributing them through a network of capillary channels embedded within the greenhouse walls and ceiling. The light, a soft, ethereal green, permeated the growing spaces, creating an ambiance that was both calming and invigorating.

"We've calculated the optimal density," Mika continued, pointing to a schematic projected onto a nearby screen. "Too little, and the light intensity is insufficient. Too much, and the algae compete for nutrients, potentially impacting crop yields. It's a delicate balance, much like the ecosystems in the wetlands themselves. We are essentially creating miniature, controlled wetlands within our agricultural zones." She tapped a specific point on the schematic. "And for supplementary illumination during Oakhaven's darker cycles, or for crops requiring a more specific spectrum, we've developed a dual-system. These secondary channels can introduce nutrient-rich water infused with a different algal strain, one that produces a warmer, amber hue. This allows for precise spectral tuning, catering to the specific needs of each crop."

The community's response was overwhelmingly positive. The idea of self-sufficient, glowing greenhouses resonated deeply with their 'future-first' philosophy. It was a tangible manifestation of Oakhaven's ability to adapt, to learn from the planet's resilience and translate it into practical solutions. The initial setup was labor-intensive, requiring careful calibration and ongoing monitoring by Mika and her dedicated team of volunteers, but the promise of reduced energy consumption and increased food security was a powerful motivator. Children, fascinated by the glowing tanks, would often peer into them, their faces illuminated by the soft light, sparking conversations about biology, sustainability, and the wonders of their transformed world.

Beyond agriculture, Mika's innovations were also venturing into the realm of ambient energy. The persistent, low-level energy fluctuations observed in the wetlands, though not fully understood, had hinted at a potential source of power. Mika theorized that the complex biochemical processes driving the luminescence also released minute but consistent quantities of bio-electrical energy. Her goal was to find a way to tap into this, not on a large scale, but for localized, low-power applications that would further reduce Oakhaven's reliance on its central power grid.

Her focus was on developing bio-voltaic cells, devices that could convert biological energy directly into electricity. She experimented with different conductive materials, seeking to create a stable interface between the living organisms and the energy-harvesting components. Initial prototypes were crude, yielding only a few millivolts, but Mika's persistence was unwavering. She envisioned a future where pathways and communal spaces were illuminated by soft, glowing orbs powered by engineered microbial communities, or where small devices could be charged by discreet bio-voltaic panels integrated into furniture or building materials.

"It's about creating a distributed, resilient energy infrastructure," Mika explained during a public demonstration in the central commons, holding up a small, faintly glowing disc. "Instead of relying solely on the hydro-generators, which are vulnerable to drought or mechanical failure, we can build a network of micro-energy sources. These bio-voltaic cells are designed to be self-sustaining, drawing energy from ambient organic matter and the very air around them. Imagine streetlights that never need replacing, or personal communicators that rarely need charging, simply by being placed near a bio-voltaic surface."

She placed the disc on a small pedestal, and a tiny LED light embedded in the pedestal flickered to life, emitting a soft, steady glow. A murmur of impressed surprise rippled through the assembled crowd. Luis, sketching nearby, captured the moment in a series of swift, fluid lines, his charcoal dancing to capture the ephemeral glow of the disc and the hopeful expressions of the onlookers. Jax, ever the analyst, was already jotting down questions about the efficiency metrics and the long-term stability of the microbial colonies within the disc.

Mika's approach was always rooted in practicality and a deep respect for the natural world. She understood that Oakhaven's survival depended not on exploiting resources, but on fostering a symbiotic relationship with its environment. Her innovations were not about grand, sweeping gestures, but about incremental improvements, about weaving sustainable practices into the fabric of daily life. She was a master of adaptation, her ingenuity flowing directly from her understanding of the planet's own remarkable capacity for change.

She also recognized the importance of safety and community well-being in all her endeavors. Every new technology, every proposed innovation, was subjected to rigorous safety assessments. Her research into bio-voltaic energy, for instance, included extensive studies on the long-term viability and safety of the microbial strains used, ensuring they posed no risk to the environment or human health. The luminescent algae for the greenhouses were carefully chosen for their non-toxicity and their ability to thrive within a controlled system, preventing any uncontrolled spread into the surrounding Oakhaven ecosystem.

"We are not trying to force nature to conform to our needs," Mika often emphasized during her presentations and workshops. "We are learning to work *with* it. The luminescence of the wetlands, the resilience of the soil, the very air we breathe – these are not just resources to be extracted. They are lessons. They are opportunities to build a more sustainable, more harmonious future. Every innovation we develop must enhance, not diminish, the delicate balance of our world."

Her reputation within Oakhaven had grown beyond that of a brilliant scientist; she was seen as a visionary, a steward of Oakhaven's ecological future. Her laboratory, once a place of solitary contemplation, had become a hub of collaborative innovation. Volunteers from all walks of life – former engineers, botanists, even artists – contributed their skills and perspectives, drawn by Mika's unwavering dedication and her infectious optimism. They understood that her work was not just about science; it was about hope, about building a future where humanity and nature could coexist, not just survive, but truly thrive.

Mika's ongoing research also delved into water purification systems, inspired by the natural filtration processes observed in the healthy wetland ecosystems. She was developing bio-filters utilizing specific plant species and beneficial microorganisms that could efficiently remove contaminants from Oakhaven's water supply, reducing their reliance on the energy-intensive chemical purification methods previously employed. These bio-filters were designed to be modular and self-sustaining, requiring minimal maintenance and further contributing to Oakhaven's goal of complete resource independence.

"The wetlands, in their pristine state, are a testament to nature's own purification systems," Mika explained during a community forum discussing water resource management. "The reeds, the specific types of mosses, even certain microbial communities, all play a vital role in filtering and detoxifying the water. We've identified some of these key players and are developing engineered bio-filters that mimic these natural processes. These won't just clean our water; they'll improve its mineral content and potentially even imbue it with some of the subtle beneficial properties we've observed in the wetland's ecosystem."

Her commitment to long-term ecological balance was evident in every project. She advocated for closed-loop systems, where waste products were not discarded but reintegrated into the ecosystem as valuable resources. This philosophy extended to her work on energy, agriculture, and water management, creating a holistic approach to sustainability that was the hallmark of Oakhaven's evolving identity. The glowing wetlands, once a symbol of the unknown and potentially dangerous, had become the wellspring of their most promising and sustainable innovations, a constant reminder of the planet's enduring capacity for life and light. Mika, with her blend of scientific rigor and intuitive understanding of natural systems, was the embodiment of Oakhaven's adaptive spirit, a beacon of ingenuity guiding them towards a brighter, more resilient horizon.

She represented the enduring human capacity to learn, to evolve, and to create a future that was not only technologically advanced but deeply, intrinsically connected to the living world. Her work was a testament to the belief that even in the wake of profound devastation, innovation, guided by wisdom and a reverence for life, could indeed promise a new dawn.

Luis's hands, once calloused from the harsh realities of scarcity and the frantic scramble for sustenance, now moved with a practiced grace across the soil. The sun, a familiar, yet newly benevolent presence in Oakhaven's sky, warmed his back as he knelt beside a row of robust, deep-green leafy vegetables. These weren't the wilting, nutrient-starved remnants of emergency rations; these were the vibrant fruits of intentional cultivation, a testament to a philosophy that had shifted from mere survival to a flourishing coexistence. His agro-ecological systems, initially conceived as a means to bolster Oakhaven's food security, had evolved into something far more profound: engines of ecological regeneration.

The patch he worked was a microcosm of this transformation. Interspersed among the rows of kale and chard were clusters of nitrogen-fixing legumes, their roots a bustling network of symbiotic bacteria that enriched the soil with every growth cycle. Tiny, almost imperceptible hummingbirds, drawn by the vibrant hues of strategically planted wildflowers, flitted between the edible plants, acting as natural pollinators and pest deterrents. This wasn't a garden; it was a carefully orchestrated ecosystem, a testament to Luis's deep understanding of the interconnectedness of life, honed by countless hours of observation and experimentation since the Calamity. He had learned to read the land not as a resource to be plundered, but as a partner to be nurtured.

The soil itself was a living entity, a stark contrast to the depleted earth that had greeted them in the early days. Luis's composting initiatives, a community-wide effort he had championed, transformed organic waste into rich, life-giving compost. He had refined the process, incorporating specific microbial cultures discovered in the less-affected pockets of the old world, strains that accelerated decomposition and enhanced nutrient availability. Now, the soil teemed with a diversity of earthworms and beneficial fungi, their presence a visible indicator of a healthy, balanced environment. He had even developed a method for inoculating the soil with spores from the resilient, bioluminescent fungi found in the fringes of the re-emerging wetlands, a subtle incorporation of Oakhaven's unique bio-signature that seemed to imbue the crops with a faint, almost imperceptible vitality.

"Look at this, Elena," he called out, his voice resonating with a quiet pride. Elena, a young woman who had apprenticed under him for the past year, approached, her own hands stained with earth. She carried a basket filled with plump, ruby-red tomatoes, their skins glistening in the sunlight. "The mycelial network is thriving here. You can almost feel the energy flowing beneath the surface."

Elena knelt beside him, her eyes widening as Luis gently brushed away the topsoil, revealing a delicate, white web of fungal hyphae threading through the dark loam. "It's like seeing the planet's own nervous system," she murmured, her voice filled with awe.

"Exactly," Luis affirmed, a broad smile spreading across his face. "We're not just growing food; we're helping the earth heal itself. This network allows nutrients to be transported efficiently, and it strengthens the plants' resistance to disease. It's a partnership, Elena.

We provide the organic matter, and the soil, with the help of these tiny allies, gives us back life."

His success extended beyond the communal gardens and into the reclaimed agricultural lands surrounding Oakhaven. These fields, once barren and scarred, were now a patchwork of thriving crops, rotated and managed with an ecological sensibility. He had introduced drought-resistant strains, cross-bred for resilience and nutritional value, drawing on salvaged seed banks and his own painstakingly developed hybrids. His methods eschewed the heavy machinery and chemical inputs of the old world, favoring a more holistic approach. Cover crops were planted to prevent erosion and replenish soil nutrients, and integrated pest management, relying on beneficial insects and natural deterrents, kept harmful populations in check.

One of the most striking achievements was the revitalization of a small, meandering stream that bordered the southern farmlands. Previously a sluggish, polluted trickle, it was now a clear, flowing waterway, its banks lined with native reeds and aquatic plants that Luis and his team had carefully reintroduced. These plants, selected for their phytoremediation properties, actively filtered impurities from the water, creating a cleaner environment for the crops and a habitat for returning aquatic life. Dragonflies, their iridescent wings shimmering, now danced over the water's surface, a sure sign of a healthy aquatic ecosystem.

"The water quality reports are incredible, Luis," Mika had told him just the other day, her eyes alight with scientific curiosity. "The levels of pollutants have dropped by nearly seventy percent in that stream. Your bio-filters are performing beyond our initial projections. It's not just about irrigation; you're actively restoring hydrological cycles."

Luis had simply nodded, a quiet satisfaction settling within him. He knew that the wetlands, with their inherent purification capabilities, had provided the initial inspiration, but it was the application of Oakhaven's own resilient flora, guided by his understanding of ecological principles, that had achieved such tangible results. He had cultivated specific strains of wetland grasses and reeds, nurturing their growth in carefully controlled nurseries before transplanting them along the stream banks and in designated filtration zones within the farmlands. These plants acted as living filters, their root systems trapping sediment and absorbing excess nutrients, preventing them from reaching the main water sources.

His approach to livestock also reflected this commitment to integration. Small herds of hardy, native breeds of goats and sheep grazed on designated pastures, their presence managed to prevent overgrazing and soil compaction. Their manure, a valuable source of nutrients, was meticulously collected and added to the composting system, closing the loop in a truly circular economy. He had even begun to experiment with silvopasture, integrating fruit-bearing trees and nitrogen-fixing shrubs into the grazing areas, providing shade, supplemental fodder, and further enriching the soil. The gentle bleating of the sheep and the contented chewing of the goats became a familiar, soothing sound on the fringes of Oakhaven, a counterpoint to the hum of Mika's innovations.

"It's all about mimicry, you see," Luis explained to a group of younger children who had accompanied him on a field visit to one of the restored farmlands. He pointed to a grove of young apple trees, their branches laden with nascent fruit, interspersed with rows of hardy fescue grass. "Before the Calamity, farmers had huge machines that churned up the earth and used chemicals that hurt the soil and the water. We learned that nature already has the best ways of doing things. These trees, their roots hold the soil firm. The grass keeps the moisture in and provides food for our sheep. And the sheep, their droppings feed the soil, which helps the trees grow even better. It's a circle of giving and taking, and everyone benefits."

The children listened intently, their faces a mixture of curiosity and wonder. They had grown up in a world where ecological balance was not an abstract concept, but a daily reality, a fragile tapestry they were learning to weave. Luis's ability to translate complex ecological principles into simple, relatable lessons made him a beloved figure, not just as a provider of food, but as an educator and a steward of their shared future.

His efforts had also indirectly contributed to the re-establishment of certain insect populations that were crucial for the broader ecosystem. By creating diverse habitats rich in flowering plants and natural nesting sites, he had attracted a wider array of pollinators beyond the hummingbirds, including a variety of bees and butterflies. These insects, in turn, played a vital role in the pollination of wild flora in the surrounding areas, contributing to the overall biodiversity and resilience of the Oakhaven region. Even the predators, like the small, iridescent beetles that patrolled the vegetable rows, were a welcome sight, a sign that the food web was reasserting itself.

The impact of Luis's work extended beyond the purely agricultural. The visual beauty of his flourishing gardens and fields had a profound psychological effect on the community. In a world that had witnessed so much destruction, these verdant landscapes were a powerful symbol of hope and renewal. They offered a tangible connection to the earth, a reminder of the planet's enduring capacity for life and beauty. People would often take leisurely walks through the fields, finding solace and inspiration in the vibrant colors, the gentle rustling of leaves, and the sweet scent of blossoms.

"When I walk through Luis's fields," remarked an elder of the community, her voice soft with emotion, "I feel a sense of peace I haven't felt since before... before everything changed. It's like seeing a garden bloom after a long, hard winter. It reminds us that spring always comes, if we tend it carefully."

Luis, however, remained grounded, never forgetting the lessons learned from the past. He was acutely aware of the delicate balance they were striving to maintain. His integrated systems were designed to be adaptable, to withstand potential disruptions, whether they be shifts in weather patterns or the unforeseen challenges of a post-Calamity world. He constantly experimented with new crop varieties, sought out indigenous species that showed promise for resilience, and maintained detailed records of soil health, water usage, and pest activity. His approach was one of continuous learning and refinement, a quiet, persistent dedication to the land and its inhabitants.

His philosophy was one of abundance, not in the wasteful sense of the old world, but in the sustainable abundance of a healthy ecosystem. By fostering biodiversity, enriching the soil, and working in harmony with natural processes, he ensured a consistent and reliable food supply, reducing the need for Oakhaven to expend precious energy on resource-intensive food production. This freed up Mika and her team to focus on other critical areas of innovation, creating a synergistic relationship between their scientific advancements and Luis's ecological stewardship.

One of Luis's most ambitious projects involved the creation of a "seed bank sanctuary" – a protected area dedicated to preserving and propagating a wide variety of plant species, both cultivated and wild. This wasn't just about storing seeds; it was about creating a living archive, a place where genetic diversity could be nurtured and maintained. He worked with botanists and ecologists to identify and collect seeds from rare and endangered plants, as well as heritage varieties of crops that held significant cultural or nutritional value. The sanctuary also served as an outdoor laboratory, allowing him to study the long-term adaptability of different species in Oakhaven's unique environment.

"This sanctuary," Luis had explained at its inauguration, his voice carrying a sense of solemn responsibility, "is our promise to the future. It's a repository of life's potential, a safeguard against the fragility of memory and the capriciousness of fate. We are not just preserving seeds; we are preserving possibilities."

His legacy, therefore, was not measured in monumental structures or groundbreaking technological leaps, but in the quiet, persistent hum of life that resonated from his cultivated lands. It was in the vibrant green of the crops, the clarity of the streams, the buzz of pollinators, and the contented sounds of livestock. It was in the renewed connection the people of Oakhaven felt to the earth, a connection that had been severed for so long. Luis, the quiet farmer, the astute ecologist, had become a cornerstone of their revitalized world, a living testament to the power of working *with* nature, even in its most altered and unexpected forms. His flourishing legacy was not just in the food he provided, but in the very health and vitality of the land that sustained them all. He was a gardener of not just plants, but of hope, nurturing it from the soil up, ensuring that Oakhaven's horizon would indeed be one of promise, built on the firm foundation of a healed and thriving earth.

Jax's fingers, still bearing the faint scent of developer chemicals from the makeshift darkroom, traced the outline of a photograph. It was a portrait of Anya, her face weathered but alight with an inner fire, captured mid-sentence as she recounted tales of Oakhaven's early days. Beside it lay another, a landscape that showed the tentative blush of green pushing through the charcoal-grey of the ravaged earth, a stubborn defiance against the memory of fire. These were not mere images; they were fragments of a narrative, pieced together by a lens that sought not to condemn, but to understand.

He sat in the quiet hum of the generator that powered Mika's workshop, the rhythmic thrum a familiar counterpoint to the beating heart of Oakhaven. The photographs, meticulously printed and dried, were spread across a salvaged metal table, each one a testament to the arduous journey they had undertaken. His gaze drifted from the faces of his companions – Liam, his brow furrowed in perpetual contemplation; Sarah, her hands steady as she mended frayed equipment; Kai, his youthful exuberance undimmed by the harsh realities of their world – to the wider panorama of their evolving home.

There was the shot of the revitalized stream, its waters now clear enough to reveal the smooth, river-worn stones beneath, a far cry from the toxic runoff that had once choked it. Dragonflies, their wings gossamer miracles, danced in the sunlight that dappled the water's surface, a vibrant sign of life returning. He had spent hours by that stream, waiting for the perfect light, the perfect moment, to capture its rebirth. The patience had paid off, yielding an image that spoke of renewal, of water's primal instinct to cleanse and sustain.

Then there were the crops. Luis's fields, a riot of greens and earthy browns, sprawled across land that had once been a desolate wasteland. Jax had captured the intricate patterns of mycelial networks beneath the soil's surface, thanks to Mika's specially designed low-light photographic filters. These images, rendered in ethereal whites and greys, revealed the unseen architecture of life, the silent, subterranean collaboration that sustained the visible bounty above. They were a stark reminder that growth often happens in ways that defy immediate perception. He had even managed to photograph the faint, otherworldly luminescence of the fungi Luis had introduced, a subtle magic blooming in the Oakhaven soil, hinting at a future where even the darkness held its own unique illumination.

His focus sharpened on a particular series of images depicting the return of wildlife. A family of deer, cautious but unafraid, grazing at the edge of the reforested zone. Birds, their plumage brilliant against the muted tones of the recovered landscape, nesting in the branches of young trees. These were not captured through the stealth of a hunter, but through the patient observation of a documentarian, his presence a silent acknowledgment of a world that was slowly, tentatively, reclaiming its own. Each creature, in its own way, was a vote of confidence in Oakhaven's future.

He remembered the early days, the pervasive sense of loss, the gnawing fear that had settled deep in their bones. The ash-grey landscapes, the skeletal remains of buildings, the hollowed eyes of survivors – these were the images that had haunted his initial work. But as Oakhaven had taken root, as the community had painstakingly rebuilt not just structures but systems, his lens had begun to shift. He still documented the scars, the reminders of what had been lost, but now they served as a counterpoint, a frame that amplified the resilience and ingenuity that had taken their place.

A photograph of Kai, his face grimy with exertion, helping to hoist a solar panel into place, captured a raw, unvarnished optimism. Another showed Anya, her hands stained with ink, meticulously sketching designs for new irrigation systems, her concentration absolute. These were images of purpose, of people actively shaping their destiny. They were not victims of circumstance, but architects of their own future, their collective will a tangible force against the backdrop of a damaged world.

Jax understood that his role was more than just a photographer. He was a storyteller, a chronicler of Oakhaven's resurrection. His images would be the visual memory of their struggle, the proof that humanity, even after facing unimaginable devastation, could not only survive but thrive. They would serve as a beacon, a testament to the enduring spirit that refused to be extinguished, a testament to the quiet heroism woven into the fabric of everyday life.

He picked up a photograph that encapsulated this spirit. It was taken at dusk, the sky ablaze with hues of orange and purple, the silhouettes of the rebuilt structures stark against the dramatic backdrop. In the foreground, a group of children, their laughter echoing in the twilight, chased fireflies, their small hands cupping the ephemeral lights. In the distance, the wetlands shimmered, a vast, dark expanse punctuated by the faint, otherworldly glow of bioluminescent organisms – a silent, pulsing testament to the persistent pulse of life in the heart of their transformed world.

This was the glimpse of tomorrow he wanted to capture, the one that held the echoes of sorrow but was illuminated by the boundless potential of a future actively being built. It was a future where the green reclaimed the ash, where familiar faces bore the marks of resilience, and where even the deepest darkness held its own promise of light. His photographs were an offering to that future, a visual symphony of hope, resilience, and the enduring, unyielding human spirit. He knew his work was far from over; Oakhaven was a story still unfolding, and he intended to capture every vibrant, defiant chapter.

He carefully gathered the prints, his movements deliberate. The weight of the images in his hands felt significant, each one a piece of Oakhaven's soul. He imagined them displayed, not in a sterile gallery, but integrated into the fabric of their community – perhaps adorning the walls of the communal hall, or even projected onto the very structures they had helped to build. He wanted these images to be a constant reminder, not of the hardships they had endured, but of the incredible strength they had found within themselves and in each other.

There was one photograph in particular that held a special place in his heart. It was a wide shot, taken from a high vantage point overlooking Oakhaven. The settlement, nestled amongst the newly verdant hills, glowed with the warm light of countless windows. The surrounding fields, a patchwork of cultivation, seemed to breathe with life. And in the far distance, stretching towards the horizon, were the wetlands, their ethereal glow a subtle, yet undeniable presence. He had waited for an evening when the sky was clear, when the stars were bright, and when the luminescence of the wetlands was at its peak. The resulting image was breathtaking. It showed a community not just surviving, but thriving, a small beacon of life against the vast, mysterious canvas of the post-Calamity world. The resilience of Oakhaven was palpable in that image, a quiet testament to their collective will to endure and to flourish.

Jax felt a surge of pride, not for his own skill, but for the people he had documented. Their courage, their adaptability, their unwavering hope – these were the true subjects of his art. He had merely provided the frame, the perspective, that allowed their story to be seen. He looked at the photograph of the children chasing fireflies again, their innocent joy a powerful symbol of what they were fighting for. It wasn't just about rebuilding; it was about recreating a world where such simple, unadulterated happiness could exist.

The distant hum of the generator seemed to grow louder, pulling him back to the present. Mika's work, Luis's cultivation, Anya's ingenuity, Sarah's quiet strength, Kai's infectious energy – all of it contributed to the vibrant tapestry of Oakhaven. His photographs were a way of weaving these individual threads into a cohesive whole, creating a visual narrative that celebrated their interconnectedness. He understood that the future was not a destination to be reached, but a continuous process of creation, a journey undertaken together. His lens would continue to follow that journey, capturing the moments of hardship and triumph, the quiet determination and the explosive bursts of joy, always searching for the light that promised a brighter tomorrow. The glow of the wetlands in his photographs was more than just a visual phenomenon; it was a metaphor for the enduring spark of life, a testament to Oakhaven's promise to never let the darkness extinguish its light.

VOCABULARY

Calamity: The catastrophic global event that led to widespread environmental collapse and societal breakdown.

Oakhaven: The fictional settlement meticulously rebuilt by survivors in the wake of the Calamity, characterized by its focus on sustainable living and community resilience.

Mycelial Networks: The intricate underground web of fungal threads that play a crucial role in nutrient cycling and communication within ecosystems, utilized in Oakhaven's agricultural practices.

Bio-filtration: An ecological engineering approach that uses living organisms, such as plants and microbes, to purify water and air.

Bioluminescence: The production and emission of light by a living organism, observed in Oakhaven's wetlands as a sign of returning ecological health.

Reclamation Zones: Areas of land that were heavily damaged by the Calamity and are now undergoing systematic efforts to restore their ecological functions and biodiversity.

Generator Hub: The central location in Oakhaven where power is generated and distributed, primarily through a combination of salvaged and new renewable energy sources.

494